D0485070

Family Skeletons

BAKER CITY: HEARTS & HAUNTS 3

JOSIE MALONE

FAMILY SKELETONS
Copyright © 2021 by Josie Malone

ISBN: 978-1-953735-00-3

Published by Satin Romance
An Imprint of Melange Books, LLC
White Bear Lake, MN 55110
www.satinromance.com

Names, characters, and incidents depicted in this book are products of the author's
imagination or are used fictitiously. Any resemblance to actual events, locales,
organizations, or persons, living or dead, is entirely coincidental and beyond the intent of
the author or the publisher. No part of this book may be reproduced or transmitted in
any form or by any means, electronic or mechanical, including photocopying, recording,
or by any information storage and retrieval system, without permission in writing from
the publisher except for the use of brief quotations in a book review or scholarly journal.

Published in the United States of America.

Cover Design by Lynsee Lauritsen

PART I

FEBRUARY 2019

CHAPTER ONE

Sullivan Barlow glanced from the handwritten—make that *scribbled*—disposition form in front of her to the typed version on the computer screen. She'd thought the high school students during her last practicum had crappy penmanship. So, did this guy. She squinted at the signature block again. Yes, it was Master Sergeant Tate Murphy. If she ever met him in person, she'd suggest he repeat third grade and learn cursive.

Oh, wait a minute. A lot of elementary schools no longer taught it. That couldn't be the case with him. He had to be older than she was, and she learned it back in the day in Liberty Valley. So, she'd give him hell. She took a deep breath. No, she wouldn't. She was a Sergeant First Class, an E-7, after all. She'd be polite and recommend he find a pharmacist to decipher his hieroglyphics.

Okay, it was official. She was definitely having a bad day. She pushed back from the desk and leaned down to rub her aching left leg. She'd worked in worse conditions than Major Harper's office. For a moment, she remembered dust, sand, and overwhelming heat. Then, she shook her head.

No, Sully. Concentrate on the moment. Think about here and now.

The room was large with two desks facing each other. Weak February sunshine filtered through the mini-blinds on the windows to her right, laying patterns on the carpeted floor. The American flag stood neatly in the stand to her left, accompanied by the Washington state flag and the one for Fort Clark. Looking at the Stars and Stripes always reminded her of that last flight home and the tri-folded flag on her lap.

She choked on the rising lump in her throat. She'd sat and held that flag on her lap on the entire flight, refusing the meals and beverages the overly sympathetic flight attendants offered.

I wish things were different. I want a do-over. If I could only go back in time… Oh, Raven, I'm so sorry.

She closed her eyes for a moment, blinked hard before she focused on the computer screen again. She always tried to avoid glancing at the U.S. flag and the glassed-in bookcases behind the stand. File cabinets lined the wall that held the same door to the hall and the break room where she could find a cup of coffee. That was if she wanted to try walking that far when her ankle throbbed in its own rhythm, pressing against her combat boot.

Okay, she'd upgrade the day from being bad to officially sucking. Her leg hurt. She had a stack of reports from a moron to type. She repeated her mantra. *Don't complain, things can always be worse. At least nobody is trying to kill me.*

"Haven't you finished those reports yet? You've been typing for three days."

Sully looked from the stack of paperwork to the blonde fashion plate in front of the desk. She was slipping. She should have heard the click of high heels in the hall before Anise Tyler, the civilian clerk in charge returned to the office. "It'd go faster if you helped instead of disappearing to the breakroom every hour."

"Speaking of that, it's a mess." In a clinging light blue dress that matched her heels, the civilian liaison sauntered across to her desk and eased into the leather chair behind it. "I told Mr. Edwards you'd clean it up. You'll find the mop in the utility closet at the end of the hall."

"Excuse you." Sully counted silently to ten, the advice one of the other sergeants in her company had given for dealing with idiots. It didn't work this time. "You're joking, right?"

"Do I look like it?" Anise smiled, but it didn't touch her pale blue eyes. Pleasure filled the lovely face. "You can go clean it now. Then come back and finish those reports."

"I don't think so." Sully rose to her feet, leaning on the desk for support, and pinned Anise with an icy glare, hoping the other woman didn't see the actual physical weakness in her stance. "Let me make one thing *perfectly* clear, Ms. Tyler. I am a Sergeant First Class. I've done three tours in the *sandbox* and I was reassigned here for light duty when they no longer needed me in the Finance section. I don't scrub floors, wash windows, or take out your trash. I don't give garbage. I don't take garbage. I am not in the garbage business. I'll do your correspondence. I won't do your dirty work. Got it?"

The sound of slow applause drew Sully's attention to the door and away from the sputtering woman on the other side of the room. A tall, dark-haired man in camouflage fatigues stood in the doorway. Oh crap, Sully thought. She was in for it now. She should have remembered she was here temporarily and controlled her temper, not actually told the full-time office manager where to go. Of course, there'd been an audience.

I never catch a break. What a hell of a time for the major to arrive.

From his smile to the dark blue of his eyes, she knew she'd seen that ruggedly handsome face before. Where? A memory fluttered. A deep voice rumbling with laughter, a strong hand reaching across her to pour two glasses of golden Chardonnay, a sweet wine kiss, then another, deeper. She shook her head. She was losing it. He was a stranger. He had to be a stranger. And he was a rude one too. He hadn't even come into the office. He just stood in the doorway staring at her like she was the most entertaining show in town.

"And you are?" Sully asked.

"Master Sergeant Murphy. Are you the person who has been transcribing my reports and emailing them back to me? I didn't recognize your initials, '*sb*'." His smile faded and he looked toward Anise. "You did check her security clearance before passing on my notes, didn't you, Ms. Tyler?"

Red mottled under her makeup as Anise gulped for air. She hadn't followed procedure and the three of them knew it.

Pity stirred in Sully and she cleared her throat. "I am qualified to type these bloody reports in every way, Master Sergeant Tate Murphy but I have to say it would be much easier if you'd learned to scribe a coherent hand."

Where had that tone come from? Gawd, she must be channeling the university professor who supervised her practicums and would be organizing the last of her student teaching when she got off active duty. The old biddy made her crazy at the best of times and today wasn't one of them.

Murphy arched one eyebrow and Sully struggled not to laugh at her own outburst. As a broad smile spread across his face, the memory pinged at her again. She'd seen him before, hadn't she? Why did he look so familiar? She studied his face. High cheekbones, a nose that had been broken, probably in a brawl—he was a soldier after all. A strong jaw and that mouth… Why did she know he'd be terrific at kissing? The ghost of firm lips, his tongue parting hers and sweeping into her mouth.

Sully's breath quickened as her body involuntarily responded to the phantom memory. She looked away to escape his steady gaze and gain control of her rampaging senses. Taking a deep breath, she squared her shoulders and lifted her chin as he entered the room, followed by a shorter, sandy-haired stranger.

Her gaze fastened on the black oak leaf on the tab of the older man's camo shirt. The major! She stepped to the right to stand next to the desk and snapped to the position of attention.

And her treacherous left leg collapsed.

She fell hard. Pain shot through her from the ankle to the hip. She hadn't broken it again, had she? Tears burned and she forced them back. No, she wouldn't cry. She was a combat soldier, damn it. Her stomach swirled and she tasted the oatmeal she'd had for breakfast. It wasn't any better the second time. *I'm not hurling here.*

Before she struggled to her feet, Tate Murphy stood in front of her. He leaned down, caught her elbow. He pulled her up, wrapping an arm around her waist, to steady her. "So, do you always throw yourself at the feet of an officer, Sergeant Barlow? Faith, with service like that, it makes me wish I went to O.C.S."

"Not too late, Murphy." Major Harper frowned thoughtfully. "I'll sign your application anytime."

"I'd need an age waiver. Thirty-five is too old."

6

Not for me, Sully thought. *He's only six years older than I am.* Okay, mind back on duty and off the hot guy holding her.

"What happened, Sergeant? Is the floor wet? Why did you fall?"

"I'm sorry, sir." Sully felt heat rush into her face. "I broke my leg, sir. The cast was removed last week before I came here. It's all right now, sir. I just moved too quickly."

"Sick call, Murphy." Major Harper glanced at his aide, then turned his eagle eyes on her. "I want a second opinion, Sergeant Barlow. From a doctor."

"What about the correspondence?" Sully slipped out of Tate's grasp, even though she didn't want to. Where had that idea come from? She put a hand on the desk to brace herself. "I'm not finished."

"Yes, you are." Major Harper said, in even tones. "We'll see you when the doctors release you to return. Paperwork doesn't disappear, Barlow. There will be plenty for you to do later."

"Yes, sir." She watched him stride into the adjoining office, then limped around the desk, still resting a hand on the wooden surface. "All right. Let's get this over with, Sergeant Murphy."

He chuckled. "It may come as a shock, but I actually do out-rank you, Barlow. I should issue the orders."

"Someone ought to have told you that *'should'* only applies to six-year-olds," Sully retorted. "And if you move along, I'll be back here before lunch."

Another low chuckle. "My father would call you a real spitfire." Tate gazed quickly across the room. "Don't save my reports for her, Ms. Tyler. You better get on them because I'm sure the doctors will assign Sergeant Barlow to quarters."

"Good luck with that." Sully measured the distance between her desk and the door. It looked as dangerous as a street in Kabul. *Nope, not going there*, she told herself. *Just take one step at a time.* She could do it. She'd faced worse. Hell, she walked on a broken leg for more than a week before the doctors realized she'd been one of the proverbial 'walking wounded.' Granted, she'd depended on a lot of wine to get her through but there'd been plenty of troubles to drown.

Raven. No, don't think of her. Not here and not now.

"Shall I send for a wheelchair?" Tate asked.

7

"No. I can handle it." Sully took a step, another and her leg buckled. "Damn it."

His arm clamped around her waist. "Well, if you don't want a wheelchair, then you'd better lean on me."

"That's probably what she wanted in the first place," Anise sniped from across the room.

"Start typing if you don't want to be here till midnight," Sully said sweetly. She let the other non-com help her to the door, past the dreaded flag, and down the hall. "Thanks."

"It's the least I can do." He lowered his voice. "Now, what is your name? Your real name? It's not Vanna."

"What?" She choked, stopped, stared up at him, and almost fell into the cobalt sea of his eyes. "Who are you?"

"Tate Murphy." A wry smile twisted his mouth. "Okay, so you had a few when we met in that hotel bar outside Tacoma. And then we split two bottles of Chardonnay downstairs and another when we got to my room, but I can't be that forgettable."

Sully gaped at him. She shivered when he trailed a finger over her cheek, down to her chin. She'd been off base in Tacoma almost seven weeks before, determined to avoid the holidays with her family. And after a hellacious, horrible day at a memorial service in Liberty Valley, followed by a military funeral, where family and friends had barely spoken to her, clustering around her oldest stepbrother, she'd gotten blitzed in a bar. She'd seen a gorgeous guy and made a move on him. It was stupid, risky behavior, but at least he'd had a box of condoms. "You were in civvies."

"So were you," Tate said. "I hope you still have that red dress. It was something. You were something."

"I was drunk." Sully took a deep breath. Wild, fabulous sex. It was supposed to be a cure-all for heartbreak. It hadn't worked. The next morning her head hurt. Her leg hurt. She was still hiding at a hotel, avoiding everyone who really knew her, barely making it to the base in time to jump through a dozen hoops. It was all part of Army procedures when soldiers came back alive to CONUS, one of which was the physical exam with the doctor who discovered she was walking on a broken leg. "I was drunk. You got me past a bad time."

"And you gave me a phony name, a disconnected number and faded like smoke. I woke up and you were gone."

"Hey, it was what every guy wants. A one-night booty call with a stranger." She watched his eyes widen, his jaw tighten, and decided she didn't feel guilty. She wouldn't feel guilty. And she certainly wouldn't tell the poor man that she barely recalled him except in dreams. Nobody needed to hear he was so inconsequential. "No commitment on either side. Now, can we go to sick call?"

"Yes." He guided her to the elevator. "I went back to that hotel several times looking for you and I still want answers to my questions about you."

"And I want a million dollars. Guess I better buy a lottery ticket."

She was spunky and not nearly as tall as she'd been in the spike heels and halter-necked red silk dress that skimmed her thighs. It should have clashed with her waist-length copper hair, but somehow it didn't. He'd seen her across the bar and watched her cut other men dead. Then, she turned on her stool and he found himself going to her. He'd asked her to dance and she refused.

She said she'd come to drink and that was what she intended to do. Her emerald green eyes were heavily made up. He'd wondered what she looked like without the cosmetics, figured he'd find out the next morning when she agreed to come to his room. The bartender had *Wheel of Fortune* on the TV and it'd taken her too long to answer when Tate asked her name. Why hadn't he put things together and realized she'd lied?

Granted, she wasn't the first woman he'd picked up in a bar, but she was the last. Somehow, nobody else matched her smile or quick wit. He'd always enjoyed bantering with smart-mouthed women. The elevator doors opened on the first floor and he ushered her toward the main entrance. Well, he'd finally found her again and the two of them could start over. They might even talk to each other instead of just falling into the nearest bed. Then again, maybe not.

"Murphy, I didn't know you were back from the field. Is Major Harper in his office?" A balding man strode toward them, frowning at the woman next to Tate. "What's your problem now, Sergeant Barlow? Ms. Tyler called and told me that you refused to clean up the breakroom."

"Considering the sergeant can barely walk, she has no business even considering doing such a thing." Tate swept the older man with a disgusted look. "And don't send my noncoms to mop floors. They don't do janitorial work. They've paid their dues and they supervise junior enlisted. If you want somebody higher up the food chain to do it, you can have one of the ROTC cadets."

"What happened to her?" Mr. Edwards asked. "She was fine when Army Finance sent her here to do office work."

"Afghanistan," Sully said in icy tones. She obviously didn't like being talked over as if she weren't standing in the hall between the two of them. "Kabul. IED. I walked away. Found out when I got home that I'd broken my leg."

Utter silence fell. Tate stared at her, then at the senior civilian liaison. "Major Harper ordered her to the dispensary and that's where I'm taking her. I'll assign someone to deal with the breakroom when I return."

"You don't need to." Mr. Edwards ran a hand over his thinning hair. "I'm sorry, Barlow. I talked when I should have listened. And Anise—"

"Always has issues when you send another woman to the Major's office," Tate said, "especially a competent one."

That earned a bark of laughter before the man returned to his own office. Now, Tate had more questions. "Was your leg broken when…?"

"We were together?" She nodded. "Yes. So, I drank more than I normally would."

"You must have a really high pain threshold. Didn't you know?" He shook his head. "Never mind. That was stupid. If you'd known, you'd have gone to the doctor or come to the hospital at the main base."

"Exactly." She didn't speak again until she was in the front seat of the Army sedan he drove on duty. "I'm not a real pain in the backside most of the time, Murphy. If there weren't any lower-ranking enlisted and my leg didn't hurt, I'd clean the breakroom."

"I don't doubt that, but neither condition applies. When you return to duty, there's plenty of paperwork around here with all the college kids training during their spring breaks, not to mention the reserve units coming home and out-processing." He started the engine. "Now, about your first name? I can't keep calling a woman I slept with by her last one."

She laughed. "Sullivan. Sully for short."

He cruised through the parking lot, catching another glimpse of the classic, bright pink Mustang Fastback parked by itself in one corner. "I do like that name better than Vanna."

"And I'm supposed to care what you like?"

"I thought you did last Christmas and you will again."

"Don't bet on it, Murphy."

Three hours later, Sully stared at the prescriptions in her hand. Returning to work was out of the question. The doctor had taken one look at her badly swollen leg and yelled for X-rays. Whirlpool treatments followed until the swelling was reduced. It seemed like everybody poked and prodded at her until she could scream. They put a temporary splint on her leg which made the damn thing hurt even more and she'd said so. The doctor told her the resultant discomfort was because she'd overstressed the leg, but he'd write a prescription for pain relievers.

The nurse was much more tactful. She had stuck around to help Sully pull on her loose camouflage fatigue pants before vanishing back into the clinic. Quarters! She grimaced. She was stuck in her room for two days and what was she supposed to do there? She wondered if she could get a ride to the liquor store on post and load up on Chardonnay. Wait a second. Hadn't that gotten her in trouble before? She'd opted for way too much alcohol to dull the pain and ended up in bed with Murphy.

She heard a knock on the door. "Come in. Everyone else has."

Tate Murphy sauntered inside, holding a pair of crutches. "How do you feel?"

"Like a total idiot." Sully shot a glare at him. "They're sending me to my room as if I'm a problem teenager. I'm not staying on base to sit around and do nothing. Even when my leg was in a real cast, I worked at the Finance Processing Center, doing payroll for returning soldiers. Okay, so my unit is training in California and I can't join them. But you could let me go to Supply to help inventory the equipment they've sent back from Afghanistan before it goes to our home base at Fort Bronson in Seattle."

He gently closed the door and leaned against it. "You are in a snit, aren't you? And before you ask, I won't bring you a laptop or send you to work anywhere. I have my orders and so do you. Two days of rest and then light duty back in Major Harper's office so we can keep an eye on you. If you have family close by, the doctors agreed you could have a two week leave at home until your unit arrives."

She shook her head. She wouldn't explain why she didn't want to be in Liberty Valley right now. She couldn't. Granted, her relatives barely called or wrote or *Skyped* when she was overseas. She wasn't their favorite. That status had always belonged to Raven.

This guy didn't have the proverbial 'need to know' what a failure she really was, Sully thought. *Everything is wrong with me, my hair, my eyes, my body, my behavior, my choices. They hate me and I don't blame them. Nobody's barely spoken to me since the funeral.* "I'm not going there. I'm staying on post."

"Then, we'll have a lot of fun."

"I don't think so, Murphy. Haven't we been that route already?"

"You bet and I can't wait to do it again."

CHAPTER TWO

A long, three-story brick structure with two wings, the Bachelor Enlisted Quarters, reminded Sully of an old motel on a lonely stretch of highway. She'd stayed here since Christmas, but she preferred the dilapidated office building and the nearby bare-bones World War Two barracks that her unit called home at Fort Bronson in Seattle. The main advantage to the BEQ at Fort Clark, this combined Army and Air Force base the size of a small town, was the transient population of soldiers coming and going. There wasn't time for anyone to try to make real friends with her and she was grateful for that.

Sully waited while Tate came around to her car door. She eased out of the sedan, using the crutches to support her weight. Gawd, she hated these things. She'd been so glad to be rid of them last week. Heaving a sigh, she led the way to the main doors. "You don't need to see me all the way to my room."

"I'll just make sure that someone is here to help if you need it."

"Wonderful." She hoped her tone didn't sound as sarcastic as she felt.

Master Sergeant Hathaway, the NCO who ran the BEQ had assigned her a small bedroom with a private bath on the ground floor when she arrived right before New Year's. He warned she might be bumped if or when a higher-ranking soldier arrived for a lengthy stay, but these were transient rooms and it wasn't highly likely, especially since she was injured. Most of the noncoms were only here for a few days or perhaps a week before they shipped out to new assignments or were reassigned to one of the military schools with their own housing. Some arranged to rent apartments off-post in one of the nearby communities.

Tate Murphy had parked as close as he could to the doors that opened onto the parking lot. He walked beside her while she made her way inside to the front desk, not showing any signs of impatience at how long it took with the damned crutches.

Behind the counter, Corporal Ferguson, a young man in fatigues, glanced at her, then stood. "What happened, Sergeant Barlow? I thought you said you were ready to charge the wall."

"I am, but this stupid leg isn't." Sully managed a polite smile at the boy who was barely out of his teens. "The doctors have me on Quarters for the weekend."

"Do you have someone to send to the shoppette if she wants anything?" Tate asked. "She'll need meals brought from the nearest DFAC."

"We'll take care of her." Corporal Ferguson returned his gaze to Sully. "Your car? Do you want someone to bring it here?"

"I do." She watched the dark-haired boy quiver, excitement in his big brown eyes. "It means everything to me. It doesn't go above twenty-five miles an hour. I know what's on the odometer. It's three miles between the parking lot at HQ and here."

He nodded. "I'll have one of the guys drop me off at HQ when I'm off duty."

"Nobody else rides in it." Sully reached in her pants pocket for the ring of keys. "I don't eat in it and no one else had better either. If I have a problem when I see it again, you'll clean it with a toothbrush inside and out."

"No problem, Sarge." Corporal Ferguson held out his hand, barely breathing. "I swear."

"Park it under the light. I want to see it from my window." Sully slowly drew out the keys. "And bring these back to me as soon as the car is here."

"If it's that big a deal, I can ask one of the M.P.s to bring your car to the BEQ," Tate drawled.

"I don't know them," Sully said, removing her room key from the ring and tucking it back into her pants pocket before passing the others to the young man on the other side of the counter. "After being here since December, I know Ferguson. He screws up and Hathaway can feast on the scraps I throw him."

"Sounds fair," Tate said.

"It is." Corporal Ferguson tucked the keys into his shirt pocket. "Thank you, Sergeant Barlow. I'll be careful. Did you need anything from the shoppette now? Snacks? Soft drinks? Water? I'll send a runner."

"Nothing at the moment." Sully headed toward the wing of rooms primarily reserved for noncoms. She wasn't surprised when Tate followed. For some reason, he seemed to be interested in her and she didn't think it was due to an overwhelming physical attraction. It was probably just male curiosity mingled with perversity. If she told any of her four stepbrothers, they couldn't have something, they busted their tails to prove they could.

At her door, Tate looked up and down the length of the short, quiet hallway. "You rank pretty high with Hathaway. Normally these rooms are for E8s and above."

"He said there were larger rooms on the second and third floors, but I'd have to share with another female noncom and some of the whiners would bitch when I used the elevator and they had to climb stairs."

"Sounds like him. He's been around forever and doesn't have much patience." Tate smiled down at her. "You have your prescriptions. You added my number to the contact list on your phone so you can call me if you need anything else. Do you want me to bring back something besides dinner in a few hours?"

Sully glanced at him. "A bottle of Chardonnay. Bring two glasses and I'll even share."

"Not with those meds." He laughed. "I'll see you later, Sarge."

"Not if I see you first," Sully muttered, feeling more childish than ever as she stepped inside and locked the door behind her.

The room carried on the same old motel feel. A full-length mirror was screwed next to the closet that was a step up from the wall locker she had in the *sandbox*. No, she wouldn't think about the room she and Raven shared there. Shaking her head, Sully opened the left-hand door to the bathroom. Hathaway and one of his team must have closed it after the Friday inspection, but she preferred to know she was alone and not worry someone might be lurking in the shadows. In the event of an assault, she kept a hoof pick in her pocket.

Sully advanced further into the room. She paused by the closet, removed her shirt, and hung it on a coat hanger. Again, not because she was Ms. or Sergeant First Class Clean. Putting away the shirt allowed her to check the closet for an intruder, another security precaution. She glanced around the remainder of the square space. The single bunk was against the left-hand wall, a nightstand beside it. She always made the bed in proper military fashion, blankets tucked in with hospital corners. It meant she could tell there wasn't anyone underneath it with a single glance.

On the right, a mini-fridge squatted next to the wooden bureau that sported the tiny microwave Ferguson had commandeered along with a coffeepot. The kid was correct when he told Tate Murphy that they looked after her here, frequently bringing her frozen meals from the shoppette when her leg hurt too badly to try to go to the dining facility or DFAC as Tate called it. She might not say so often enough, but she did appreciate their efforts.

She heaved a sigh. The pain wasn't as bad when she supported her weight on the crutches. Still, they made her feel helpless. Her phone vibrated against her leg. Leaning the crutches against the wall, she sat down on the edge of the bed and pulled out the cell. It was her mother. Dreading the barrage of complaints that would be forthcoming, Sully didn't answer.

Deciding to clear the queue, she scrolled through the list of missed calls from her mother and deleted the three messages she'd already heard. She had four others from the university, undoubtedly about the upcoming semester and the last bout of student teaching at the high school in Lake Maynard. She'd deal with them later.

Supporting herself with one crutch, she limped to the window and closed the blinds, blocking the weak afternoon heat of the mid-February sun. Light still filtered through the slits and she took a moment to glance around the square room. She'd aced the Friday inspection again, easy enough since she didn't hang pictures on the wall or the bulletin board. She always made a point of returning any library books on Thursday nights and didn't check out new ones until Friday afternoon. She winced. It'd be a long, dull weekend without something to read.

Her uniforms hung in precise order in the closet adjacent to the hallway door. She scrubbed down the bathroom every day, not only to keep it clean enough to adhere to Army standards but also because it was a habit from her time in Afghanistan. She didn't like creepy, crawly things sharing her shower, a reason she carried a hoof pick everywhere even when she'd sold her last horse years ago.

During their first tour in Iraq, a woman from a different unit was assaulted in the showers. When nothing beyond a few lectures was done to prevent future attacks, Raven had her mother send an assortment of hoof picks in the next box from home. She and Sully passed them out to the other enlisted women in their company. They didn't have enough picks, but Ann Barrett received more from her father who bred champion Morgan horses. When battalion Command Sergeant-Major Jenkins learned what they carried with them, he asked what protection the tool provided.

Sully explained that a short-handled piece of wedge-shaped metal sharp and strong enough to pry packed dirt, rocks, sticks, and other crap from a horse's foot could do serious damage to an assailant's face and make him easy to identify later. The senior non-com had simply nodded and thanked them for looking out for the troops. Later, Sully learned from the company deputy commander that he was supposed to tell them to throw away their country-style defense, but it wasn't Jenkins' style.

She missed the sarcastic old man. Hell, she missed everyone, but she'd have been a liability to them with her leg in a cast. They'd be home before she had her health back and could be an effective member of the team. She sighed. At least, she couldn't gripe about the weather or the insects here. For a moment, she remembered the joke Raven's grandmother always told about western Washington State. "There are only two seasons, the rainy one and August."

Sully shook her head, blocking the unwanted memories. She

wouldn't think about Grandma Driscoll or the fabulous homemade snickerdoodles she kept in the moonshine-jug shaped cookie jar, the ones that only Sully and Raven loved since their older brothers preferred chocolate chip or peanut butter.

No. Don't think about Raven. Stop it. Remember this morning and plan how to jump the hot guy with those cobalt blue eyes and that dangerous smile.

The laptop on the desk caught her attention for a moment and faint amusement trickled through her. Murphy might think he was the boss of her, but nothing could be further from the truth. She didn't need him to bring her a computer. She had one of her own. If he thought he oversaw her activities, he was wrong. Nothing could be further from the truth. She might not be able to type his silly reports about training exercises and the performances of the individual soldiers but that didn't mean there wasn't work for her to finish.

She needed to put together the lesson plans for the unit she was supposed to teach on *To Kill A Mockingbird* and forward them to the cooperating teacher at the high school as well as her university supervisor. Just the idea of talking about the book Raven loved to reluctant tenth graders who would undoubtedly have issues with even reading the classic novel made Sully's eyes burn with unshed tears. She took a deep breath. No, she wasn't crying. Instead, she'd figure out how to get Tate back in her bed. Sex with him might not be the answer, but it'd keep her mind from racing like a hamster on its wheel.

She returned to the single bed. Crutch against the wall, she sat down on the bunk and unlaced her combat boots, grateful the temporary splint didn't cover her entire foot like the previous cast. She'd nap away the afternoon and hope the pills kept her from dreaming. If not, she'd go to the smaller Common room near this semi-private wing and watch TV. It wouldn't be one of those sappy *Hallmark* movies that Raven adored with their happy-ever-after endings.

No, I'll watch Judge Judy and let her kick butt on stupid people who don't have moral compasses to define the differences between right and wrong.

Sully stretched out on top of one blanket and pulled the second over her. She'd close her eyes just for a moment, see what happened.

She drew one deep breath, exhaled just as deeply, took another breath. Tension seeped out of her shoulders. She turned her cheek into the coolness of the pillow.

A knock on the door woke her. She yawned, glancing at the radio clock on the nightstand, automatically converting the digits into military time. Almost five p.m. made it sixteen-forty-five. She reached for one of the crutches as the visitor rapped again. "Just a moment."

Supporting her weight, she stood and hobbled to the door. She unlocked it, opened it to find Tate Murphy standing there. "What are you doing here?"

"Supper." He held up the distinctive red and white sack from her favorite restaurant on the highway outside the base, a cardboard carrier with two cups of coffee in the other hand. "I asked Corporal Ferguson and he told me what you preferred."

"My car? Is the kid off-duty yet?"

Tate pulled out the set of keys. "If I'd realized we were talking about that '68 classic Mustang, I'd have finagled a way to drive it, even if it is hot pink. Automatic or stick?"

"Automatic," Sully said before she thought. "I wanted a five-speed, but Raven was the one who found the car at her grandpa's wrecking yard. She called 'dibs' before I even got there. And it's, *Passionate Pink,* not *Hot Pink.*"

"Dibs?" Tate asked, a smile edging his mouth. "Why dibs?"

"Between us, we have ten older brothers. They got everything first. If one of them saw that Mustang, we'd have lost out. This way we had Grandpa Driscoll on our side, although he winced a bit when we chose a girly color to keep the boys away from it."

Tate chuckled. "Sounds like my family. My youngest bro, Lock always pitched a fit when we tried to leave him home, but he was such a baby."

"How big is your family?" Sully wanted, needed to change the subject from her own. The past was behind her, and she couldn't bear to remember. "How old is Lock?"

"He just turned thirty." Tate led the way to the table in the far corner. He put down the bag. "Sit and eat before your omelet gets cold. I'll open the blinds so you can scope out the car."

"Well, they'd better get their acts together." Picking up her fork, Sully cut into the omelet. "Otherwise, it will be a total culture shock when they end up in the *sandbox*."

"We're downsizing. By the time these kids graduate from high school and college, they won't be headed to Afghanistan."

"There will be another hot spot somewhere and we have a volunteer military with a commander-in-chief that hasn't served a day in uniform. So, those kids will be leading troops into battle. They'll be just as expendable as we are." Sully held up a hand when it looked like he might interrupt. "Sorry, I have issues, especially when I've missed lunch. Let me eat and I won't be so grumpy."

CHAPTER THREE

He drank coffee while she ate. Sergeant First Class Sullivan Barlow had opinions and he respected that. He found it easier to deal with a woman who did than one who didn't. He enjoyed looking at her and the way the t-shirt clung to her body. The dog tags on a silver chain around her neck drew attention to the curve of her breasts as if he didn't remember them already. They'd been perfect, filling his hands.

He suddenly realized he'd talked more to her today than he had that night in the hotel. Back then, he'd been caught up in the fantasy of taking a stranger to bed. He hadn't considered her agenda, although he knew she must have had one. Everyone came with baggage whether they admitted it or not. He certainly had his share.

Something about her reminded him of his mother. It wasn't their height. At about five-feet-five, Sully was taller than his mom. Even with that mane of copper red hair subdued into a braid and pinned into a neat tight bun, Tate remembered it wild, free, flowing down her back. Bronwyn Murphy was a petite, silver-haired dynamo who complained about her propensity for putting on weight because she snuck chocolate chip cookies at Pop's Café in Baker City. When she went on a diet, the entire family ate salad or else.

Amused, Tate wondered what his mother would think of Sullivan Barlow. Would they get along or argue? And what about Quinn? His twin never hesitated to share her opinions of the women Tate dated. It'd caused more than one argument in the past when she met what she called, 'Ranger groupies.'

"Why are you smirking at me?" Sully demanded. "What have you done now, Murphy?"

He laughed at the tone. "That's it. You sound just like my mother."

"Oh, way to impress a woman. How many have you told that?"

"None, because nobody else channels her." Tate leaned back in the chair. "What about yours? What did she say when you told her you were joining the Army?"

"I should marry the boy next door and unite our farms in Liberty Valley the way my step-dad wanted. I didn't need to go to college to find a husband. I had one waiting in the wings for me to grow up."

Tate eyed her, fascinated. "That sounds medieval. What did you say?"

"Oh, I was a typical teen diva. I went all screaming meltdown on the poor woman's head." Sully finished her toast, pushed back from the table, and picked up the cup of coffee. "I was going to college and I'd get the Army Reserve to pay for it since she and her husband wouldn't."

"Did your folks come around when you graduated?"

"Well, before that. My stepdad, Gil was impressed when I made the President's Honor Roll my freshman year." Sully flinched. "Of course, I ended up in Iraq for my first tour before I finished my bachelor's degree. My mom totally freaked."

"Anyone's mother would." Tate put his empty cup on the table. "Dad said that mine did the stoic routine and cried outside in the rain every time I shipped out. She didn't want anyone to know."

"My dad died in the first Gulf War," Sully said. "She never laid that on me when my unit prepped for the first tour in the *sandbox*, but it was the proverbial elephant in the living room. We both knew it was there, even if neither of us mentioned it."

A shadow crossed her face and Tate opted to change the subject. He wouldn't ask her to share war stories yet. He'd done his tours in Iraq and Afghanistan too. He knew she'd undoubtedly seen what he had. Instead, he asked. "Didn't your dad have insurance to pay for your college? If he was military, you should have had his benefits."

"He didn't marry my mother or claim me as his kid. She said they'd split up before he died. She married Gil Barlow, a widower with four sons. I'll give him credit. He tries to treat me like I'm one of his kids, but he couldn't afford to send the boys to college either. There isn't much money in dairy farming now."

"Not in any kind of farming," Tate said. "Lock runs my dad's place. The two of them are always watching the pennies." He grinned. "Because the dollars—"

"Are already spent," Sully finished, smiling back at him. "Do your folks have a garden?"

"Oh, sure. When I'm home on leave and sass Mom or Dad, she sends me to pull weeds."

"My step-dad does that too." Sully laughed. "It's better than a time-out or being grounded."

"Got that right." Tate leaned back in his chair. "And college? How long did it take to get your degree?"

"Almost seven years with all these little breaks to go to war." Sarcasm laced her tone. "I applied for graduate school because I figured I'd finish my master's degree and then find a job. Maybe, I should have listened to my mom. It's been more than ten years, almost eleven and I'm still a college student. If I'd married straight out of high school and started popping out babies, I'd be safe. She wouldn't be losing her mind whenever my unit left for the Middle East."

"And you'd be the one going crazy."

"True and Falcon Driscoll is a good guy who deserves a wife that actually loves him."

"What about you?" Tate stood and cleared away the table. "Shouldn't you have a guy who thinks you make the sun rise and set?"

"Careful." This smile didn't touch her eyes. "Won't you lose your *man card* for being too sensitive?"

"Oh, I think I can handle it." He put the disposable plate and plastic ware in the garbage, went into the bathroom, and came back with a damp paper towel to wipe the table. "Okay, you're squared away for tonight. Do you need anything else? Corporal Ferguson said he'd bring you breakfast tomorrow, and I'll check in on you at lunchtime."

"Wow, am I lucky or what?" She stood, bracing her weight on the back of the chair. "I can take care of myself. There's a whole string of fast-food places just outside the gate and now that I have my car, I can drive to one of them."

"Not when you're restricted to quarters, Barlow. The doctors want you to rest that leg. You have your orders and so do I."

"Is that all this is, Murphy? Orders?"

"For now." He watched speculation rise in her green eyes. She tilted her head and he nodded in response to the unasked question. "I'm interested in what comes next too."

"A kiss goodnight?"

"Another time." He snagged the liner from the small garbage can, tied the corners, and backed toward the door. "It's too soon."

"For you?" She started across the room. "Funny. You didn't say that a few weeks ago."

"I'm saying it now. I want to get to know you." He escaped to the hall, closing the door behind him.

If Quinn had seen him flee from a woman, Tate would never hear the end of it. Of course, his twin would have had a list of names to call him for picking up a woman in a hotel bar, starting with, "You slut-puppy," and ending with, "You used a condom, right?"

Tate eyed the closed door. Why was Sully willing to sleep with him when she barely knew him? Half of the time she acted like they were strangers and now, she made the moves like she really wanted him. It didn't make sense. Who was the real Sully? Had he even met her? Would he want her when he did? Okay, stupid question. He wanted her, but this time it had to last more than a few hours that ended with the morning sun.

She glowered after him. Wow, that was different. She'd expected him to stick around for a heavy petting session at the least and a romp in bed at the most. What was wrong with the man? He admitted he was interested, but he'd turned her down although he hadn't been stupid enough to give her that line, *It's not you, it's me.* And it wasn't like she was the only one who enjoyed herself back in December. She'd rocked his world too.

She took a deep breath. What was the matter with her? Had she lost her mind since she returned from Afghanistan? Would she have jumped Murphy if he acted the least bit receptive? That wasn't her style. When she was in high school, she'd dated Falcon Driscoll for a few weeks. They experimented with an occasional kiss, but it hadn't worked for them. Neither of them was too attached. Too much brother and sister affection, not enough passion.

He'd gone after a tall, blonde, basketball champion and she'd opted for the debate captain. She'd lost her virginity to the guy on Prom night, but that hadn't seemed like a big deal either, more a rite of passage. One boyfriend in college and their kisses had been a fun way to end intense study sessions. They'd only slept together a couple of times since both of them had roommates and weren't much for spending money on motels.

All right after dating a half-dozen guys and only sleeping with two of them, she couldn't sign up to be a nun. Still, she wasn't like Raven who'd dated her way around the college campus in Bellingham and kept a scorecard on her laptop. She claimed she intended to sleep with the five-star guys, not that there were many at their university. One-stars never got more than a coffee date. Two-stars meant she might consider meeting them at the university dining hall for dinner, but they had better plan on paying.

Three stars and all of them would go to the movies when Sully had time away from her books. Four stars and Raven actually spent time alone with the guy, usually bringing back leftover Chinese food or the remains of a pizza for her and Sully to share later. Five stars and the fellow had better have money for a hotel room, or he'd lose out because Raven wasn't sleeping with anyone in a college dorm.

No, she wouldn't think about her best friend now, or the way she said that only Sully's oldest stepbrother, Kord rated a six. It wasn't time. Focus on Tate Murphy instead. Their night together before Christmas had been an aberration. *Still, I could use a distraction and he'd be a good one. Then, I wouldn't have to think about anything else until tomorrow. Okay, let's stop playing Scarlett O'Hara.*

Sully drew a deep breath. If she wasn't doing something that she privately considered cheap and slutty, she'd gimp her way down to the dayroom and watch *Bones* on the big screen TV, rather than viewing an episode on her laptop. Solving the fictional murder would block the memories and she wouldn't have to analyze her issues with Murphy. She also wouldn't feel guilty about not designing the unit lesson plan for *To Kill a Mockingbird*. Maybe one of the other non-coms would show up with booze or she could have someone bring her a bottle of wine from the nearby mini-mart, still commonly called the shoppette.

She left her room, locking the door behind her, and slowly hobbled down the hall. She bypassed the pool tables where most of the off-duty soldiers clustered and headed to the adjacent lounge. Surprisingly she was the only one there, but somebody had left on the TV. Sully picked up the remote, then sank into a recliner, leaning back until she could prop up her injured leg. She pressed the button and changed channels until she found an episode of one of her favorite shows. It began with the discovery of a body in the woods, then cut to sharp, witty dialogue between the characters.

She glanced toward the door as a slender brunette wearing hospital scrubs strolled in and commandeered the other recliner. Sully nodded at her and waited until a commercial break before she said, "Hi. I'm Sully Barlow."

"Jeannie Sanders. I've seen you around. Weren't you at the clinic today?"

"Yeah, my leg acted up." Sully pointed to the offending limb. "So, I'm on quarters for the weekend."

"Let me know if you need anything and I'll bring it back for you."

Sales pitches over, the show started again. Sully decided to wait before she mentioned her favorite wine. It wasn't like she needed it right away. A few hours wouldn't make much of a difference.

On the next set of commercials, Jeannie resumed the conversation. "Are you assigned here for long?"

"Only until my unit finishes out-processing in California. They should be back to Washington State in two or three weeks. Then, we'll hopefully be Stateside for a while. What about you?"

"Oh, I'm permanent here, at least for the next year. I'm looking for off-base housing but haven't found an apartment yet."

"Where did you come from?"

"Anchorage." Jeannie heaved a sigh. "I was stationed there for two years and I miss it. I arrived last month. In Alaska, we have about seven hours of daylight at this time of year."

"Join the Army and see the world?"

"Something like that, but I didn't expect it to be Washington State." Jeannie smiled. "So, what do they have you doing while you wait for your unit?"

"Do you know Anise Tyler?"

"Of course. Who doesn't? She comes in and freaks out all over us whenever one of the clerks assigned to her office in HQ goes on sick call. How are we supposed to stop them from exercising their rights to escape her corner of Oz? Did she trip you or hit you with her broomstick?"

"No." Sully grinned, appreciating the witchy references. "I was assigned to work with her, so she had me typing all of the reports for Major Harper."

"Sounds like her. If she spent more time working, she could do them herself."

"Where would the fun be in that?" Sully glanced at the TV, but the show hadn't started yet. Instead, a famous actor extolled the benefits of reverse mortgages.

"I swear the commercials last longer than the bits of the show," Jeannie said. "How do you stand it?"

"By analyzing the persuasive techniques to get me to buy crap I don't want. So far, I've seen five slogans, two bandwagons, one expert opinion, and now—"

"Testimonial," Jeannie finished. "So, what are you in the real world, Sully?"

"An English, Science, and History teacher or I will be soon. I have my last segment of student teaching next quarter and a final course where I complete various projects and take certification tests during this summer. I'll have my master's in teaching degree in August and be looking for a position at a high school."

"And you didn't go for your commission? Why not? With that much college, you could easily be an officer."

"I could." Sully shrugged. "But at the time, it seemed like too much hassle and I'm happy as a noncom. I know several who are college grads."

"Yeah, we have our share in the medical field too." Jeannie reached in her pants pocket and pulled out a cell phone. "You up for pizza? I ordered a large combo already and my room-mate is stopping for beer on the way here."

"I'm in," Sully said. "Any chance she can pick up a bottle of Chardonnay?"

"No worries. I'll text her."

When she woke the next morning, her stomach burned. She remembered the sour taste of the Chardonnay the night before and grimaced. It had been a bottle from her favorite local winery and normally they had great quality, so what happened? The second and third glasses hadn't been much better than the first. She hadn't said anything to Jeannie, but the pizza hadn't been that wonderful either. Instead of having two or three pieces, Sully hadn't finished her first slice. Was she growing up after all this time and losing her affection for junk food?

No, that couldn't be it. She'd just been full of the omelet that Tate brought her. She'd pig out the next time there was pizza or KFC on the horizon. Since she didn't have to report for duty, there wasn't much point in getting out of bed. She flipped the pillow to the cool side, drew the blanket over her shoulders, and tried to sleep. It was quiet here, too quiet. She listened hard, waiting for the thumping of helicopters overhead, traffic sounds, conversations in the hall, anything...

No sounds. Sweat beaded on her forehead. She sat up, letting the blanket fall. Okay, if she wasn't going to sleep, then she'd take a shower, put on clean clothes. She was assigned to quarters, so it didn't have to be a uniform. She could probably get her comfy jeans over the splint on her leg. She eyed the door to the bathroom warily. It was open, revealing the empty room. It was safe. She was safe.

She shifted, swung her legs off the bunk. Okay, she'd do it. Shower and change her clothes. She took a deep breath. Why make such a big deal of it? She reached for a crutch, stood up, and unbuttoned her camo pants. It took a few minutes to slide them off her legs since she had to work them over the splint. She dropped the pants on the floor. She'd pick them up later.

Meantime, the blue splint had to go. The doctor had told her she could take it off when she bathed, a definite improvement from the one she'd had on before. She'd needed to wrap that cast in trash bags when she couldn't avoid the shower any longer.

This contraption had a series of nylon straps that wove through rings and fastened on themselves. She sat on the bed and proceeded to work her way through them, from top to bottom. She probably could have removed it last night, but what was the point? She needed to keep the leg stabilized or it wouldn't heal, and she'd be trapped in her room that much longer. She wanted to return to the office, even if Anise Tyler was a pain in the backside. Sitting around gave Sully too much time to think, to remember and she tended to avoid that whenever possible.

Before she headed into the shower, she decided to brew a pot of coffee. It'd be ready when she was, and she'd spend the morning on the lesson unit. Like Raven used to say, "Sooner to it, sooner through it." Nothing would be resolved by continuing to dread the work and this way, Sully could email off the draft to all parties concerned. If they wanted changes, it'd be fine because she wasn't throwing her heart and soul into the project.

Decision made, she filled the canister with water, set the glass carafe in place on the warmer. She opened the plastic lid on the can of coffee. Nausea rose in her throat. She barely made it into the bathroom before her stomach finished its rebellion. There wasn't much to up-chuck. She hadn't eaten anything since that pizza last night. She stepped back, filled a glass with water, and rinsed her mouth.

She stared in the mirror on the medicine cabinet. "Okay, Sullivan Barlow. What's going on with you?"

CHAPTER FOUR

A knock on the door jarred Sully awake. She sat up, glimpsing the radio-clock on the nightstand. Thirteen hundred hours. Showering, washing her hair, replacing the splint, and dressing in sweats and a sloppy t-shirt had sapped all her energy so she'd opted for a nap before she started on the lesson unit. She hadn't planned to sleep until one in the afternoon, but oh well.

Another knock. She sighed, grabbed the crutches, and headed for the door. "Who is it?"

"Tate Murphy."

"Really?" Sully heaved another sigh. What was he doing here? She unlocked the door but didn't unhook the security latch, cracking the door a bare inch. He stood in the hall, brawny and beautiful in his fatigues. "You so have to get a life."

"What would you gripe about if I did?"

"Oh, I'd find something." She opened the door wide. "Come in and tell me why you bailed on work on a glorious Saturday. Don't you have to go see what your little princesses need?"

He chuckled, held up a cardboard takeout box. "When I checked in with Ferguson at oh-six-hundred hours, he said you didn't answer at breakfast time, so I brought you lunch."

"How kind of you." She suppressed the urge to roll her eyes at the sight of the familiar cartons the Army dining facility used. "Please tell me it's something edible."

"Healthy too." He grinned, mischief sliding into his eyes. "Caesar salad with chicken, ranch dressing on the side, and chocolate chip cookies for dessert."

She turned to limp toward the table. "Why does that actually sound good?"

"It is." He put the box on the table. He reached into one of his pant pockets and pulled out a bottle of water. Silverware came out of another pocket.

She nearly asked if he was always prepared and decided not to push it. He was being kind and she should accept his efforts in the spirit they were intended. She opened the box and found a neatly arranged salad on a disposable plate. She removed the cover, picked up the small cup of dressing and proceeded to decorate the greens. "Are you staying or going?"

"I'll stick around a while and then I'm headed out to the field to check on the troops and see they have all the equipment they need for the rest of the weekend." Tate drew out a chair. "Ferguson will bring you dinner. I'll be back tomorrow morning. Would you like to go off post for a few hours?"

"I'm confined to quarters, remember?"

"I checked in with the doctor and he agreed that if you took it easy, we could go to a movie or somewhere else."

She opened the napkin, studying him across the table. If she was totally evil, she'd insist on visiting the giant bookstore at the mall. She considered the idea. Replenishing her reading stock sounded like fun since the post library had a super small selection of fiction although the librarian always offered to order whatever mysteries Sully wanted. "Do guys shop?"

"When Quinn is taking her step-kids school shopping, I do." Tate shrugged a broad shoulder. "How bad can it be?"

"Way to sound enthusiastic." Sully laughed. "Okay, you're on. What time?"

"I'll pick you up at noon. We can have lunch off base and go wherever you like. Do I get to drive the Mustang?"

"Only in your dreams."

He shrugged again. "It was worth a try."

"Nothing ventured, nothing gained."

The platitude earned a wicked grin and he stuck around while she ate. Afterward, he collected the garbage and headed out without so much as a meaningful glance goodbye. Sully sighed and straightened the covers on her bunk. She ought to deal with the lesson unit, but it seemed like too much trouble. She checked for messages on her phone and saved the ones from the university, grateful her mother hadn't called again. Leaving the laptop on the table, Sully limped down to the Commons and took over the TV for some mid-day justice.

The next morning, she woke to Ferguson tapping on the door. She ate the oatmeal he'd brought and dumped the coffee down the bathroom sink when it tasted terrible. What had the cooks done to it? Normally, the coffee was strong, black, and indestructible. It even tasted good when she warmed it in the microwave hours later.

Oh well. There was nothing she could do about it. She'd get Murphy to run through the espresso stand near the main gate if she needed more caffeine. She showered, washed her hair, and then tried to decide what to wear. It wasn't like she could choose a dress and heels when she had to contend with the knee-high splint. So, she'd go the opposite route and opt for comfort instead of trying for sexy.

Most of her civvies were still at Raven's house in Liberty Valley which limited the choices available. In December, she'd found the Mustang outside the church and realized her stepbrother must have brought it to the wake for her, but her mother was the one who'd loaded the trunk with two suitcases filled with Sully's clothes and shoes. Tears stung and she blinked them away.

I'll think about that later. Right now, I have a date. What should I wear? I wish you were here to advise me, Raven. I have more uniforms than anything else, but no way am I putting on my fatigues. Normally, Sully would have opted for boot-cut blue jeans, but they wouldn't fit over the stupid contraption on her left leg and were too heavy to wear under it.

She selected lightweight, flared black slacks, and a black western-style cotton top with a Southwestern print. She braided her waist-length, red hair, added earrings, and applied makeup. Okay, if Murphy didn't kiss her today, she'd jump him. Well, at least she'd try. She might have to trip him with her crutches, but a woman did what she had to do.

He arrived exactly at noon. She silently gave him points for the decision. He wasn't too early so she would be embarrassed when she wasn't ready. He wasn't late so she would have to wonder if he was really coming or if she'd been stood up. He'd chosen to wear jeans and a blue checked shirt that made his cobalt eyes look amazing. They headed for the lobby since regulations meant she needed to sign out at the front counter with the soldier assigned to C.Q. duties. This time it was a pretty blonde in camo fatigues who pushed the clipboard forward. Sully nodded at the young woman. "I didn't realize Ferguson had the day off, Adams."

"He had the night shift, and he went off duty at seven. He'll be back tonight. Call the desk if you need anything while he's gone, and I'll send someone to get it for you."

"Thanks, I will." Sully already knew she wouldn't ask for favors and Private First-Class Joyce Adams wasn't the type to volunteer for extra duties. She mouthed all the right words, but never stepped up to do more than the bare requirements of the job.

Outside in the February sunshine, Tate gestured to the dark blue Subaru by the curb. "Here we go."

"Why do I think this isn't your regular ride?" Sully shot him a long look. "What's up with your own car? Is your P.O.V. in the shop? Raven and I installed the engine and rebuilt the tranny in the Mustang. It was basically a shell when we got it and we literally restored it from the ground up. I do all the P.M.s, the preventative maintenance now. If it's not hyper-technical, I can help you."

"I have a Ford 150 and I'm like you. I look after my rig. If I need help, Egan lends a hand when he's not on the road. He's a long-haul driver. My pickup doesn't get to a garage often." Tate shook his head, smiling. "I figured you'd have too much trouble getting in and out of it and I'm not supposed to take the major's assigned car off post for leisure activities, but privately-owned vehicles are different."

"That all makes sense, but next time let's take your P.O.V. You don't have to rent a car for me," Sully said, easing into the passenger seat. "I don't expect special treatment."

"You should." Tate took the crutches from her and put them in the back. "Lunch first and then the mall or do you want to do it the other way around?"

The rumble of her stomach answered, and they both laughed. "Okay, which restaurant are you thinking, Murphy?"

"I swung through the deli and figured we'd picnic out by the lake. If you'd prefer a sit-down meal, we can do that instead."

"I'd much rather be outside." She didn't say noisy restaurants made her nervous and he didn't ask. If she intended to eat in one, she chose the odd times of days or nights when the places weren't packed. The same went for grocery stores. Security was easier when she could see anyone approaching. He was a combat vet. Did he feel the same way about crowds?

They were off the base, heading north on the freeway before he spoke again. "What's it going to take for you to call me by my first name? You did that night."

"Shut up, Tate." Heat flooded her cheeks. "Picking up a guy in a bar and screwing his brains out isn't my usual style. I had a horrendous day and you benefited by it."

"I'd say we both did."

"If I agree it was consensual, can we change the subject?"

"Are you ever going to tell me why the day was horrible? Why did you need to drink at an airport hotel? And why did you pick me?"

She shrugged. "Like you said, it was close to an airport. I thought you'd be leaving in the morning for a business trip and we wouldn't see each other again. Why were you there?"

"We'd checked in the previous night because Quinn wanted to Christmas shop before the flight to Anchorage. She couldn't stay on post when I'm at the BEQ and Aunt Heidi already had a houseful of relatives."

"That makes sense." Sully leaned back in the seat, relieved that Tate wasn't the kind of guy who hung out in hotels looking for women to jump. "Why was she going to Alaska?"

"She didn't want her step-kids flying back from their mom's by themselves. Even if her husband and his ex are cool with depending on the airline to monitor the kids, Quinn has issues."

"How old are the kids?"

"Ten, twelve, and thirteen. Two girls and a boy."

"Is he the oldest or the youngest?"

"The youngest."

"I agree with your sister. The flight attendants are overloaded during the holiday season even when things are going well. They don't need the added responsibility of three unattended minors and the oldest girl is probably focused on her phone, not her siblings."

"That's what Quinn says. Lyle doesn't get it, but we ignore him."

"Is that the husband?" At Tate's nod, Sully smiled. "I'd ignore him too. You and Quinn are really close, aren't you?"

"We're twins," Tate said as if that was answer enough.

Sully waited until he changed lanes. "And yet she didn't enlist?"

"No. The Army is my thing. We're not joined at the hip."

"You just visit each other a lot," Sully teased. "I'll bet you email every day."

Tate grinned. "Quinn texts me too. Some people say we're too close. Luckily, Lyle isn't one of them, but his ex and oldest daughter are."

"You're twins. Tell them to grow some brains."

That earned a chuckle and he kept driving north on the freeway. She frowned when he passed the exit for the park bordering American Lake. "I thought you said something about picnicking."

"My uncle has a place on a privately-owned lake near here," Tate said. "We won't have to share our lunch with anyone except the local four-legged wildlife and possibly the dogs my aunt rescues."

"I can go with that." Sully felt herself relaxing even more when she caught glimpses of blue water shimmering through a fringe of pine trees. "Are you introducing us?"

"It will undoubtedly be a requirement since the old man can smell fried chicken from ten miles away." Tate took the next exit from the freeway. "My aunt is very health conscious."

"Does your uncle have issues?"

"No, Aunt Heidi was diagnosed with adult-onset diabetes. She controls it with diet and exercise which means Uncle Arnie eats organic foods too. He says it's worth it. Nothing tastes better than home-grown tomatoes."

"And he gets the occasional piece of deli chicken when his nephew comes to visit."

"Exactly." Tate signaled and turned into a long gravel driveway blocked by ornate black metal gates. Barely off the road, he unrolled the driver's window to tap in a code on the keypad attached to a post. The large set of gates that blocked the entrance slowly swung wide.

They drove through and when she glanced over her shoulder, Sully saw the gates close behind them. "No visitors?"

"Aunt Heidi enjoys having family visit, but before my uncle installed these gates, they always had strangers showing up wanting access to the lake to picnic on the shore, or swim, or launch their boats. Entertaining the masses wasn't why they retired here, and my aunt didn't like them upsetting the dogs."

"Sometimes people don't know when they overstep the boundaries," Sully said.

"And sometimes they don't care."

Which is why I need to install a set of gates or build walls to protect my heart, Sully thought, *and where do I find a contractor for that?*

A carpet of neatly mown grass unrolled in front of them, dotted by clusters of evergreens. Three collies bounded to meet the car, barking. Tate parked in front of a sprawling log house. "Be right back. I'll go tell them we're here in case they haven't heard the doggie doorbells."

Amused, Sully watched him pet the dogs and then saunter toward the front porch escorted by two of the canines. The third, a tri-colored youngster raced around the car, still emitting the occasional woof. She opened the door, shifted on the seat swinging her legs to make it easier to stand. It provided an advantage to greet the pup when he drew close. He was a mix. She could tell by the larger skull, blunt nose, wide-set eyes, and black mottling on his white ruff. He sat down, gave a collie grin, and held up a white-tipped, black-speckled paw for her to shake.

She laughed, obeyed, and then stroked his black and gold head. "Yes, you are cute, and I'll bet you know it."

Another little bark and the half-grown pup closed his brown eyes blissfully while she petted him. She hadn't thought about it before, but now that she was home and wouldn't be returning to Afghanistan for at least a few years, maybe she'd get a dog. It felt good to have someone who was happy to hang out with her, somebody who didn't ask questions, make demands, or find her wanting.

She glanced around the yard as the dog tensed under her hand. She spotted someone coming from the rose garden off to the far left. A wiry, white-haired man approached the car, a friendly smile on his wrinkle-lined face. She nodded a greeting. "Hello."

"Hi there. I see you met Bo. His sister will be around soon."

"Does she look like him?" Sully asked.

"She's a sable, gold, and white. My wife found them at a shelter, days before their time ran out. The pups constantly play with each other. Between that and their tight bond to each other, it makes training them a challenge."

"I'll bet." Sully glanced past him and saw Tate coming toward them, accompanied by a petite woman wearing ironed jeans and a crisp red-checked blouse. Her cap of black hair didn't show any gray or a hint of curl, although she had to be in her mid-sixties. More dogs escorted the pair. A small yellow and white female eyed Bo, then charged him. He tore off to race laps around the yard, his sister in hot pursuit. The chase evolved into a fierce tug of war as they found a rope toy.

Sully laughed. She put one hand on the back of the seat, the other on the door frame, braced herself, and levered up to a standing position. Her mother always called it, "making her manners," but Sully didn't want to be introduced when she was sitting like a queen on a throne. She met the older woman's golden-brown gaze. "Hello. I'm Sully Barlow. Thanks for letting me visit."

"Heidi Hogan." She held out her hand. "You like dogs. Want a puppy?"

"In a few weeks when I get off base and have a place to live," Sully said, gripping the other woman's fingers. "Will that work?"

"The new litter will need at least that much time before they're old enough to leave their mother." Heidi glanced at her husband, then added. "We have an apartment over the garage. Tell Tate to show it to you when you finish eating and only give Arnold one piece of chicken.

It's hell on his cholesterol. I'll show you the puppies later. Come to the house. Use the back door."

"Yes, ma'am." Sully didn't take offense at the brusque tone or the orders. It would be easier to deal with someone like Heidi than her mother whose sweetness grated on every nerve. "Thank you."

Heidi nodded. "Take the chicken bones with you, Tate. Don't let the dogs get them."

A muscle twitched in his jaw and Sully struggled to hide her smile. From the short time she'd known him, she'd noticed that he didn't mind giving orders, but he apparently wasn't much for taking them. It made him seem more human. After a few additional comments, ending with a command for Tate to call his mother, Heidi turned and headed to the garden to inspect the way her husband prepped it for planting.

Sully giggled. "I bet her kids could salute before they got out of diapers."

"We'll have to ask when she hosts the family Easter Egg hunt in a few weeks." Amusement slowly slid into his dark blue eyes. "Let me change that. You'll do the asking. I'm pretty sure my cousins can still kick my butt, especially the girls."

"You'll have to tell me about them."

"I will at lunch."

"Sounds like fun." Sully took the crutches he passed to her and waited while he picked up the bags containing their meal. She hadn't been on a picnic in forever and this one was bound to be entertaining. Granted it wasn't all that warm today, but they weren't dealing with a usual February rainstorm. Afterward, there would be an apartment to see and puppies. What could be better?

He hadn't complained about stopping at the mall on the way back to the base. She'd glimpsed a quick flash of relief when she pointed out a parking spot close to the huge bookstore three hours later. Did he think she wanted to buy clothes when she had to contend with this stupid splint? No way. She reconsidered the idea. She probably did need to purchase a few things before school started, but she could wait to pick up some new blouses.

"Are you serious about a puppy?" Tate asked, switching off the motor and pulling out the keys. "Which one did you like?"

"Bo." Sully leaned back in the passenger seat for a moment. "Your aunt says he is five months old. He's already housebroken and doing some obedience work."

"It'll break Diddly's doggie heart if you take her brother away."

"I know. I'm figuring out a way to have both. Heidi was receptive to the idea."

"I'll bet." Tate laughed. "She undoubtedly promised them a home together. Now, shall we go shopping? What do you like to read?"

"Mysteries, science-fiction, and historical novels when they're accurate. I throw them across the room when they're not."

"Thanks for the warning. I'll duck."

Browsing through the mystery section would have been difficult by herself when she had to maneuver the crutches, but Tate picked up a basket and hovered nearby while she selected books. She'd intended to choose paperbacks, but that was before she discovered two of her favorite authors had recent hardcover releases.

Ten books later, she was comfortably and contently ensconced in a chair at a table in the coffee shop, the crutches tucked neatly against the nearby wall, slightly out of her reach. For some reason, coffee didn't sound good, not even her favorite mocha so she opted for a cup of decaf peppermint tea and a huge snickerdoodle.

Engrossed in the first chapter of what would undoubtedly be a gruesome murder in Amish country, she barely noticed when an older woman stopped by the table. "Sullivan Barlow, is that you? I didn't know you were home. Why haven't you or Raven contacted me about your last student teaching assignments in Lake Maynard? Spring quarter for the university starts the first week in March."

CHAPTER FIVE

He saw the tension in Sully's body as soon as he entered the coffee shop attached to the bookstore. Grimacing, he swept the two older women with his gaze as he approached. The civilians didn't look all that threatening to him. About his mother's age, both dressed more for comfort than style in dark slacks, sweatshirts, and walking shoes. When he neared, one glanced over her shoulder, turning slightly to scan him, her gray eyes measuring him and finding him wanting.

He nodded a greeting. "Hello. I'm Tate Murphy. And you are?"

"Leslie Dunaway." The woman who appeared to be in charge held out her hand to shake his. "I'm Sullivan and Raven's supervisor from Cascadia University. I'm setting up their last quarter of student teaching now that they're finally ready." She gestured to her short, plump gray-haired companion who would have looked like a stereotypical grandmother if it hadn't been for her fierce scowl. "This is Maureen Evans. Raven will be in her English—"

"Raven's gone." Sully gestured to the crutches. "Get those, Murphy. We're out of here."

"Gone? What? How? Did you girls have an argument?" Shock and bewilderment filled Leslie's face. "Where is she? How do I contact her?"

"I have no idea." Tate put his shopping bag on the chair next to Sully's and eyed her. The tight jaw and narrowed green eyes revealed she was almost in tears although the other women probably didn't realize it. "Barlow will be in touch when the Army releases her from active duty."

He passed her the crutches. As soon as she had them, she headed for the exit. He took a moment to collect their bags before he followed, nodding politely to the women.

Maureen Evans, the gray-haired plug of a woman caught up with him. "What happened to her?"

"An I.E.D. in Kabul."

"I'm sorry. Was Raven there too?"

"I don't know." Tate strode toward the door, not saying he'd find out, but that was next on his list. He suspected if the crutches had been within reach, Sully would have already left the store and been trying to hitch a ride back to the base. Luckily, he didn't have to look for her. He spotted her by the rental car. Using the key fob, he unlocked it as he approached.

She must have heard the locks disengage or seen him do it, because she opened the passenger door, sitting in the seat and swinging her injured leg inside before he arrived. He put their bags in the back, laying the crutches on the rear seat.

She wasn't crying, at least not yet. She stared out the windshield. He passed over the small box of tissues provided by the rental company. "Who is Raven?"

"Drive, Murphy."

He slid the key in the ignition, started the engine. "And Raven?"

"I'm not talking about her."

He let the silence build between them until they were on the freeway and he was at highway speed. "Have you told anyone what happened?"

"Not your business. Take me to the BEQ."

"I didn't think so. Not trying to piss you off, Barlow, but the Army has counselors for a reason. You should talk to them."

"Did you?"

"What?"

She spaced out the words as if it was the only way he'd understand them. "Did you talk to the shrinks when you heard about your friend?"

"Touché."

He parked close to the front of the building. Turning off the motor, he walked around the vehicle and opened the back door. She headed inside as soon as he handed her the crutches. Collecting her bag of books, he followed. She faltered for an instant when she spotted a brawny, brown-haired civilian at the counter chatting with PFC Adams who all but drooled over the man. He easily topped six feet and looked like a truck driver in faded jeans, well-worn cowboy boots, a plaid flannel shirt, and a fleece-lined denim jacket.

Sully stiffened for a moment. Then, she swung forward on the crutches. "What are you doing here?"

"Looking for you." He eyed her. "What happened?"

"Nothing."

"Yeah, right. You've always been pigheaded. Did you get in a fight? Win it? Lose it? Need a lawyer?"

"Shove it." She signed in on the clipboard Joyce Adams handed her, then disappeared down the hallway before either of them could follow.

The stranger stared after her for a moment, then turned a dark-eyed gaze on Tate. "I'm Kord Barlow, Sullivan's older brother. You're…?"

"Tate Murphy." He stepped forward to shake hands. "Sully is assigned to our office. She took a fall on Friday."

"How?"

"Her leg isn't as healed as she'd thought and it went out on her."

"Whoa. Hold up there." Concern filled Kord's features, landing in the dark brown eyes. "What happened to her leg?"

"She broke it. Wait a second." Tate held up his hand. "She told me she was injured in Kabul. An I.E.D. Why don't you know that?"

"She hasn't come home since the week before Christmas and even then, she didn't stay long in Liberty Valley, and only a few hours in Seattle." Kord gestured to the lounge on the right side of the lobby with its chairs, tables, and couches. "Not really for public consumption. Let's talk over there."

"Works for me." Tate waited while the other man collected a good-sized, clear container of cookies from the counter with a last polite nod to Joyce Adams. "Why didn't Sully stay for the holidays?"

"They sucked." A shadow crossed Kord's face. "Nobody felt much like celebrating after the funeral, not even the kids."

"Hold up. Who died?" It only took a moment for Tate to put everything together. "Raven."

Kord nodded. A muscle twitched in his jaw. He clenched one large fist but was careful not to crush the cookie container. "My wife. We buried her at Fort Bronson in Seattle. Sully barely spoke to anyone at the wake before the funeral. Got lost between the graveside military service and the bigger gathering when we returned to the church hall in Liberty Valley."

"Survivor's guilt."

Another nod. "Everyone adored Raven. Nobody blames Sully around me. If they try, I won't let them."

"She blames herself. Been that, done there."

"Me too. Did my time in the Navy, then worked for Nighthawke Security. The girls didn't need to enlist. Raven wanted adventure and Sully was always right behind her."

"Is the rest of the family as supportive?"

A shrug this time. "Most aren't, but they've stopped getting in my face. I tell them people die in wars. Didn't think one would be my Raven."

"Could you have stopped her?"

"No. Birds need to fly. It's their nature and I never believed in clipping wings." Kord handed Tate the plastic box. "Take these to Sully. Raven's grandma sent them. They're Sully's favorite snickerdoodles. She doesn't answer when the Driscolls, or Dad or I call, but we're glad one of our girls came home, although we'll always miss the one who didn't."

"She'd say the wrong one lived."

"Maybe, you can convince her otherwise. This war's gone on too long. Can't keep sending the same troops back to combat again and again without casualties. Even the best among us loses the edge."

"Are you seeing someone?" Tate studied the former soldier. "Does your counselor have you on drugs? You're fairly together for what you lost."

"Some folks think that." Kord's smile didn't touch his eyes. "My therapist is a little too *woo-woo* for them. She doesn't believe in prescribing meds to prevent emotions. She says people need to feel in order to heal."

"That doesn't sound *woo-woo* to me."

"Yeah, well when I told her that I haven't slept alone since Raven died, Estelle never asked if I'd been cheating on my wife. She offered to have one of her daughters *cleanse* my house in some sort of new-age ceremony to get rid of Raven's spirit." Kord shrugged again. "May sound crazy, but she'll go when she's ready and I'm not having someone else order her around. She's not in the Army now."

"I'm from Baker City." At the incomprehension on the other man's face, Tate added. "We have our share of ghosts. There's a reason why we hosted a haunted town last October and it wasn't obvious, although most folks figured we wanted to raise money at Halloween. My mother's in on the plans for the memorial next month when we'll honor those who died in the avalanches that nearly wiped out Baker City more than a hundred years ago."

"All right then." Kord glanced toward the hallway to the NCO wing. "Consider taking Sully. By that time, she may be ready."

"I'll keep it in mind. Mom tells me attendance is mandatory."

"Send me the date and I'll be there too. Don't know if Raven will come or not. She was always independent. Death hasn't changed her." Kord pulled out his cell phone. "What's your number? Call if Sully needs me."

"Wow and I thought I was pathetic." Raven Driscoll-Barlow sauntered around the room. It was too *bare bones* to suit her, too G.I. and too squared away. If she'd been the one living here, she'd have thrown one of her grandma's patchwork quilts on the Army cot, put fresh flowers in a vase on the table, planted a giant box of brightly colored condoms on the nightstand, hung her poster of a cluster of yellow ducklings on the wall, the one proclaiming, 'Lead, follow, or get the hell out of the way!'

It'd have given the inspection team something to bitch about on a weekly basis, not that she'd have listened to their sniveling. She'd have offered the ranking NCO or officer a roll of toilet paper to use in lieu of their forms even though most of them had no sense of humor and she always ended up with extra duties. It'd amazed her when she was promoted ahead of Sully this last time and appointed to the position of company first sergeant. Her B.F.F. adhered to every regulation regardless of how stupid the rule was, but she had Raven's back regardless.

"Hey, doofus." She flicked a glance at her best friend huddled in a chair. "I'm the one who died. What's up with you?"

No answer, of course. It wasn't as if Sully heard her. Raven wandered into the adjoining bathroom. It was odd to look in the mirror and barely be able to see herself. Her hip-length black hair, tall, rail-thin frame made her look like a tree in camo fatigues. Kord never complained about her small boobs and narrow hips. If he had, she'd have castrated him, and he knew it.

He was damn lucky to have her. She'd told him that more than once when she was a kid, crushing on him and again on their wedding night. He'd looked so hot in his Navy uniform. He was the first to admit he was hers and even if she was dead, that didn't mean she'd share him with someone like the blonde bimbo at the front desk on Sunday C.Q. duty.

Raven sauntered back into the bedroom, crossed to the chair, and eyed the splint on Sully's leg. "Well, hell. What happened to you? Talk to me, girlfriend."

Sully stirred slightly, tears filling the green eyes. "I'm so sorry, Raven."

"For what? Me being the immortal asshat who thought we'd live forever? Me insisting we talk to the stupid Army recruiter who promised us the stars, the sun, and the moon, not just college bennies so we could get our teaching degrees and save this sorry world? Get over yourself, Sullivan Barlow. Own what's yours to own."

Of course, her best friend didn't listen to the advice. Sully buried her face in her hands, shoulders shaking while she sobbed.

"Crap. Now, what am I supposed to do?"

A knock interrupted, but Sully didn't move, didn't leave the chair by the desk. A second knock, more determined this time. Raven

his. "I'll get cleaned up and let's hit the Chinese place by the main gate before the Sunday dinner rush."

"Works for me."

Raven waited until the pair left on their dinner date before she drifted over to the bed. It took little more than a thought to empty the bag of books. She grimaced at the stack of murder and mayhem stories. Trust her best friend to load up on suspense novels, rather than the romances Raven preferred. She sorted through the paperbacks, opting for the one with the most innocuous cover. She wished she could enjoy a couple of her grandma's cookies along with the book, but that wasn't going to happen.

She eyed the pillow, shifting it against the wall so she could lean against it. She'd go home to Kord after she made sure that her sister by more than marriage came back okay from the dinner date. The guy was hot and if Sully got lucky tonight, the last thing the two of them needed was an audience.

"I wasn't much for clapping rhythm when I was alive. I sure as hell am not doing it now."

CHAPTER SIX

For the most part, she'd enjoyed the afternoon with Tate. Granted, there'd been the stress of running into Dr. Leslie Dunaway, the prissy and pissy university professor as well as Raven's mentor teacher at the bookstore and Kord's visit, but she didn't have to let anyone else ruin her life, Sully thought. She did a good enough job doing that herself. She'd enjoyed the picnic and playing 'fetch' with the puppies.

Tate Murphy proved to be a surprising companion, especially when he knew how to comfort her while she cried, a skill none of her stepbrothers or stepfather had.

They arrived at the Chinese restaurant before the dinner rush started. They didn't have the place to themselves, but she didn't feel surrounded by a crowd of hungry diners. Their waitress had been attentive without being obsequious and Tate rewarded her with a large tip. Since Sully couldn't finish the huge portions provided in the combination dinner of chicken, subgum, and fried rice, she had leftovers for lunch tomorrow.

When they got back to her place, she unlocked her bedroom door and led the way inside coming to a halt when she saw the pile of novels on the bunk. "Somebody's been here."

She glanced to her left, into the empty bathroom, then swung on the crutches to the wall locker. Leaning on one crutch, she opened the closet door, prepared to use the other one to batter an intruder. "I don't see anyone."

"Don't sound so disappointed." Tate scanned the room, then put the cardboard container with Sully's almond fried chicken in the micro-fridge. "How do you know someone visited while we were gone?"

"Look at the books." Sully turned around, gesturing to the pillows positioned against the wall, the paperbacks piled haphazardly on the foot of the narrow cot, the two hardcovers barely out of the sack. "Someone's been on my bed, reading my books before I do."

"Well, at least they didn't eat your cookies, but if you had any porridge you could be in trouble."

"Ha, ha. Not very funny, Murphy." She cast another look around. "It had better not be PFC Adams or I'll kick her scrawny butt from here to Tacoma and back, although I'm not sure the girl can read anything beyond what's on her smartphone."

"Your laptop is here, Sully. So is the coffeemaker, fridge, and microwave, so nobody broke in and stole anything." He shrugged. "I don't think anyone other than the noncom in charge of the BEQ has master keys to the rooms. Hathaway usually locks them up in his office if he goes off post on the weekend, so it probably wasn't the junior enlisted on duty as fireguards or C.Q.s. Do you want me to contact the M.P.s?"

"And tell them what? Someone came into my room, looked through the books I bought, and apparently skimmed a couple?" She crossed to the bed and counted the novels, then picked up the receipt and verified what she already knew. Whoever had unpacked them hadn't taken any. It was as if the visitor checked them out and found her taste in fiction lacking. "This visitor is like Raven. She always pitched a fit when I went to one of the few brick and mortar bookstores that are still around and didn't buy any romances."

"Are you upset or scared? I'm serious. If you want the cops, I'll call them."

Sully shook her head, glancing around the small room and then at the man leaning against the wall by the door. "No, I'm fine."

"You have my number so you can call me if you change your mind or need someone to throw out a bibliophile."

She laughed. "Or scrape up the mess after I beat up the critic with my crutches."

"That too." He grinned. "Reminds me of the story Lock told me about Jeff Ransom."

"Who?"

"Durango Hawke's second in command. Ransom runs Hawke Construction now, but he was a POW in one of our undeclared wars. Shortly after he got home, he was at Pop's Café in Baker City. A bunch of drunken visitors, we call them flatlanders, decided to take on the locals in the bar and one of them thought a crippled guy on crutches wasn't a threat."

"I suspect your brother's friend taught him differently."

"When the cops arrived, they found two city slickers hiding under the pool table while Ransom stood at the bar drinking his beer. He hadn't come to fight, but he intended to enjoy his beer and make it last most of the night."

"Makes sense to me." Sully crossed the room, stopping in front of him and putting one of the crutches against the wall beside him. "If I promise not to go barhopping without you, will you kiss me?"

"Think I can manage that." He took a step toward her, drew her against him, placing the second crutch by its mate. He feathered a thumb over her lips. "You'd also have to promise not to sign up with Nighthawke Security. I don't want to be loved and left one more time."

"It wasn't love, just sex."

"But I want more than that."

"Too bad, too sad." She hesitated for a moment before she laced her arms around his neck, gazing up into his face. "You're a guy. You're supposed to prefer late-night booty calls without the commitment and you already know I'm good with that."

"I'll admit I enjoyed those when I was younger, but after my dad almost died on me, I realized play-time was done. A man has to grow up sometime." His head lowered. "And I was overdue."

Their mouths met in a tender kiss that wasn't what she'd expected. He didn't try to deepen it, seeming satisfied with the slow approach. She wasn't. She threaded her fingers in his short, dark hair, her lips parting beneath his.

He lifted his mouth a scant inch from hers. "We have all the time in the world, Sullivan. There's no need to rush."

"*Hurry up and wait* isn't on my list tonight."

"Too bad." He chuckled, kissed the tip of her nose. "Too sad."

She nipped his ear. "Take me to bed, Murphy."

"I will when you really want me."

"What does that mean?" She pulled back enough to see his face, his dark blue eyes. "Of course, I want you. I don't invite every guy I meet into bed with me."

"I know."

His lips brushed hers and then he eased back to find one of her crutches. She stared at him as she fitted it into position under her arm. "Are you serious? You're actually leaving?"

"Yes. I'll be here in the morning to take you to sick call."

In a few moments, he was out the door and she locked it behind him. "What a jerk."

They'd had a good day together. The only thing that would have been better was if he'd stayed over. Yes, the Army bunk was narrow, but they could have humped like proverbial bunnies, cuddled between bouts of sex and she'd sleep for at least an hour or two in his arms. Good sex meant no nightmares and she didn't want to remember Afghanistan or think about the way she'd failed her best friend.

Sully shook her head. *No more memories. T.V. time*, she thought, glancing at the radio clock on the nightstand. Eighteen-hundred hours meant the nightly news would be on, but she didn't have to listen to the weekend wrap-up of headlines. She'd channel surf and find something to watch. "And it definitely won't be a romcom. I don't need the headache when there's no sex in the offing."

Tate wasn't surprised to see the line of texts from his twin. He'd been incommunicado most of the afternoon, except for sending her a couple of lines while he was book hunting at the mall. He read through the messages, shaking his head when he saw the warning that his aunt had contacted his mother about Sullivan Barlow. His mom never bought the line that if the Army wanted him to have a wife, he'd be issued one.

None of his brothers were married or engaged so their nuclear families couldn't entertain her, and Quinn's three step-kids weren't enough for Bronwyn Murphy. She wanted more grandchildren to spoil and daughters-in-law to share her interests. When thirty-three-year-old Dougal pointed out that she might not like her sons' choices in potential wives, she threatened to send him to the woodshed with his father. Her theory was simple. If a woman was smart enough to love one of her boys, then she already had something in common with Bronwyn Murphy and the two could build their own relationship from that starting point.

Tate sent a quick 'thanks for the heads-up' to his sister and then asked about the beauty shop she'd started in Baker City. He didn't care about cuts or perms or fake fingernails, but the second salon was his sister's newest venture and any questions regarding the business would normally distract her. The ploy didn't work this time. She came back with more demands to know about Sully.

Tate gave up and sent her a picture of Sully playing with the pups at Aunt Heidi's. That brought a question about the crutches and his response about her injured leg silenced his twin for a moment. Another text showed up as he parked at the car rental agency.

Looks like you've found a hero. You'd better elope before Mom arranges a wedding since Aunt Heidi already approves.

She decided not to wait for Tate the next morning, telling herself that the Mustang G.T. needed the exercise even if the short drive around the base wouldn't do much for the vintage sports car. Besides, after turning her down all weekend he deserved the rejection. Since she expected to go to the office after seeing the doctor, she opted for camo fatigues and her combat boots. Well, she wore one and carried the other. If she promised to be careful, she could leave the splint and crutches at the clinic for someone who really needed them.

Soon after she arrived, Jeannie came to escort her to an examining room. Sully smiled at the other woman who wore bright blue scrubs, not the usual uniform. "So, how was your weekend? I didn't see much of you."

"I got off post as soon as I could Saturday morning to go skiing with friends. I learned a long time ago in this woman's Army that if I stick around, I'll be one of the first called in for an emergency. If you hadn't been laid up, we'd have invited you to join us."

"Next time. I may not be able to get up on the slopes, but I can sit in the lodge and drink hot chocolate with the best of them."

Jeannie laughed. "That's always a winner." Gesturing to the chair, she added, "Take a seat. The doctor will be along soon."

"I know the drill." Sully chose a magazine from the assortment in the wall rack and settled down to wait. It didn't matter if it was a military clinic or a civilian one. Doctors were notoriously overbooked, but at least she wasn't out front in the lobby.

Halfway through the first article, Jeannie returned. "I need to draw some blood. The test results weren't what the doctor expected, and he wants to check them again."

"It's my leg." Sully lowered the magazine. "Why do you vampires need blood when I just need a quick once-over and a release to go back to work? This doesn't make sense."

Jeannie shrugged, removing a small tray from the cupboard. "It's the Army, Sully. Does logic ever enter the picture? It's easier to 'go along to get along' if the battle doesn't matter. Which arm?"

Sully put the magazine on the exam table. "The right. Anything else?"

Jeannie nodded, putting a plastic cup on the counter. "He wants a urine test too."

It was a 'puzzlement' as the middle-schoolers used to say during her last practicum before she went onto student teaching at local high schools, but she'd wait and cross-examine the doctor when he finally arrived. Maybe, he wanted to make sure nothing else had been missed. After the explosion, the medics had quickly accepted her 'walking away' and prescribed a short run of antibiotics to prevent infection from the various cuts which required a minimal amount of stitches.

However, when he arrived, the doctor zoomed through the exam of her leg and told her to come back the next morning to learn the results of the tests. If she continued to wear the splint, use the crutches, and practiced reasonable precautions, she could return to work at Major Harper's office.

"This is ridiculous," Sully told Jeannie at the end of the visit. "What is he looking for? I don't do drugs. Even if marijuana is legal in Washington State, it's against Army regs to use it and I wouldn't."

"Count yourself lucky that it's only going to be a few hours to get the results. It could take days if we had to use an outside lab not the one at the main hospital on post."

"Don't you ever get tired of being the proverbial 'voice of sweet reason,' Jeannie?"

"No, that's why I'm a nurse. A bunch of us are going to the movies tonight. Want to come?"

"Okay, but I hate romcoms. What are we going to see?"

"Some sci-fi thing my roommate chose. It'll be fun."

"I'm in, but I don't share my popcorn."

Jeannie laughed. "You're just a fun date, Sully."

"I try."

She parked the Mustang in the lot adjacent to the headquarters building deliberately not using one of the handicapped slots. Yes, it meant she had to go a bit further to the doors, but this way she could see the car from the office windows and the spot she'd have taken was available for someone who needed it more than she did. She headed across the lot to the sidewalk that led to the front entrance.

At ten in the morning, the day was well underway. Official vehicles rolled on the main base highway, soldiers practiced drill and ceremonies on the parade ground, marching to the cadence calls of sergeants. Three flags fluttered in the breeze and she glanced away from the Stars and Stripes, still unable to look at it without remembering the one covering Raven's coffin. Nope, not going there. She was headed to work. Focusing on the word processing in the Major's office would prove enough of a distraction.

As if her thought conjured up the man, she saw the officer approaching followed by Tate Murphy. She stopped, adjusted the crutches so she could raise her right hand in a respectful salute. When he returned it, she realized he was only about four inches taller than her five feet, five inches. Silver threaded through the short bristles of his hair. She met his dark eagle gaze. "Good morning, sir."

He nodded. "Morning, Sergeant Barlow. We're headed out to the field. I told Ms. Tyler to bring you lunch. Take it easy today. We'll see you this afternoon."

"Thank you, sir. I'm glad to be back to duty. I'll get those reports completed."

"I'm sure you'll do your share and so will Ms. Tyler."

Sully wasn't as certain of that but knew better than to say so. He headed off to the parking lot and she glanced up at Tate. "Anything else I should know?"

"Isn't that my question? What did the doctor say?"

"To continue wearing the brace, using the crutches, and not to overdo." She grimaced. "He wants to see me again tomorrow morning."

"I'm glad they're taking such good care of you. Keep me posted. I'll see you later. Do you want to go off-post for dinner?"

"Not tonight. I'm going to the movies with Jeannie and her friends."

"Then, add me to your social calendar for tomorrow night."

"Sounds good."

The next morning, she was one of the first patients to arrive at the dispensary. A different nurse took her back to an exam room. A few minutes later, Jeannie entered followed by the doctor.

Sully began to remove the splint and her friend held up a hand. "There's no need for that. You're just here for the results of the tests."

"What are they? What's wrong?"

"It depends on how you look at it." Jeannie and the doctor shared a glance before he continued. "We ran the tests twice to be sure. You're pregnant, Sergeant Barlow."

CHAPTER SEVEN

Not ready to go to headquarters and act like typing military forms was her be-all and end-all, she drove off post to the nearest doughnut shop. One or two maple frosted crullers always helped her deal with stressful situations and a surprise pregnancy counted as one of those. When she'd asked the doctor why her birth control pills didn't prevent conception, he explained the antibiotics she'd been given after her injuries interfered. Condoms couldn't be guaranteed either.

She grimaced, stirring honey into the cup of hot peppermint tea. She didn't look forward to telling Tate Murphy the news. Their one-night booty call had resulted in unexpected consequences. What was she going to do about it? She could hardly keep it a secret when she was almost two months along. As part of her job, Jeannie had detailed all the available options, but Sully immediately waived abortion.

Adoption was out too. She loved children even if she preferred snarky tweens and teens to little munchkins who tried to boss her around. It was why she chose to become a teacher. She'd keep her baby. She was almost thirty years old and she certainly didn't need Tate to support her or their child. Still, she had to share the news with him. The question was when. The sooner, the better. She'd do it tonight at dinner and hope he didn't do what her own father had, hightail it for a combat zone.

Okay, so that probably wasn't fair to him. After all, he'd been a soldier when he and her mother started dating. But, if they were old enough to date and sleep together, why weren't they mature enough to think about what could happen? Sully drew a deep breath. What was she doing? Blaming her parents when she'd made the same mistake? She'd seen a hot guy and jumped him without thinking about the possibilities.

She grimaced, then forced a smile when the counter-person came over with a fresh pot of hot water for the tea and ordered another cruller. She might be off caffeine for the duration, but it didn't mean she had to give up doughnuts or sugary treats. Her cell phone buzzed, and she winced when she recognized her mother's number. More criticism would be forthcoming when Helene Barlow learned about the surprise pregnancy.

I couldn't do anything right when I was a kid. If I didn't hear I was the 'bad seed' from her, I heard it from the entire extended Barlow contingent. The only one who was decent was Gil and he never let his boys pick on me. They might have been a bunch of macho jerks like Kord. They still treated me like a little princess even when they tried to leave me behind.

I wish Raven were home to help or at least to listen and offer advice. Of course, if she were here, I wouldn't be pregnant because I wouldn't have been in a hotel bar, jumping a hot guy. Time to grow up, Sullivan Rafferty Barlow. You're having a baby. You don't get to be one.

Tate eyed the text message on his phone again. Normally when another soldier offered to buy him dinner, they met at one of the dining facilities on base. He hadn't seen the brilliant pink Mustang parked adjacent to the nearest DFAC utilized by the soldiers staying at the BEQ when he passed the cafeteria on his return to headquarters. He suspected that wasn't what Sully had in mind. He'd probably find her at the family-style restaurant off post that served breakfast twenty-four, seven. Corporal Ferguson had said the place featured several of her favorite meals.

It didn't take long to read through the reports waiting on his desk and to sign them or to email Major Harper and provide a 'sitrep'. Tate dropped the paperwork on Anise Tyler's desk, adding a quick note for her to forward the copies to the appropriate parties. Now, it was off to dinner with Sully.

He spotted her car strategically stationed in the far corner of the restaurant's parking lot, taking up two spaces so nobody else could harm the classic vehicle. He pulled in next to it, amused by the passive-aggressive technique, and wondered what her best friend would have thought. Too bad he wasn't the *O'Leary*, the town medium in Baker City, and couldn't ask Raven Barlow himself.

Inside he spotted Sully waiting in a corner booth in the dining room and went to join her. "Have you been here a while?"

"Just long enough to get seated and order ice water and hot tea. How are the troops?"

"Finishing up their field exercises." He eyed her. She hadn't stopped off to change from her fatigues and combat boots. Neither had he. A few strands of copper-red hair escaped from the bun on the back of her head, but he wouldn't point it out. "Does alcohol interfere with your meds? We're both off-duty. Do you want to share a bottle of Chardonnay?"

"Not tonight, Murphy." She twirled a straw in her ice water, then shrugged. "Go ahead if you want."

"I'm fine. I don't drink that often."

The waitress arrived and he ordered coffee as well as a glass of water, then opened the menu. "Any ideas of what's good?"

"I can eat breakfast regardless of the time of day. I'm going for the steak and eggs special."

"That sounds great, but I think I'll go for the steak dinner with salad and a baked spud." Decision made, he put the menu aside and turned his attention on her. "You weren't in the office when I left for the field today. Was your leg bothering you?"

"No, I had to go back to the clinic for the results of the tests they ran." She took a deep breath before managing a weak smile. "It's not important. Tell me about your princesses. How'd they do these last few days? Don't they have crucial tests to complete?"

He watched her closely as he described the competitions at the obstacle course. Something was on her mind, but she apparently wasn't ready to share it. Sooner or later, the final report from the clinic would land on the Major's desk and unless it was extremely confidential, Tate would hear the details. However, he didn't want to wait for his C.O. to tell him what he needed to know, and he wouldn't.

———————

Gutless, Sullivan Rafferty Barlow, you're a gutless wimp. Soldier up, woman.

Despite the mental orders, she couldn't make herself do it. Instead, she ate her dinner, forcing herself to chew the steak instead of attacking it in giant mouthfuls. At least, now she knew why she could barely choke down breakfast in the early morning and why coffee turned her stomach. She might not have expected the results of the tests, but answers to unasked questions were easier than not knowing.

Out in the parking lot, she unlocked the Mustang and put the cardboard container holding the slab of cheesecake he'd bought her on the passenger seat. "We have to talk."

"The worst words a guy wants to hear." He eyed her narrowly. "What's wrong, Barlow?"

"How do you know something is? Never mind," she held up her hand. "If you do the touchy-feely, sensitive crap, I'll lose it." She took a deep breath. "I'm pregnant."

Utter silence while he stared and obviously processed the information. He rubbed his jaw, dark blue eyes narrowing. "How far along…?"

"Nearly two months." She met his gaze. "I don't sleep around, Murphy. The last time was…"

"With me." He shook his head. "We used condoms."

"They failed." She shrugged. "So did the birth control pills because I was on antibiotics for my injuries."

"Will the baby be affected by those?"

"The doctor says not likely."

"Good to know."

She took a deep breath. "I'm not getting an abortion."

"Didn't ask you to, Barlow." He took a step toward her, obviously intending to draw her against him for a hug.

She backed away, scowling up at him. "Don't even go there. I said, no touchy-feely crap."

"Okay, got it. You're the boss." He almost smirked, then hastily hid it behind his hand.

Another long silence. He folded his arms, leaned against the side of his pickup. "So, do I propose now or wait even longer?"

Heat flooded into her face. "I didn't expect that, Murphy. I expected you to demand a D.N.A. test to prove the baby was yours before you offered child support."

"If you knew me at all, you'd know that wasn't my style." He stepped forward, caught her chin in calloused fingers. "I'm not talking about in the sack, Barlow. We've spent time together and my kid has my name."

"We don't need marriage for that."

"I do." He smiled, feathered his thumb over her lips. "What kind of ring do you want?"

Tears stung and she blinked hard. "Again, not necessary."

"It is to me. You choose or I will."

She measured the sincerity on his rugged features. He was serious and she wasn't sure what came next. She didn't know if she wanted to get married, even if she was drawn to him and eagerly anticipated jumping his bones again. "I need time to think."

"We'll go shopping at lunch tomorrow."

"I don't think so."

"You have tonight to become accustomed to the idea."

Before she could avoid it, he bent his head and brushed her lips with his. She broke free, gaping up at him. "You're taking this far too well. We only got together again a few days ago. You don't know me either. I could be lying about not sleeping around and you being the dad."

"Are you?"

"Hell, no! My step-dad always said that lying compromised a person's integrity and nothing was worth the cost. I'm pregnant and it's your fault for being so sexy."

"Likewise." He chuckled. "I want you to have my Army benefits for the baby, so we'll get married."

Still stunned by his reaction, she hastily climbed into the Mustang. Back at the B.E.Q., she opted to head for the lounge off the dayroom and the big screen TV. Grateful most of the enlisted soldiers appeared to be at dinner, she picked up the remote, clicking through the channels before settling into the most comfortable recliner.

She was in the middle of an old *Criminal Minds* episode when Jeannie arrived, still wearing her clinic scrubs, brown hair neatly pinned up in a bun. She carried a party-sized bag of plain potato chips and a six-pack of ginger ale. She sat down in a nearby chair. On the next commercial break, Sully muted the volume and nodded to her new friend. "That was a total surprise today."

"I can believe it." Jeannie tore open the bag of potato chips, took a handful, and then passed the bag to Sully. "You didn't make an appointment to see the clinic OB/GYN this morning before you left. Do you want me to arrange that tomorrow?"

Sully hesitated and then nodded. "Sure. That'd be great."

During the next commercial, Jeannie asked, "Did you text the father?"

"He's on base so we had dinner." Sully fished out a few plain chips and handed over the bag. "He wants to get married."

"Really?" Jeannie laughed, shaking her head. "Did you tell him it's 2019, not 1919?"

"A commitment was the last thing on my mind when I met him. He was incredibly hot, and I wanted a one-night hookup." Sully heaved a sigh. "Now, I have to decide what comes next, and if I want to get hitched to an old-fashioned man like my step-dad."

"Guys with codes of ethics are few and far between in the real world. He may not be a nutcase."

"I haven't called him one yet and you're preaching to the choir, girlfriend." Sully clicked the volume button as the show resumed and the detectives continued the hunt for the killer.

Later in her room, she pulled out her cell phone and eyed the message queue. Did she want to talk to her mother or not? What would Helene Barlow say when she knew she was going to be a grandmother? Everything she heard was shared throughout their small farming community. The woman lent new meaning to the phrase, 'bucket-mouth' and Sully didn't want her name bandied about.

Gawd, I sound like an old-timer! Tate Murphy isn't the only person out of sync with the real world!

"You've been quiet all morning, Murphy. What's on your mind?"

Tate glanced in the mirror at his boss in the rear seat of the sedan, then turned his attention to the road. "I'm marrying Sergeant Barlow before I ship out."

"Well, that isn't much of a surprise. I've seen how you look at her." The older man put a file back in his briefcase. "What do you need from me? My permission isn't required anymore."

"A weekend pass for both of us. I want to take her to Baker City to meet my family and the town is beyond the seventy-five-mile limit we're allowed off base."

"You've got it. When's the wedding?"

"Sometime in the next month. It'll be small. She's still getting over losing her best friend in the *sandbox* and won't want a big celebration."

"We know what that's like." Major Harper drew out another folder. "You can always have a reception next year when you get back."

"That's what I'm thinking." Tate grimaced. "I just have to get my mom and sisters on the same page."

"Good luck. Pick up the license today and use it this weekend at your local church in Baker City. I'll extend the pass for a few more days and then you lovebirds can have a honeymoon."

"And an elopement keeps Mom happy." Tate grinned appreciatively. "Thank you, sir."

She heard footsteps in the hallway and men's voices at the same time. Sully focused on the computer screen and continued typing in the needed information on the current form. She flicked a glance at Tate and then at Major Harper who followed him into the office, waving at her to remain seated.

"Good morning, sir."

"It's almost lunchtime." The shorter, sandy-haired man in camos smiled at her. "I hear congratulations are in order, Sergeant Barlow. I hope you and Sergeant Murphy will be happy together."

Heat flooded her face until she decided it must look as red as her hair. She mumbled a response, hoping it sounded like a *thank you* and struggled not to glare at Tate. She ought to smack him with her crutches. Glancing across the room, he paused in front of her desk. "Where is Anise?"

"Ms. Tyler is at lunch. I told her I'd cover the phones while she's gone, and she'll bring me back a sandwich."

"Not necessary. We can grab something while we're out and the Major can have the sandwich, or you can eat it later."

"It may come as a surprise, Murphy, but you aren't the boss of me."

"You're wrong there, Barlow. I outrank you and I am. Let's go."

Damn, she hated it when she was wrong. She hastily saved the document, shut down the computer, and reached into the bottom drawer for her purse before taking the crutches he handed her. "Anything else I need to know?"

"I'll tell you when we get to the parking lot." He walked beside her to the elevator. "Have you decided what kind of ring you want?"

She glowered up at him. "I guess I could say anything will do."

"You could but I won't believe you."

"And I suppose if I don't choose one, you will."

"That's about right. As my dad says, 'things don't need all the thought folks want to give them.' I've always liked emeralds and it'd match your eyes."

"Charm won't get you anywhere."

He chuckled. "I'll keep trying anyway."

She wasn't sure how she ended up at a small, upscale jewelry store a few miles from the base when she didn't want to admit how emotionally vested she was in this enterprise. She hadn't agreed to marry him, but somehow, they were shopping for a ring. Despite the array of elaborate designs, her gaze continually returned to a beautiful solitaire ring crafted of polished yellow gold with an antique setting. The center stone was a large emerald in a classic six-prong head.

Tate held up a tray containing a ring showcasing an emerald surrounded by sparkling diamonds. "I like this one."

"You're not wearing it." Sully gestured to the unique vintage ring she preferred. "I want that one."

"I can afford something more elaborate."

Sully pointed to her choice again. "Murphy, I'm sure either your dad or mom told you at some point that a 'happy wife makes for a happy life.' If not, one of them should have."

CHAPTER EIGHT

Once they completed their shopping, they stopped at Tate's favorite deli to choose a variety of salads, fresh fruit, bottled water, and crispy fried chicken for a picnic lunch. Then, he drove out to his aunt's and uncle's place. Rain misted the windshield and he parked near the gazebo, close enough that the wet grass wouldn't mar their boots when they walked across it. Surprisingly, none of the dogs came to greet them and she wondered where Bo and his sister lurked.

"What's on your mind?" Tate handed her a paper plate and a plastic fork once they'd sat down at the picnic table. "You keep looking for something."

"The dogs."

"In the house when Aunt Heidi and Uncle Arnie are gone. As soon as they get back and let out the canine contingent, we'll undoubtedly be attacked."

"Great. I knew we should have stopped at a pet store for doggie toys and treats."

Tate chuckled. "We can do that on our way to the courthouse."

"Why do you want to go there?"

"To get a marriage license." He met her gaze evenly. "I'm expecting orders to go to Kentucky for training next month. When I'm part of a

Ranger team, I'll ship out to Afghanistan again. Before I head out, I want to marry you."

She struggled for a deep breath. *I'm a soldier*, she reminded herself, *and so is he. We do what most people don't.* "That sounds like you expect the worst."

"No, I expect the best, Sully, but I'm preparing for the worst. If something happens and I don't make it home alive, I want you and my child to have my benefits. The two of you will need a support system. My family and the folks in Baker City will provide a good one for my wife, but they're old-fashioned. My fiancée might not get as much respect."

A lump rose in her throat before she managed a nod. She'd intended to convince him they had all the time they needed before making a huge decision that would affect both their lives, but it sounded like they didn't. "What if you get back and we're not compatible?"

"Then, we'll file for divorce, but I'm not a kid. I'm thirty-five, old enough to be a good father and husband. It's worth a try. I'm worth a try. So are you." He pushed the carton of chicken Caesar pasta salad toward her. "Now, eat something. You and the baby need food."

Their visit ended with a quick tour of the furnished two-bedroom apartment above the two-car garage. She hadn't seen it the first time they were here because she hadn't wanted to try climbing the staircase to the screened-in porch that opened into the loft, but she was in control of the crutches now. They entered a large living room with a view of the kitchen, so she supposed she could call it 'open concept', although it wasn't a fashion statement. There was only one bathroom, but she could live with that. The short hallway directly in front of the bath opened onto the bedrooms that were approximately the same size, thirteen square feet, one for each of them.

To make it appear larger, someone, probably Heidi had painted all the walls soft ivory. Cream drapes hung at the windows in the living room. Golden-brown carpet covered most of the floors, with matching gold tile in the bath and kitchen. A red teakettle on the stove, red throw pillows on the old couch, red striped towels all provided accents.

"What do you think?" Tate stood in the bedroom doorway watching her check out the large closet. "Could you live here?"

"Easily." She smiled at him. "Later, we could adapt the second bedroom into a nursery."

"Whatever you want." He glanced at his watch. "Let's go. We need to get back to HQ before your Mustang turns into a pumpkin in the parking lot."

She laughed and teased, "Whatever you want although we skipped orange as a color because our brothers really liked *The General*, that *Dodge Charger* in the *Dukes of Hazzard*."

On the way back to his truck, she spotted Arnie unloading groceries in the carport. He waved and came toward them. "What did you think of the apartment?"

"I like it," Sully said. "Will I be in big trouble if the puppies come up?"

"Just don't let them bump into you on the stairs until you're steady on your pins."

"I'll be careful." Sully paused as Bo ran to meet her, tail wagging and a collie grin in place. She petted the young tri-color pup, then gave the soggy ball he dropped at her feet a toss into the yard. "How much is the rent?"

"Heidi and I will talk about it. When do you want it?"

"Next week." It was Tate's turn to hurl the tennis ball. "We're going up to visit the folks this weekend. Sully has a classic Mustang Fastback. She'll want to put it in the garage. Is that okay?"

"Sure. Nobody else parks there. Heidi and I prefer the carport. It's closer."

After she threw the ball a few more times and he brought it back to her, Bo abandoned them for the puppy snack that Heidi had prepared, and Sully hobbled to the truck. "I'll be glad to get off these crutches and use the cane the doctor promised to give me this Friday. It will make it easier to go up and down the stairs at the apartment."

"And to get around my parents' farm on Saturday," Tate said.

"That too."

In her room that evening, she contemplated the afternoon with him. Yes, she'd enjoyed the time they'd spent together. They'd purchased two wedding rings along with the emerald engagement one she wore, had lunch, explored an apartment, played with a puppy, picked up the marriage license and Tate still hadn't kissed her again. She knew he had a libido. Wow, did he! If he hadn't, she wouldn't be in her situation with a baby due in September. She grimaced. She wasn't looking forward to being pregnant during the hot summer days, but she'd manage. She'd survived worse.

She eyed the laptop on the table and contemplated continuing the work on the literature unit plan for student teaching. It seemed like too much trouble. She stretched out on the bunk. She'd take a nap first. Afterward, she'd finish off the fried chicken and potato salad Tate left for her supper. Then, she'd take a fresh look at the lessons she'd use to teach Raven's favorite novel.

Just the idea of having someone on her side warmed Sully's heart. Nobody had wanted to take care of her in a long time, nobody except Raven. A guy like Tate was far different from her childhood best friend. She reminded herself that even if he weren't going off to war, he'd abandon her as soon as he realized how flawed she was. *It's not like I'm loveable. I learned that a long time ago.*

Raven strolled across the room and glanced at her dozing friend. The emerald ring on the third finger of Sully's left hand demanded attention. "Well, what a surprise, girlfriend. I didn't know you were so hung up on that hot soldier."

Sully shivered. She snuggled deeper into the pillow and Raven eyed the extra blanket on the foot of the bed. It only took a thought to unfold it, to cover her bestie. "Okay, now what have you been doing?"

Her attention on the computer, she scanned the first lesson and grimaced at the introduction of *To Kill A Mockingbird.* "Oh, come on, Sullivan Rafferty Barlow. You're the one with the History degree. You can do better than this. Let's engage them with an interactive project about Depression Era America in the 1930s before they actually start reading the story. Then, they'll be somewhat familiar with the setting."

She skimmed through four of the lessons, grimacing at the university designed template that required so much formal language and details about the essential requirements for each hour of class. It reminded her of the forms she always had to complete for the military. She rarely did. She generally convinced Sully to type the paperwork for both of them in exchange for doing all the filing. If Leslie Dunaway, their teaching supervisor ever had any imagination, she'd lost it long ago and Maureen Evans was a walking irritation who lectured as if everybody else was a total idiot.

When she'd refused to let Raven observe her classroom prior to the last practicum, it was the final affront. Granted, the older woman had a ton of excuses about the effect of visitors on her students, but Raven hadn't bought any of them. She'd told Leslie to find a different placement for her, that there wasn't much point in putting up with a complete control freak if she wasn't in combat.

"You need to tell those two witches that you're not planning to be part of their coven, girlfriend. They're an utter waste of time and space."

Sully sighed in her sleep but didn't awaken.

"Okay, let me see what else I can do to brighten up these teaching strategies, so the kids have a good time and learn why racism is evil before I go home to Eagleville. You're lucky Kord's on a long haul to Montana right now. Hanging out in the semi on a never-ending road trip is majorly boring when he can't hear me, so I'll stick around the base for a couple of days and harass you instead."

Yawning, Sully shifted on the single-size cot and slowly raised on one elbow. She didn't remember pulling the extra blanket over herself, but she must have in her sleep. She eased into a sitting position, collected the crutches, and headed for the bathroom. When she returned, she paused to look at the waiting laptop. Had she loaded up the lesson unit before she abandoned it to take a nap?

Undoubtedly. After all, she was the only one here. She clicked the 'escape' button and watched the screen come to life revealing various links to the fictional town of Maycomb, Alabama. "I don't recall doing this."

"I was looking for the interactive site our teacher used back in

72

middle school, but I couldn't find it," Raven said. "Everything changes. You know what I mean, girlfriend."

Sully frowned thoughtfully, recalling an assignment she'd had eons ago. It wasn't one that she'd done at the university in any of her classes, but Raven had loved clicking on the various buildings and learning facts about them. "Hmm, I wonder if any of these links will take me there."

"I wish you could hear me." Sulking, Raven floated over to sit on the foot of the narrow bed. "It's the worst part of being dead. Nobody listens to me."

Two lesson templates later, Sully emailed the entire package with its attachments to the university supervisor. If Leslie Dunaway approved of the unit, she'd forward it to the school and mentor teacher. Of course, if she had ways to improve it, she'd return it with suggestions for changes to incorporate. Sully always figured she had to jump through the various hoops and didn't bother to argue each and every point, unlike Raven who thought she knew best and refused to make the required adjustments.

"Okay, it's TV time. I've earned a reward." Opening the mini-fridge, Sully collected the fried chicken, potato salad, and a bottle of ginger ale, packing her supplies into a small backpack. "I need some murder and mayhem."

"No way," Raven grumbled. "I'm not watching that stupid FBI team try to capture serial killers. I hate seeing gruesome crime scenes."

The backpack strap slung over one shoulder, Sully limped down to the dayroom, determined to enjoy *Criminal Minds* on the big screen TV. She headed to the adjacent lounge, leaving the pool tables to the more able-bodied soldiers. When she was up to it, she'd hustle a few games and earn some extra bucks. It wasn't the money she enjoyed, although that always came in handy at the bookstore. It was more fun to teach wannabe macho guys to suck eggs as Raven's grandma said. Sully picked up the remote, then sank into a recliner, leaning back until she could prop up her injured leg.

She twisted the cap off her soda, sipped and put the bottle beside her on the little table, fished a drumstick from the bag of chicken. The stream of commercials ended and a long-haired brunette in comfy clothes sighed dreamily gazing at a hometown hero in a flannel shirt and jeans. "What the hell? Which one of you is dying?"

"Neither," Raven replied with a snort. "You know I hate blood and guts. There's enough of that crap in the real world."

As the duo on the TV exchanged blissful, romantic dialogue, Sully grimaced, trying not to gag at the saccharine story. She pressed buttons on the remote, surfing back to murder most painful.

The cops had just discovered a battered, bloody human carcass in the woods when Jeannie arrived with a huge bag of corn chips and a partial six-pack of beer. As usual, she hadn't stopped by her room to change from her blue scrubs. She plopped down in the other recliner. "Pizza's coming. The clinic was crazy busy, so I missed lunch and dinner."

"It amazes me that a health professional eats so much junk food."

"Bite me." Jeannie ripped open the sack of chips. "This is an appetizer and they're organic, made from non-GMO corn. Want some?"

"You know it."

"What are we watching?"

"*Criminal Minds.* There's a serial killer on the loose in the Pacific Northwest."

"Doesn't surprise me. If it doesn't stop raining, we'll have more than one. I'll volunteer. I have a list. Everybody is super grouchy because of the weather, not just the patients." Jeannie frowned as a couple on the big screen kissed. "Why doesn't this look like dead bodies everywhere?"

"What is happening tonight?" Sully clicked back to her show. "I swear this TV is totally messed up. It keeps losing my channel."

"Tell Master Sergeant Hathaway to call repair."

"I will if it continues screwing with me." Sully munched corn chips. "So, what happened at the clinic today?"

"The hell with that." Jeannie pointed to the ring. "Tell me about your latest news. I'm liking the baby daddy more every minute. Way to step up!"

"Baby?" Raven zapped the remote, so the TV shifted to one of her favorite Hallmark romances. "I want to hear this, girlfriend. What have you been doing with soldier hottie—like I don't know? When did this happen?"

The next morning Sully had an early appointment at the clinic. She paused at the front desk nodding at Corporal Ferguson. He smiled, passing her the sign-out log. She printed her name in the first box. "I was having trouble with the TV in the lounge last night. It kept reverting from the channel I wanted to watch to a different one."

"That's new." He took the clipboard from her. "I'll tell Sergeant Hathaway. He can fix almost everything around here and if he can't, we'll call in the cable company. We should have it repaired by the time you get back from work."

"Thanks. I appreciate it." She remembered the proposed trip with Tate to meet his family. "Are you on duty this weekend?"

He nodded. "It's my turn. Let me know if you need anything and I'll be happy to pick it up for you at the shoppette."

"I'll be out of town and the Mustang needs a babysitter, or should I say a car-sitter?"

"That's me." Excitement filled his dark eyes. "Do you want me to take it to the carwash?"

"No way, Ferguson." She laughed, shaking her head. "It never goes to one of those places. I don't want those automated brushes marring the finish. I wash and wax it by hand. I only use the good stuff, higher-quality handwashing soap, and all finishing products—sealants, wax, polish, proper rags, sponges, orbital polisher, wheel care products, chrome polish, interior conditioner…"

"I can do that too after I hit the auto parts store."

"Only if it stops raining and Sergeant Hathaway agrees you can leave the building. I don't want to be sleeping in the base dungeon." Still amused, she turned toward the door and headed for the parking lot.

Her appointment at the clinic didn't last long. The doctor seemed pleased by her progress, changing the temporary splint for a walking one. She happily traded the crutches for the quad cane with four rubber-tipped feet and a rectangular base. Even though it was easier to walk, she still opted for the elevator at the headquarters building rather than climbing the stairs. In the office, she found Anise Tyler sorting and filing reports.

Sully nodded a greeting, then headed for her desk. She came to a halt when she saw the huge stack of paperwork waiting for her. "What's this?"

"Correspondence that needs to be completed by close of business today, so you'd better get started."

Sully took a deep breath, then sat down and began sorting through the documents, putting them in "suspense date" order. Unless she intended to be here until midnight, she doubted she'd be able to type all the responses, but she'd complete the most crucial ones first. She debated asking why there was so much to do, then decided against it. Obviously, Anise hadn't done much of the work when she was alone in the office, but there wasn't any point in bitching at her for being such a slacker. Nothing would change and it'd be a complete waste of breath.

Three hours later, Tate strolled into the office, looking gorgeous in fatigues and combat boots. He stopped on the other side of the desk. "What did the doctor say?"

"I have a walking cast and a cane. If I keep progressing, I'll be able to wear two shoes next month."

"Sounds like a winner. Are you ready to call it a day? I want to hit the road early so we avoid rush-hour traffic."

"That's not happening, Murphy. I'm up to my eyeballs finishing the major's answers to these requests. The earliest we'll be able to go is tomorrow morning."

"No. I told my mother we'd be home in time for supper tonight and if we're late, I'll be mucking pigpens all weekend." He collected the stack of papers on the far side of the desk. "I told you not to save your work for Sergeant Barlow last week, Ms. Tyler. If you didn't hear it then, I'm telling you now."

CHAPTER NINE

Downstairs, they crossed the lobby, heading for the front doors and the parking lot.

Before they reached the door, an older man in camouflage fatigues entered the building. Sully had no trouble recognizing the sandy-haired visitor as the most influential non-com in her reserve battalion, Command Sergeant-Major Jenkins.

He looked her up and down, his brown gaze narrowing on the walking cast and the cane. "What happened to you, Sergeant Barlow? I thought you were ready to rock and roll, not on the sick, lame and lazy list."

"The leg gave out on me last week," Sully said, her tone even. "So, I wasn't as much on the mend as the doctors and I thought."

"And what's the plan now? Lunch?"

"We have a weekend pass so I'm taking her to meet my family and spend a few days with them." Tate took a step forward, holding out his hand. "Tate Murphy, Sully's fiancé."

"I didn't know you were engaged, Barlow." Another slow dark-eyed look as the two men shook hands. "When's the wedding?"

"As soon as she agrees," Tate said. "Since her unit is back from overseas, she doesn't need permission from her commander."

"Not that you'd ask anyway right, Barlow? You and Driscoll always told us what life was about whether the cadre liked it or not. You two lent new meaning to the phrase, 'it's better to seek forgiveness than ask permission.' Good sergeants are always missed."

Sully struggled to manage a weak smile at the mention of her best friend, then decided to be gracious about the intended compliment. She nodded in agreement. "I guess you're correct. Did you need to talk to me, Sergeant-Major?"

"No, I'm just checking in on the advance party folks and making sure everything is ready for the unit when they arrive next week. You'll be back on Monday, won't you? I'll stop in then. I'll need to speak to your supervisor too."

"Make it Thursday morning," Tate said. "Our passes are good through Tuesday and we won't be back until Wednesday at lunchtime."

"Sounds fair." The senior non-commissioned officer strode toward the receptionist's desk.

Sully took a deep breath and headed out the door beside Tate. "Pretty sure you're not the supervisor he'll speak to, but I hope it's not Ms. Tyler. She's not going to be a happy camper since she has all that paperwork to finish this afternoon."

"It will be Major Harper. He has the records showing that you followed the doctor's orders and were assigned to quarters for a few days. That can't be held against you and Anise always has issues with reservists."

"From your lips to God's ears." Sully came to a stop beside her car, unlocking the door. "I'll need time to change and pack."

"Me too. We'll stop for lunch on the way to Baker City."

Although she'd lived in western Washington State most of her life, she'd never actually visited Baker City in the Cascade mountains before. Tate drove north on the freeway for almost three hours. They passed the various exits for Liberty Valley and continued toward the Canadian border. Finally, he turned onto an east-bound highway. It narrowed from four to two lanes after they passed through Lake Maynard, but Tate kept going.

"Are we there yet?" Sully teased. "Or do we continue until we reach the end of the world?"

"No, but you can see it from here." He chuckled. "Actually, we're getting close. The Murphy farm is on the east side of Baker City. It borders the Madison's place, a fancy Morgan horse facility. Back in the day, my mom's first foster girl used to run away and hide out in their barns. Lock would track her down and drag her home."

"What was the big deal? Did the owners complain?"

"No, Frank Madison always offered to hire her."

The name sounded familiar and Sully frowned thoughtfully. "I think he's the dad of one of the noncoms in my company. Ann asked him to send an assortment of hoof picks to us when we were in the *sandbox.*"

"Why?"

"Because we weren't supposed to keep pocket knives for protection and the showers weren't exactly safe."

Tate's hands tightened on the steering wheel. "Did you have a problem?"

"No, but I'm comfortable using a hoof pick to take out a guy's eyes, nose, and a few other things he might want to keep. I have four stepbrothers and they taught me to kick butt before they let me date any of the guys in Liberty Valley."

"Good to know."

As they headed into the town a short time later, she spotted a large barn on the right-hand side of the street. A sign painted on the building proclaimed, "Summer's Feed and Tack." On the left, was another large structure, the Baker City Mercantile. Tate continued past the café, two bars, the church, a cemetery, and a vintage schoolhouse. More cedar shake buildings of varying sizes lined the roads.

Tate glanced at his watch. "We'll explore Baker City tomorrow. We should head straight for the farm to make it in time for dinner."

Outside of town, it only took a few more minutes to reach the Murphy home. After they crossed a narrow, arching private bridge over the river, she saw black Angus cattle grazing in pastures that lined the evergreen-shrouded driveway. Sully liked the look of the farm. It reminded her of the ones she'd seen in photographs or paintings. The gravel drive swirled around and eventually, Tate stopped in front of a three-story house with a tower, balconies, and even a wraparound porch.

He'd no sooner switched off the truck motor when the back door opened and a short, silver-haired woman in jeans and a flowered top hurried across the porch toward them. Smiling, she greeted Tate with a prolonged hug and a kiss before turning to Sully. "I'm Bronwyn Murphy. Welcome to my home."

"Thanks for the invitation. I'm Sullivan Barlow, Sully for short." She held out her hand, but Bronwyn ignored it, drawing her into a warm hug. Sully felt tears prick her eyes and hastily blinked them away.

"Tate will take your things to the guest room. Come with me. We're putting dinner on the table right now." Bronwyn put an arm around Sully's waist, urging her toward the back porch. "I hope you like spaghetti. On Fridays, my daughters cook and it's the easiest thing for them to make."

"It sounds wonderful. Lunch feels like forever ago and I'm starving."

"Oh, good. I like women who aren't afraid to eat, not the scrawny ones that Dougal brings home who are on bizarre diets. I never know what to fix for them."

"Not my problem." Amazed and oddly delighted by the older woman's affection toward a stranger, Sully walked beside her in the direction of the house. Had she finally found a home? Could Baker City be as wonderful as Tate claimed?

Tate watched the two women walk toward the kitchen door, glad they seemed to like each other. Humming softly, he opened the rear door to the truck's super cab and removed his duffel and her suitcase. He hadn't needed to be told that his mother wouldn't let them share a bedroom yet, that was understood. Sully would be in the room she'd reserved for company on the second floor and he'd be banished to his old bedroom on the third floor.

Hearing voices, he glanced toward the barn and saw his younger brother approaching, their father beside him. Both topped six feet. Broad shoulders and a wide chest filled out a dark blue work shirt that matched Lock's eyes. He wore jeans and boots, unlike their dad who still opted for faded overalls. Joe Murphy lifted his hand in a wave and grinned, the smile lighting up the rugged good looks he'd passed onto all his sons.

Tate went to greet them, unsurprised when Lock grabbed the bags so Joe and Tate could hug each other. "Hey there. Why are you late for supper?"

"Had to fix one of the pens so the old sow wouldn't lie on her new litter," Joe said, glancing around. "Your mom told me you were bringing company. Where is she?"

"Mom already took Sully into the house." Tate elbowed his brother. "Bet you're missing Mariah again. She had a knack for rescuing the little ones."

"She's been gone seven years ever since she graduated from high school." Lock scowled. "Do you think we can get through one weekend without you picking a fight?"

"No." Tate grinned at the younger man. "I live to harass you. It's my favorite thing."

"Boys will be boys no matter how old they get." Joe chuckled. "Put those bags upstairs, Lock and let's head for supper before your mom comes looking and we're all in trouble."

Raven followed the three men into the house, sniffing the aromas of tomato sauce, garlic bread, and something that smelled like chocolate. She spotted Sully in her white ruffled blouse and knee-length skirt of red floral lace making nice with two teenage girls, one African-American and the other Asian. The girls wore fashionably torn jeans, tight-fitting crop tops that revealed belly button rings, enough makeup for an entire cheerleading squad, plus plenty of earrings in their actual ears.

If she'd shown up for dinner like that, her mother would have heaved her martyr sigh, and her granny would have asked if Raven planned to sell herself on a street corner. Obviously, Tate's momma knew how to choose her battles. Raven drifted through the downstairs, a large country kitchen, a dining room, a parlor for special occasions, a living room with comfortable furniture, and a huge flat-screen television. A study, sewing room, and library with jam-packed shelves and a half-completed jigsaw puzzle on a table.

Framed family photos marched along the hallway walls beginning with sepia pictures of an old-time couple with their children, then more of the following generations in different fashions including fancy wedding shots of brides and grooms. There were soldiers in various uniforms, and she recognized Sully's fiancé in his dress blues. More contemporary ones showed other family members in up-to-date attire. She paused when she recognized a younger version of their company supply sergeant and wondered why there wasn't a photo of her twin sister. Mariah Stevens had said once that she was raised in foster care after her father died in a car accident but rarely discussed her past.

Back in the kitchen, Raven spotted one of the younger men scowling at the teens. She nearly asked what his problem was, then recalled she was dead, and he wouldn't be able to hear her. Mariah probably wouldn't agree, but there was more than one way to shoe a horse.

Sully stopped putting silverware around the table when the African American princess named Naveah signaled her. "Come meet Dad, Joe Murphy, and the guy his older brothers call the greatest lawgiver since Moses, Lock."

Hiding her smile, Sully shook hands with the older man first, then the younger one. "I'm Sullivan Barlow, but I prefer to be called, Sully...."

"Soon to be Sullivan or Sully Murphy," Tate said. "This is when I say, 'speak now,' Lock, but it'd be better if you didn't."

"I haven't said anything yet." Lock eyed her narrowly, scowling at his older brother. "Welcome to our home, Sully. I don't know why you came with him because I'm sure you could do better on a bad day. Aren't there more men than women in the Army?"

Sully laughed. "Shades of my brothers. Do guys ever grow up?"

"How many brothers do you have?" Chantrea asked, skillfully placing folded cloth napkins at each place setting. "We have five..."

"Here at the Murphy's," Naveah interrupted. "We haven't added in our other sibs."

"Well, maybe I can meet them another time," Sully said. "I have four older brothers and they always think they know best especially when it comes to me, but they still squabble with each other about it."

"Squabble." Joe pulled out a chair and his wife sat down. "That's a good word for it. Since it's time to eat, the boys will behave appropriately."

Sully struggled not to laugh at the quick look of disgust that passed over Tate's ruggedly handsome features, mirrored on Lock's face. Obviously, neither of them appreciated their father's description. They undoubtedly thought they were adults, but their dad didn't see them the way they saw themselves.

Once they began eating, topics of conversation shifted to the spring festivals Bronwyn's quilting group planned to attend, the crops Lock intended to plant, Joe's activities with the local Grange, and what the girls planned to do over their upcoming spring break. Lock claimed to have lots of tasks for them at home which promptly began another round of quarreling.

"You'd think you'd have learned better than to start World War Three after your battles with Mariah," Tate said.

"You mean *perfect* Mariah?" Naveah asked. "We get so tired of hearing how wonderful she was. We screw up a lot, but she never did."

"That's an unusual name. I've only met one woman called Mariah," Sully commented, "and I wouldn't say she's perfect. Obsessive, perfectionistic, and quick-witted, but never perfect. She always gives the senior noncoms heartburn and I'm the one who smooths everyone's ruffled feathers when the first sergeant threatens to transfer Sasha to a different company."

"I thought you were talking about Mariah. Who is Sasha?" Chantrea tilted her head to one side. "I never heard of her."

"Oh, she and Mariah are twins and if you want anything from Supply, you'd better stay on their right sides or you'll never get another pair of socks or boots." Sully teased out a piece of tomato from the greens in her salad and stopped at the sudden silence. She glanced around the table at the other adults. "What's wrong? Did I say something out of turn?"

Tate touched her shoulder gently. "No, sweetheart. Our Mariah came here ten years ago when she was barely fifteen and whenever she got in trouble with Mom, Dad or Lock, she always claimed Sasha was the one who did it."

"Sounds about right. Sasha does the same thing when I chew her out, except then it's Mariah Margaret Stevens who did the evil deed. I don't envy their college professors."

Tate leaned back in his chair. "Are they in your teaching cohort?"

"Oh, no way. Mariah Stevens is one of the go-to farriers in Liberty Valley. She and Sean Killian are who you call if you want your horses shod for three-day eventing or showing. If we hadn't been in the *sandbox*, Sasha would have been a contender for the equestrian Summer Olympics next year."

Another moment of silence before Bronwyn asked, "Then if they do that, why are they in college?"

"Veterinary medicine costs a lot, so Mariah started shoeing horses to earn money for tuition. Sasha told me their family comes from a long line of international champions and she's been groomed to compete since she was a teenager. Their grandfather went ballistic and refused to spend family money on their education so the two of them enlisted in the Army Reserve for the benefits."

"No wonder they talk to you." Tate passed the serving platter of garlic toast to her. "You have so much in common."

"Except I went through the horsey stage when I was a kid and didn't stay there for the rest of my life." Sully smiled at him. "And I'd much rather teach school than doctor sick animals."

Chantrea heaved a sigh. "I'd love to learn to ride, but I have to wait until I'm 18 and age out of the system."

"Hey if *perfect* Mariah could do it, so can you." Naveah bumped her arm. "You only have three years to go."

"Two and a half," Chantrea said.

CHAPTER TEN

After supper, Sully helped clean the kitchen, loading the dishwasher while Tate disappeared with his brother and father to do stock work in the barns. If she weren't stuck with the walking cast and a cane, she'd have joined them. When she was a kid, it took the proverbial *Act of Congress* or the occasional order from her step-dad to stay inside and give her mother a hand when it wasn't her favorite thing.

Sully reminded herself she was an adult and she needed to act like one. She did her best to smile and be cheerful while she did what she thought of as *girly* chores. Once they finished tidying the kitchen, the teenagers chorused polite goodnights and vanished to prepare for their Friday night dates.

On the way to the family room, Bronwyn Murphy showed off framed family photos in the hallway. "We were told Mariah was an orphan when she came here. It won't do much good to call her social worker at this late date."

"Or you could just contact her when our battalion returns to Washington State next week," Sully said. "She'll be around a while. Why didn't you stay in touch after she aged out of foster care?"

"I tried, but she and Lock never did get along. He'd start lecturing her and she'd storm off in a huff." Bronwyn heaved a sigh. "So, I don't know why Naveah and Chantrea have the impression that she was perfect."

"They undoubtedly heard it from someone." Sully lingered to look at a picture of a woman in an old-time prairie dress with her husband and several children. "Why don't you sign Chantrea up for riding lessons? You could find the same type of barn my step-dad did, one that insists the students do horsey care in addition to grooming and saddling their own mounts."

"Oh, between the organic gardens, the orchard, and livestock, we have enough farm chores around here for the girls. We don't do horses. They're too much trouble and they don't bring in money like the pigs, beef cattle, sheep, goats, chickens, ducks, and turkeys."

"You didn't say anything about dogs."

"Because we don't have any right now. Of course, Mariah took hers when she left."

"I see." Sully saw a lot but had the good manners not to say so. When she was growing up on the Barlow farm, her older stepbrothers usually brought home any strays they found. Their father, Gil did the same thing when he went to the hardware or feed store. Her mother never seemed to notice when their menagerie grew to include another dog or two or three, or the extra cats and kittens in the barns. Of course, she also pulled out dishes and food for the additions.

Maybe, I'd better cut the woman some slack instead of always screaming at her for favoring the boys over me.

Tate left his muck-covered boots on the back porch beside the pair belonging to his brother, then followed Lock and their father into the kitchen. They found Bronwyn Murphy assembling the customary evening snack of small toasted club sandwiches and chocolate chip cookies.

"Where is Sully?" Tate asked.

"She dozed off on the couch in the family room, so I covered her up and left the poor girl to rest. You soldiers work too hard."

"That's what I keep telling you." Controlling the urge to laugh, Tate sauntered into the living room. Sully continued to sleep while he gathered her into his arms and carried her to the stairs and the guestroom. He'd let his parents think whatever they wanted. It'd be up to Sully when they announced the fact that she was pregnant.

Five bedrooms including the master suite and two bathrooms took up the second floor of the old house. The one set aside for Sully was definitely intended for female guests from the flowered comforter on the queen-sized bed, to the papered walls, to the lacy curtains at the three windows and the fancy, antique bowl, and its pitcher on the bureau. A rocking chair stood in the far corner, a table beside it with an old-time pole lamp behind them.

He felt her stir against him and lowered her to the bed, dropping a kiss on her forehead. "Do you need help unpacking?"

She yawned, then opened her eyes to stare up at him. "I was watching TV with your mom while you did the farm-boy routine. You didn't tell me she was into Hallmark movies. That might be a deal-breaker, Murphy. Of course, she is a total sweetheart so I may have to overlook the sentimental shows."

"You passed out on her." He chuckled. "She thinks soldiers work too hard."

"Well, please don't tell her otherwise. I'm not ready to share my business. Our business."

"I'm good with that. Did you have a tour upstairs yet?"

When she shook her head, he gestured to her suitcase on the wooden luggage rack at the foot of the bed. "Well, there's your clothes." He waved across the room. "The bathroom is through that door and you don't have to share it since nobody is staying in the other guest room. The remote for the flat-screen TV is on the bureau. The girls have their own latrine further down the hall and they keep it clean, so they won't bother you."

Someone tapped on the doorframe and he spotted Lock standing in the hallway with a tray containing a club sandwich, three cookies, and a cup of hot chocolate. Tate took the tray and carried it over to the nightstand. "Mom must have sent you."

"She thought Sully might prefer a snack up here rather than joining us."

"Thank her for me," Sully said, sitting up to lean against the pillows. "It was very sweet of her."

"I'll tell her you said so." Lock leaned against the doorframe. "You're coming back downstairs with me, aren't you, Tate?"

"After he brings up my cane," Sully said in a sugary tone. "I know this is a walking cast, but I don't trust it and the doctor at the base needed my crutches for a different patient."

"You've got it." Tate eyed her. She'd obviously intended to make a good impression on his family by wearing a white ruffled blouse, knee-length red skirt, and one low-heeled, lace-up leather boot on her right foot while she had the walking cast on her left. "Do you need help with your boot?"

"No, I can handle that, and I probably should so I don't get dirt on the bedspread."

"Works for me. I'll be back in a few minutes."

When he returned, he found Sully sitting on the edge of the bed, her boot neatly beside it. She took the cane he offered, then gestured to the cup of hot chocolate. "Help me out here and drink that."

"Why?"

"Like coffee, it nauseates me. I don't want to pitch it even if your mom doesn't know I can't drink it."

"Okay, I'm on your side."

"I'll remember that." She stood and headed to the bathroom. "You can have the sandwich and I'll share the cookies with you in a few minutes."

Late morning sunlight streamed through the lace curtains and awakened Sully. It must be spring after all, not a wintry Saturday in February. She slowly sat up, waiting to see if her stomach would rebel, but it didn't. Was the morning sickness over? She shifted the blankets aside and headed for the bathroom. She'd shower, dress, and then go downstairs remembering her company manners. She wanted Tate's mother to like her. It'd make the future easier for all of them, especially when the woman had to do the 'grandma' thing.

Sully had barely glanced at the bathroom the night before when she used the toilet. Now, she took the time to glance around the room. Someone had a decorating good time tying in the icy blue and white, then reversing the colors in the bedroom with its cream walls and blue accents. The floor was made of dark blue tiles. An antique wood vanity held a farmhouse-style sink. A stack of striped, huge towels was on the bottom shelf. There wasn't a tub but instead a huge walk-in shower with two shower heads, the bigger one a rainfall style and handrails.

She returned to the bedroom long enough to pull clean clothes out of her suitcase, blue jeans, a hip-length cream sweater, underwear, and one running shoe. When she went back to the bathroom, she turned on the shower, then sat on the toilet and removed the walking cast. Like the previous brace, this one had a series of nylon straps that wove through rings and fastened on themselves. She worked her way through them from top to bottom. She found herself wondering who'd lived in the guestroom and used the bathroom before. Even if she didn't ask his parents, she might see if Tate knew the answer to the question. *I must be super snoopy.*

Almost an hour later, she went downstairs. She heard voices in the kitchen and found Bronwyn Murphy talking to a tall, curvaceous brunette in faded jeans and a purple sweatshirt. Both women glanced toward her.

"Sully, this is my daughter, Quinn Murphy-Chapman." Bronwyn smiled, friendliness all over her face. "Quinn, this is Sullivan Barlow—"

"Sully for short. Tate has told me about you, Quinn."

"Same here, Sully. My brother is chatty, but only with me."

"I hope some of it was good."

Quinn laughed. "All of it was."

Bronwyn crossed to the counter. "We have an early breakfast and lunch is two hours away. What would you like me to fix for you? Scrambled eggs? Bacon? Sausage?"

"I'm a light eater," Sully said. "Just toast and tea." She looked around the room. "Is Tate out helping on the farm?"

"Along with my dad and brother," Quinn said. "The girls are out in the greenhouse."

"It's time to start the tomatoes and peppers." Bronwyn began to cut slices from a loaf of homemade wheat bread. "The girls are planting seeds right now. Your munchkins could have come and helped, Quinn."

"Not on Saturday. It's their day with Lyle and I'm not interrupting their daddy time."

"Especially since you want to do your own thing."

"You've got it." Quinn turned on the teakettle. "After this, do you want to go to Baker City with me, Sully? I need to visit my salon and sign some checks for the manager."

"Sounds fun." Sully limped over to the table and drew out a chair. "What do you offer at your salon?"

"We do the three basics, hair, nails, and skin treatments."

While she ate the toast between sips of peppermint tea, Sully listened to detailed descriptions of the various services ranging from shampoos to conditioning to hair dyeing to perms to extensions, wig care, and custom events. After that, Quinn went on about manicures and pedicures, then facials, skin treatments including eyelash extensions, tattooing, and makeup.

"I just visit Quinn's Haunted Hair Emporium when I need a cut and color," Bronwyn said, "but Naveah gets her hair braided by one of the technicians and Chantrea constantly goes for acrylic nails. They don't hold up very well on the farm."

"I'll have to wait for those until I'm off active duty. The Army has regulations about everything, so I must pin up my hair above my collar when I'm in uniform. I could use a trim, but I haven't been back to Liberty Valley since Christmas."

"I'll call and see if Haisley is on today," Quinn said. "She's phenomenal with long hair."

Returning home to the Murphy farm always meant repairing and mucking pig pens, building fences, feeding livestock, and basically following Lock's orders about what needed to be done. Tate enjoyed being outdoors but had to admit he was accustomed to being in charge, not doing as he was told on a regular basis, especially by his baby brother.

The aroma of homemade vegetable soup filled the air when they entered the house. He allowed his brother and father to precede him to the bathroom and focused on his mother. "Is Sully still sleeping?"

"No, Quinn took her off to Baker City to visit the salon and go shopping. I told them to stop at the new bakery and bring home dessert. Twila Garvey makes better cakes than I do."

"I'll text them and see where I can catch up with them after lunch," Tate said.

"We finished our chores in the greenhouse." Naveah carried a bowl of fruit salad to the table. "Can we ride into town with you?"

"If it's okay with Mom, it's okay with me." Tate headed to the nearest bathroom to wash up for the meal, leaving the teenagers to convince Bronwyn of their desperate need to go hang out with their friends.

While they were eating, the afternoon plans drew Lock's attention. "I need help to finish up the pastures for the ewes that are lambing soon."

"You'll have me and the rest of the family tomorrow after church," Tate told him. "Today, Sully and I have to meet Reverend Tommy while we're in Baker City."

Silence fell and his parents gaped at him. Then, his father asked cautiously. "What are you saying?"

"I've told the whole Murphy clan my orders came through. I'm shipping out to Kentucky in March. Sully and I are getting married before I go."

Another long silence while everyone stared at him before his mother passed the platter of grilled ham and cheese sandwiches to him. "How does Sully feel about going to Kentucky so soon after coming back from Afghanistan?"

"She can't. She'll be training with her unit at Fort Clark for a couple of weeks when they arrive. After that, she's student teaching at the high school in Lake Maynard to finish her degree."

"Our school?" Chantrea stared at him. "Oh, my gawd, she'll be our aunt and our teacher? That's freaking amazing."

"I don't know what classes she has. You'll have to talk to her about it."

"Definitely." Naveah beamed at him. "We are so passing the word to everybody when we get to town. They better be nice to her or we'll kick their butts."

"Does she have a place to stay in Lake Maynard?" Lock swallowed the last of his coffee. "You don't expect her to drive back and forth to the base, do you? Traffic's terrible during rush hour. It takes forever. You should ask if she'd like to live here with us, Mom. There's no reason for her to be at the Army base without Tate."

Bronwyn nodded in agreement. "I will. It'd be much safer for her and give us all the opportunity to know one another."

"Besides, then you could bring her up to speed on all of Tate's hijinks," Joe added, "and what to expect when they have kids."

"Thanks a lot, Dad."

"It's the least we can do for family," Lock said. "Are you passing on those sandwiches or eating them all yourself?"

An hour later, Tate dropped the teens near the café in Baker City so they could locate their friends. They'd promised to be home in time for supper since the family rule was, they could either date Friday night or Saturday night, but not both nights. He cruised through town because he hadn't seen his sister's fancy SUV parked near her salon. He spotted it at the feed store and pulled in beside it.

Inside, he found Sully talking to a woman about her age. Something about the way the other woman held herself screamed military although she wore civilian clothes, faded blue jeans, and a red Washington State University sweatshirt that should have clashed with her strawberry blonde hair but didn't. Clinging to her hand was a little dark-haired girl.

Sully smiled at him as he approached. "Tate, this is Captain Endicott and a daughter of one of our noncoms."

"What's a noncom?" the child asked. "Auntie Margo says my mama's a sergeant."

"That's a shorter way to say noncommissioned officer which is what we call your mom," Margo Endicott said. "I borrowed Devon from her grandparents because I need to spoil her, and her mother won't be home from a training school for a few more weeks."

"Makes sense," Sully smiled at the pair. "This is my fiancé, Tate Murphy. We're visiting his family for the weekend."

Devon tilted her head to one side, hazel eyes filling with curiosity. "Are they the same Murphys who live next door to my grandpa and gramma? Mrs. Bronwyn lets me help feed the lambs when I visit and

Lock gives me baby piggies to hold, 'cept Gramma Ginger won't let me have one for keeps."

"That makes sense too," Sully said, amusement trickling into her voice. "I'm pretty sure piglets want to be with their moms."

"Yup, that's what Lock tells me." Devon tugged on Margo's hand. "I've been good a real long time. Can we look at the toys now?"

"Yes." Margo started away, then glanced over her shoulder. "Keep me posted on how the practicum goes, Sergeant Barlow. Before all of us returned to the *sandbox* this time, Ann and I both taught in Lake Maynard and we've got your six."

CHAPTER ELEVEN

Sully glanced up at Tate where he stood beside her, a tall, dark-haired hunk. In jeans, a flannel shirt under a denim jacket and boots, he looked like a lumberjack, a sexy one. *Mine, all mine.* She tiptoed up, brushed her lips over his, and then teased. "How was life on the farm?"

"Anything but laid-back when Lock's in charge." Tate grinned at her. "So, what did you think of Quinn? Are you two going to be good buddies?"

"Be afraid, very afraid. Your sister is almost as wonderful as your mom." Sully turned slightly so he could see the shining curtain of her hair, newly trimmed in a gentle U. "Her salon is terrific and so are the people who work there. I'd shampooed and conditioned my hair before we arrived, but Haisley decided it'd needed more treatment and went bonkers on it."

Tate laughed, his dark blue eyes amused. "That's why I stay away from Quinn's place. I don't want her crew coming after me. What did you do with her?"

"She's getting dog and cat food and I told her I wanted to look around. Then, I ran into Captain Endicott which put a stop to that."

"What do you want to see? The toys?"

"No, the clothes. I need a few more civvies unless I want to take a trip to Liberty Valley to pick up the rest of mine and I'm not ready for that. Being chastised by everyone I know there always puts me on the self-pity pot."

She gestured to the display racks of outdoor clothes, gloves, riding boots, and barn boots off to the left. Shelves of gifts and souvenirs, including a few used paperback novels on a spinner took up the front right corner. Pet gear, horse tack, medicine, and farm equipment filled the back-half of the store. Feed was through the back door in the adjacent warehouse. "Let's do some browsing."

"Okay, but I must tell you I'm a guy and I don't shop. It isn't my thing."

"I'll keep that in mind, but I don't believe you, Tate Murphy. You have the patience of a saint when it comes to putting up with all my angst."

"Now, I know we need to spend more time together so you figure out what an asshat I can be before Quinn and my mom share my idiosyncrasies."

"Still don't believe you." Laughing, Sully led the way to the western blouses. While she sorted through the various shirts, Tate wandered a short distance away to the children's section. The next time she looked, she saw him checking out the baby clothes. He was so cute. He'd be a good daddy, although they had a little more than six months to go.

The next time she glanced away from the tops, she saw Quinn had joined him. Sully hastily chose three of the flared, flowing tunics, one in a blue paisley print, one in green, and a third in red. Any of them would be appropriate for teaching school since she could wear them with jeans or leggings. She hustled across to join the twins. "What's happening?"

"You tell me." Quinn folded her arms, eying Sully. "Am I going to be an auntie?"

Heat flooded into Sully's face and she elbowed Tate when he snickered, then smirked. "Men. None of them can keep a secret and it's too early to announce anything."

"Okay, then I'll keep my mouth shut." Quinn snagged a pink and white onesie that declared, 'Yes, it is my first rodeo.' "Tate's orders came through, so I'll be your coach while he's gone, and I get to throw the first baby shower plus I'm the chosen babysitter."

"That's a lot to offer. Why would you when we've barely met, and I can be a real witch only I spell it with a 'b'?"

"You're just like me and I can too." Quinn shrugged. "Tate's my twin. He knows I really want a baby of my own, but my husband, Lyle already had three kids when we got together. He refuses to have any more. I may be out of luck, but I'll spoil your babies rotten."

Tate drew his sister against him in a quick hug. "Does he know how you feel?"

"Yes, but it doesn't matter. We've worked through it. I have the salons, your soon-to-be wife and baby to love." Quinn winked at Sully. "How much are you going to pay me to keep my mouth shut around Mom and Dad?"

"A lot." Tate kissed her forehead. "Sully gets to decide when we make the baby announcement. You don't."

"Got it, but you know Mom will want to knit and crochet a ton of stuff, so tell her early enough that she can get started."

"We will," Sully said, "but I want to wait a couple more weeks to be sure."

"Good luck with that." Quinn eased away from Tate and slid her arm through Sully's. "Are you two kids okay if I head out? I have a few errands to finish."

"We're fine," Tate said. "I called Reverend Tommy and we're going to meet him at the church. Mark your calendar. We want to get married Monday afternoon and I need you to stand up with me."

"I'm your twin. That's always going to be my job."

Once they'd paid for their items, the three of them headed for the parking lot. Quinn passed a bag to Tate, then sauntered across to her elaborate rig, unlocking it with the key fob. Two waves later and she was gone.

Sully waited while he opened the passenger door. "I like her. She's super sweet and wow is she smart. I'd have asked her to be my witness if you hadn't nabbed her. Now, I still need one. I wish I knew for sure that Jeannie got leave. I'll have to text her and find out."

"If she's not available, we'll get someone else you like. I have a ton of relatives."

"I can't wait to meet them if they're all like your family." Sully drew a deep breath. "Have to warn you again that my relations weren't real fond of me before Raven died and now, they really have issues."

"They'd better not share those concerns because I'm not willing to listen to the haters. I'm not the jackass whisperer."

Sully laughed and turned to brush his lips with hers. "That's almost enough to make me run away and marry you tonight."

"We better wait until Monday or my mom will ground me."

After parking in the lot adjacent to the church, the two of them walked toward the over-sized carved wooden doors where a silver-haired elderly man stood waiting. He didn't wear the traditional dark suit associated with most preachers, but a plaid, flannel shirt tucked into faded jeans. He nodded a greeting to Tate and smiled at Sully. "Hi there. I'm Reverend Tommy. Welcome to Baker City."

"Thank you. I'm enjoying my visit."

"Good. Tate tells me the two of you want to get married. Let's talk and see what we can manage."

To Sully's amazement, they had everything arranged by the end of the afternoon. She'd met the minister's wife who promised to decorate both the church and the reception hall for the wedding. Twila Garvey, the new local baker who turned out to be the widow of one of Tate's Army Ranger buddies agreed to provide a cake. Pop MacGillicudy, owner of the town café said he'd call Tate's mother about a buffet meal served in the community room at the church.

"What's next?" Sully looked at the clock on the dashboard. "Shouldn't we head for your folks' place so we're on time for supper?"

"Not yet. Quinn told me the new owners of the Cedar Creek Guest Ranch are fixing up their cabins. I thought we could check it out and see if we can rent one Monday and Tuesday night. I really don't want to spend our wedding night at my parents' house."

"Works for me. Let's do it." She giggled. "I guess I better not tell you that after six kids your folks probably know what we'll be doing then."

"It doesn't mean I want to think about that."

A mile outside of town, Sully saw a bright pink and purple sign that read Cedar Creek Guest Ranch. Tate turned into a gravel drive. He slowed to point out a row of small cabins with lawns that sloped down to the creek, running deep with snowmelt. He parked near the vacation homes, waving to a copper-haired woman strolling toward them from a nearby porch.

"That must be the owner. Quinn said she'd call her."

Sully eyed the other woman. She wasn't particularly dressed for big-city success but wore a blue tank top under a man's flannel shirt, loose, faded jeans, and running shoes. "I don't think I've said it often enough. I do like the down-home atmosphere in this place and everyone seems so nice."

"They're good folks. I always planned to move back here when I retired from the Army."

"I can certainly understand why."

Collecting her cane, Sully opened the truck door and slid out of the seat, starting around to join him on his side of the pickup. She paused and glanced over her shoulder, heaving a mental sigh when she had to return to close the passenger door. She'd thought it'd swing shut behind her. She'd pushed it, hadn't she? Apparently, not hard enough.

"Hi there. I'm Cat McTavish. You must be the couple Quinn Murphy called about."

"Yes, I'm Tate, her twin brother and this is my fiancé, Sully. We'd like to talk to you about renting a cabin for a short honeymoon."

Cat looked past them for a moment. Her emerald green eyes narrowed, then she nodded. "That's what Quinn told me. Well, let's take a look-see. I've already rented the biggest one to an Army officer fresh from Afghanistan. We're still working on the next one and it's not ready yet. The third cabin is basically one room with a bath and teeny-tiny kitchenette, kind of like a rustic, cheap hotel room. If you want fancy, you need to go to Seattle or Bellevue."

"Oh, we don't do fancy." Sully laughed. "It totally isn't me."

"Or me either," Tate agreed. "We'll go for comfortable."

"Fair enough." Cat gestured toward the third cabin. "After you. The door's open. Go see what you think. I'll wait here and that way we won't all crowd inside. You can tell me if it will be suitable."

Raven floated behind her bestie and the hot soldier. Who'd have thought that Sullivan Rafferty Barlow would be pregnant and married in a matter of days? *Not me, that's for sure. Too bad I'm dead and can't hassle her.*

The tall redhead stopped halfway to the cabins and held up her hand. In a low voice, she said, "Hold it right there."

Raven felt her insubstantial legs quiver and her feet freeze to the ground her shoes no longer touched. "What the hell? Who are you?"

"I'm the O'Leary and those are my questions. Answer them or—"

"Or what?"

"Or I send you where the bad ghosts go." A faint smile touched Cat's mouth, but not the green eyes. "I'm the O'Leary and this is my place. Baker City is my town. What do you want with Tate Murphy?"

"Hey, come on. I'm married. I like looking, but I'd never cheat on Kord Barlow. It took me long enough to rope and hogtie that man, plus months to get him to the altar."

"Where is he? Alive or dead?"

"He's alive. So was I until that I.E.D. in Afghanistan just before Christmas last year."

Cat frowned thoughtfully, turned to look over her shoulder at the cabin. "Is that where Sully hurt her leg?"

"You betcha. She walked away, but I didn't. She's my little sis by marriage, my best friend. I have to make things right for her."

"Why?"

"Because I'm the one who talked her into enlisting in the Army Reserve to get money for college when her parents bailed on her and mine didn't have enough bucks to send me. The scholarships we had wouldn't cover all the costs. She wanted us to apply for student loans, but we'd be paying them for the next hundred years once we got our teaching degrees and jobs."

"That isn't the way it works." Pity stirred in Cat's eyes and she lowered her hand. "What's your name?"

"Do you have to know to send me away?"

"No, I have to know because I'm insatiably curious. We're going to get along simply fine. I'm not dissing you and you won't be disrespecting me or my husband, Rob. He's like me and he can send you away too. I need to tell him who you are, so he understands you're not a threat."

"That actually makes sense. I'm Raven Driscoll-Barlow."

"Okay, Raven. Let's go check out the honeymoon suite and learn if the lovebirds like it."

The cabin had an Alpine appearance with a steep roof that sloped over the wraparound porch and its Adirondack wooden chairs. Barely six-hundred square feet, it was compact and cozy. Tate rested his hands on Sully's shoulders. They'd entered through the kitchen door. Straight ahead was the bathroom and off to their right, a combination sitting area with a queen-size bed. "What do you think?"

"I like it." She shifted on her cast and leaned back against him. "We'd better not tell Master Sergeant Hathaway about it or let him see the place. He'll be redecorating the barracks."

"I think it's bigger than both our billets." Tate chuckled and dropped a kiss on top of her head. "We could live in something like this."

"Yeah, but we'd need more closet space for our uniforms."

At the sound of footsteps on the porch, Tate turned slightly and spotted Cat McTavish coming to join them. "It's perfect."

"I'll have bigger cabins ready by summer if you decide you want to be here longer than a few days and your families make you bonkers."

"I only met his family yesterday and they're genuinely nice. Mine is in Liberty Valley."

"That's pretty close. Will they be here for the wedding?"

"We'll see," Sully said, her tone even. "I'm not one of their favorite people right now."

Cat tilted her head as if she listened to something more than what was being said, then nodded. "It's up to you, but I love weddings and my kids will be in school on Monday."

Tate studied her for a moment. "You're the new O'Leary, aren't you?"

"I thought she said her name was McTavish," Sully said.

"It is, but she comes from one of the founding families here in Baker City, the O'Leary's and they have gifts." Tate drew Sully closer. "We have our own stories here and they sound strange to outsiders."

"What kind of stories?" Sully flicked a sideways glance at the other woman. "What isn't he telling me?"

"That I'm a medium and as they say in Hollywood, I talk to dead people."

Sully blinked hard. "You two are crazy weird."

"Yup, that's what Raven said you'd say. You're seriously lacking in the imagination department."

When she tried to pull away from him, Tate tightened his grip on her. "Just listen to the woman, Sully."

"Are you insane?"

"No, but I'm the one who talked to your older brother and he said he knew he wasn't alone, that Raven was still with him."

Another silence before Cat nodded agreement. "She's not ready to leave him or you yet, Sully. She says you were her maid of honor when she married him and the two of you always intended for her to be yours."

"Yes, but that was before she died."

"She says she's still here and she wants to stand up for you on Monday. Oh, and you should call your mom instead of being such a dweeb. You know the woman has the broom she rode in on and nobody wants to listen to her pitch a fit for the next hundred years or hear her calling you all sorts of a slut in Liberty Valley. As your mother says, 'whores get paid,' and only a cheap chippie like you gives it away." Cat winced. "Sorry about the language, but I quote exactly what they tell me."

"So, Raven isn't the only ghost you claim to see?"

"As my daughters say, there are lots of them in Baker City and they are not quiet. When they want something, I hear about it."

"And my best friend wants my family at the wedding?" Sully yanked free, staggered for a moment, then steadied herself with the cane. She glowered at Tate. "I can't believe you're going along with this nonsense."

"Hey, I was raised in Baker City. There are some things we don't do in our town and ignoring the O'Leary is one of them. You must call your relatives even if they sound horrible."

"And if I don't?" Sully lifted her chin. "Is the wedding off?"

"Stop being silly, Barlow. Our kid is half Murphy. She or he will follow the same rules the rest of us do in Baker City."

"You can kiss my—" Sully stomped to the door, then stormed outside, calling back over her shoulder. "Those people hate me because —I'm not telling them anything."

"Well, that went splendidly." Cat heaved a sigh. "I'm sorry, Tate. I didn't mean to make trouble between you."

"It's okay. Kord Barlow told me Sully blamed herself for what happened to Raven."

"And vice versa," Cat said, after a moment. "If you have Kord's number, Raven says *you're to* call and invite him. He'll round up those in the family who want to come and who can be trusted to behave appropriately. Oh, and she says that Helene Barlow, Sully's mom will call her daughter all sorts of names when the two of you meet, not just the ones I already said."

"She'll only try it once." Tate met Cat's gaze. "No wonder Sully is overwhelmed by my folks. She isn't accustomed to being treated with civility."

"No, but it doesn't mean you should avoid your potential in-laws. As the saying from that old movie goes, 'keep your friends close and your enemies closer.'"

"Is that what Raven wants?"

"Yes. I speak for the dead, Tate Murphy. I don't just see and hear them."

CHAPTER TWELVE

It'd started to rain again while they were in the cabin. She wasn't going to get soaked in the early spring downpour. He hadn't locked the truck, so Sully climbed into the passenger seat, propping the cane next to her. What on earth was wrong with the two of them? Cat McTavish was obviously insane, and Tate Murphy seemed to be going along with her fantasies. Did they actually believe in ghosts? He hadn't seemed nuts when they met or during their time together at Fort Clark. Was this something that happened only in Baker City?

She swept a scathing glance over him when he opened the driver's door. "Do you seriously think I'll go along with this crapfest? Raven's dead."

"Nobody is saying she's not." Tate started the engine, switching on the windshield wipers, and shifted the truck into gear. He turned the pickup around and drove back toward the small mountain town. "Baker City was established by the O'Learys, the McElroys, the Sweeneys, the O'Connells, the Garveys, the O'Neills, and the O'Sullivans. Seven Irish boys met on a ship bound for America. My family, the Murphys, came after World War One so we're somewhat respected, not total newbies like the MacGillicudys who are Scots-Irish and didn't get here until the 1940s. They don't count for much to some of the folks who live here."

"And you're telling me the O'Leary's have always been mediums?"

"That's right. The family always has one person, the *O'Leary* to maintain peace, order, and keep everyone calm and happy in Baker City. My mother told me the town didn't have a medium for a long time after her grandmother passed, but then Ed and Adam Williams found Cat last fall when she entered their essay contest and won the dude ranch."

Despite knowing better, Sully asked, "How does she maintain order? She didn't look like a cop to me."

"She's not. Dick O'Connell is the chief and keeps that sort of law. He wouldn't even try to do what the *O'Leary* does. Cat O'Leary manages the ghosts who haunt Baker City and runs interference between the living and the dead."

"I'm sure you're about to tell me why there are so many."

"Yes. We'll be living here and you need to know." Tate drove past the mercantile and feedstore coming to a halt by the church and the cemetery behind it. "In February 1910, it snowed until there were drifts more than ten feet deep. Clouds couldn't get over Mount Carmody. A foot of snow fell each hour and it continued day after day, night after night. Valentine's Day, it suddenly warmed up, and the snow changed to rain. Then, the avalanches started."

"How many?"

"Five in total. Two big ones hit the town, wiping out the train station, the hotel, the school, three shops, and five homes. Sixty people died. It took months to dig out all the bodies. The last funeral was for Mrs. Doireann O'Sullivan, the schoolteacher who'd come from Ireland. After her husband died in a farming accident, she'd returned to teaching and remained at the school until her death."

"No wonder people want to believe in ghosts."

"No wonder," Tate said drily. "Come on. Let's take a walk."

"Why? Are you going to show me where the Murphys are buried?"

"Yes, along with other founding family members. My great-great-grandfather bought one of the O'Neill farms after the disaster. He married a Sweeney girl, so I'm related to pretty much everyone in town."

"Even the *O'Leary*?" Sully mocked.

That earned a stern look before he said, "Indubitably. My mother could tell you all the connections."

Sully forced a scowl when he gripped her elbow to steady her. Why did she still enjoy his touch when she thought he'd lost it? She didn't tell him that as he guided her toward the oldest section of the cemetery.

Someone had spent a great deal of time maintaining gravel walkways between the graves. She began to read the engraving on the tombstones. They had different names, different birthdates, but the majority had died around February 16th, 1910. She still didn't believe in ghosts, but she could understand how a tragedy like this would mar a town and make people want to think there were spirits. Granted, it didn't answer the question of how Cat O'Leary McTavish knew about Raven Driscoll-Barlow who'd lived in Liberty Valley and wasn't even buried in Baker City.

"I'm sorry about what happened here, Tate."

"But you still figure I'm bonkers for believing in my town's culture."

"Pretty much, but I don't have to be a witch about it." She took a deep breath, trembling when he tipped up her chin. "Now, what?"

He dropped a kiss on her forehead. "According to your brother, there are witches in Liberty Valley."

"Yeah, Kord has a load of stories he's heard from the old-timers. Raven's grandpa says a pack of werewolves lives in one of the northeastern towns in the valley. You don't want to go there on the night of a full moon because you'll be dinner."

"Do you believe that?"

"Oh, hell no! I think it was just a story to keep me and Raven from running amuck since we were little troublemakers and worse ones when we hit our teenage years. We partied all over the valley and he didn't want us going too far from home." Sully sighed and pressed close to Tate. "Our kid needs a dad. Are we still getting married even if I don't believe in ghosts?"

"As long as you don't make fun of me because I do."

"I can handle that."

Two sweet kisses later, they started back toward the pickup. Sully realized the path intersected a newer section of the cemetery and stopped as the names filtered into her mind. Each and every tombstone marked the grave of an O'Sullivan. A white marble marker like the ones she'd seen at the military graveyard at Fort Bronson where they buried Raven caught Sully's attention. This one read, 'Rafferty Gallagher O'Sullivan, Sgt, U.S. Army, Grenada, Panama, Gulf War, 1964-1991, Beloved Son, Brother, and Friend'.

One more long look and then she walked beside Tate to his truck. Was that her father? If so, he'd obviously died in combat when she was about two years old. She remembered her mother saying they'd split up and he'd left before Sully was born. Apparently, he hadn't visited when she was a toddler either. Some guys weren't cut out to be fathers. She slipped her hand into Tate's. "Sorry to be so touchy."

"When you are, I'll tell you."

They arrived at the Murphy farm in time for Tate to help with the evening chores. Her hair and clothes were damp from the rain. She went upstairs to change before she did the 'good guest' thing and jumped in to help Bronwyn with supper. Sully tucked the cute onesie for the baby into her suitcase and hung the new tops in the closet. She removed her favorite floral pullover dress from the hanger. Caramel-brown, it had a flowing fit and flare-type style with an adjustable back tie and cap sleeves. Crochet lace trimmed the V neck. She took it and a pair of brown tights with her into the bathroom so she could dry her hair.

Back in the bedroom, she draped her jeans over the rocking chair and hung her sweater in the closet. She reminded herself that she needed to go downstairs, but somehow, she lacked the energy. Instead, she crossed to the bed, unfastened the various nylon straps that wove through the rings of the walking cast, and stretched out for a nap. She'd doze a bit and then go help in the kitchen.

Watching her best friend sleep, Raven sank into the rocking chair. It'd have been majorly boring to stay at the base by herself, but she'd never expected to meet someone who could see and talk to her. Now, she felt lonelier than ever. She stood, crossed to the bed, and drew the hand-crocheted afghan over Sully. There were other ghosts in Baker City and Cat O'Leary had told Raven not to limit herself. All she had to do was think about where she wanted to be, and she'd end up there.

Saturday night meant live country music at the town café and even if she couldn't dance with Kord, she could still enjoy a party. *Okay, so I'm dead. That doesn't mean I'm dust, at least not yet.*

Dinner was homegrown vegetables around a beef pot roast. While he waited for his turn to wash up, Tate scanned the kitchen. "Where's Sully?"

"Upstairs. I sent Chantrea to call her." Bronwyn carried a platter of steaming biscuits to the large oak table. "You two must have really toured the area. The girl is worn to a frazzle."

"She's sleeping," Chantrea reported, coming into the room. "I didn't wake her up. I just turned on the bathroom light and came back downstairs. Is that okay? Or do you want me to go back and get her?"

"Let her sleep," Bronwyn said, eyeing Tate. "Is there something you want to tell me, son?"

"Not that I can think of." Tate started for the adjacent bathroom, then glanced over his shoulder. "Virginia Thompson said she'd touch base with you about flowers for the church. Do you have some in the greenhouse we can use for the wedding?"

"Good distraction, but it won't work, young man. I put Naveah in charge of them. She's going to meet up with Virginia at church tomorrow. Chantrea, get another jar of strawberry jam out of the pantry please."

"I'm on it." Smiling, the teenager walked away.

After the meal, while the girls cleaned up the kitchen and Lock loaded the dishwasher, Bronwyn put together a plate of food for Sully. Following her directions, Joe made a cup of peppermint tea and poured a glass of milk. Tate oversaw serving up dessert, a slice of homemade apple pie surrounded by three chocolate chip cookies.

"When she's eaten, bring the dishes back downstairs, Tate,"

Bronwyn said. "Tell her if she's not up for church in the morning, we'll see her afterward."

That comment earned puzzled looks from Lock and the two girls, but Joe nodded wisely in agreement. "Your momma knows what's what around here."

"Well, I don't," Lock said. "I have to be half-dead or one of my pigs does before she lets me off the hook. Church and Reverend Tommy's sermons are mandatory on Sundays."

"What he said," Naveah agreed. "Is she going to be a new fave around here, Mom?"

"Don't be so thick." Chantrea elbowed her. "Come on. We're done here and Mom's gonna help us knit."

"Knit what?" Lock asked. "That's old school."

"You're a guy. You don't get it." Chantrea said. "We'll be in the sewing room."

Bronwyn laughed, wrapping an arm around each girl. "What she said. Let's do it. You guys can watch TV until it's time for you to make the late-night snacks."

Carrying the supper tray, Tate headed for the stairs. He suspected his mother and foster sisters already knew what was happening with Sully although he hadn't shared the secret. Quinn wouldn't betray him. She never had, but he'd text and let her know about the knitting party. She'd want to be involved with it even if quilting was more her preferred craft and she'd undoubtedly be hitting her favorite stores for material tomorrow after church if she hadn't gone to Lake Maynard already.

Sully yawned, slowly coming awake. She glanced at the radio-clock on the nightstand, stunned to discover it was almost seven-thirty at night. What happened? She'd meant to nap a few minutes, not a few hours. *Oh, my gawd. Tate's mom is going to think I'm the most useless female alive. And now, I've got to pee like a racehorse.*

When she returned from the bathroom, she found Tate setting up a tray on the table next to the rocking chair. She allowed herself the privilege of standing and leering at him for a long moment. If she thought he was a hunk in his uniform, she had to admit he looked amazing in blue jeans and the flannel shirt that emphasized broad shoulders and muscled arms. Wow, she couldn't wait until she had him in her bed again, his legs tangling with hers, his feet against hers and—

"You're staring."

"I can't help it. There's something so sexy about a guy bringing me dinner. I bet your mom thinks I'm totally worthless. I meant to help her, but I didn't make it downstairs."

"She figures we spent too much time walking around Baker City." He pulled the rocking chair closer to the table. "Eat your dinner while it's hot, Sullivan Barlow soon to be Murphy."

"Only if you help with the chocolate chip cookies. They're good, but they aren't my be-all and end-all. Then, I won't have to share the pie."

"You got it, sweetheart."

After she ate dinner, they cuddled together on the bed sharing dessert while watching an episode of her beloved *Criminal Minds*. She'd almost told him that she didn't like being called his 'sweetheart' when she obviously wasn't. She could remind him that he'd only proposed because she was pregnant. It all sounded so nasty and mean-spirited. She could do better, be a better person. She opted not to pick a fight with him. He was trying hard and the least she could do was meet him halfway.

Besides, he looked majorly hot doing the cross between the lumberjack and logger routine with five-o'clock shadow edging his jaw. She heaved a sigh, pressing her cheek against his chest. "Am I totally evil if I dread calling my mom tomorrow about the wedding?"

"Not evil, scared. Will she really be rude to me or my family?"

"I'm afraid so. Your mom has been super sweet to me. My mother isn't like her. She critiques me nonstop, well except when she's talking to Raven's mom or someone, she considers a friend or acquaintance which is pretty much everyone she knows in Liberty Valley. Then, she reads them my pedigree and they hear about all my sins from potty-training to college. It wouldn't be so bad except she never does that to my stepbrothers or says anything negative to their various girlfriends. According to her, they walk on water."

"And Raven? She's your sister-in-law. Does your mom do that to her?"

"No, she adores Raven. She always praises her to the skies too." Sully blinked hard to hold back tears, then turned her attention back to the television drama. "I couldn't bear to be around my mom after the funeral, not when she acted like I'd deliberately killed—"

"And the wedding? Will she blame you for what happened to Raven then?"

Sully nodded. "It's why I don't want her there. I want one day that's about me. Okay, I'm being selfish. I should say about us."

"I won't keep my mouth shut if somebody, even your mother says bad things about my wife before or after the ceremony." He feathered a thumb over her cheekbone, down to her lips. "Captain Endicott and Sergeant Barrett aren't the only ones who have your six. I've got it twenty-four, seven."

Sully pressed her lips against his thumb. "And I have yours too, so I guess this is where I suck it up and drive on."

"Easier to do when you're not alone."

"True." Sliding her arms around his neck, she reached up to kiss him. She threaded her fingers through his short black hair and brought his mouth close. For once, he didn't hold back. Their lips met and hers parted beneath the pressure of his mouth. His tongue tangled with hers in a passionate duel. One kiss led to a second, then a third. She trembled when his hand cupped her breast. His thumb teased an ultra-sensitive nipple through her dress and bra. She moaned softly.

He lifted his head. "I should go."

"I'm not telling you that."

"No, but I don't want my parents grounding me for life if they catch us necking in their guest room."

She laughed, looking down at his hand still on her breast. "Aren't you supposed to be a big, bold Army Ranger?"

"Yes, but my mom even scares Lock and he did Recon in the Marines."

Sully eased across Tate, sitting on his lap. Her dress hitched up and she felt his erection press into her, right where she wanted him most. Her panties dampened at the idea. She nipped his lower lip. "Stay with me. I dare you."

"You're too tempting." He rocked against her.

She pushed back, brushed her mouth over his, and trailed a line of kisses to his ear. "Have me."

"I will Monday night." He gripped her waist and lifted her off him. "You'll be hotter then and so will I."

CHAPTER THIRTEEN

She'd set the alarm, so she'd wake up early enough to attend church with the Murphy family. After her faux pas of missing dinner the previous night she didn't want to repeat the mistake. She wanted Tate's parents to like her, not think she was some sort of diva. She pushed the blankets aside, reached for her cane, and then eased out of bed.

Her ankle-length, long-sleeved granny nightgown swirled around her as she stood and swayed for a moment. Her stomach rebelled at the movement. She hurried across the room, barely making the toilet in time to heave.

Dimly, she thought she heard someone, but when she risked a glance, she didn't see anyone behind her. Then, her stomach clenched, and she threw up again. She huddled over the toilet, half-afraid to leave it. Someone collected her flyaway hair, holding it at the nape of her neck.

She caught the scent of spicy aftershave and hurled for the third time. "This is your fault and I hate you."

A low deep chuckle and a male voice said, "How can it be when we only met Friday night?"

She flicked a glance over her shoulder and saw Lock Murphy, a younger dark-haired version of his soldier brother. "What are you doing here?"

"Naveah came to call you for breakfast and heard you being sick. Are you done?"

"I think so."

He helped her stand and Sully staggered to the sink to rinse her mouth while he flushed the toilet. "In case you wonder, I really hate your older brother almost every morning and when I barf at night, I hate him then too."

"If I was puking my guts out as soon as I moved, I'd join the club." Lock squeezed toothpaste on the toothbrush and handed it to her. "I'll get your robe. Fair warning. I sent for Mom and at least now I know why she excused you from church."

"Thanks a lot." When they left the bathroom, Sully saw Bronwyn Murphy placing a cup of steaming peppermint tea on the table along with a package of soda crackers. "I'm sorry to be so much trouble."

"Why would you think that?" Bronwyn adjusted the placement of the rocking chair. "Come sit down and try to nibble some crackers. They'll settle your tummy. Back in the day, I was told if I had morning sickness, I was less likely to miscarry."

"Did Tate tell you we were having a baby?"

"He didn't need to." Bronwyn gestured to the chair again. "Honey, I knew as soon as I met you. I've had six healthy babies and the stork didn't bring them."

Sully's lips quivered into a smile and she limped to the seat. "Thank you. I hate missing church. I really wanted to hear Reverend Tommy's sermon."

"There will be other Sundays and you'll be up for it after your first trimester. Eat your crackers. Drink the tea and then take a nap. We'll be home by lunchtime." Bronwyn paused to stroke Sully's hair. "I'm extremely excited about being a mom-in-law and a grandma. Now that I'll have one of my boys married off, I'll have help to find matches for the others."

Sully smiled and reached for the cup of tea. "Tate didn't tell me that was a requirement."

"He didn't know and I'm getting out of here before you two start hunting up a fiancée for me," Lock told them. "I'm happy with things the way they are."

"Not for long," Sully said and nestled into Bronwyn's warm hug.

Mama Murphy is so sweet, Raven thought, watching the pair cuddle. *And you need a real mother, not somebody who constantly finds you wanting, and makes most of Liberty Valley hate you, sis of my heart. I don't care what that woman has told you forever, you're a good person and you deserve love.*

From the time she was a child, Raven knew she had to be careful with her bestie's mom if she didn't want Helene castigating her all the time the same way she did Sully. And since she'd fully intended to marry Kord Barlow from kindergarten on up, making a friend out of Helene Barlow was pure necessity.

And I did, but wow it wasn't easy. That woman still has the vacuum cleaner she traded her broom for, Raven thought. *Still, she must at least be invited to the wedding even if she doesn't come or she'll browbeat Sully about it for the next fifty-plus years until we, Sully, and I put her in the ground.*

The door opened and she saw Joe Murphy enter with a brown ceramic teapot. He crossed to the table and carefully topped off the cup. "So, I'm going to be a grandpa."

"How did you know?" Sully stopped taking cautious bites of the saltine. "I never said a word."

"You didn't have to." He winked at her. "I'm the daddy of six kids and I always knew before Bronwyn did when we were adding to the family."

"And we'll be spoiling your little one rotten when we're babysitting before we send him or her back to you and Tate," Bronwyn said. "Be afraid, darling. Be very afraid."

Sully sniffed and blinked hard in an obvious attempt not to cry. "But I'm not scared, not at all. I want the whole family to love our baby, for it to have what I never did."

"They will." Bronwyn hugged her again. "I'll see to that. I promise."

"Me too." Joe smoothed Sully's bright red hair. "No worries. We'll take good care of you."

"About time," Raven told the older couple although she knew they didn't hear her.

Tate followed his family toward the over-sized carved wooden church doors where Reverend Tommy Thompson stood waiting to greet his parishioners. Even if it was Sunday morning, he still didn't wear the traditional dark suit associated with most preachers. Instead, he wore his usual plaid, flannel shirt tucked into faded jeans and battered cowboy boots.

After greeting his parents, brother, and foster sisters, the minister glanced toward Tate. "Where's Sully today?"

"Sleeping in," Bronwyn answered before Tate could. "That poor child has been working too hard on the base. Little wonder she's barely healed up from her injuries in Afghanistan, so Joe and I insisted she rest up while she visits us."

"Do you want to hold off on the wedding tomorrow?"

"We want it then," Tate said. "When I saw Sully before we left this morning, I promised to confirm the time with you. The Army's sending me for training later this month. I'll be back for a few days before we ship out to Afghanistan."

"Sounds like a plan." Another smile and Reverend Tommy walked away to say hello to Cat O'Leary McTavish and her family.

Tate had barely sat down in one of the pews when his sister slid in beside him, accompanied by her husband, Lyle Chapman, a local business executive who always wore a dark suit, and her three stepchildren. The blonde stair-steps always opted for more formal attire than their peers, dresses and heels for the girls, slacks, a collared shirt, and a tie for the boy. It meant when they came to Sunday dinner, Quinn would be the only one ready to visit the farm in her jeans, lace-up boots, and W.S.U. sweatshirt.

She pulled out her phone. "I have pics I want to show you and Sully."

"Who's Sully?" Lyle asked.

"I told you again at breakfast this morning, but you probably didn't hear me because you were on your laptop. Tate's engaged." Quinn scrolled through photos, glancing sideways at her twin brother. "I was at the fabric store last night and picked some samples for you to approve."

"You need to ask Sully what she likes," Tate protested. "It's a girly thing."

"It's a surprise for her. Suck it up, buttercup, and tell me what you think."

"And when I screw up and piss her off, I'll be the one she nails to the wall."

"Welcome to the club." Lyle laughed, amusement in the dark brown eyes and on his handsome face. "Every married guy knows that rule."

Quinn scowled at the two of them in turn before she brought up a photo of a pink and white floral quilt. "This is a variation of an *Irish Chain* pattern and since it's strip piecing, I can make it super quick. Granted, this one is more feminine than you might prefer, Tate but I can incorporate other colors."

"I thought you were making—" Tate paused and looked down the bench at his mother.

"Mom and the girls were knitting last night."

"I know. Chantrea texted me a pic of her new project, but this is a wedding gift, one for your bedroom. I can wait on the other quilts until Sully goes shopping with me to choose the material." Quinn scrolled to a different picture; a quilt made of three types of triangle-shaped pieces. "Okay, so this one tries to create an old-fashioned appearance, almost a vintage appeal. It works with florals and solid fabric, or stripes and solids."

"Like a pool game," Tate said, shifting to avoid the elbow she nearly smacked into his ribs. "Why am I in the hot seat?"

"It's a present for the two of you. Man up."

Tate tried to look interested as she showed him a few more brightly colored handmade blankets. He was glad when the music started, and the minister approached the pulpit. Maybe the sermon would get him off the proverbial hook. Then, he glimpsed tears shining in his twin's dark blue eyes and put an arm around her shoulders. "Show me the second one again."

"Is that your favorite?"

"Yes." He squeezed her, a quick hug. "And pick out some blues and greens, not only a bunch of flowery crap."

"I will. You'll love it, Tate. So will Sully. I already called Vanessa

Sweeney and set up the time for our quilting group to help me piece, bind, and finish it when I complete the squares. Aunt Heidi volunteered to visit and she's always so creative. We'll be able to give it to you and Sully before you ship out in May. By then, you'll have a rough idea of where you'll be living when you get back from Afghanistan."

"We'll love it." He hugged her again. "And I'm counting on you to take good care of Sully for me while I'm gone."

"You know I will."

After the service ended, the small congregation headed to the reception hall for refreshments. They'd barely chosen doughnuts and beverages when Virginia Thompson, the minister's wife, a stately woman with silver-streaked dark hair arrived at the Murphys' table. She exchanged greetings with everyone, but her attention was on Naveah. "Is now a good time to organize the flowers for tomorrow?"

"Sure. Mom said Chantrea and I could skip school for once."

"Why? What's going on?" Cressida Chapman tilted her head curiously. "We're seeing the high-school basketball team off to State competitions tomorrow morning."

"Tate's getting married." Chantrea's focus was apparently taken up by the maple bar in front of her. "And we're helping with that."

"What?" Lyle gaped at Tate. His bewilderment was mirrored on the faces of his daughters, but his ten-year-old son barely looked away from the conversation he was having with Lock. "When did that happen?"

Quinn heaved a sigh. "I told all of you when I got home last night and again at breakfast, but obviously nobody was listening."

"I was," Finlay announced, rolling his dark eyes. "But, like you said, Dad was on his computer doing emails, Cressy was texting the other cheerleaders on her cell, and Letty was reading a book when she was supposed to be setting the table this morning."

"Thanks a lot." His middle sister glared at him. "You don't need to rat out everybody."

"I'm not. Quinn said we didn't pay attention to her news, only I did." Finlay glanced at his father. "Can I miss school too and go to the wedding? It'll be fun and I bet there's gonna be cake."

Tate chuckled. "Yes, there is. Sully and I picked it out yesterday."

"You don't know her, Finn," Cressida shot him a glare. "She probably won't like having you spoil the day."

"I won't spoil it. Can I come, Quinn?"

"I'd love it, but I'm standing up for Tate, so you have to sit with Lock and make him behave appropriately."

"No worries. We're buds and I will."

"Now, I'm scared." Lock winked at Virginia. "So, who is standing up with Sully? Are you?"

"No, I'm playing the organ. The O'Leary is. She'll be over to talk to you in a few minutes, Tate." Virginia gestured to Naveah again and the two of them walked away, followed by Chantrea carrying the remnants of her maple bar.

That news earned him a long look from his brother-in-law before Lyle said, "I have a sales meeting in Portland tomorrow, so I won't make it back in time for the ceremony. If I'd had more notice…"

"Getting leave from the Army isn't always easy to arrange," Tate swallowed some coffee, "much less a four-day pass."

"So, how does a soldier find a woman to marry him on a long weekend?" Cressida inquired, her tone super sweet, too sweet. "Isn't it a big deal to be an Army wife?"

"It's a bigger deal for me to be an Army husband." Tate winked at the thirteen-year-old. "As long as we're stationed on the same base, we'll be fine."

"You mean she's a soldier too?" Letty asked. "Why isn't she here?"

"Because she's still recovering from a run-in with an I.E.D." Cat O'Leary McTavish announced, arriving in time to hear the question. Accompanied by a tall, dark-haired man who she introduced as her husband and two little red-headed girls, the woman gestured to an adjacent table. "Bring that over here, Rob. My daughters want to ask you something, Tate."

He eyed the pair who were definitely twins. "Hi, I'm Tate Murphy and this is my twin sis, Quinn, and her family."

"I'm Sophie and she's Samantha and we wanta come to your wedding. Raven said we could be flower girls. That means we can wear the fancy dresses our gramma brought us. Daddy will take our pictures and send them to her and Grandpa Dave at their condo in Hawaii."

"What?" Tate shook his head, then eyed their parents. "When did all this happen?"

"Last night at the café. We like to go to Pop's for dinner on the weekend." Rob and Lock finished carrying over chairs and arranging them around the second table. "There's always live country music on Saturday nights and the girls were talking to some of the folks who showed up for it."

"And Raven was one of them?"

Samantha nodded. "The mayor was telling her the rules for being in Baker City and when he finished, she saw us."

"And we told her who we were and asked who she was, 'cause she's new here," Sophie finished, "so she told us she came with you and Sully and about your wedding."

"That was enough for them to insist they should get to miss school and be there for you two," Rob added, smiling around the table, and oozing laid-back charm. "Are you good with it? Will your fiancée agree?"

"I'll tell her when I get home." Tate held up his hand to quell his mother's and sister's protests. "I outrank her, and this is a great swap-ortunity as they say on TV. I get the twins and her mom doesn't get to ruin the day."

"You still gots to invite her or Raven says she'll browbeat Sully forever." Sophie slid into the chair her father held out for her. "Daddy, what's browbeat mean?"

"Bully. And it's not a smart thing to do to a soldier, especially one who just came home from combat." Rob rested his hand on Cat's shoulder for a moment. "Another maple bar for you and milk for the girls?"

"That works." Cat smiled at him. "Thanks, love."

"Nobody likes bullies," Samantha decided, joining her twin at the table, "and some of the teachers at school make you stay inside at recess and write sentences when you do it."

"Good to know these things." Tate wondered if Sully did that to the teens at the high school and decided he wouldn't be surprised if she assigned extra work to troublemakers. "This wedding is getting bigger and better all the time."

"That's one phrase for it." Quinn frowned as a slender blonde woman followed Rob toward them. "Oh, for heaven's sake, here comes trouble, Tate. Did you warn Sully about your past and Dommi?"

"No worries. That was high school. She dumped me when I enlisted." Tate stood to greet the newcomer, the perfect fashion plate in a light blue dress that clung to every curve and matched her eyes. Stilettos made her almost as tall as he was. "Dominique MacGillicudy, I didn't know you were in town."

She brushed an air kiss over his cheek. "Tate Murphy, as handsome as ever. I hear congrats are in order and I'm just the gal you're looking for."

He chuckled. "My fiancée would have something to say about that."

"Yes, but she's going to want a house of her own and I'm flipping foreclosures for Daddy. I can so find the perfect place for you."

CHAPTER FOURTEEN

When she went downstairs shortly after eleven that morning, she found breakfast waiting on a covered plate on the table along with a note from her soon-to-be mother-in-law to expect Quinn's family as well as the 'regular suspects' for Sunday dinner that afternoon. Grateful for the info, she was glad she'd opted for her favorite floral pullover dress and brown tights today as well as the one lace-up boot she could wear.

She nuked the scrambled eggs and bacon in the microwave and brewed a cup of tea. She'd never tell Bronwyn or Joe Murphy, but Sully appreciated the solitude of having the house to herself. While she ate, she scanned messages on her phone. She skipped over the ones from Leslie Dunaway, deciding she'd contact the university supervisor later.

After she finished eating, Sully put her plate and silverware in the dishwasher. She took a moment to check the ham in the oven. It didn't need anything, gravy bubbling around it in the roasting pan. The brown sugar glaze and pineapple rings topping the meat made her hungry all over again. *Good thing I'm pregnant,* she thought, *or I'd have to run five miles a day to work off these calories.* Right now, she needed to call her mother and let her know about the wedding tomorrow.

I'm not sure if Raven's haunting me or not, but Cat O'Leary was right about contacting Mom. The woman bears a grudge longer than a politician.

With a fresh cup of peppermint tea, Sully sat down at the kitchen table and skimmed through the contact list, choosing her mother's number, and waiting for her to answer.

"It's about time you called, Sullivan. What were you thinking?"

A thousand answers came to mind, but she didn't use any of them. "I'm sorry. I was busy working."

"Do you expect me to believe the Army kept you so busy for the past two months that you didn't have five minutes to call me?"

Sully counted silently to ten, determined to remain calm. "That's right, Mother."

"I had to put your presents in the attic when you didn't come for Christmas."

More guilt as if she didn't already feel enough. "Again, I'm sorry."

"You keep saying it. Why are you sorry now?"

"Shall I make a list?"

A long silence and then her mother said, "Kord told us you were hurt, that you broke your leg when Raven died. Why didn't you come home?"

"I couldn't. I didn't want to impose."

"For heaven's sake, Sullivan Rafferty Barlow. We're your family. Where was your head? We'd have looked after you."

"The Army did."

"You should have demanded leave. They'd have granted it after what happened to our Raven."

"It wasn't necessary, and I could still work. I needed to work." Sully drew a deep breath. "Did Kord tell you about Tate Murphy?"

"No, who is that?"

Sully calmly threw her oldest stepbrother under the proverbial bus. "My fiancé. We're getting married tomorrow in Baker City before he ships out."

A gasp, followed by a wail. "Sullivan, what are you thinking?"

"I'm just calling to invite you, Gil, and Kord to the wedding as well as any other family members who have time to attend."

"I can't believe you. I don't believe you. How can you do this to us? We don't even know the man."

"Kord does." Sully paused. "The Murphys are all that and the so-called bucket of chips here in Baker City. They've pulled all the necessary strings to make the ceremony special. All you have to do is show up at the church after lunch."

"What are you going to wear? Your clothes are all here at home, packed away in our attic or at Kord's and Raven's house."

"I'll go shopping this afternoon with Tate's mom and sisters. We'll find something at the feed store."

"Oh no, Sullivan. Take some time. Don't rush into anything and we'll go to Seattle and get you a real dress if you want to marry this man."

"I am marrying him. Tomorrow, Mother. Be here or don't. It's your choice."

Before there were more recriminations, she heard footsteps on the porch and then voices as someone unlocked the back door. "I have to go, Mother. Leave a message and let me know if you're coming."

"Of course, we are. You're my daughter and Gil and I love you. I'll tell your brothers."

Tears stung for a moment. She hastily managed to swallow the lump in her throat. "I love you too."

She ended the call and blinked hard, forcing a smile as Bronwyn led the parade of family members inside. The older woman beamed at her. "Oh good, I'm glad you're feeling better. How are you at peeling potatoes?"

Sully laughed weakly. "I grew up on a farm in Liberty Valley. I learned ages ago."

"Wonderful. Tate can wash them for you. We need a lot to feed this crew." Bronwyn glanced over her shoulder at the youngsters piling in the door behind her. "Chantrea, take the other kids with you to the greenhouse for veggies. Move it, move it, all of you."

"We aren't dressed to get muddy," a blonde teen queen complained.

"Then, it's a good thing Lock refreshed the gravel walkways this past week." Bronwyn waved her hand. "Go, kids, go."

"She's the one who should be a teacher," Sully murmured to Tate when he came to stand beside her. "She has the voice and the power."

"She's a mom." He tugged gently on her waist-length braid and leaned down to brush her lips with his. "How many spuds do you want?"

"Pounds and pounds and a paring knife."

"Two paring knives," Joe said, sitting across from her. "And a newspaper for the peels."

"What do we do with those?" Sully asked.

"Save them for my pigs," Lock said. "I'll set the table in the dining room. Come help me, Quinn, and I'll let you tell me all about the wedding present you're making for these two crazy youngsters."

"We don't need a present," Sully said.

"Speak for yourself, woman. I know better than to argue with my sister." Tate gestured to Lyle. "Come on. I'll let you help me tote the potatoes."

That evening Sully cuddled up next to Tate on the couch while all of them supposedly enjoyed a Christmas movie that Bronwyn had chosen. Sully hid a smirk when Lock and his dad both grimaced at the cheesy dialogue between the romancing couple. On the next commercial, she whispered, "I bet a murder mystery would go over better."

"Or a baseball game, but Mom doesn't much care for sports even when the Mariners are playing." Tate's voice was low, and Sully was the only one who heard him. "As for football, forget it."

Sully giggled as the show started again and Bronwyn glowered at them over her knitting needles. "We're being quiet, but I have to tell you the book was better."

A few minutes later, there was another long commercial break and it was Chantrea's turn to comment. "There's a book? Who's it by? What's it about? Why do you prefer it?"

"I'm a sucker for stories narrated by animals and much of the book was told by the cat."

Wearing his dress blue Army uniform, Tate waited outside the Baker City church. He, Lock, and Finlay were in charge of meeting, greeting, and sending people to find seats inside. His mother had made it clear she expected guests on both sides of the main aisle, not separated by family ties. When Sully's mother arrived, she was to be escorted to the room where her daughter waited for the ceremony to start.

Three cars pulled into the parking lot. He recognized Jeannie Sanders, Sully's favorite nurse coming toward him in her dress uniform. She waved when she saw him. Tate lifted his hand in greeting. "Glad you could make it."

"I wouldn't miss it, although it took until this morning to get permission to leave the base. Thanks for asking me." Jeannie nodded to Lock. "Jeannie Sanders. Where's Sully?"

"In the room with the other girls 'cept my big sister. She had to go to school 'cause she's a cheerleader." Finlay beamed at her. "We get to have cake later."

"Best part of a wedding. Do I have time to check in with the bride?"

"Finn will take you there and then show you where we're sitting." Lock held out his hand. "Lock Murphy, brother of the groom."

Tate waited until the two were out of earshot. "Are you hitting on my fiancée's friend?"

"Of course. Women always get romantic at weddings. Do me a favor and don't tell her I'm a pig farmer. Very few girls find that sexy."

Tate chuckled. "You got it."

A few moments later, he glimpsed a brawny, brown-haired giant striding toward him, accompanied by an older silver-haired version of himself and a petite strawberry blonde woman in a sage-green outfit. Her hair color undoubtedly had help now, but Tate bet nobody dared to say as much. The two men had dressed up for the wedding in dark suits and Tate stepped forward to greet Kord Barlow who introduced him to his father, Gil, and Sully's mother, Helene.

She scanned him with narrowed hazel eyes. "So, you're the one who talked my daughter into this nonsensical wedding?"

"That would be me," Tate agreed. "I'm a lucky man."

A long silence as she looked him up and down, still glaring. She and Sully resembled each other in size and hair color but the fierce expression made them strikingly similar. "Wow, I'm impressed. She got her beauty from her mother."

She scowled at him. "That charm may work on my daughter. It

won't on me. Where is she? I'm going to talk some sense into her. She's not getting married to you or anybody else today."

"Lock will show you where she's getting ready. I have to stay here and follow my mom's orders."

"Thanks a lot," Lock mouthed silently, then pasted on a polite smile and escorted Helene Barlow into the building.

Kord grinned appreciatively. "It's not going to do her any good. Sully's as stubborn as her mom."

His father stuck out a hand to shake Tate's, eyeing Kord at the same time. "I notice you didn't say that where she could hear."

"I'm not stupid and I have to ride home with you two."

"There will be more room when we unload Sully's things into Tate's rig." Gil rubbed his jaw ruefully. "When Helene's not a happy camper, we all take the route of least resistance. You're lucky. Sully may look like her mom, but that's as far as it goes. She's a sweetie."

"And she doesn't bear grudges most of the time," Kord added. "If my brothers and I couldn't drive her around the bend, nobody else will. Of course, if she's not happy, we'll kick your butt from here to Texas. The guys couldn't get the time off work, but I promised to pass the word."

"Good to know," Tate said, smiling at the other man.

As soon as Sully saw the floral lace appliqued ankle boots with the metallic thread and sequins, fancy stitching, and decorative ankle straps at the feed store, she'd known they'd be perfect for the wedding. She eased into the left one, then carefully zipped it around her slightly swollen leg. She added the right boot, hoping the smile she gave the photographer looked genuine.

Jeannie Sanders rolled her eyes. "Tell me again why you're doing this, Sully Barlow. It's insane."

"I couldn't agree more." Helene Barlow closed the door behind her and stalked across the dressing room. "I'm glad one of your friends knows this is a crazy stunt, Sullivan."

"I'm talking about her going down the aisle without her cast and cane," Jeannie said. "What are you bitching about?"

"Me, ever marrying at all. I'm supposed to spend my life alone as some sort of penance for being born."

Sully stood, shaking out the skirt of the fun, flirty ruffled halter dress. It was lightweight blue cotton with a v-neckline, empire waist, and lovely ruffle high-low bottom hem that landed above the knee and draped backward. It was perfect for a wedding and she could wear it later for a date night or to one of the local holiday fairs with her new husband if he were home in time for Christmas next year. "She thinks I should join a convent."

"You're not canceling the ceremony, are you?" Dominique MacGillicudy lowered her elaborate professional camera. "Virginia Thompson will have a major fit and so will I because I need her help to get the old MacGillicudy family homestead so I can flip it."

"Don't stress." Sully steadied herself by gripping the back of the chair. "Take lots of pictures so we have something to remember today. When you finish with me, find Cat O'Leary and her daughters."

"Okay. I need more photos of Bronwyn and Tate's sisters. I don't know if the rest of the Murphy hunks of burning love have arrived yet or not."

Sully smiled. "Is that what his brothers are actually called? I've only met Lock."

"The rest of them are older and just as gorgeous," Dominque said. "Tate used to lose it when I flirted with all of them. He thought because we were dating, I shouldn't kiss other men."

"Go figure," Jeannie said. "What is wrong with that man? Fidelity is so over-rated."

"Exactly." Two pictures later, Dominique lowered the camera. "Okay, I'm off to find other family members. I'll see you at the church."

Jeannie waited until the door closed behind the fashion-savvy blonde in the tight-fitting, bright red dress. "Do you kick me out if I say it looks like Anise Tyler has a twin?"

"Of course not." Sully laughed. "And I barely know Dominque so I can't tell you if she's a sleaze or not, but she was up-front about Tate being her high-school *squeeze* and she only dumped him when he joined up. Besides, all I've heard about Anise is she doesn't like having other women in *her* office and nothing about her being the proverbial camp follower."

"I'll tell you more when you get back to the base." Jeannie pushed the chair forward. "Sit down until they call you."

"And then we can talk about this foolhardy decision." Helene advanced on them. "I don't see the necessity."

"Really?" Jeannie shook her head. "Have you had your vision checked? If Tate Murphy sizzles in his fatigues, you should see him in dress blues, his beret and jump boots, Sully. He takes my breath away, total eye candy."

"He's mine. I called 'dibs' and you saw my engagement ring right after I got it." Sully poked her friend. "Be nice and do me a favor."

"What?"

"Go find Tate's sister, Naveah, and my bouquet. She'll be in the church finishing the flowers with the minister's wife. Then, my mother can pitch a fit in private."

"The things I do for love." Jeannie heaved a sigh. "If she talks you out of the wedding, fair warning. I'm nabbing Master Sergeant Hot Stuff."

"In your dreams." Still amused by her friend, Sully waited until she was alone with her mother. "We haven't seen each other since Raven's funeral. Why don't we start over? Will you hug me and tell me how you are? How is the family?"

Helene stalked across the room. "Then, will you listen to common sense instead of your hormones?"

"Possibly, but I'm not promising anything except to marry Tate Murphy in exactly thirty-nine minutes."

Of course, no one saw her and the other ghosts drift into the church in time for the wedding. Raven sighed, impressed when she saw the decorations fastened to the end of the pews, small bouquets of roses tied with white and blue ribbons, combined with tulle streamers. More flowers covered the altar. Simple but effective, she thought, especially when she considered how quickly the ceremony had been planned, all the way down to the trimmings.

She watched the minister's wife take her seat at the piano. The groom, accompanied by his twin sister, took their places. The reverend wore a dark suit for once at the lectern. Oh yes, Sully deserved this ceremony. Raven hastened to one of the forward pews, obviously reserved for family members where she saw her husband sitting alone, the spaces on his left for his stepmother and father, although neither had joined him yet.

She sat next to Kord, pleased he'd left an empty place beside him for her. She just wished he knew she was still with him, wished he knew how much she loved him, wished he could hear her whisper his name, feel her fingers brush his hair out of his face. Then, she heard his low bass rumble.

"Little bird, don't you think I know when you're near?"

CHAPTER FIFTEEN

The ceremony started without a hitch. Cat O'Leary's twins almost waltzed down the aisle, casting rose petals from their baskets. In what the owner of the feedstore called, 'barn dance gowns,' lovely ivory cotton and appliqued lace dresses, Naveah and Chantrea followed them. Sully clung to her stepfather's arm as he escorted her, not merely for support. She'd been surprised and touched when Bronwyn brought him to the waiting room, but her soon-to-be mother-in-law insisted Gil Barlow wanted to participate.

Sully didn't know how true that was, but still whispered 'thank you' when he passed her hand to Tate's. "I'm glad you came."

"Me too." Gil kissed her forehead. "Be happy, honey."

"I'll make sure of that," Tate promised, drawing her close.

Two and a half hours later, the reception in the community hall was well underway. She'd chosen her favorites from the buffet lunch and shared them with Tate, danced with her new husband, stepfather, and father-in-law. She'd posed for a stream of photos with her family, his relatives, and their wedding party. It was time to cut the elaborately decorated cake, but she didn't immediately see Tate.

She spotted Jeannie and crossed to her, trying not to limp or wince when her leg throbbed. "Do you know where Tate went?"

"He's in the parking lot with his brothers, his uncle, and your stepdad and bro." Jeannie narrowed her eyes, studying Sully. "Okay, you've had enough being the glamor girl. I'm getting your cast and cane."

"I don't need them yet."

"I'm the physician's assistant and I say you do. Let's find a chair and you stay there."

"Okay, but I need to hit the restroom first."

As the old saying went, he'd been up the hill, over the mountain, and seen the varmint, but he couldn't remember ever dealing with someone like Sully's mom who'd filled an SUV with her daughter's belongings and brought them to a wedding. Luckily, each carton was labeled and that gave Tate a rough idea of where to send it. Housewares, boxes of 'keeper' books, and personal items went into Uncle Arnie's rig to be delivered to the apartment near the base. School clothes, shoes, teaching materials, and more books went to his brothers' various vehicles. They'd take them to the Murphy homestead.

While Garvin carried the last box to his pickup, Kord locked up the SUV. "Sully has more belongings in the guestroom at our place and when she wants them, the two of you can fetch them. I'm not into drama."

"Why didn't she leave everything there?" Tate waited for his brothers and uncle to join them before they headed back to the reception. "Why take anything to your folks?"

"It was Raven's idea. She always played 'peacekeeper' between Sully and Helene. Raven figured if Sully brought everything to our house, the breech would be permanent. My wife did the 'go along to get along' game with Helene and agreed with whatever my stepmother wanted, said, and did."

"That must have been interesting."

"We had a few intense discussions until Raven finally informed me that Helene's whims didn't affect the outcomes. Raven would do whatever she thought best, but she wasn't going to squabble with my mom and since Helene raised me and my brothers for damn near thirty years, she was our mother so I could just get over myself."

Tate laughed. "I wish I'd met her." He paused, held up a hand. "I know the O'Leary said she was here, but it's different meeting someone in real life, not just hearing from the town medium."

Kord's jaw tightened. "Introduce me to her. I have things I want to say to Raven and I never got the chance."

"When we're inside."

Raven heaved a sigh as she followed what she considered the 'boy scout troop' back into the church hall. "I should have known Helene would stir up a ruckus."

"She always did like to make things exciting." A sandy-haired man in camo fatigues strolled up beside her. "The fireworks were fun for a while, but it got wearing when we weren't in bed."

"Ick. Way too much information." Raven held up an insubstantial hand. "I don't want to think about my mother-in-law having sex."

"Sorry to shock you, but it wasn't invented by you youngsters."

Raven did some mental calculations, then eyed the stranger again. "You're Sully's dad, aren't you?"

"Nope. That honor is all Gil Barlow's. I'm just the guy who slept with her mother and ran away when I heard there were consequences."

Raven blinked. "That's what Sully's mom always said."

"Hey, she was right about me. I'm not into monotony."

"Or monogamy," Raven shot back. "You undoubtedly did the slut-puppy routine throughout Baker City, didn't you?"

"And Liberty Valley and Seattle and most of Washington State when I was home. And alive. Yes, I slept around when I was stationed elsewhere, not that we ever did much sleeping. I wasn't into spending my nights alone when I had a choice. Rafferty O'Sullivan at your service."

"No thanks." Raven shuddered. "I don't know if ghosts can get STDs, but I'm not taking any chances. You're just creepy."

A woman dressed like an Army nurse, appearing as if she'd just stepped out of the old TV show *MASH* laughed. "She's got your number right, Rafferty. Still up to the same games, aren't you? Careful, I don't think the O'Leary cares for cheaters—even dead ones." She nodded to Raven. "I'm Bridget McElroy. Welcome to our corner of the world."

"I'm not staying," Raven said, glancing around the parking lot at the other ghosts. "I'm going home with my husband later."

"Be careful." This time it was the mayor who spoke. "The witch in Liberty Valley may not ask what you want. She may just send you to Summerland, her version of Heaven and it could take a while to return to yours."

"Thanks for the heads-up. I'll be careful."

They'd cut the fancy cake with swirls of white frosting, saving the top tier for their first anniversary. Bronwyn Murphy offered to take it home to her freezer until they'd found a place to live and Sully gratefully accepted. She glanced around the reception hall, noticing Kord standing near Cat McTavish while she chatted with her daughters who then left her and came over to Sully.

"We're taking flowers to our teacher at the school and Mommy said we should 'vite you to come too," Sophie announced.

"It's 'cause you're a teacher and all the O'Sullivans are teachers, 'cept Mr. Rafferty who's a no-count." Samantha tilted her head, apparently curious about the notion. "Don't all grownups know how to add and 'tract numbers? And mult-ply and divide?"

"They're supposed to." Sully collected her cane and a paper plate with a slice of cake, guessing whoever judged her father and found him wanting meant to say, 'no-account' but the eight-year-old had misunderstood. "Let's go. Why didn't your teacher come to the party?"

"She says she doesn't care for fuss, frills, and furbelows," Samantha explained. "It's okay if some folks don't like parties. Daddy tells us that life would be danged dull if everyone was the same."

Sully grinned appreciatively. "He's right."

The afternoon sun shone, making the clouds look like puffy white marshmallows against the pale blue spring sky. The puddles on the sidewalk had evaporated as they walked toward the vintage two-story building with the cupola on the shake roof. The twins bypassed the stone staircase and the main entrance, going to a side door.

It stood slightly ajar and Sully followed the girls inside to an empty office. An antique wood and gold hand-held teacher's bell sat on the old maple desk and she smiled at the sight. She glanced around, then put the plate beside the bell. "Where is your teacher?"

The twins shared a long look and Sophie said, "She's here, but it's okay if you don't see her. Most people don't, 'cept us and Mommy and Daddy."

"And it uses lots of energy for her to make other folks notice her, so she doesn't bother too much," Samantha finished. "She only comes out when it's needful or when Mommy says she wants Mrs. O'Sullivan's help like when our grandpa stole us."

"Really?" Sully heaved a sigh, glancing around the empty office. "I guess it's inappropriate for me to say I don't believe in ghosts."

"Especially in Baker City where we have so many of them," a deep voice said behind her. "Hello, girls. Who is your friend?"

"Hi, Mr. Smitty. This is Sully. She married Mr. Tate today and Mommy said we had to bring her to the school, 'cause she's one of your kith and kin, an O'Sullivan," Samantha said. "What's a kith and kin?"

"*Kith* means *known* so those are your friends and *kin* are all your relatives." A tall, solid-looking, mixed-race man in a dark suit, his close-cropped, once black hair now totally gray, Smitty O'Sullivan eyed her and Sully returned the favor.

"According to what the O'Leary says, you're one of ours. Mine and Mrs. Doireann O'Sullivan, the first of us schoolteachers who emigrated from Ireland to teach in Baker City."

Another long glance before he asked, "And who are your kin?"

"Other than you?" Sully leaned more heavily on her cane. "My mother's maiden name was Helene Walsh and my father was Rafferty Gallagher O'Sullivan."

"That makes us distant cousins. He always intended to join the Army and leave Baker City well behind. I don't know if he came back after he died in the first Gulf War." Smitty gestured to the hallway behind him. "Sorry I missed the wedding, but if all of the O'Sullivans came, we'd overflow the church. Now, that you've married Tate Murphy, you'll get to know the whole kit and kaboodle of us. Do you have time to tour the downstairs or do you have to get back to the reception?"

"I have a few minutes." Sully glanced at the twins. "Are you two okay if we stay a little longer?"

"Yes, we like visiting with Mrs. O'Sullivan," Sophie said. "We want to come to school here too."

"Well, before you can do that, the rest of the school board and I have to find teachers for you." Smitty smiled at the girls, then at Sully. "Let's go talk about school. We're planning to start classes in the fall unless we pull it together in time for next quarter."

"I wouldn't be able to be here then since I need to finish my last session of student teaching for my English and History endorsements at Lake Maynard Middle High. I've already completed the requirements for my secondary Science certification. Next week is the last session for my English and History endorsements, and I'll have my master's degree when I graduate in August. After that, I'd be interested, but I can't promise to stay for more than a year. It all depends on where Tate's stationed when his tour ends in Afghanistan."

"Once you know where you're going, you can let us know." Smitty led the way toward the classrooms, gesturing to his left. "That's the main entrance." He pointed to the old-fashioned wooden staircase on their right. "That takes you up to the rooms for the older students. The upstairs is a mirror image of the downstairs, so we don't have to climb up there until you're a hundred percent."

"Makes sense to me."

Two large rooms opened, one on each side of the hallway. There weren't any lockers, just old-style cloakrooms at the far end of the classrooms. She paused in the doorway of the right-hand room. Instead of individual desks, there were several tables lined up in neat rows, each with three chairs, enough space for thirty students.

"The restrooms are in the addition near the principal's and secretary's offices. There's a kitchen where the cook makes hot lunches, but the kids eat in the classrooms. They go outside and run around town and the cemetery for P.E. Once we refurbish them, we'll have the soccer field and baseball diamond."

"I was on the softball team in high school."

"Wonderful. That means you can coach the girls here."

"I'd like that." Sully didn't mention her pregnancy. She'd have the baby sometime in September. When she saw the OB/GYN, they'd figure out her due date and it'd be soon enough to decide what she'd do in the fall. Perhaps, she could return part-time to school in October while she waited for Tate.

She glanced at her watch. "I'm the bride and I'd better head back to the church if the girls are finished with their conversation."

"I'll join you."

"You've only been married a few hours, so what did you do with your new wife?"

Tate forked up another bite of the vanilla cake and eyed his amused aunt. "The O'Leary's twins took her off to see the Baker City schoolhouse. Is it okay if we move into the apartment Wednesday night after work?"

Heidi shrugged. "I'm good with it. Do you want me to lock up the dogs?"

"Not necessary for me. If they're out and about, they'll entertain Sully while I'm carrying up everything. With that bunged up leg, she has limitations even if she doesn't admit it."

"You're a very smart man."

"Smart enough to ask who you arranged to have doggie-sit so you and Uncle Arnie could come today and not have to rush home. One of my cousins?"

"They're good with the dogs, but not terrific. No worries. My favorite sitter was back in town."

"Another favorite?" Tate watched a faint blush enter his aunt's cheeks. "You always claimed Mariah was the best and the only person you trusted with your puppies."

"Shut up, Tate. Your mouth is open again."

"It has to be if I'm having cake."

"Yes, and if you're not careful, I'll be the one breaking my word to my sitter. I don't want to go there, not when she and her sister just came home."

Tate frowned thoughtfully, looking across the room as the door opened and Sully entered, followed by the O'Leary twins and an older man that he recognized as the vice-principal of his high school back in the day. "Are you telling Mom that Mariah's home?"

"Not here. I'll bring it up later when we're alone. Now, it's time for you and Sully to leave for your honeymoon, isn't it?"

Tate finished his cake, then checked his watch. "You're right. We'll bring dinner when we come on Wednesday."

"Okay and I'll make dessert."

Tate put his saucer on the table, kissed his aunt's cheek, and went to meet Sully. "What have you been doing?"

She smiled up at him and introduced the man with her. "This is Smitty O'Sullivan, the head of the new school board. We toured the Baker City school and he offered me a teaching job in the fall."

"I like that." Tate slipped his arm around her waist. "You'll be close to my family when I'm gone."

"Will they tell you everything I do?"

"Probably not." He dropped a kiss on top of the brilliant red hair. "I hardly ever hear any gossip from Quinn unless I totally pin her down for details and Mom only tells me positive stories about the girls, my brothers, and Dad. Of course, she called when he had that heart attack because she knew I'd want to come home for him."

Tate felt Sully heave a sigh and relax. "Good to know. I don't want you to worry about me when you're in the middle of a combat zone."

"That's my girl." He winked at Smitty. "Best thing about marrying another soldier is she can take care of herself when I'm not there to watch her six."

"You don't have to worry too much," Smitty replied. "She's an O'Sullivan and we look after our own."

CHAPTER SIXTEEN

She opened her eyes, slowly becoming aware that she was lying on the queen-size bed in the honeymoon cabin. What happened? She recalled leaving the church with Tate, hurrying through a crowd of well-wishers. They'd gotten into the pickup and driven out of Baker City. Then, what? At some point on the way to Cedar Creek Guest Ranch, it was 'lights out' for her.

Kid, I'm a grownup. I haven't fallen asleep in a moving vehicle in years. Pushing the afghan covering her aside, she sat up, swung her feet to the floor, and grabbed the cane. Bathroom first. Then she changed into more comfy clothes, sweatpants, and a white tank-top. When she hung her wedding dress in the closet, she saw Tate's uniform beside two sets of camouflage fatigues, his and hers.

A few minutes later, she found him sitting in one of the large Adirondack chairs on the front porch watching the moon rise in the night sky. The sight of him looking all barefoot 'sexy farmer' in blue jeans, a flannel shirt amused her. "Sorry, I zonked out on you. I guess the events today wore me out more than I thought."

He grasped her hand and drew her down on his lap. "We have all the time in the world, Mrs. Murphy and my mom said she napped a lot when she expected one of us."

She sighed, breathing in the scent of lime aftershave. "I know we planned it very quickly, but the wedding went off really well. I'm so glad my mother didn't pitch a fit or embarrass me in front of your folks. I was terrified she'd rip into me when she had a new audience."

He stayed too quiet for too long.

"She tried something, didn't she?" Sully felt him tense against her for a moment before he relaxed again. "What happened? What did you do?"

He described his response to the arrival of her belongings and told her where to find them. "I just ran a little interference."

"You had my six." She kissed the strong line of his jaw. "Thanks for letting today be special and not allowing my mother to do her drama diva routine."

"You'd have covered me. We're a team."

"Got that right." Sully turned her face into his neck. "I'm not telling her about the baby for a while."

"No need to share the news yet."

They had a homestyle dinner of chicken fried steak, mashed potatoes with gravy, and green beans provided by Pop's Café, and then snuggled together on the bed to watch TV. No cable meant no local channels, but there were plenty of DVDs and they enjoyed a classic mystery movie. She fell asleep while Audrey Hepburn verbally sparred with Cary Grant as the two of them attempted to discover who murdered her husband. Sully woke in time to see the film credits roll. "I keep missing things and it's all your fault."

"How do you figure that?"

"Because I'm either sleeping or going to the bathroom or throwing up if it's morning." She paused, "except when I do it at night."

Tate chuckled. "Think positive. It'll give you something to harass our kid about when she or he is a teenager. Rob Hendrickson told me he'd stocked the fridge and freezer. Ready for ice cream?"

"Definitely." She snagged her cane and headed for the bathroom. "No chocolate sauce, but I'll take a different topping if there is one."

When she returned, she found a bowl of vanilla ice cream topped with caramel and whipped cream waiting for her. She dug into the sundae while he set up another movie, this time one of her favorite romantic comedies. "How did you know how much I love this?"

"I was guessing. You're a girl and whenever Quinn visits, we have to watch Inigo Montoya get his revenge."

Sully laughed and cuddled up next to him. "That's one of my favorite lines, but I really like the rest of the dialogue too."

"Good, then maybe you'll stay awake for the whole thing."

"No promises." She leaned close to brush her lips over his before scooping some of the whipped cream off his sundae. "But I'll try."

He dropped a kiss on her forehead. "No worries if you don't make it."

"I'll keep it in mind."

This time she remained awake for the entire movie. It undoubtedly helped that he kissed her whenever she cringed, distracting her from the villain's hijinks. As always, she enjoyed the scene where he got his final comeuppance. At the end of the film, she slowly laced her arms around his neck. "Where do we go from here?"

"I have a few ideas after all this time, Mrs. Murphy." He lowered his head. "I haven't kissed you enough tonight."

She melted against him and their lips met with a soft, teasing pressure. She sighed when he kissed the side of her neck. Did he feel her nipples stabbing into life against her bra and tank top? Or hear her ragged breathing? She unfastened the top two buttons of his shirt, sliding her fingers against the skin of his shoulders. "It took you long enough, Murphy. I've been trying to get you back in bed for weeks."

"We'll see what happens tonight." He nipped her ear, then trailed a line of kisses to the rise of her breast. "There's no rush."

"Want to bet." She pulled him nearer and found his mouth with hers. Her tongue teased his into a passionate duel.

Between kisses, they slowly began to undress each other, their shirts, and her bra ending on the floor. She gasped when he sucked gently on her nipples, wondering when they'd become so sensitive. It must be due to the pregnancy, she thought, but he was oh so careful when he cupped her other breast, rubbing the nipple with his thumb. She arched toward him, quivering under his touch. It reminded her of their first night together when he set her nerves afire.

He lifted his head, caught her mouth with his for a moment. "Time to lose those sweatpants, darling."

"When you take off your jeans."

"I can do that."

More kissing, more caresses as she learned what pleased him again, exploring his chest and muscled arms. She moaned when he stroked the curls between her legs. She trembled at his touch, anticipating what came next. She clutched at his shoulders when one finger slid inside, then out of her, joined by a second while his thumb rocked against the small bud of flesh. Her hips rose and fell, joining in the dance he'd started. She clung to him, kissing his neck, nipping at his ear. "Don't stop."

"I won't." The movement continued while he sucked on her nipples again.

She cried out as the climax claimed her and heard his low chuckle before he lifted his head. "Now, we'll see what else you like."

"Are you serious?"

"You'll find out." He began to explore her body with slow, gentle touches and followed his fingers with his mouth, searching out each curve until he finally reached what obviously was the goal. He parted her legs and his lips claimed her. He stroked upward with his tongue, exploring the folds of skin with soft strokes before diving deep. He kept lapping, licking, and finally drew the small bud into his mouth and sucked. She convulsed again, calling his name.

Afterward, she stared into his face while he held her. He dropped a kiss on her forehead, his calloused hands smoothing her hair. "That was amazing for me, but what about you?"

"I'm looking forward to no condom tonight. I've never had sex without one."

She laughed, brushed his lips with hers. "You're a very responsible man."

"I try." He feathered his thumb over her lips. "Tell me if anything I do hurts you or the baby."

"I will, but so far you haven't."

"That might change." He shifted to lie flat on the bed and drew her on top of him. "Let's do it this way."

"Only if I get to choose how we do it next time." She adjusted her position, slowly sliding down until he was buried deep inside her. She leaned forward and met his lips with hers. She rose, fell against him. "I didn't expect this."

"I live to surprise you." He moved under her, guiding her through a series of long, leisurely strokes. He kissed her as he began a new pattern of his thrusts, but they were still steady, still careful. He was in control. She wasn't. Some movements were deep, others shallow, and then his pace increased.

So, did hers, sliding up and down, moving faster and faster. She met him, motion for motion. They ascended, higher and higher. Each thrust took them further and further. Despite what he'd said earlier, he was in charge and she could only go with him. He smiled, drawing her closer and his lips claimed hers. His tongue plunged into her mouth as he drove her beyond the universe. Their hips met, clashed and they achieved fulfillment in an explosive moment.

"Wow, not what I expected." She stared down into his rugged features, the dark blue eyes before she lowered her lips to meet his, remembering the middle name she'd learned when they exchanged vows at the church. "You're special, Tate Joseph Murphy."

"So are you."

They cuddled together. She felt complete, safe in his arms, and sleep claimed her. When she woke, they made love again. Oh, she could grow accustomed to this, to being with him. She just hoped he wanted her as much as she wanted him for the rest of their lives. She wasn't sure if she loved him or not, but she didn't intend to lose him.

The next morning Tate left her to sleep. He took his first cup of coffee out to the porch to watch the sunrise. Unfortunately, he couldn't see it through the clouds and the intermittent late February drizzle. He was a married man. He shook his head, bemused by the notion. He'd always told the other Rangers on his team that if the Army wanted him to have a wife, he'd be issued one.

However, he hadn't expected to meet Sullivan Rafferty Barlow, much less have one night with her lead to them having a baby. What kind of father would he make? As good as his own dad or his uncle? No way to know, but at least he could ask them what to do when he got stuck in a quandary.

While he drank a second cup of strong black coffee, he saw Rob

Hendrickson drive up and park in front of the larger cabin a short distance away. Carrying the mug, Tate went to check out what the other man was doing. "Morning."

Nodding a greeting, Rob opened the tailgate and gestured toward the largest cabin. "The hot water tank died yesterday and flooded the place. I helped Margo Endicott clean up the mess and promised to switch it out today. Want to give me a hand?"

"Sure. I've never enjoyed sitting around and Sully's still asleep."

When he returned to their smaller A-frame cabin two hours later, he found Sully in the small kitchen. Still wearing her purple fleece robe, she sipped a cup of peppermint tea, a piece of toast on a saucer beside her. Grimacing, she scrolled through emails on her phone. He put his mug in the sink and crossed to her. He leaned down to kiss her.

"What's going on?"

"I answered the emails from Dr. Dunaway, my university supervisor, and told her that I want to see the classroom and the kids before I start teaching at Lake Maynard Middle High next week. She says I've been reassigned to Maureen Evans as a student teacher and the woman is too busy to have guests this week. I'm to show up and start teaching next Monday, but in the meantime, I need to swing by the district office and get an I.D. badge."

"We can do that this afternoon while you're in civvies," Tate said, "unless you want to wear your fatigues."

She smiled. "No, that's okay. What the hell? If I could do more than a year-long tour in the *sandbox*, I can do fourteen weeks at Lake Maynard Middle High."

"That's my girl." He kissed her again. "Want to go for breakfast at Pop's Café in Baker City?"

"Isn't it closer to lunchtime?"

"It is, but my wife once told me she could eat breakfast all day and half the night. I know Pop serves omelets and pancakes until mid-afternoon."

"Okay." She put her phone on the table. "I'll hit the shower and get dressed."

"I'd offer to scrub your back, but then we'd never leave the cabin."

"Promises, promises." Laughing, she reached for her cane and hobbled from the room.

A short time later, Tate parked his truck in front of a large cedar shake building in Baker City and they walked toward the café. He held the door for her, nodding to the assorted customers. A wiry, balding man behind the counter waved at them, then gestured to an empty booth. "Have a seat, kids and I'll bring you coffee and menus."

"I prefer decaf tea," Sully said, limping toward the red bench-style seat. "Do you have any raspberry or orange pekoe?"

"Both. I'll have my daughter bring over the sampler and you can choose what you like."

In a few minutes, Linda MacGillicudy, a plump brown-haired woman hurried toward them carrying a tray with white ceramic mugs, a steaming teapot, and a cardboard caddy with various types of teabags. She smiled at them. "People are still talking about the wedding yesterday. They really enjoyed the buffet and Dad's talking about including more catering options. It'll boost our business."

"It was wonderful, and the food was amazing." Sully chose orange spice and listened politely as the older woman continued to rave about the ceremony the previous afternoon.

A bell jangled as the front door opened and a tall, muscular blond man in his late thirties entered, followed by Dominique MacGillicudy who was her usual blonde fashion diva self. She didn't seem to have a problem, unlike the man who appeared to be avoiding her. "All I'm saying, Durango, is that I can do wonders for that old house, even if you won't sell the place."

"It's not mine." Durango sounded weary as if he'd argued the point a hundred times before. "Heather inherited the McElroy farm and all I did was pay the back taxes. If she wants you to remodel the house, the two of you can work out the details. Until I hear from her, it stays as is."

"Well, if you give me her phone number I'll call and make the arrangements."

"If I had it, I wouldn't." Durango hitched up on a stool and gestured to Pop. "Coffee, please."

"You got it." The spry oldster took a mug that read 'Hawke Construction' from a display on the wall, put it on the counter between them, and filled the cup. "Dominique, I've told you not to harass my customers for the last six months. If you're here to eat, find a place to sit and I'll get you a menu."

"I only came to talk to Durango about fixing up his house."

"Heather's house."

"Then, there's nothing more to say." Pop pointed to the door. "Go or stay, but you know the rules."

A long dramatic sigh as Dominique scanned the room. Her attention landed on Sully and she advanced across the room on red-soled spike heels, a black V-neck, long-sleeved, tuxedo jumpsuit clinging to every curve. She looked totally 'big city' in her attire and Sully felt even more 'small town' in her black slacks and paisley print tunic top but they were professional enough and more than suitable to visit the school district office.

"Is now a good time for me to show you the pictures I took of the wedding?"

"Certainly." Sully scooted over a little so the other woman could sit beside her in the booth. "But only if you've brought your camera and agree to Pop's rules. I'm new to this town and I don't want to make waves."

"All of the food here is so fattening," Dominique complained. "I never eat at Pop's Café."

Sully pointed to the page listing different types of salads. "Stop your sniveling. Nobody wants to listen to it."

Tate grinned appreciatively. "And you think my momma sounds like a teacher. So, do you, Mrs. Murphy."

CHAPTER SEVENTEEN

The rest of the afternoon flew by. After their meal, they drove to Lake Maynard so Sully could fill out paperwork at the school district office and obtain an identification badge with her photo and her new name of Sullivan Murphy. Then, they drove back to Baker City and the Murphy farm. She began to unpack the boxes of clothes in the guest room while Tate and Lock brought down two bookcases, a file cabinet, and a small desk from the attic. Once the girls arrived home from school, they ferried blouses, slacks, and jackets to the laundry room where Bronwyn started the washer.

Sully sorted through the carton containing her dresses. She glanced across the room at Tate who arranged paperbacks on the bookcase. "I really appreciate the help. I thought it'd take days to organize everything."

"That's why we have a family," Tate said. "Everybody pitches in on big projects. I told Lock you'd need somewhere to keep your *Barbie* car and he's going to clear out one of the bays in the garage."

"It isn't a *Barbie* car. We only painted it bright pink to keep the guys from driving it."

"What guys?" Lock lingered in the doorway. "I thought you settled for my big brother."

"My brothers and Raven's. Between the two of us, we have ten of them. After we got our hands on the Mustang, we weren't letting them near it."

"What kind of Mustang?" Lock drifted closer. "A new one?"

"Don't be silly." She shook out a blue floral and lace dress. "It's a '68 Mustang GT Fastback with Shelby rims."

"Pink ones to match the hot pink, *Barbie* car."

Sully heaved a dramatic sigh. "I told you already, Tate Joseph Murphy. We painted it *Passionate Pink*, not *Hot Pink* which is a totally different color. Of course, we ordered pink wheel covers from the dealership and paid to have them custom made. The goal was to keep our baby safe from the Barlow and Driscoll boys. It worked. They're too macho to drive a pink car."

"But if you ever want to sell it, you need to repaint it to an original Ford color," Lock said. "You'd get more buyers and more money for it."

"Never selling it so that doesn't matter." Sully carried three dresses to the door and passed them to Chantrea standing in the hallway. "Lock, I'll also need a storage locker for all the supplies I use to maintain the car."

"Okay." He gave her a long look from the narrowed dark blue eyes so much like his older brother's. "I tune-up Mom's and Dad's cars plus the vehicles we use here on the farm. Not a hassle to add in yours."

"You can dream, Lock Murphy. It's not happening. Nobody touches the Mustang, except me and Raven."

"When do we meet Raven?" Lock asked.

"You don't unless you're the O'Leary." Tate shifted hardcover novels on the second shelf. "She didn't make it back alive from Afghanistan."

"I'm sorry." Lock turned toward the door. "I'm headed for the garage to sort out room for your rig, Sully. I'll find a place for your tools and supplies too."

"Thanks. If nobody's ever told you before, you're wonderful and I'm really grateful."

A quick smile and he was gone. Sully walked across the room to kiss Tate. "Do you have the slightest clue how lucky you are? All of them are so great."

"You don't know all of them yet." He drew her close. "You barely met a handful of them at the wedding. Wait until there's a real holiday, a party, a picnic, or an emergency. Sometimes, they're a major pain in the—"

"They show up," Sully repeated, outlining his mouth with an index finger. "I was always an outcast to most of the Barlows. They told Gil he shouldn't give me as many presents as he did his sons or come to my school events or 4-H activities. They left me out when they invited the boys to visit."

"And your mother went along with that?"

"She was his second wife and they never let her forget she was pregnant with another man's child when Gil married her. She did the 'go along to get along' routine with them and because she was my harshest critic, they accepted her when they threw me to the proverbial wolves."

"It's not the Murphy way."

"Obviously not." She laced her arms around his neck. "I'm so glad to be a Murphy now. When we get back to the base tomorrow, I want to order new nametags for my uniforms."

"I'm good with it, but I think I have a few Murphy name-tapes in my dresser if you want to sew one on your shirt and a second on your hat tonight."

She grimaced. "I can't. My sewing machine is at Raven's house."

"Ask my mom if you can use hers. If she agrees, I'll run back to the cabin at Cedar Creek and get your uniform before dinner."

"You're the best." After a prolonged kiss, she headed for the door. "Be right back."

She found Bronwyn Murphy alternating between fixing supper and doing laundry. When Sully asked about using the sewing machine to change the names on her Army uniform, it took almost twenty minutes to convince the older woman not to do the task for her. Bronwyn finally agreed to persevere with the laundry and only help with the new nametags if needed. After that, Sully sent Tate off to bring back her camouflage fatigues and proceeded to set the table for dinner. Then, she helped Naveah chop vegetables for a salad.

"Dominique MacGillicudy is going to bring by the photographs from the wedding." Sully added green onions to the large wooden bowl. "She said she has her broker's license and she'll find a house for me and Tate."

"Tell her you're not interested in a heartache." Bronwyn removed a bowl from the refrigerator and carried it to the sink. "She's always flipping foreclosures. You don't want a house someone lost because he couldn't pay the mortgage or taxes."

"No, I don't."

"Especially in Baker City." Naveah began to slice mushrooms. "Around here, there are plenty of ghosts so tell her you want the O'Leary to do a walk-through and make sure the place is clear of haunts."

"Good idea." Bronwyn removed the chicken breasts from the brine and started rinsing them. "Nobody wants uninvited guests, especially the spectral ones who throw things around at night."

"Dominique didn't say she has trouble like that."

"She's not exactly sensitive." Bronwyn arranged pieces of meat in a baking dish. "If she was, she wouldn't be trying to convince the rest of the MacGillicudys to let her flip their ancestral home."

"Do you think they'll go for it?" Sully cleaned a green pepper before cutting it into strips. "That was one of the houses she wanted to show us."

"Don't hold your breath. Pop MacGillicudy isn't shy about his opinions and he says the place is staying with their family."

It was after ten when they arrived at the honeymoon cabin. Bronwyn had offered up the guest-room, but Tate insisted on returning to Cedar Creek Guest Ranch, claiming he didn't want to lose the money he'd paid for the room. Sully doubted his veracity and knew his parents did too. She waited for him to open the truck door and slid out into his warm embrace. "I'm sure your folks know what we're doing tonight."

"Undoubtedly, but I'm not confirming or denying anything."

She laughed, then gasped when he swung her up in his arms, closed the truck door behind them, and carried her toward the cabin. "I can walk."

"I know, but I want us to get there before midnight."

She laughed again, nipped his ear. "I think you've been watching too many classic romantic movies where the hero sweeps the woman off her feet and carries her away to his lair."

"Whatever works."

Still charmed, she asked, "Are you planning to have your wicked way with me?"

"Yes, and I'll make sure you enjoy it."

———

They hit the road early the next morning since they had a four-hour drive back to Fort Clark, the Army base south of Seattle. While he drank coffee and drove through the rush-hour traffic, Sully slept in the passenger seat. Entertained by the sight, Tate shook his head. Then, he continued driving, keeping a watchful gaze on the other vehicles on the highway. Before they left for the long weekend, he'd discussed coming in late on Wednesday with Major Harper and the officer agreed they could start work after lunch.

Sully woke as he pulled up to the main gate behind a row of cars and trucks. "Wow, that was a quick trip."

"For some of us." Tate chuckled. "I figure we'll move out of the barracks tonight and go to the apartment at Aunt Heidi's and Uncle Arnie's. Does that work for you?"

Sully nodded, pulling down the visor to check her hair. "Yes. I only have a few clothes, books, and my laptop. Do you want to contact Sergeant Hathaway at the BEQ, or shall I?"

"R.H.I.P., sweetness. I'll do it since we want to check out after hours."

She grinned, tucked another pin into her red hair before putting on her hat and adjusting it to the proper position. "First time I've heard another sergeant admit *Rank Has Its Privileges*, but I'll let you handle it. Do you want to eat on base, or should we find something off post? Neither of us will want to cook if we're moving into a new place when we have to work tomorrow."

"Let's order take-out from your favorite restaurant. We can use a home-cooked meal even if neither of us fixes it."

"Works for me."

Once through the entrance, he followed the main drag toward the office building a short distance away. He stopped as close to the front doors as possible, parked, and went around to open the passenger truck door. "Wait for me in the lobby and we'll go up together."

"Sounds good." She limped through the soft drizzle toward the entry.

———

It wasn't a surprise to see the giant stack of correspondence waiting for her and Anise Tyler nowhere in sight. The other woman must have gone to the breakroom for coffee or else stepped out for lunch. Sitting at her desk, Sully logged in, pulled up the word-processing program, and began typing the responses as quickly as possible. What on earth did Anise plan to do next week when she'd be alone in the office? Who was going to handle all the reports after Sully left? Would Mr. Edwards, the civilian supervisor find someone else to pick up the slack? She suppressed a smile, deciding she wouldn't ask the older man on her way out the door.

She heard boots on the tile floor and glanced up in time to see Tate entering the office, a cardboard cup in one hand and a bag from the dining facility in the other. "What's this?"

"Lunch. You slept most of the way back and missed breakfast." He eyed the files and paperwork on her desk. "You've got to be kidding me."

"No, but I have it handled. I'll do what I can today and tomorrow. Friday, I need to out-process so I won't be in the office at all."

The comment drew Anise's attention as she entered. "What does that mean?"

"You've been on base long enough to know that it takes a full day to transition from being a soldier to a civilian." Sully adopted her sweetest tone. "I'll be visiting the doctor, going through finance, checking out with supply."

"Changing your identification, having the Mustang inspected so you can come on post whenever you like as a military dependent to visit the PX or Commissary." Tate gestured to the sandwich. "Eat something, Sergeant Murphy."

Anise gasped and stared at them. "I thought—"

"We got married on Monday," Tate told her. "That's why Major Harper signed off on the long weekend pass. Sully has a civilian job starting next week. So, as my grandpa says, you'd 'better grab a root and growl', or you'll be up to your eyeballs in documentation."

While she prepared to move out of the barracks later that afternoon, the situation continued to amuse Sully. Anise had jumped in to help with the correspondence, obviously determined to show she wasn't a total slacker. She'd tried hard to be friendly, a little too hard, asking about the wedding and the civilian job. Sully had played along, careful not to give away any details that might come back and bite her in the butt. She didn't have 'stupid' tattooed on her forehead or anywhere else for that matter.

She'd just finished filling her rucksack when she heard a knock on the door. She limped over to it, expecting Tate. Instead, Corporal Ferguson beamed at her. She found herself smiling back at the young, dark-haired soldier. "Hi, what's going on?"

"Sergeant Murphy is clearing out of his room and Sergeant Hathaway is upstairs ready to do a walk-through. I offered to carry your things out to the Mustang."

"You sure have feelings for my car." Sully laughed, then gestured to the Army green duffel bag and large plastic case. "Those are ready to rock and roll if you are. Thanks for the help."

"And the keys?"

"Oh, you're right." She pulled the ring out of her pants pocket and handed it to him. "Thanks again, Ferguson."

"I'm glad to do it. Sergeant Murphy said you'd be back most weekends and if I played my cards right, you'd let me wash and wax the Mustang. I couldn't detail the inside when I *car sat* for the last few days because I didn't have the keys."

"Good point." She met his brown gaze. "I'll have to consider that. I notice you didn't call it a *Barbie* car."

"If I did, you'd never let me near it."

"Good thinking. You're smarter than my stepbrothers. *Passionate Pink* worked to keep them away from it."

"I knew you had a good reason to opt-out of the standard range of Ford paint colors."

"Yes, and since I don't plan to ever sell it, I'm not changing to one of those."

"Makes sense." Carrying the canvas duffel bag, Corporal Ferguson headed out the door.

Two hours later, she followed Tate's truck into the driveway at his aunt's and uncle's place. They weren't the only visitors. An older red Ford Excursion sat in the driveway close to the sprawling log cabin. Tate pulled up close to the garage and she parked behind him. Switching off the engine, she reached over to the passenger seat and collected her cane. First, she'd let Heidi and Arnie know they were here and then it'd be time to offload the stuff in the rigs.

Three rough-coated collies bounded to meet the car, barking and she waited to pet the greeters. Bo and Diddly chased after them rushing toward her, Bo carrying his favorite green tennis ball. The tri-colored youngster raced up to her, somehow managing the occasional woof. Laughing, she leaned down to pet him, earning a collie grin and the ball dropped by her boot. His sister, Diddly, a gold and white collie crouched down and yipped in excitement when Sully bent down to pick up the soggy tennis ball. She hurled it across the carpet of newly mown grass. Both pups tore off in pursuit, while the older dogs looked on in adult amusement.

She'd barely finished petting them when she saw the back door open and Heidi Hogan approach. As usual, the petite woman wore ironed jeans and a crisp western blouse. Her cap of black hair didn't show any gray or a hint of curl. Behind her, came two slender redheads both dressed in similar attire, mirror images and Sully recognized the Stevens twins.

She bypassed the dogs to limp toward them. "Hey, girls. When did you get here?"

"Last night, Sarge." Mariah nodded a greeting. "We're glad to see you."

"Which means you want something." Sully took the ball Bo offered and tossed it again. "How can I help?"

"First, we should say, hello and we're glad to see you," Sasha said, a smile lighting up the sky-blue eyes. "Since we're in civvies, we can hug you."

"Now, I know you definitely want something." Laughing, Sully hugged each of the twins and they returned the favor. "I'm glad you're back safe and sound. Now, what do you need?"

"You to explain to Command Sergeant-Major Jenkins that if we leave for Pullman now, our instructors will cut us slack for missing the first six weeks of the semester since we've been on active-duty," Mariah said. "We can study together and stay on the Dean's List, the honor roll. That helps us get scholarships too."

"And we'll be able to finish up our classes by the end of the summer and start our next set of clinical rotations at an equine vet practice in the fall," Sasha added.

"That makes total sense. Where's the problem?"

"He thinks we should decompress with the unit for another month here at Fort Clark, Sarge." Mariah took a deep breath. "He doesn't get it. We don't have time for that and since the First Sergeant isn't here to go to bat for us, we figured you'd understand."

"Yes, I do." Sully threw the ball again and then gestured to the nametag on her uniform. "You help me out with more Murphy tags, and I'll take care of you."

"O.M.G!" Mariah's bright blue eyes widened. "What did you do, Sarge?"

"Married your foster brother, Tate Murphy and it's a small world." From the corner of her eye, Sully glimpsed Heidi's approving nod. "That makes me your sister-in-law and according to their rules, Murphys look after one another."

CHAPTER EIGHTEEN

Tate lingered by his pickup to watch Sully interact with the other women. Of course, he knew his aunt, but it took a few minutes to recognize the slender woman with shoulder-length, strawberry-blonde hair as Mariah Stevens, his former foster sister. She wore fashionably torn jeans and a crimson Washington State University sweatshirt. Standing next to her, bumping her arm was a *doppelganger* that he didn't know, another skinny redheaded girl in the same sort of civvies, but apparently, Sully knew both of them.

He strode across the driveway and hugged his aunt, then stood next to his wife and nodded at Mariah. "It's been a while. How are you?"

"Fine." She looked him up and down before she flicked a sideways glance at her double. "Sasha, this is one of my foster brothers, Tate Murphy."

An assessing blue-eyed scan before her counterpart spoke. "Hey, nice to meet you. I've heard a lot about your family."

"I hope some of it was good," Tate said.

She shrugged. "Well, it wasn't all bad."

"Damned with faint praise." Sully gestured to the Mustang. "Are you two headed somewhere or can you help us carry things to the apartment over the garage?"

"We can help, Sarge," Mariah said. "We're staying with Aunt Heidi until you get us cleared to blow this popsicle stand."

"Where are you going?" Tate asked. "Mom and Dad will want to know how to touch base with you."

"I send them Christmas cards when I'm Stateside." Mariah turned and walked in the direction of the classic sports car. "Come help me, Sash. We want to get out of Dodge by tomorrow night or Friday morning so we can settle in over the weekend, Sarge. Our old roommate says she'll clean our rooms for us."

"Our grandfather paid the rent while we were gone so we didn't lose our place," Sasha added. "Decent rentals are always at a premium in college towns especially when you have children or pets."

"I'll see what I can do to make it happen." Sully scooped up the tennis ball and heaved it across the yard for the puppies. "Thanks for jumping in."

"Where are they going?" Tate asked again. "The family really has been missing Mariah."

"That's their issue, not yours," Heidi said. "Your mom has problems with what she does for a living, but the girl isn't selling herself on a street corner. She was horse-crazy from the time she arrived at your farm."

"What does that have to do with anything?" Tate demanded, narrowing his gaze on the older woman. "So, she loves horses. Who cares?"

"Your mother. She's always made it plain that it's either her family or horses and the two will never meet. No compromise."

It was Sully's turn to ask the question. "Why? Bronwyn didn't seem hidebound when I met her."

"One of our brother's boys, Tate's cousin was killed by a pony." Heidi heaved a sigh. "Granted it was a tragedy, but I always figured animals have reasons for being ornery and the child should have been supervised, not turned loose with a creature larger than he was."

Sully gasped and Tate wrapped an arm around her shoulders, drawing her close. He wanted to promise nothing would happen to their baby but decided to wait. "Well, that explains why you and Uncle Arnie could stay for the reception. When did Mariah and her sister arrive?"

"Sunday night. We looked after Mariah's dog while she was overseas."

"Another conundrum," Tate drawled. "Lock has problems with dogs that might chase his pigs or the sheep or the steers he raises for the organic beef market."

"And if he built dog-proof pens and fences, then he could chill out." Frowning, Heidi folded her arms, obviously annoyed at the family drama. "It means you can't take the pups to the Murphy farm, Sully."

"So, what's the answer?" Tate glanced at Sully, trying to read her emotions, but she didn't seem too concerned. "Suggestions?"

"I'll do some house-hunting after school when I'm doing my last practicum at Lake Maynard Middle High." Sully picked up the tennis ball at her feet and passed it to him, pointing to the bouncing half-grown collie pups eagerly anticipating another chase and capture of the toy. "Your turn, Tate. Throw the ball and I'll call Dominique MacGillicudy next week to start weeding through her listings. What kind of house do you want?"

The next afternoon, she was in the middle of the never-ending pile of correspondence when Command Sergeant-Major Jenkins strode into the office, an imposing sight in camouflage fatigues. Sully stood up to greet the most influential non-com in her reserve battalion but before she spoke, he waved her back to the chair behind the desk.

He drew up one saved for visitors and sat down across from her. "No need to stress that leg, Sergeant." He paused and looked at her nametag. "Wow, okay let's make it Sergeant Murphy. Major Harper asked if you could do your drill weekends here in March and April to help with the spring training reports. I don't have a problem with it. Do you?"

"No, I'd appreciate the opportunity to spend time with Tate before he ships out for training and then to Afghanistan." Sully smiled at the older, sandy-haired man. "Thanks for thinking of me."

"Looks like you didn't wait for the wedding either."

"We didn't have much time," Sully said, her tones even. "Tate goes to Kentucky in two weeks."

"Ouch. That's hard since you just got back. Aren't you lined up for student teaching in a few days?"

Sully nodded. "I start next Monday. I'll be in Lake Maynard on weekdays but come back here on weekends, or Tate will come up to Baker City if he can get a weekend pass."

"Another good reason to do your two days of drill in this office. I'll talk to Major Harper and tell him you'll be available to pull duty after your new husband leaves for Kentucky, not before."

Grateful for his intervention, Sully blinked hard and drew a deep breath. "Thank you, Sergeant-Major. It will make it easier on me and give me a place to be after he goes."

"It's tough being a soldier but my wife tells me her job isn't a walk in the park either. Anything else you need?"

"You to clear Mariah Stevens and Sasha Chevalier to return to Pullman."

"The twins who run Supply for your company? I never did understand why they have different last names when neither of them is married."

"After their parents divorced, Mariah was raised by her father until he died, and she went into foster care. Sasha was raised by her mother. They met in college."

"Sounds like that Disney movie my daughters love, but those twins met at summer camp."

"Yes, but this is real life. Mariah and Sasha want to finish up their courses and be on time for their clinical internships. They could only complete just so many online university classes while we were overseas."

"They're studying medicine, aren't they?"

"Veterinary medicine and they'd have their degrees if we hadn't been called up. They need to return to their real lives, so they don't lose their chances to intern at a premier equine clinic in September."

"Okay, I'll call and tell them to go, or you can but first they need to give you a clear status report for the new Active Guard-Reserve tech to take over Supply."

"That's Ann Barrett, isn't it?"

"We're hoping so, but we haven't received the final word yet. She's at a Finance School back East right now so she can handle payroll when she takes over your company in mid-March."

Sully nodded. "I'm qualified in that MOS, and I'd be happy to help her if she needs me."

"I'll keep it in mind when you come back to us in May."

Tate hadn't returned from the field when she was ready to leave that afternoon, so she texted him that she'd be picking up dinner at the local Chinese restaurant. She spotted the Ford Excursion still in the Hogan's driveway. After parking the Mustang in the garage, she collected the bags with their meal and headed upstairs to the apartment glad she'd bought enough food for all of them. She hadn't told Tate that she'd arranged for the twins to finish the unpacking. As the Army saying went, he didn't have *a need to know*. Raven always claimed, *turnabout was fair play* and if people wanted something from her, they should be willing to do something for her.

Sully opened the apartment door and called, "Hey there. I'm home and I brought dinner."

"Sounds great." Sasha came to greet her, Bo tagging at her heel, his black tail gently wagging. "Kitchen is unpacked, and dishes are done. I broke down the boxes and put them with the recycle-able cardboard. Mariah is finishing up the laundry. She's already put away your clothes. Shoes and boots are in the closet. Diddly's helping her."

"Wonderful." Sully headed for the kitchen. "I talked to the Command Sergeant-Major today. Let's set the table and I'll bring the two of you up to speed. Then, one of you can invite Heidi and Arnie to join us."

<hr />

After helping his uncle tune up the lawn tractor that night, Tate climbed the stairs to the apartment. He heard the rise and fall of voices in the living room when he entered. He paused in the doorway. Sully sat in the recliner. Bo curled up on one side of the chair while his doggie sister slept on the other. Mariah and her twin shared the couch, each with a glass of wine.

He eyed Sully and her ever-present cup of tea. "I brought home the makings for old-fashioned banana splits. Any takers?"

"Me." Sully glanced at the two younger women. "What about you?"

"We're in." Carrying her glass with her, Mariah stood. "I'll help scoop ice cream while Sasha snivels about being left behind that day."

"What day?" Tate asked.

"We run Supply, so we're called *fobbit's* by some who don't appreciate the support troops who aren't allowed to go off the base," Sasha said.

"Not by me or anyone in our company. We wouldn't have had what we needed in supplies or equipment if it weren't for you two gals." Sully rocked gently in the chair. "And I know Raven never allowed it."

"Top respected everyone," Sasha agreed. "She was great."

"Who else did you lose?" Tate removed four sundae dishes from the cupboard. "Besides Raven?"

"She was our first sergeant." Mariah put her glass on the counter and opened the freezer to collect three quarts of ice cream in vanilla, chocolate, and strawberry flavors. "Specialist Luis Ramirez. Corporal Javonte Jackson and an officer, a lieutenant from HQ. What was her name, Sash?"

"Trish Powell," Sully answered before Sasha did. "She was a decent kid, could have learned to be a good officer."

"What were you doing?" Tate eyed Sully. "I didn't know you were in a combat unit."

"Our company is part of a Personnel Support Battalion. That day, we were just going to inspect some reports, shuffle papers, and update records at a smaller unit's HQ after dropping off donated supplies at a girls' school. We primarily make sure that everything's in order if there are casualties, so soldiers' beneficiaries inherit without a hassle."

"The scuttlebutt around the *FOB* was the battalion C.O., the Colonel was warned there could be trouble," Mariah said softly, "but he sent out our people anyway."

"Stuff happens especially when you don't expect it." Tate peeled a banana, slicing it lengthwise and placing it in the glass dish before he slid it to her. "Need to listen up."

"He didn't. Our folks died. Sasha took it hard. She and Ramirez were tight, although he had something going with a half-dozen different women, not just the ones in our battalion. She said they were just friends."

Tate nodded, fitting a banana into the next dish. "And you? Are you dating now?"

Mariah shook her head, adding a scoop of vanilla ice cream to the boat-shaped bowl. "If I get serious about a guy, it interferes with my studying for classes and they're hard enough. I can't let anything distract me or my GPA could drop from a four-point and that screws with my scholarships."

"Makes sense." Tate glanced sideways at her. "So, when are you leaving?"

"Tomorrow, after we do our *sit-rep* for Sully. She says we can email it to her, and she'll add her comments, then forward it to Master Sergeant Waller, the lead civilian tech at the battalion, and the Command Sergeant-Major tomorrow afternoon."

Tate looked across the room. "What's happening tomorrow morning? Aren't you going into the office?"

"Doctor appointments in the AM," Sully said. "I already told Ms. Tyler and she'll let Major Harper know."

"I'll go with you." Tate began to add toppings to the ice-cream. "I want to hear the news about your leg."

"You're not the only one. I'm hoping to get rid of the brace before I start teaching next week."

———

To her amazement, she didn't have to deal with a rebellious stomach the next morning. Tate brought her a cup of tea and a slice of dry toast before she got out of bed. A short while later they headed for the clinic. She'd told him that she also had an appointment with the OBGYN, and he wanted to be with her for that, so he'd go to the office after lunch while Sully completed out-processing.

The busy Friday ended with the two of them sharing a supreme, whole-grain pizza they'd picked up at the deli. He'd added more veggies before baking it. Over dinner, they discussed the baby's due date in September and the house-hunting she planned to do the following week after school. If she found something, she thought they might like, they'd tour it the next weekend. If not, there would be more time to look and she could always email him photos.

"We'll want at least a two-car garage," Tate said. "Three would be better since you need space to work on your *Barbie* car."

She tilted her head. "Are you trying to annoy me, Murphy, or is that just an added benefit?"

"Your defense strategy of painting the Mustang bright pink to keep away the guys amuses me." He pushed the pizza toward her. "You should eat more. Do I have to be worried that you'll run amuck with a spray can at our new place?"

"Only if you overstep the boundaries." She snagged another slice. "I want a one-story house with bedrooms close to each other. I don't want the baby's room far away from ours."

"Makes sense." He topped up her glass of ice-water. "When do you want to buy a crib? Before I go to Kentucky or when I'm back on leave?"

"When you're back. By then, we may have a house to furnish."

"Sounds good."

She cleaned up the kitchen while he walked the puppies. By the time, the three of them returned, she was comfortably ensconced on the couch in the living room ready for a peaceful night of television. He sat down next to her, dogs flopping on the floor. She fell asleep in the middle of one *Criminal Minds* episode and woke as the team hunted a different serial killer.

They spent Saturday at the apartment, and he helped her detail the Mustang. She still didn't let him drive it to the grocery. Sunday afternoon, he carried down her small wheeled suitcase and laptop loading them onto the back seat.

"Call me when you get to Baker City."

"Yes, Dad."

"I'm serious."

"I know." Smiling, she tiptoed up to kiss him. "Keep me posted about next weekend."

"I'll ask for a pass tomorrow morning. I don't want you to drive back and forth so much. The traffic's a killer."

"And you're a worry-wart."

"That's Master Sergeant Worry-Wart to you, Mrs. Murphy."

Tenderness swept through her when he gently placed his hand on her tummy. She didn't have a baby bump yet, not really. She covered his hand with hers. "I'll be careful. I promise. And I'll talk to you at least once a day."

"More than that. I want much more than that."

"Then we'll work on that too." She kissed him again. "Stay safe with your princesses."

"You too."

PART II

MARCH 2019

CHAPTER NINETEEN

She avoided the temptation to ignore the speed limits on the way to Baker City. A brilliant pink Mustang always attracted the notice of the cops and the last thing she needed or wanted was a ticket. Raven had flirted her way out of at least a dozen speeding violations over the years, but it wasn't Sully's style. Hell, she couldn't even cry on demand. So much for being a manipulative female. She'd have to work on her womanly wiles.

The thought amused her as she pulled into the driveway and parked in front of the large Murphy home. Bronwyn must have been watching for her because the older woman was out the back door and headed toward the car before Sully even switched off the engine. Naveah and Chantrea were hot on their foster mom's heels. Three warm hugs later, the teens grabbed the bag with her laptop and suitcase, and they trooped toward the house.

"Tate called and told me when you left Heidi's place," Bronwyn said. "You made good time. We baked snickerdoodles and we stocked up on several varieties of decaf tea when we went to the grocery."

"The first thing I need is a bathroom." Sully laughed. "Then, I'm ready for a cookie break."

"Tate also emailed Mom a long list of what you're allowed to eat and what you're not," Chantrea reported. "And we're supposed to remind you to take your prenatal vitamins every morning."

"Are you serious?" Sully gaped at them. "I can't believe he did that. I'm a grown woman and I take personal responsibility for what I do."

"He's a control freak." Bronwyn wrapped an arm around Sully's waist as they climbed the steps to the back porch. "He comes by it honestly, but it's not my fault. He's just like his father. Joe always tried to order me around when I was expecting."

"What did you do?"

"Left him home with the kids when I had to go see Doc MacGillicudy for one of my appointments. It doesn't work with the first baby." Bronwyn frowned thoughtfully. "Well, it might. You could switch to the Baker City clinic since you're up here and he's the closest physician. Then, Tate wouldn't know everything the doctor tells you. Of course, it wouldn't stop him from researching on the Internet."

"Get thee behind me, Satan." Her phone buzzed and Sully pulled it out of her pocket in time to see a message from Tate. It was a picture of him and the puppies. She smiled and quickly texted a reply that she'd arrived safe and sound. She'd wait until she saw him and then chew his ears for trying to control her.

The next morning the girls insisted on riding with her to school. They informed her it was better than taking the bus, but since they'd be getting out before she did, they'd ride it home. For the first time in years, she felt like part of a family. The Barlow relatives always treated her as an outsider despite Gil's insistence that she was his daughter although the Driscolls who lived next door seemed to consider her one of them.

However, Sully couldn't bring herself to visit them, not after Raven died. They might have condemned her for the loss of their *real* child and even if they didn't, Sully still blamed herself. She took a deep breath. Kord had told her they wanted to send wedding gifts, but she wasn't registered at the usual outlets. Once she knew what she needed for her life with Tate, she was supposed to contact them. Tears burned and she hastily blinked them away. Teach first, she told herself sternly. Cry later.

She found a spot in the staff parking lot for the Mustang, then collected the canvas tote bag she used as a briefcase. It was large enough to hold her laptop, wallet, office supplies, papers, planners, grade books, numerous colored pens, and other miscellaneous items. Mentally, she called it her *school bag*, although she'd heard Dr. Dunaway refer to it as a *teacher bag*.

Taking a deep breath, Sully locked the vehicle before heading to the office. *Fourteen weeks*, she told herself. *Seventy days, sixty-nine after today. I can handle it. Hopefully, I won't be in a warzone.* It felt odd to wear something other than camouflage fatigues and combat boots. Determined to make a good impression on her first day, she'd chosen navy slacks that fit comfortably under the brace on her left leg, a white and blue pinstripe blouse, and a navy blazer. She had an assortment of other jackets, cardigans, a couple of cute dresses, and three pairs of flats so she could mix and match whatever she wore to teach.

In the front office, she introduced herself to one of the secretaries, a young fashionably dressed blonde at the front desk, and was immediately directed to Security where she registered her car. From there, she was sent to the principal who took her on a quick guided tour that included meeting the three assistant administrators, one of whom offered to escort her to the wing of the building where she'd find the English and History classes. He eyed her brace and the cane, then showed her the elevator, telling her to use it to access the third floor.

Upstairs, she entered the second classroom on the right, nodding to her new mentor teacher, Maureen Evans. The short, plump, gray-haired, squatty-bodied woman in the gray suit reminded Sully of a troll. "Good morning."

"You're late." Maureen snapped. "Teachers start a half-hour before students arrive for classes."

"There were a few details to take care of in the office." Sully kept her voice even and calm. "From now on, I'll be here at oh-seven-hundred."

"See that you are." Maureen stalked across to a second desk in the front corner of the room. "This is yours. You'll be teaching four middle school English courses and one Washington State History, beginning Wednesday. Today and tomorrow, you'll observe me and take notes. Are we clear?"

"Yes, ma'am." Sully took a deep breath, then carried her bag over to the assigned desk. She eyed the textbooks before glancing at the stacks of completed student work waiting to be graded. How was she supposed to take notes and correct all these assignments at the same time? She didn't ask.

Instead, she turned her attention to the other teacher. "Do you have copies of the seating charts and your classroom procedures, so I'll be on the same page with you?"

Maureen heaved a dramatic sigh. "I don't do seating charts. You'll have two days to learn your students' names and how I run my classes. If you have questions, write them down and we'll go over them at the end of the day."

"Yes, ma'am."

Sully struggled to stay awake while she watched Maureen Evans teach an assortment of approximately ninety students during the first three periods that morning. The woman ran the classroom like a drill sergeant, rapping out orders, and never answering questions about the curriculum. Different older teens arrived each period, taking attendance and grading some of the waiting assignments. One of the girls introduced herself as Octavia Butler and told Sully that she'd be responsible for entering grades in the computer.

They had a half-hour lunch break after third period and Maureen Evans promptly left the room. Sully didn't go with the older teacher, deciding that by the time she struggled downstairs to the faculty lounge and back up again, she'd have used up most of their break. Instead, she made a quick trip to the nearest restroom, then ate in the classroom and continued to line edit the various summaries of the short stories the students had obviously read during the past month. She didn't find a rubric and opted to hold off on scoring the work. She added a question about that to her list.

After lunch, more seventh graders arrived. She recognized Quinn's oldest stepdaughter, but the girl was too busy with her cheerleader friends to notice Sully. Like the students in the earlier classes, these read two episodes of *Homer's Odyssey*, then filled out worksheets that promptly landed on her desk, the same as the others had in the morning. Sully grimaced but didn't say a word. It was going to be a hellacious fourteen weeks. Fifth period, Washington State History was the last class of the day, at least with students. This time, the kids read a chapter in the textbook and answered the questions at the end. Once more, they turned in their work. Sixth period turned out to be teacher planning time when they'd prepare for the next day.

Sully listened to the older woman's lecture and again took more notes. She learned how to enter the grades into the computer and that the T.A.s would file the student work in their folders the next day. Asking for a rubric to judge the short story summaries elicited more impatient sighs, but at least she received permission to create a checklist since Maureen claimed not to have one. Sully explained she wanted to let the students know how she judged their work and the levels of quality.

Another huge sigh and Maureen said, "I suppose you can create a form, but show it to me before you pass it out to the kids."

"I'll have it for you before school tomorrow."

Classes ended sharply at 2 PM, at least for the teens, but Sully had to stay another two hours. It gave her time to enter grades in the online school system. She arranged the work in separate stacks for each period. When she left the room, she met the janitor who promised to lock the classroom after cleaning. In the office, she asked the senior secretary about a key and was told she'd have one waiting in the morning.

The friendly older woman introduced herself as Della Lowry and wanted to know if Sully had everything she needed. She glanced cautiously around the empty office, then asked if it'd be possible to have a copy of the attendance for each class she was expected to teach. Della nodded and promptly printed off the forms including pictures, apologizing that the photos weren't up to date because they'd been taken the previous October.

"Let me know what else you need," Della said. "When Dr. Dunaway was here, she told me you'd be starting as soon as you got off active duty for the Army. I don't know if you've heard it yet, but I appreciate your service."

Tears stung and Sully caught her breath determined to maintain control. "Thank you."

"No, thank you, honey." Della passed her the pages, then pulled out a paper showing the staff parking lot. "You certainly have a pretty car and Brian Wright, the head of Security promised he'd keep an eye on it for you. He's assigned it a spot, number thirty-three, directly below one of the cameras. Park it there tomorrow."

"I will. Thank him for me."

Della nodded. "I will. Dr. Dunaway told us your sister-in-law didn't make it home. I'm so sorry."

"Me too." Sully slipped the papers into her canvas tote. "I'll see you tomorrow." She hesitated, then asked. "Who is the Humanities Department Chair?"

Della blinked. "Sandra Young. She was at a training workshop today, but she'll probably stop in to meet you and visit this week. Why?"

"I need rubrics when I grade student work to ensure I'm adhering to school policy."

"Oh, you don't need Sandra for that." Della hustled over to a file cabinet, opened a drawer, and removed a notebook. "Here's the seventh-grade handbook. We give copies to our students and their parents at the start of the school year. Anything else?"

"No, this is terrific. Where do I get copies of the essay rubric to attach to the papers I'm grading?"

"Which one do you want? I'll have enough here for you in the morning."

Sully flipped through the book and quickly found the form she needed. It showed students their work was judged on the usual standards of *purpose, organization, details, voice, and mechanics* with ratings from one to four. Best of all, the footnote declared it was intended to be used English department-wide and that meant she didn't have to reinvent the proverbial wheel.

Della promptly went to a different set of shelves, these on the far side of the room, and removed a stack of colorful postcard-sized rubrics, bringing them back to the counter. "Here you go. Let me know when you require more."

Sully tucked the cards into her bag. "Why didn't Mrs. Evans go to the training? Wasn't it for all the Humanities teachers?"

"It was, but we have a limited number of substitutes in the district, so we couldn't get one for her. She intended to leave you in charge of her classes, but Mr. Ames, the principal told her it wouldn't be reasonable to expect you to take over without notice."

Sully took a deep breath and started to explain that although she did work as a substitute teacher in Liberty Valley, university regulations didn't allow her to perform those duties when she did a teaching practicum. She opted to keep her mouth shut and decided to let Dr. Dunaway break the bad news that a student teacher wasn't a *free* dogs-body, babysitter, or servant. She'd had her share of crappy assignments in Liberty Valley, but never one where she wasn't paid for attempting to teach the curriculum.

Halfway to the Mustang, two guards approached, both in blue and black uniforms, badges proclaiming they worked for Nighthawke Security. The petite, dark-haired woman smiled politely and the man with her, a sandy-haired, muscular giant waved a greeting. They might act friendly, but Sully knew better than to judge by appearances. Her older brother, Kord worked for Nighthawke Security after leaving the Navy and these two had undoubtedly served as well.

"I'm Sullivan Murphy." She showed them the ID badge she wore on the lanyard around her neck. "I just started student teaching here today."

"Bianca Powell and this is Dak Marshall." The woman assessed her with a narrowed, dark-eyed gaze. "You look familiar."

"So, do you." Sully leaned on her cane studying the other woman, then recognized her. "You came to my sister-in-law, Raven Driscoll-Barlow's funeral in December."

Bianca nodded. "Yes. She and my sister died in the same ambush. You were with them, weren't you?"

"Yes, I was. I'm sorry. There wasn't anything I could do to save them." Sully drew a ragged breath. "Trish was a good person. She's missed."

"Not just by the folks in your unit." Bianca paused. "I'm on swing shift this week. Maybe, we can go for a drink tomorrow."

"Tea would be better," Sully said. "I'm pregnant and off booze for another six and a half months."

"That's do-able." Bianca agreed.

"So, what are you naming the baby?" Dak asked, obviously trying to change the subject.

"Raven."

"And if it's a boy?" Dak kept going. "What then?"

"Raven," Sully repeated.

"That works." Bianca turned to glance at the vintage car. "I remember seeing it at the funeral."

"Raven and I rebuilt it and my older brother looked after it for us when we were overseas." Sully limped toward the vehicle accompanied by the two guards. "Della told me that the head of Security had a special place for it."

"Yup and we've all gotten the word to keep it safe and sound," Dak told her. "We'd have done it anyway because it's a classic beauty, but we'll give it extra attention now since you served with Bianca's sister."

"Thanks." Sully unlocked the car and put her tote bag on the passenger seat, placing her four-footed cane in the back before she slipped behind the wheel. "I'm staying in Baker City with my in-laws. Do you want to join me for dinner at Pop's Café tomorrow night, Bianca?"

"Sure. I'll bring Dak too. He can be my designated driver."

"I live to serve," Dak said.

"Yeah, well right now we'd better get back to our rounds or we'll hear about it. Stay safe, Sully."

"You too." Sully slid the key in the ignition. She waited until they'd headed off to patrol the campus, inspecting buildings and access points. Then, she started the engine and drove toward the highway. She remembered Tate telling her to gas up in Lake Maynard since it'd be cheaper than buying fuel in Baker City.

Even with a short stop, she was at the Murphy farm in plenty of time to put away her school bag, change to jeans and a sweatshirt before helping Bronwyn prepare dinner. Sully felt the phone vibrate in her back pocket and pulled it out in time to recognize the caller.

"It's Tate."

"Go talk to him in the living room. You can finish the salad when you get back." Bronwyn winked. "Tell him I'm being good. I'm not serving undercooked meat, or fish and you washed the veggies."

Laughing, Sully obeyed. She waited until she plopped down on the couch to carry on a real conversation. "You're going to be grounded for life, Murphy. Your momma's been running her kitchen forever. She doesn't need you bossing her around and neither do I."

"Want to bet?" He chuckled. "I missed you. Tell me about your day and then I'll tell you about mine."

CHAPTER TWENTY

That became their pattern over the next three days, working during the day and talking in the early evening. She went to the school arriving on time, carefully dressing for success, and not telling Maureen Evans what the parameters were for student teachers from her university. Dr. Dunaway hadn't returned her call, but Sully decided it didn't matter yet since she hadn't been put in the proverbial *Catch-22* situation and didn't have to refuse to substitute teach at Lake Maynard Middle High.

She told Tate a little about the dinner with Bianca and Dak, promising to introduce the pair to him when he visited. Sully shared more about the lessons she'd taught, adhering to the classroom procedures modeled by her mentor teacher. Vocabulary games weren't allowed which made it difficult to teach the Greek roots of words. Neither were exit slips when the students left the room so she couldn't assess what they'd learned in the daily lessons. Reading was done by rote and so were the worksheets she had to grade. When he asked, she admitted she hadn't met many of the other teachers because lunch periods were so short, but said she hoped to do so before her practicum ended.

Late Thursday afternoon, she took notes while Maureen lectured about the shortcomings in her classroom management style. Since the older woman usually left the room as soon as the bell rang, it was a mystery how she knew what was taught during the various classes. Sully opted not to ask, instead murmuring, "I'll do better tomorrow."

"Fridays are half days," Maureen announced. "The students will perform presentations in front of their classes and be graded by you and their peers."

"What presentations?" Sully asked. "They haven't had time to prepare."

"They do it as homework. They'll act out the next two episodes of the *Odyssey* and you'll enter their grades afterward."

"Is there a rubric for that?"

"You can make one for them tonight and have the TAs get copies in the office tomorrow before school starts." Maureen folded her arms. In the gray suit with poofy, gray hair, she looked more like a children's toy troll than ever. "Any questions?"

Sully leaned back in her chair, hoping her eagerness at an early escape from the high school and Maureen's environs didn't show. "What time do we finish tomorrow since it's a half-day?"

"The students go home at ten-thirty. Why?"

"My husband doesn't have a weekend pass yet. If I leave early, I'll avoid rush-hour and be back at the base before traffic gets bad."

"I'll see what I can do."

The older woman left the room so quickly that Sully didn't have time to thank her. There were plenty of assignments to grade, but she took the time to remove her phone from the school bag and check for messages. She spotted two from Tate and hit the speaker button so she could hear what he had to say while she worked.

His deep voice rumbled in the empty classroom, brightening the afternoon. "Hey, Mrs. Murphy, your battalion Command Sergeant-Major stopped in and told me to let you know the *sitrep* completed by your supply gals worked for the unit technician. Anise and the Major both want to know when you'll be here to save the day and catch up on the D.F.s. Can't wait to see you. I don't have a pass yet, but I'm working on that too. The pups and I are missing you, sweetheart."

She laughed, amused yet touched by the endearment. Weren't they supposed to have a so-called 'marriage of convenience'? Instead, he'd obviously tried to make it *real* for both of them. She marked the scores and attached a rubric to the summary she'd finished red-penciling while setting the message to repeat. The sound of heels clicking on the tile floor in the hallway drew her attention and she glanced toward the door to see a lovely, well-dressed African-American woman in her late thirties enter the room. "Can I help you?"

"You must be Sullivan Barlow, our new student teacher. I'm Sandra Young, the Humanities Department Chair. I wanted to give you time to get settled before I introduced myself."

Sully clicked off the cell phone, unwilling to share Tate's message with the newcomer. "Actually, it's Sullivan Murphy. I was married last week."

"Wow, Maureen didn't share that." Sandra turned a chair and sat down across from Sully. "What are you grading?"

"Short story summaries." Sully put her red pen on the desk. "I don't mean to make waves, but what is the standard timeframe? When do students have to turn in their revised responses?"

Sandra frowned thoughtfully. "Since they've already started their new literature unit, they should have done that before. Did you want to give them the opportunities to raise their grades?"

"It'd only be fair when most of them didn't write passing papers."

"Okay." Sandra picked up one of the graded essays and read through the corrections. "You've really done a thorough job here and now I see how you've been spending your time when you aren't teaching. You haven't joined us for lunch or during your prep period. I know the other teachers are looking forward to meeting you."

"I barely have enough time to eat and hit the bathroom at lunch." Sully managed what she hoped was a polite smile. "And Mrs. Evans likes to counsel me on my performance during our prep periods."

"You'll meet everyone tomorrow. We have a potluck lunch as soon as the kids leave and then department meetings for the rest of the day."

Sully glanced down at the stack of papers on the desk, determined not to show her disappointment. Damn Maureen Evans and her predilection for games. Why couldn't the woman have simply shared the school's expectations earlier? Was it the same reason she didn't say the English rubrics were already in the office and all Sully had to do was ask the secretary? "Would it be possible to get a copy of the weekly schedule for teachers?"

"Of course. I have one in my room. If you'd like to come with me now, I'll get it for you."

"Thank you." Sully pushed back enough to brace herself on the desk and stand. She tucked the cell phone in her blazer pocket, then reached for the cane. "Let's do it."

Sandra stared for a moment, then gestured to the walking cast. "What happened? A car accident? Or…?"

"Didn't Mrs. Evans or Dr. Dunaway or the principal tell you I'm an Army Reservist? I just came off active duty after a tour in Afghanistan and I broke my leg when our patrol was hit by an I.E.D."

"Nobody told me." Sandra slowed her pace, so they walked together out of the room. "If you need anything, send a teenager. They all know how to find me."

"Thanks, I will. I'm not standoffish. It just takes me forever to get places right now. Once the doctors at the Army base clear me for reasonable exercise, I'll be back to running at least two miles every day."

"You'll have to share that with the track coaches. They're always looking for more help."

Sully laughed. "Oh, the first thing a soldier learns is not to volunteer, but I'll be happy to run with the students." She flicked a sideways glance at the taller woman. Time to give one mentor teacher a lesson in *suck eggs!* "So, how do I arrange to go to the base next Friday for my doctor's appointment without stepping on anyone's toes?"

"What two classes are you teaching? Tomorrow, we'll find someone to cover them or Maureen can."

"I teach all day," Sully said. "Four seventh-grade English classes and then Washington State History."

"That's not right. You're supposed to start with one class each week and build up to all five after spring break in April. I'm amazed you've been able to do all five periods."

"It probably helps that I have my emergency substitute certification and I'm accustomed to teaching all day when I'm in Liberty Valley."

179

"You're paying big bucks to your university to do a practicum, not being paid to teach one-hundred-fifty students from the start. Granted, Maureen is doing her own administrative supervisor practicum with the assistant principals this semester so she can become a principal before she retires, but it sounds like I need to provide more guidance for you."

"I'd appreciate that." Sully pasted on what she hoped was her sweetest smile. "Dr. Dunaway told me it was against university policy for me to substitute teach during my practicums, but she didn't say anything about when I was expected to take over all five classes."

"Oh, you can substitute here when you're cleared to teach all day if you have your emergency cert and you already do, but we have to pay you. No freebies, Sullivan."

"I'll keep that in mind."

When Tate drove by Lake Maynard Middle High School on Friday afternoon, he spotted the flashy pink Mustang in the staff parking lot. He glanced at his watch. It was almost sixteen-hundred hours. He'd escaped from the base three hours ago, not bothering to change out of his fatigues and combat boots once Major Harper agreed to give him a weekend pass. Tate recalled Sully mentioning it was a half-day, but apparently that was for the students, not the teachers. It reminded him of the joke his father told about farmers only working half days and either twelve hours would do.

He signaled for the right turn, pulled into the lot, and parked behind the classic sports car, proceeding to *hurry up and wait.* Thirty minutes later, he glimpsed her limping toward him, leaning heavily on the four-footed cane, weighed down by her laptop and a tote bag obviously crammed full of work.

Opening the pickup door, he slid out and went to meet her, appreciating the floral print dress that clung to her curves and swirled around her knees. When she spotted him, a smile dawned on her face. "You're here."

"I wasn't sure I'd make it until after lunch when I finally got the

OK." He took the black canvas computer bag and then the tote before he leaned down to kiss her. "Had to talk fast."

"And I'm sure you're good at it."

"Definitely." He slung the straps over his shoulder, then pulled her close. His mouth claimed hers in a longer, slower kiss. When he lifted his head, he saw tears sparkle in her emerald eyes. "What's wrong?"

She shook her head, then heaved a sigh. "It just sucks being at a place where my mentor teacher hates me and constantly tries to sabotage me. She spent the afternoon criticizing me non-stop in front of the other English teachers in the department meetings. Even the cookies your mom sent for the potluck lunch didn't improve her mood."

"But it's all verbal, right? Nobody's actually shooting at you yet and I know you can kick civilian butt and take names, Sarge." He feathered a thumb over her lips. "Let's go to Pop's for dinner and you can tell me all about it."

"Okay." She sniffed hard. "I really want at least one glass of wine, but I can't have one of those."

"Not for another six and a half months." He wrapped his arm around her waist. "Should I say I'm not sorry about the baby?"

"If you start smirking at me, Murphy, I'll slug you."

"That's my girl." He guided her to the Mustang. "So, what's in the bag? Bricks?"

"A bunch of performance reviews and lit packets I have to grade over the weekend. It wouldn't be so bad if the kids had been taught to write coherently in the past seven months, but it's impossible to find the main ideas or topic sentences in most of them."

"I guess I should be glad you only bitched about my lousy handwriting when I was out in the field taking notes."

"You're lucky you're sexy or you'd be in trouble."

He chuckled while he waited for her to unlock the driver's door of the vintage car, then tucked the bags on the back seat. "Remember to stay under the speed limits on the way to Baker City, Mrs. Murphy, and let's get the hell out of Dodge."

"I will if you do. Did you let your mom know we wouldn't be at the farm for supper?"

"Yes. I said we'd be there for brunch tomorrow because we're spending the night at Cedar Creek. I'm not comfortable sharing the guest room with you in the old family home and I know you don't want to walk up to the third floor and sleep with me there."

She smiled, tiptoed up to kiss him. "Let's hit the road and I won't tell you again that your parents know all about babies and how to make them."

"You're an evil woman." He tugged gently on her braid. "I'll let you have your wicked way with me tonight."

"I can't wait."

A mile outside of Baker City, Sully saw the bright pink and purple sign that read Cedar Creek Guest Ranch. She followed Tate down the gravel drive stopping in front of the cabin they'd used the previous week. He waved to the woman in camo fatigues and combat boots striding toward them from a nearby porch.

Sully pulled in next to his truck and parked. She snagged her cane, then got out to greet the Army officer. "Hello, Captain Endicott. I didn't realize you were the person that Cat McTavish mentioned when we were here before."

"I put my stuff in storage and ended my lease when we shipped out, so I needed a place to stay when we returned home," Margo said, handing over a set of keys. "I told Cat I'd meet you two and give you these so you can get into the cabin. How is the student teaching going? Ann always pitched a fit about the admin at the high school. Are they treating you right?"

Sully shrugged. "I met the principal and his assistants last Monday. I haven't seen them since. I've been busy teaching four English classes and a Washington State History course. By the time I leave school, they're long gone."

"And she has a ton of homework to grade this weekend." Tate eased an arm around her waist. "If I thought I'd get to spend time with my new wife, my mistake."

Margo laughed. "Oh, the joys of teaching full-time. Yes, the two of you can be together when you help her. I've got a date tonight, but I'll show you the quick and dirty way that *real* teachers do grading tomorrow afternoon."

"That must be a secret I don't know. I've substituted for years but I didn't have to do much grading then and I left shortly after the kids did."

"Well, those days are over. See you tomorrow at fourteen-hundred hours." With a friendly wave, Margo strolled away toward her own house.

Relief washed through Sully as she turned and walked beside Tate to the small Alpine style cabin. After she unlocked the kitchen door, he gestured for her to sit in one of the Adirondack chairs on the wraparound porch while he unloaded the car and truck. She knew she ought to jump up and help but decided to let him play the *big man* and take care of her. It'd been a long five days.

"Ginger ale on the rocks." He handed her the icy glass, then sat down beside her with his own drink. "I figured it'd be worth my life to drink alcohol in front of you, so I opted for safety first. I'm ready to do the sympathetic ear thing. Quinn taught me that women want good listeners, not solutions."

"I love your sister. She should offer classes to all men who want their relationships to work."

"I'll tell her you said that."

She hadn't thought sharing her experiences at Lake Maynard Middle High would help, but somehow it did. Tate was true to his word. He didn't say anything. He just sat, drank his soda, and let her spew out all the miserable details. When she finished, he asked what she'd do if she could really teach and she vented about the strategies she was forbidden to use. By the time they'd shared a box of snack crackers and she'd drained two glasses of ginger ale, she felt human. No, he couldn't help her in the classroom, but knowing he believed in her was what she needed to hear.

"Okay, you're a credit to your twin sister. Let's go have dinner at Pop's Café."

"Does that mean I get to drive the *Barbie* car?"

"Are you serious? Don't push your luck, Murphy. Stop making fun of my Mustang. Being sexy only gets you so far."

He stood, collected their glasses. "Well, I'm hoping it gets me laid tonight."

"Anything's possible especially since I feel better now." She eyed him. "Tell the truth, Sergeant Tall, Dark, and Handsome. Was that the real reason for the charm?"

He grinned, then winked at her. "I'm not talking, or I'll be abstinent way too long."

CHAPTER TWENTY-ONE

When she woke late the next morning, she decided the steak dinner at Pop's Café the night before followed by dancing in the lounge and finishing off the evening by jumping Tate when they returned to the cabin at Cedar Creek was the perfect way to end what had been an awful week. Luckily, she didn't have to wear the same clothes she'd worn to school the previous day. He'd done his Master Sergeant in charge of the world routine and hit her closet at the garage apartment.

She had clean underwear, comfy pull-on white capris, a pink-checked, western-style shirt, and sandals. Granted, she could only wear one shoe, but she wasn't complaining. After she showered and dressed, she found him sitting on the porch enjoying a cup of coffee. She sat down in the Adirondack chair next to his and sipped peppermint tea. "Okay, it's your turn. Tell me all about your week with the princesses, the latest office drama with Ms. Tyler and Major Harper, and the puppy adventures at your aunt and uncle's place."

Laughing, he followed directions. His stories still made her smile as they headed for his parents' home a short time later. They opted to take the pickup this time. "I didn't have a chance to meet with Dominique MacGillicudy this week, so she said she'd show us a few houses today or tomorrow. What works best for you?"

"Since we have an appointment to work with Captain Endicott at two o'clock today, let's do it tomorrow after church. We can invite Quinn to join us and then show up for Sunday dinner at the folks' place."

"Works for me." Sully pulled out her phone to text the realtor while he used his phone to contact his twin sister.

Brunch at the Murphy farm meant good food and conversation. She showed off the bay in the garage set up for the Mustang. Tate oohed and aahed appropriately over the large metal cabinet Lock provided for the necessary supplies to maintain her classic car. When she tired of Tate's teasing, she thumped him with her cane. He promptly pulled her into his arms and kissed her. One kiss led to another and could have gone further if his younger brother hadn't interrupted.

Still amused by their antics when they arrived at the cabin, Sully led the way inside. She made a fresh pot of coffee and turned on the teakettle while he set out the cookies his mother sent along for the grading session. Margo tapped on the door precisely at two o'clock and Sully went to greet her. "I'm glad you're here."

"I hope you still agree when we finish." She gestured to the tall man in comfortable civvies who accompanied her. Built like a truck driver, he undoubtedly wasn't military now but had been at one time since he had the proverbial *high and tight* haircut. "This is Jared Williams. We're taking in a movie tonight, so I drafted him to help us. What are we grading?"

"Literary packets for the first half of Homer's Odyssey, worksheets critiquing the performances the English classes did yesterday, and three chapter reviews completed by the kids in Washington State History."

"Wow, your mentor teacher really wanted to use up your weekend, didn't she?" Margo gestured to the kitchen table. "Okay, let's get started. Give everybody a red pen and three Odyssey packets."

Sully blinked. "Why? I've been assessing them one at a time and it takes forever when there are approximately a hundred and twenty to grade, or there would be if all of the students had turned in the assignment on time."

"Not any longer, Sergeant Barlow-Murphy. I'm teaching you the way that *real* teachers grade." Margo pulled out a chair and sat down.

"We'll do a compare and contrast between them, so the grades are consistent."

Sully followed directions. Once everyone had three packets, they turned their attention to Margo who talked them through judging the covers, then the first few pages. The coffee finished brewing before they finished the original three packets and Tate stood, pouring cups for himself, Jared, and Margo. Sully had her favorite tea.

When Margo and Jared were ready to leave three hours later, the scored assignments sat in neat stacks on the table, arranged in class order from first through fifth periods. Sully took a deep breath. "Wow, as soon as I enter the grades tonight, I'm done."

"No." Margo held up her hand. "You have a life tonight. You don't enter the grades in the school programs until tomorrow night. Take a nap after dinner Sunday night. Get up and start about twenty-two hundred hours."

"It takes me at least four hours to get everything posted," Sully protested. "I'll still be doing it after midnight."

"That's the idea," Margo said. "Let your mentor, her department chair and the administrators think you were up all night after grading all weekend. Think *boot camp* and you'll have the basic idea of what this last practicum is like. They want to torment a student teacher, so don't let them know you have a strategy or a life."

"That's a fair point." Tate gathered the cups, carrying them to the sink. "And since we're done, do you want to go out for dinner?"

Sully nodded. "Sure. It's either that or cook something and I'd rather eat at Pop's Café."

"Okay, then let's hit the road."

"We'd invite you to join us in Lake Maynard," Jared drawled, running a hand through silver-blond hair, "but Margo says you're teaching there so it's better if you don't socialize in a town where you work."

"Another good point." Sully smiled at them. "Thanks again for the help."

"No worries." Margo started for the door, then paused. "Your battalion has reserve duty next weekend. I'll see you there at Fort Bronson and you can tell me how things are going."

Sully shook her head. "No, I'll be at Fort Clark. I have a doctor's appointment on Friday and the Command Sergeant-Major arranged for me to work on base so Tate and I can be together until he ships out a week from Monday."

"Then stop by here on Tuesday night after school and let me know the latest," Margo ordered. "Tell your university supervisor you need that Monday to take him to the airport and see him off."

Tate leaned against the counter, obviously eyeing the officer. "We don't want to make waves when Sully needs to finish this practicum to complete the qualifications for her teaching certificate and get a full-time position."

"Your wife needs to take you to the airport." Margo straightened to her full height, rapping out the order. "She'll arrange it, or I will. Got it?"

"Yes, ma'am." Sully pulled out her cell phone and proceeded to text the professor. No response came, but at least the request was out in cyberspace.

They didn't go to the lounge to dance after dinner. Instead, they returned to the cabin and sat on the porch to listen to the early spring chorus of frogs croaking, the water splashing and rushing over the rocks in Cedar Creek, and to watch the stars play hide and seek among the clouds in the night sky. Sully leaned back in her big wooden chair, heaving a sigh. "I dreaded this weekend when Maureen Evans dumped that crapload of work on me yesterday afternoon. I nearly started crying but I wasn't going to give her the satisfaction."

"Did it help when Captain Endicott said it was like basic training?"

"Hell, yes! Granted, I was with Raven and she had my back, but we survived it together. I know I can make it through this, even if it is longer than *boot camp*. One week down and thirteen more to go until I finish in June."

"You'll make it." He stood, crossed to her, and held out his hand. "Come on, Mrs. Murphy. It's my turn to jump your bones."

"I can't wait."

The next day started with breakfast at the café, then church where they met up with the rest of the Murphy clan. Sully enjoyed a cup of decaf tea and a maple bar during the social hour while she listened to the chatting family. Glancing across the room, she spotted Dominique and waved to her.

The fashion diva, in yet another tailored dress and stiletto heels, promptly joined them, opening her laptop. "I have so much to show you."

Sully eyed the screen saver that revealed a three-story, Gothic wonder behind a black wrought-iron fence. The elaborate structure had a stone staircase and double doors, big bay windows that extended from the ground floor to the top towers. "That so isn't my house. What did you find for us? I want a one-story Craftsman."

"This is the old MacGillicudy place," Dominique said. "I inherited it along with my cousin. I want to flip it for a million plus, but I have to wait until he gets here, and we have a meeting of the minds about the work that needs to be done."

"Where is he?" Sully sipped the last of the tea. "In the States or abroad?"

"Working. He's a writer and he sent word he'd be along after he finishes his book tour. It's okay. It gives me time to plan the updates." Dominique clicked the mouse and proceeded to pull up views of a series of reasonably priced bungalow-style homes. "These are three or four-bedroom houses, all with two or more bathrooms. Which one would you like to see first?"

Sully gestured to Tate who came to stand behind her while Dominique showed them one property after another on her computer. After discussing it, they opted to see five different properties. Two of them had large fenced yards, but one was nestled in the middle of five acres on the other side of Baker City. Although she didn't admit it to him, it sounded like the best to her.

Collecting her cane and purse, Sully stood and left with Tate and his twin sister. In her usual Sunday attire of jeans and a sweatshirt, Quinn sauntered next to Sully on the way to the parking lot. "Cressida says you're teaching her English class. How is she doing?"

"Do you want the truth, or shall I do the *go along to get along* routine?"

"Truth, please. I know her grades are good, or she wouldn't be able to be a cheerleader."

"I'm entering the scores for the last two assignments tonight. She hasn't rewritten her short story summaries yet from the last unit and those are due no later than a week from tomorrow, next Monday."

Quinn winced. "Why do I have a feeling all hell is going to break loose at home? Lyle loves bragging about his daughter, the teen dream cheerleader but if her grades are low, she'll be off the squad."

"Well, she'd better turn in those summaries on time," Sully said, her tone even. "According to the freshman handbook, I'm supposed to mark down late assignments five percent for each day."

Another grimace. "That means if she doesn't step up and get it done right away, she'll fail even if she turns in the work."

"Exactly." Sully unlocked the passenger door to the Mustang. "Do you want to ride with us or Dominique?"

"Definitely with you." Quinn flashed a smile that reminded Sully of her brother. "And now we can focus on the houses. This is going to be fun. If we don't find one today, we can always look after school next week."

"Famous last words. I'm usually worn to a complete frazzle by the time I arrive at the farm."

To Sully's amazement, Dominique turned out to be a fantastic realtor. When they toured Baker City, she showed off the simple homes built of natural materials, hand-crafted wood, and stone trim scattered throughout the town. Each house had the quintessential qualities of the one-story Craftsman home with prominent exterior features including low-pitched roofs with wide eaves, large front or wrap-around porches, and numerous windows, some with leaded or stained glass. Sully liked all the buildings, but the last home spoke to her heart.

Vinyl fences and green pastures lined the paved driveway leading up to the two-story white house. At just under 2,000 square feet, it was trimmed out with blue shutters and stone on two of the front-facing walls. They crossed the wrap-around porch to the grand foyer, Tate closing the double doors behind them. Sully admired the open layout. A large study opened off to the left and to her right, she saw two bedrooms with a full 'jack and jill' bath between them.

Dominique continued walking as she described the spacious family room and then opened a set of glass French doors that allowed plenty of light before opening onto the rear patio and a fenced yard, perfect for Bo and his collie sister. Off the family room to the left was a country-style kitchen and dining room with an adjacent butler's pantry, a laundry-mudroom, and doors to the three-car garage. To the right was a huge, gorgeous master suite complete with its own entrance onto the patio.

"As you saw, each bedroom has a walk-in closet and while the other two rooms share the bath, yours would have a fantastic private one and you have a sitting area when you want to get away from the kids or guests."

Sully tucked her hand in Tate's and tiptoed up to whisper. "It's also perfect for a nursery. I don't want the baby alone for the first year."

He nodded agreement and leaned down to brush her lips with his. "Like you say, '*a happy wife makes for a happy life.*' I'll go with whatever you want."

"There's a basement and two upstairs bedrooms with a full bath. The family used one room as a den and the other as a gym, but—"

"I'm hearing *man cave*," Quinn announced. "Come on, Dominique. We'll leave these two alone to canoodle and you can show the basement and upstairs to me."

"There's also a small barn near one of the pastures and a chicken house as well as an orchard and berry patch on the other side of the driveway," Dominique said. "The previous owners kept a pony for their kids."

"What happened to them?" Tate asked. "Why are they selling?"

"His job transferred him to California, and he'll be there at least three years so the whole family ended up moving."

"Along with the pony?" Sully leaned into the warmth of Tate's side. "Does he like California?"

"The listing agent brought me here to see the place and we found animals still living here including the pony. When I contacted them, the sellers said they'd arranged for him to go to a relative, but it didn't happen. He was a cute little guy and I sent him to live with Cat O'Leary McTavish and Rob Hendrickson. I thought he'd be perfect for their daughters, but they already have ponies. Dray MacGillicudy, Linda's son took on finding homes for the cats and the dog."

"That was decent of you," Quinn said. "I have a few choice words for people who abandon animals."

"I do too," Dominique said. "Between stray animals and kids, they destroy property values. I still must get rid of a feral cat colony that's taken up residence at the MacGillicudy house. Pop and his daughter completely lost it when I offered to have county Animal Control come in and remove them. They've been feeding and trapping the stray felines for Doc's granddaughter. She's the new local veterinarian and she's fixing and vaccinating them. That's an exercise in futility since she turns them loose again after treating them. They're a nuisance and she should just put them down, but she screamed her head off when I suggested it."

Tate chuckled. "Let's go look at the pastures and barns, Mrs. Murphy. Mom will want to help you plant a garden this spring and Lock will put in a greenhouse for you. If you don't want to deal with the chores that come with chickens and a cow, we can get eggs, milk, and meat from the family."

"Sounds great." Sully waited until they were outside before she asked. "What amused you?"

"Dominique. Whenever I think she may be a human being, she shows me she's not. Only she would get rid of a pony because it was detrimental to the price she wants for this place and pitch a fit about feral cats."

"Well, she may not have saved the pony for the reason you or I would have, but she did do the right thing."

"True." He guided her along the driveway toward the white barn with the gambrel roof. "We'll want a structural inspection of the house and outbuildings, but I agree with my family. We all want Cat O'Leary McTavish to do a walk-through."

"You really think she talks to dead people?"

"Of course, she does. She's the O'Leary."

Sully heaved a sigh. "You're so weird, but it won't hurt anything if she approves of the place or not. I really like it here."

"I do too. Maybe, we've found a home."

"I hope so." She snuggled closer. "So, get out your phone and call the local *Ghostbusters*."

Tate left for the base at oh-dark-thirty after a steamy kiss goodbye. He'd loaded the Mustang for her, but she still took a few minutes to wash up their breakfast dishes and wipe down the counters before leaving the keys on the kitchen table. Cat McTavish had promised to meet Sully that afternoon to walk through the house and barns at the farm and make sure it didn't have any malignant ghosts. Personally, Sully didn't think it was needful, but she'd decided to do the *go along to get along* routine with Tate. It wouldn't hurt and it'd make him feel better about making an offer on what would be their new home.

When she arrived at the school, she headed for the office to check-in, then went onto the classroom. She'd barely finished placing the stacks of graded work in front of the crates that held student files when Maureen Evans stomped inside, followed by Dak Marshall, looking young, fit, and handsome in his Nighthawke Security uniform.

Sully smiled politely at the pair. "Good morning. How was your weekend?"

"Not as good as yours," Maureen sniped. "Brian Wright, the Chief of Security, and Mr. Ames, the head principal said they had you on camera necking with some man in the parking lot on Friday."

"Are you serious?" Fury rose and Sully clenched her fists, struggling to keep her tone even and civil. "For your information, my husband secured a weekend pass and met me here. Yes, we kissed but nobody was here, not any students or staff. I was the only one since you told me I had to stay until sixteen-thirty hours every day."

"Sixteen-thirty? What's that?" Maureen demanded.

"Four-thirty in civilian time," Dak said helpfully. "And Chief Wright is tired of having to reset the security alarms when Sully leaves late. Teachers are supposed to clear the buildings by fifteen-thirty unless they make special arrangements to help with after school activities and they're on his rosters."

"I didn't know that," Sully told him. "Are you for real?"

"Sure am, Sarge," Dak said. "I'll let the chief know you're not on the graveyard shift anymore."

"Thank you." Sully focused on Maureen Evans, watching irritation mount in the older woman's eyes. "I don't know if you heard, but I won't be here this Friday because I have a doctor's appointment at the Army base and I won't be here next Monday since my husband is shipping out and I'm taking him to the airport."

"It sounds to me like you're just being lazy and having a long weekend."

Enraged, Sully grabbed her cane and stalked toward the hallway door, deciding she needed a few moments in the bathroom before class to compose herself. "He's an Army Ranger. I'm seeing him off for training. If he goes to Afghanistan before I finish student teaching, I'll take a day off to see him go. And if he comes home in a box like Raven and Bianca Powell's sister did, I'll damned well take at least another day to freaking bury him."

CHAPTER TWENTY-TWO

That afternoon, she packed up a few minutes after three. Laptop bag on one shoulder, school bag hanging from the other, she collected her cane and headed for the classroom door. Maureen Evans had been conspicuous by her absence today, undoubtedly still reeling from Sully's meltdown this morning and she told herself again that she didn't miss the older teacher. She shut off the lights, closed the door, and headed for the elevator.

Downstairs, she paused to give a list of the rubrics she needed to the secretary before going to the Security office to apologize in person to Chief Wright. It wasn't his fault she'd been set up to make trouble for him. A stocky man in his mid-fifties with buzz-cut gray hair, he seemed more fit than other cops she'd met. He turned from the row of screens in front of him when she entered and nodded to her.

Sully smiled at him. "I'm taking off on time today. Thanks for sending Dak to tell me the hours for teachers here at the school. I'm sorry for the misunderstanding. Is there anything else I should know?"

"Not that I can think of." He winked at her. "Sorry if I got you in trouble for teasing Principal Ames about the guy Dak told me was your husband showing up to wait for you last Friday."

"Luckily, the principal didn't write me up for PDA," Sully retorted.

"How could he when I've seen steamier kisses between the students, and he doesn't give them detention?"

"Good point." Laughing, she left the room, limping toward the parking lot and the Mustang. She spotted a group of cheerleaders coming from the gym after practice and recognized Quinn's stepdaughter. Cressida hastily turned away before Sully lifted her hand to wave and she realized the girl wanted autonomy. Nobody in high school wanted to be related to a teacher, even one still learning the business.

When they'd spoken on the phone the previous afternoon, Sully agreed to pick up Cat at the dude ranch. Instead of stopping by the row of cabins bordering Cedar Creek, she drove up to the large three-story, wooden Victorian house with its towers, bay windows, and gingerbread trim. It wasn't her style, but then again other people might not like Craftsman bungalows either, although both she and Cat seemed to approve of wrap-around porches.

Sully parked in front of the house and spotted Cat coming toward her. Today, she wore a dark blue tank top under a navy-checked, man's flannel shirt and loose, faded jeans, hip-length copper hair neatly confined in a braid. Sully eyed the other woman, glimpsing the swelling of her stomach under the shirt as Cat opened the passenger door. "You're pregnant."

"Yup, I'm at the halfway point, four and a half months along." She slid into the seat, closing the door. "I thought you realized that the first time you and Tate Murphy rented one of my cabins."

"No, I think I was too wigged out by your claiming to see my B.F.F., Raven."

Cat nodded. "That makes sense. So, why do you want me to inspect your potential home?"

"It's more Tate's thing. He doesn't want to make an offer on the place if we have uninvited or unwanted ghostly guests."

"No worries. Let's go check it out."

They arrived at the farmhouse a short time before Dominique MacGillicudy. It gave them time to walk around the pastures, the barns, and other outbuildings. While they sat on the porch, waiting for the realtor, Cat said, "Nobody's here, at least not outside. Not every home has haunts."

"Good to know. Tate will be pleased."

"I can pass the word you'd prefer not to have spectral visitors." Cat rocked in one of the wooden deck chairs. "I have spooky friends like the local mayor who back me up. I'd rather not block Raven Driscoll-Barlow from coming to see you since she doesn't mean any harm."

"Is she here now?" Sully glanced at what appeared to be an empty, landscaped front yard. "I can't see her."

"She's not here. She went home with her husband after your wedding. It doesn't mean she won't be back to see you."

"Would it freak you out if I said it was okay if she came? We've been besties since we were little-bitty, and I miss her so much." Sully winced. "O.M.G., I sound like a total nutcase."

"Not in Baker City." Cat's voice softened. "We live with our loved ones regardless of whether they're alive or not."

The words remained in Sully's mind for the rest of the week. She and Tate discussed the house more than once while they waited to hear if their offer would be accepted. Dominique was the proverbial buyer's agent and said that the sellers wanted too much for the property, especially since they'd abandoned so many animals.

Maureen Evans was still out of sight and definitely out of mind when Sully graded papers on Thursday afternoon. This practicum was far different from the other two she'd completed. Then, she'd received regular guidance from experienced teachers, and she hadn't minded the fact that they were well-paid for their endeavors. She wondered if she could suggest to Dr. Dunaway that the university provide a discount for this student teaching endeavor when the supervisor arrived next week to do an observation.

Her cell phone buzzed. Sully viewed the screen and incoming text from Dominique. "Good news! They accepted your offer. When can we meet to finish the paperwork?"

First things first, Sully thought and texted Tate before she called the realtor. To her amazement, Dominique offered to meet them at the listing agent's office in Seattle on Saturday. "Why would you come so far south?"

"I like shopping in a real city, especially when I have a reasonable excuse," Dominique said. "And I love hanging out with Claire Rocklin, the broker who listed your new home. We were in the same sorority at the U-Dub. Meeting at her office makes sense since you and Tate will be at the Army base this weekend and I'd have to take the signed papers to her anyway."

"Okay. This all works for us." Sully glanced at the clock. "Hey, I've got to pack up and hit the road before Security has a major fit. I'm so glad we got the place and I know it will ease Tate's mind before he ships out again."

"I don't know how you manage the stress of being an Army spouse. You're a stronger woman than I am, *Gunga-Din.*"

Buoyed by the compliment and the knowledge that they had a home on the horizon, Sully gathered her things and headed downstairs. She'd keep the news about the farm to herself until she and Tate signed the final papers and then she'd start planning a huge party when he returned from training. Of course, the date depended on when they closed on the property. Her mind still on the upcoming festivities, she came to a stop in the doorway when the school secretary waved at her.

"Principal Ames wants to see you," Della Lowry said, gesturing to the administrative wing. "I'll watch your things if you care to leave them here for a few minutes."

"Thanks." Sully handed over her laptop and school bag. "I have a doctor's appointment tomorrow, so I'll see you next week."

"Don't count on making it," Della murmured. "He wants you here."

Appreciating the warning, Sully nodded, but didn't add the Army slogan about *'Want in one hand, defecate in the other and see which fills up first!'* There wasn't any point in offending her ally.

The principal wasn't alone. Maureen Evans sat in one of the chairs facing his large oak desk. Sully nodded to both and waited for the onslaught.

"Mrs. Evans tells me that you plan to take tomorrow and Monday off." A ruddy-faced, blond man in a pinstriped suit, Principal Ames looked Sully up and down. "You need to take this internship seriously."

Time to play the Army game of Last Word, Sully thought. *Let's see how many sir's I can throw into a sentence. There's more than one way to deal with an authoritarian asshat.*

"Sir, I've been teaching five classes a day for almost two weeks with minimal direction, sir, so I'd say I have been, sir." Sully leaned on the cane and met his pale blue gaze. "Sir, I have a doctor's appointment at Fort Clark tomorrow morning at oh-eight-hundred hours, sir and if I'm not there, sir, the Army will send the Military Police to bring me to the clinic, sir. Is that the sort of fuss you want, sir, at your school, sir?"

He blinked, then glanced at Maureen. "You should have changed it to a more reasonable timeframe."

"Really, sir? Did you serve in the military, sir?"

"No."

"Then, you may not realize they don't do *change*, sir. Officers issue orders, sir and subordinates obey those orders, sir. Doctors are officers, sir and they outrank me, sir. I cleared this with the Department Chair here at the high school, sir, just last week as well as my university supervisor, sir."

"You could see a local doctor and it wouldn't interfere with your teaching responsibilities."

Sully lifted her chin. "I could, sir, but since I was injured in combat, sir, I prefer to see a physician who knows how to treat injuries from an I.E.D., sir. That's an improvised exploding device, sir. I need an Army doctor, sir, not a civilian one, sir, who has never seen the results of a roadside bombing."

Another series of blinking while he obviously sought for words. "We weren't told you were—"

"That I was a soldier returning from combat, sir?" He was lying and all of them knew it, but she wouldn't say so. Instead, Sully held up her hand, barely flicking a glance at Maureen Evans. "Sir, I'm sure Dr. Dunaway told you this practicum had to start after I came back from Afghanistan, sir. She definitely shared it with Mrs. Evans, sir."

"All right, then." Principal Ames shifted in his seat behind the elaborate desk. "Tomorrow is a half-day and I certainly understand why you want to see your regular doctor. There's no reason for you to miss Monday's classes."

"Sir, my husband is an Army Ranger deploying for training and I'm taking him to the airport on Monday, sir." Sully reached in the back pocket of her slacks, pulled out her phone, and scrolled through the emails for the message from Dr. Dunaway. "I applied for permission from my supervisor to see him go, sir. I spoke to the Humanities Department Chair about it, sir, when she came to observe one of the classes on Tuesday, sir."

Maureen Evans stirred in the chair. "You didn't tell me Sandra Young visited my room then."

"If I'd seen you this week, I would have." Sully handed the phone to the principal so he could see the message from the university professor. Once he'd viewed it, she replaced the smartphone in her pocket again. "Now, I'm leaving, sir. If either of you have any further concerns about my performance, I suggest you contact Dr. Dunaway. Otherwise, I'll be back on Tuesday morning."

He worked late so he could go with Sully to the doctor the next morning and made a point of swinging by his favorite deli on the way to his aunt's and uncle's home. When he pulled in the drive, he spotted the bright pink Mustang. He saw her throwing a stuffed toy for Bo and Diddly and lingered to watch the three of them.

The pocket-sized monkey flew through the gray afternoon air and Bo leaped to catch it. His sister promptly tackled him, and puppy wars ensued until she had the six-inch, plush animal grasped firmly in her teeth. Tate laughed as he watched more collie races around the yard. Sully must have heard him because she turned and hurried to greet him.

Dropping her cane on the ground, she flung her arms around his neck and pulled his head down until their lips met. He kissed her with the same fierce intensity. Moments later, he lifted his mouth from hers. "You missed me."

"Wow, you're a smart man, Master Sergeant Murphy." Knocking off his hat, she tangled her fingers in his short hair and tugged hard. "It's been a long four days. Kiss me again, but like you mean it this time."

He laughed again, lifting her off her feet. "Don't I outrank you?"

"Pregnant women get horny." She nipped his lower lip. "Take me to bed. Now!"

"You don't have to tell me twice." He swung her up into his arms and strode toward the staircase to the garage apartment. "Anything else?"

"Kiss me, damn it!"

"I will until you beg me to stop." His lips claimed hers.

Afterward, she fell asleep in his arms. He held her until he was sure she wouldn't awaken when he slipped out of the bed. He pulled on his pants and a t-shirt, then went downstairs to unload her car and his truck, grateful it was cold enough that the deli salads and fried chicken hadn't spoiled during the wait in his rig.

Upstairs, he left her cane, suitcase, school bag, and laptop in the living room then went across the room to the kitchen. Before he stored the food in the fridge, he heard footsteps and glanced over his shoulder to see her in the entry, the purple bathrobe draped around her. "Ready for dinner?"

"Only if I get you for dessert."

He chuckled. "Who'd refuse an offer like that?"

"Not you." She hobbled toward him. "The only problem with being carried off to bed is trying to walk without my cane afterward."

He swiftly crossed the room, scooped her into his arms, and carried her to a chair at the table. "Wait here. I'll be right back."

Over a late supper, they talked about furnishing their new house. He'd contacted his mother and she'd promised to let Sully raid the attic at the family farm for tables, chairs, bookcases, dressers, and anything else she wanted. He told her about the weekend schedule and the Major's suggestion that she work on Friday after her doctor appointment and then she'd only have to put in a few hours on Saturday and Sunday.

"Did you have any trouble arranging to spend tomorrow and Monday here?"

"Not after I clouded up and rained all over Maureen Evans and Principal Ames." Sully dug into the potato salad. "I'm glad I listened to Margo Endicott and followed her advice to include my university supervisor so they couldn't chain me in the dungeon."

"Was it that bad?"

"Oh, once I had a major fit and fell in it, they backed off."

"I want to see another one of those tantrums." He reached in the carton of fried chicken for a second drumstick. "You're cute when you rant and rave."

"If you want to get lucky after dinner, you better stop being a sexist jerk."

He considered the recommendation, then shook his head. "Nope, not happening, Mrs. Murphy. Once I have my mouth on you, I'll get lucky anyway."

She blushed, her cheeks rosy. "You wish!"

"And you'll beg for more."

CHAPTER TWENTY-THREE

Monday afternoon, she struggled not to cry as she drove to Baker City. She wasn't in love with Master Sergeant Tate Murphy, was she? Of course not. He was immensely attractive, total eye candy even in camos and combat boots. Kinder than any man she'd ever known, more responsible, more thoughtful—

No wonder, she already missed him. She'd known from the start that he'd be leaving for Kentucky and four weeks of training before combat deployment. Yes, they were married, but only because she expected a baby. They'd bought a home together near his parents, again only because she was in what Gil Barlow called 'a delicate condition'.

They had a marriage of convenience, she told herself sternly, nothing more. It was convenient. He was convenient except when he abandoned her to do his duty and serve their country. Sure, she jumped his bones this last weekend. It was reciprocal. He'd hauled her off to bed a lot too. Of course, that was what caused this situation. She'd found him incredibly sexy and it didn't hurt that the man knew how to send her screaming through the rafters. She always figured Raven bragged about multiple orgasms with Kord which Sully informed her bestie was just icky. She didn't want to hear all those sex stories.

She'd warned Tate to be careful when they were at the gate waiting for his flight to be called. He'd better damn well come home safely to her or she'd kick his butt from here to Kentucky and back. He'd laughed and hugged her tight, promising he would. She couldn't face his family yet. Her so-called, stiff upper lip needed some work.

She turned off the highway at Cedar Creek Guest Ranch and drove to the cabin Margo Endicott rented. Sully spotted the Army officer sitting on the porch still wearing camo fatigues and combat boots. She parked the Mustang and went to join her. "Tate left today on the 0700 flight to Kentucky."

"And you already miss him?" Margo leaned back in the chair, gesturing to the bottle of wine on the small table between them. "I'll get you a glass."

"No, I'm pregnant. I may want booze, but I can't have it." Sully drew a deep, ragged breath and sat down. "I'm headed for the Murphy farm, but I can't put on my *party* face yet for Tate's family. If I walk in the door right now, I'll undoubtedly wail like a banshee."

"They'll understand. They love him too."

Managing to nod, Sully slumped into the Adirondack chair. She wouldn't say she loved him. She never lied, not to herself or other people. She wasn't sure how she felt about him, but the sex was out of this world. She certainly liked and respected the man, but she hadn't expected to miss him this much already. Love came with too high a cost especially since nobody ever stayed with her.

"What did you do this weekend?"

Remembering how often she'd dragged him off to bed, heat swept into Sully's face. She hoped the other woman didn't see it. "I worked in the Headquarters office catching up the word-processing after I saw the doctor about my leg. He wants me to start physical therapy this week in Lake Maynard and then see him in two weeks so he can check my progress. I have an appointment with the OB-GYN on the same day."

"That works." Margo sipped her wine. "How's school?"

"It sucks."

"Tell me about it."

"Do you really want to hear a *sitrep* about all the ways the high school reeks?"

"I wouldn't ask if I didn't." Margo stood. "Be right back. I have soda in the fridge. I'll bring you a ginger ale and some crackers. Then I won't feel guilty about drinking in front of you."

———

She was in the middle of grading vocabulary tests during prep period Tuesday afternoon when Quinn's oldest stepdaughter eased into the room. Sully smiled at the slender blonde in the short, red-pleated cheerleader skirt and red, monogrammed sweater. "Hi, how's it going?"

Cressida shrugged, glancing over her shoulder at the two girls in similar attire who followed her. "My stepmom couldn't get through on your cell last night and she wants you to call her, plus you're supposed to come to dinner tonight. She told us that she promised to take care of you for Uncle Tate and you'd probably be freaking out about him. Dad says we're all supposed to step up."

"I'll call and let her know I'm okay, but tonight might be tough. I'm starting physical therapy after school. Tate and I visited for a couple of hours when he got to the base but once his training starts, it'll be tough for us to connect." Sully shook her head ruefully. "The Army won't let him Skype and if it's like the training I've done, they'll limit when he can use his cell phone."

"I figured you'd be talking to him whenever you could since you two just got married." Cressida handed over three stapled pages and her friends did as well. "Quinn said you'd told her that you had to mark them down if we were late turning in the rewritten summaries, but we get a pass."

"It's in the handbook." Danielle, the curvaceous brunette next to her flipped the long, dark braid hanging down her back. "We get extensions on homework when we're cheering at a game."

"And our cheer coach said she'd email a list of names of the girls on our squad, so you'd know who we are." This time, Pamela, the other blonde spoke. "And then you can send our grades to her once a week for grade checks, so we aren't benched at the baseball games."

"All right, I'll follow up with her." Sully signed the pass that

Cressida gave her, and the trio trooped toward the door, chatting away as they headed back to their sixth-period class.

"I know other people do physical therapy after car wrecks, but Mrs. Murphy limps a lot," Pamela said, walking into the hall. "I didn't think she'd be ready for that."

"Your blonde is showing," Cressida informed her friend. "I guess you could call being hit by an I.E.D. in Afghanistan a car wreck, but I sure wouldn't. Where did you hear that?"

"Oh, my gawd, I like didn't have a clue. I was outside the teacher lounge waiting for Mr. Duffy and somebody inside said—"

"Well, you're not the only clueless one," Danielle said. "You just don't think of it being the teachers."

"Or of women being soldiers in combat," Cressida added. "Although since they're on TV all the time, a person would."

Their voices faded down the hall. Amused by the exchange between the teens, Sully returned to grading. Once she was alone, she checked messages on her cell phone and found several from Quinn. She texted her sister-in-law, letting her know Cressida had turned in her work and that dinner sounded lovely if she was up to it after physical therapy. Quinn promptly replied and reminded her not to overdo the exercises because of the baby.

Between teaching, physical therapy, dinner at Quinn's house, shopping for material for a baby quilt with her sister-in-law, and investigating the attic at the farm with her mother-in-law, the next two days flew by. On Friday morning, Dr. Dunaway arrived, ready for an initial observation. Instead of watching Sully teach one set of students, she ended up seeing all five classes since each one only lasted a half-hour.

Luckily, it wasn't one of the days when the kids had individual performances. Sully was reviewing their resubmitted short story summaries. She spent the first ten minutes going over the requirements according to the rubric, then used the document camera to showcase different papers she'd graded and finished by returning the assessed work to the students. They still had fifteen minutes to revise the summaries with their peer editors. It made for a chatty workshop environment, but they seemed to enjoy it, Sully thought as she circulated through the room and answered questions.

In Washington State History, she asked the students to form small groups. Then she passed out a quiz she'd designed for the seventh graders. She gave them ten minutes to work together to solve mysteries about the founders of Seattle. Granted, she already knew they wouldn't find the answers in their textbooks. It was why she'd asked the following questions determined to engage their interest in *real* history.

Who was a bigamist? Who measured Elliott Bay with a horseshoe and clothesline to see if the water was deep enough for sailing ships? Which noted pioneer married his sister? Oh, and did his younger brother do it too? Who saw to it that muddy potholes were filled with sawdust? Who were the Mercer Belles? Did a local legend inspire a popular TV show in the late 1960s and a song still played today? What woman made a fortune in what would now be considered an illegal profession, financed projects that local banks wouldn't, and left an estate to what became the King County school district?

When the time elapsed, they were completely baffled. Sully opened her copy of local historian, Bill Speidel's *Sons of the Profits* and proceeded to read his unorthodox, hilarious anecdotes to them. She began with her favorite line at the opening of the book, "I'm sure there must have been somebody who participated in the construction of Seattle without first determining whether there was a buck in it for himself, but this book isn't about him…"

She went on to tell the story about the Dennys, a known respected family in Seattle. The patriarch was a widower who'd married a widow with almost grown daughters and subsequently, his adult sons married their stepsisters. That brought groans and laughter from her class who were certainly familiar with blended families, but as one boy pointed out, there was no way he'd ever get together with his sis. "These people are gross."

"True," Sully agreed, "but so is history." She glanced at the classroom door when it opened and Maureen Evans entered, then continued with the lesson. "Real historians dig for the facts regardless of where it takes them. They record those facts. We don't have enough time today to continue with the saga of Asa Mercer, who served as the first president of the territorial university, and during the 1860s made two trips back to the northeastern states to recruit marriageable women to come to marry men in Seattle."

"Weren't there already women here?"

"Yes, and over the weekend, I want you to research what was happening in the 19th century. Why did local men pay Asa Mercer to travel back East?" Glancing at the clock, she realized she was almost out of time and closed her book. "You can use your smart devices to help find the answers and report back on Monday. For extra credit, watch an episode of *Here Come the Brides* and write a one-page summary of the plot, listing three historical inaccuracies."

The bell rang and the kids headed for the door, still discussing the subjects she'd raised. Sully waited until she was alone with the other adults before she glanced at the university supervisor. "I thought you intended to visit Thursdays and was sorry to miss you yesterday."

"I had a conflict this week," Leslie Dunaway said, "so I emailed Maureen and suggested today instead. I'd forgotten that Lake Maynard Middle High does half-day Fridays, but I enjoyed seeing your versatility and the way you're able to shift from one subject to another, Sullivan."

"Thank you." Sully eyed the professor warily, wondering if this was a civilian example of the Army tenet, *Praise in public, punish in private.* She didn't ask. Instead, she waited for the proverbial other shoe to drop.

Leslie turned slightly in her chair to include Maureen in the conversation. "I'm sure you want to share your impressions of how the internship is proceeding, so why don't you start? We'll address those concerns first. Tell me what you think of Sullivan's teaching."

"From what I've seen her skills in classroom management are seriously lacking."

"Really? How do you suggest we address that?"

Sully counted silently to ten, then twenty, then fifty as the two older women discussed her teaching. Maureen apparently hadn't heard of the *sandwich* technique of criticism the university espoused, starting with positive comments first, then listing problem areas, and finishing with more positive remarks. Her last statement had to do with the lack of daily lesson plans Sully provided.

"I see." Leslie Dunaway's professional smile didn't fade. "Sullivan, I realize you had all five classes today since it was a half-day, but what two periods are you currently teaching?"

"I teach four periods of English 7 and one period of Washington State History every day." Sully gestured to the agendas she'd written on the whiteboard for the students. "I can take a picture of that each morning and email it to Mrs. Evans."

"It's a very nice organizational tool for teenagers," Leslie commented. "However, it doesn't include all the requirements the university teaches you to use when you're planning a unit. I think you could create suitable weekly lesson plans according to our standard template and email all five of them to her no later than Sunday night, a set for the one English class you're supposed to teach and another set for Washington State History."

"Yes, ma'am." Sully struggled not to clench her fists, a giveaway she was seriously annoyed. "May I include all four English classes on one form? Or would you like separate lesson plans for each period?"

"I'm confused, Maureen. Why does Sullivan keep asking about all four English classes? This is her third week. When you and I set up the program, didn't we arrange for her to teach part-time until Lake Maynard's spring quarter starts in April?"

"She's only instructing two subjects and the seventh-grade English classes are very similar."

"I saw that." Leslie tapped a pen on her notebook. "Wouldn't some of your concerns about classroom management be alleviated by Sullivan observing other teachers and the way they handle their classes?"

More blather and Sully's irritation continued to mount. The conversation ended when Leslie ostentatiously looked at the large clock on the wall. "I have another student to observe and need to go to Liberty Valley. Sullivan, I'll email my suggestions to you, but I do expect to see those lesson plans Sunday night. When you send them to Maureen, send them to me as well."

"Yes, ma'am." Sully took a deep breath, determined to maintain control. "Should I remind you of my doctor appointment at the Army base next Friday too? He says I may get to wear two shoes although I still have to use a cane as an assistive device."

"That's a good idea. I'm glad you thought of it. Send me all the dates. You'll have some seminars to complete at the Cascadia University campus down south when the students here are out on spring break the first week of April, so arrange your schedule accordingly. I'll forward the times to you and Maureen, so she'll know when you won't be here because they start next Thursday, the last one in March. We'll do your mid-term evaluation next Wednesday."

Sully gaped at her supervisor for a moment, relishing the idea of escaping from the high school for a week and a half. Realizing the professor waited for a response, she hastily nodded in agreement. "Yes, ma'am."

Leslie stood and started for the door, then paused. "Oh, one more thing, Maureen. Since Sullivan has just completed her third week of teaching full-time, her internship here understandably will be shorter. She'll finish the second Monday in May, rather than the middle of June when your school year ends."

Maureen sputtered and hustled after the university professor leaving Sully alone in the classroom to do a mental *happy dance* since she couldn't do a physical one. She silently vowed not to share the news with anyone else until she had the opportunity to speak to Tate. Crossing to the counter at the back of the room, she paused by the bins where the students turned in their assignments and collected their papers. Yes, she'd spend the weekend grading them, but her time at Lake Maynard Middle High was winding down faster than she'd expected.

Pages tucked neatly in her school bag, she removed the package of store-bought cookies she'd purchased at the Baker City Mercantile for the teacher potluck lunch this Friday. Bronwyn Murphy had offered to bake a dessert for Sully to bring, but she'd gently turned down the older woman. Why should either of them waste their time after their efforts had gone unappreciated two weeks ago?

When she reached Sandra Young's room, Sully heard Maureen Evans complaining to the department chair about Dr. Dunaway's decision. *What goes around, comes around,* Sully thought and softly closed the door to wait out in the hall until the sniveling stopped. Pulling out her phone, she texted the good news to Tate. She'd swing by Cedar Creek Guest Ranch on the weekend and let Margo Endicott know the culmination of the practicum was in sight.

Six weeks to go! I see a light at the end of the tunnel and now I know it's not an oncoming train.

Three hours later, she arrived at the Murphy home to find an empty house. A detailed note in the kitchen said Bronwyn and Joe had taken the girls with them to Liberty Valley to do various errands. Lock had a meeting with some other farmers at the Grange Hall, but everyone would be home around supper time. Bronwyn planned to bring back Chinese food, so Sully didn't have to prepare anything. Instead, why didn't she take a nap?

"I'm a grown woman and I can do whatever I want," Sully informed the sheet of paper on the kitchen table. That decided, she grabbed a ginger ale from the fridge and a bag of potato chips out of the pantry. She headed for the family room, picked up the remote, and turned on *Judge Judy* for a dose of daily snark. Wow, she missed hearing the *Goddess in a Black Robe* giving hell to stupid people but long days teaching full-time meant she always missed the legal reality show.

She curled up on the couch, content in the solitude. *A week after Cinco de Mayo, I'll be partying hearty and able to start a full-time teaching position. I can't wait.*

CHAPTER TWENTY-FOUR

Other than a few texts and one email with a selfie of him in camo face paint, she hadn't heard from Tate in days. It shouldn't be a surprise. He'd said he'd be in the field training for combat during his last call. Waves of disappointment still swept over her every time she thought about it.

She missed him, even though she repeatedly reminded herself that she didn't. They had a marriage of convenience, strictly for their baby who needed two responsible parents. And everything else was the 'friends with benefits' cliché that had become acceptable. But, wow she really missed him!

She limited herself to three emails a day, sending one in the morning, one during her prep, and one after dinner. Okay, he was in the field. He was training. He was busy. He probably didn't even have his phone. He was her husband, her new husband, damn it. If he got his cell, he could at least send an emoji. She'd tell him what a terrible job he was doing as a military spouse.

No, she wouldn't. She had his six. She'd 'woman up' and wait for him even if she thought about sending out the Red Cross to find him at least twice a day. She really missed having him hold her in bed. He was always so tender, stroking her hair, kissing her softly, making her feel like she mattered.

Meanwhile, his family did their best to make her feel as if she belonged, as if she were a *real* Murphy, not a *jill come lately*. Bronwyn always had time to talk when she cooked supper, or when they worked together in the greenhouse. Joe told Sully stories about Tate when he was growing up. Lock usually popped into the garage to visit when she was working on the Mustang. The girls helped her organize the furniture she wanted for the farmhouse she and Tate bought. If everything went as planned, they'd close on the house at the end of April. She'd move in immediately after the internship ended. It might even happen before he came home from training.

On Sunday afternoon, she took time to drive over to see Margo Endicott at Cedar Creek Guest Ranch. Invited inside, Sully glanced around the small kitchen and watched the other woman clean and trim carrots, preparing to ride one of Cat McTavish's horses.

"Talk to me about teaching," Margo said. "I miss it more than you know."

"I love being back in the classroom, although I will admit my so-called mentor is a walking irritation. My university professor came to do an observation last Friday. She says since I'm teaching full-time, she's moving up my mid-term evaluation."

"To when?"

"Next Wednesday. On Thursday, I go to the university and start a week's worth of seminars while the students are on spring break."

"Whose idea was that?" Margo dropped the moldy tip of a long, skinny carrot in the trash. "It's smart. When I did my last internship back in the day, the school lined up one crappy job after another over Christmas break and I certainly didn't get to enjoy the time off, much less visit my family back East for the holidays. Ann still complains about the stunts her mentor teacher pulled."

"Wow, I thought I was the only one." Sully drew out a chair at the kitchen table and sat down. "I guess I shouldn't pitch a fit about having to write up lesson plans and email them to Dr. Dunaway and Maureen Evans tonight."

"O.M.G. is she your mentor? Ann used to gripe about her big-time. The woman has no clue about collaborative teaching or teamwork with the other English teachers. If she didn't have tenure, she'd be out on her butt." Margo finished up the last of the carrots and started chopping apples. "Talk to me about the lesson template you'll use."

Over the next hour, Sully listened to the other woman's advice including using the time at department meetings to grade papers, creating a master lesson plan for each class to adjust for the different assignments, continuing to enter grades at the last possible moment, and never volunteering for extra duties. Before she left, Margo told her to ask about being paid to teach full-time after a successful mid-term since she already had her Washington State emergency certification for Liberty Valley and it'd only need to be extended to include the Lake Maynard district.

She kept the words of wisdom in mind as she taught Monday and Tuesday. She asked Maureen Evans about completing the mid-term evaluation forms before Dr. Dunaway's return on Wednesday, but the older teacher refused. She said the three of them would do the paperwork after the professor observed a class on Wednesday. Unsure whether Maureen had shared that decision with Leslie Dunaway, Sully emailed her university supervisor. A detailed response arrived in her inbox a short time later and she followed directions for the self-evaluation portion of the forms.

The cell phone buzzed. She pulled it from her jacket pocket and looked at the screen for the caller's name. Tate!

At long last, it was finally him!

"I've missed you so much," Sully said. "Talk to me, Master Sergeant Hot Stuff. How was the field exercise?"

"No worries. We aced it." He chuckled. "I miss you too. We're back in the barracks now and I had time to call before chow. How are you? Not overdoing the physical therapy?"

"I'm only going for an hour after school two days a week. I'll miss the next few sessions because I'm headed to our apartment at your aunt's after my mid-term tomorrow. The kids leave on spring break Friday and I'm supposed to do a ton of seminars at the university starting Thursday."

"Sounds fun."

"I'll let you know what happens." She leaned back in the chair. "Now, entertain me. Tell me all about what you're doing. Loved the warrior pic you sent."

"Thought you would." He chuckled and proceeded to share anecdotes about night marches, ambushes, and bivouacking in the rain.

She didn't want to be overheard discussing the baby so when he asked again about the therapy routine, she told him about the easy exercises the therapist chose, keeping the pregnancy in mind. "I ride an exercise bike for ten minutes, do stretches, climb up and down on a wooden box while holding onto a counter. My favorite part is when I finish with my leg elevated, wrapped up in an icy bandage with mini electrodes attached. The therapist says it stimulates my nerves, but I generally doze off for a few minutes."

"Mom said she encourages you to take naps, but you always refuse."

"If she's ratting me out, the least she could do is tell you I fall asleep in front of Judge Judy whenever I get the chance."

He laughed. "Yeah, I heard about that. What about Quinn? Are you two shopping for the house yet? Remember we're buying a crib together. One of the other noncoms gave me a list of what we need in the nursery, bassinets, changing tables, rocking chairs, the works. Whenever I have time, I go online and look at baby furniture."

"Stop that." Sully glanced at the classroom door as it opened, and Maureen Evans entered. "Focus on your training, Murphy. I'll send you pics of what your mom is giving us. We'll buy everything else when you get home in two weeks before you ship out to Afghanistan."

"Don't stress about me. I'm fine."

"Hoo-rah! And if I believe that, Master Sergeant Hot Stuff, you'll give me some other Bravo Sierra. Now, suck it up and drive on."

"I will when you do. Tell me you love me."

She took a deep breath, thought about their audience, looked at Maureen, and said, "Of course, I do. Promise you'll be careful. Stay alert and alive. I'll lose it if something happens to you."

"No, you won't. I'm counting on you to *drive on* too, sweetheart."

She repeated his words. "I will if you do."

"You got it."

"Wait a minute while I get some privacy, Murphy." Ignoring Maureen's huge sigh, Sully rose to her feet, picked up her cane, and headed for the hallway. She closed the door behind her leaving the older teacher in the classroom. "Now, I can say it. Are you sure you want to hear it?"

"You sign your emails with the word, Mrs. Murphy."

"You got them? Why didn't you answer?"

"Because I didn't get them until an hour ago. You filled up my inbox."

She laughed, leaned against the wall. "Serves you right. I'm so lonely without you."

"Because you love me."

"Yes, I love you. Now, be careful, damn it and come back to me soon."

The bell signaling the end of school rang cutting off his reply and students began to rush toward her. She ended the call, clinging to the phone a few more minutes, then re-entered the classroom. She focused on Maureen Evans. "Did you need something?"

"Personal calls are—"

"Stop, just stop." Sully tucked the phone into her blazer pocket, gathered up the paperwork on top of the desk, and slipped it inside the canvas tote. She stood, slung the straps of her laptop bag and school bag on her shoulder. "I don't know why you have the overwhelming need to abuse me when I've done nothing to deserve it, but I've told you before my husband is an Army Ranger away for combat training and I'll talk to him whenever he's able to call."

Maureen sniffed. "This school has rules."

"And I'm not breaking them." Sully collected her cane and limped toward the door. "I can't believe that with a country being at war for almost twenty years that you, the school administration, or Lake Maynard district have issues with me talking to my husband during prep period. He didn't call during class-time, didn't interrupt when the students were here and after your rant about me kissing him three weeks ago, I had to go into the hallway to tell him I loved him. I knew you'd use it against me. Save your Bravo Sierra for someone else. I'm going home."

"It's barely two o'clock."

"Too bad, too sad. As the song goes, my give-a-damn's busted." Sully headed down the hall, blinking back her tears. Once she was in the elevator, she sent off a series of quick texts to Dr. Dunaway, explaining the situation. Sully was signing out in the office when her phone rang. She pulled it out of her bag and answered.

"Sullivan, are you all right?" Leslie Dunaway demanded.

"No," Sully drew a ragged breath. "Tate's been in the field for training for almost a week. No phones allowed and he finally called me today and—"

"I read your texts. I just need you to hold on for one more day and then you'll be here at the college with us. Can you do that for me?"

"Yes." A tear slid down Sully's cheek, followed by a second, then a third. "I'm so scared for him and he hasn't even gone to Afghanistan yet."

"But you didn't share that with him?"

"Of course not. He needs me to step up, not whine at him." Sully accepted the tissue the school secretary offered, managing a grateful smile in Della's direction, then continued to talk to the college professor. "I'm sorry. I shouldn't dump on you."

"You never have. Now, go home and finish your evaluation. Cut yourself some slack. This is undoubtedly because you lost Raven the last time you were overseas."

"I hadn't put those facts together. I know better than anyone that soldiers die every day and I'm not ready to lose somebody else I love." Sully wiped her cheeks with the tissue. "Thank you, Doctor. I'll see you tomorrow."

Della Lowry narrowed her gaze and waited until Sully put away the cell phone. "Talk to me. How is your husband?"

"He's fine. I just lost it for a few minutes when I caught hell because he called as soon as he got back to the barracks from the field." Sully adjusted the shoulder straps. "It's tough living in *The World* after being in the *sandpit* for so long. I'm not accustomed to all this civilian…" She paused, seeking an appropriate word. "…rigmarole."

"Good that he touched base with you."

"Yes, I'd have kicked his gorgeous backside from Kentucky to Washington State and back again if he hadn't." Smiling, Sully started for the front doors and the parking lot. Behind her, she heard Della's soft laughter. When Sully flashed a glance over her shoulder, she saw the older woman heading toward the administrative offices.

He'd pushed too hard and he knew better. He shoved the cell phone in the pocket of his fatigue pants, glaring around the small room he shared with another sergeant. He should have waited until he was home in two weeks to convince her it was safe to say the *real* words he wanted to hear. Yes, she'd said she loved him, but she hadn't said she was in love with him. Granted, she probably wanted to hear that from him first.

This was undoubtedly payback for all the women he'd dated over the years when he'd never shared his feelings. Of course, he hadn't been that emotionally involved with the groupies who shared his bed, any more than they were with him. Sully had intrigued him from the start. Well, maybe not a hundred percent, but when she vanished like smoke after their night together and he couldn't find her, he'd been hooked. The baby was icing on the proverbial cake. They were his and he'd get the words he wanted to hear out of Sully before he left for Afghanistan.

"Hey, Murphy. Let's march these guys to dinner before the DFAC gives us up for lost, strayed, or stolen." His roommate, Aaron Reeves, the other ranking noncom stood in the doorway. "How's your wife? Mine said to tell you to line up a laundry service for diapers."

Tate chuckled. "And mine said to focus more on training and less on shopping."

"Whoa. That's different." His buddy sauntered inside, a thin African-American buttoning his camo fatigue shirt. "I don't remember anybody else's wife saying that. My brother could use a gal like that. She have a sister?"

"Not anymore. Raven died on their last go-round in the *sandpit.*"

"No wonder yours wants you to focus." Aaron closed the door behind them and snapped the padlock in the hasp. "Well, send her the link of the baby furniture you like at that store near your new home. Even if she's telling you to *soldier on*, she'll still want to see what you have in mind."

Tate considered the idea as they walked through the barracks gesturing for other, lower-ranking soldiers to join them. "Tell you what. I'll send the link to my twin sis, and she can take Sully shopping. It'll distract her from the crapfest where she's student teaching."

"Now, you're rocking and rolling."

She'd barely sat in the driver's seat of the Mustang when her phone buzzed, and she recognized Quinn's number. "Hi, what's happening?"

"That's my question. Tate texted me and said I'm supposed to take you to the outlet mall to see the nursery bedroom set he wants for the baby. If you agree, he'll arrange to have it delivered when you two close on the house in a couple of weeks."

"O.M.G., does that man ever listen? I told him to think about training, not baby stuff."

"Yeah, like that's gonna happen. Where and when do you want to meet? I'm at my salon in Lake Maynard. Come get me and we'll shop, then have dinner and you can snivel at me about your rotten husband and I'll agree with you about my evil brother."

"He's not rotten." Sully slid the key in the ignition and started the car. "Okay, I'm on my way, but aren't you supposed to be home tonight? I thought you told me Lyle did some business thing on Tuesday nights."

"I already called him and told him to take care of the kids, fix them supper, do the homework hour with them, and make sure they do their chores. Cressy is on laundry detail. Letty has vacuuming and dusting while Finn loads the dishwasher and cleans up the kitchen after supper."

"How does Lyle feel about that?"

"Considering what he's told me about babies and how we can't have one, he'd better not say a word. Are you coming? Or do I have to call Tate and tell him you bailed on me?"

"I'm on my way." Smiling, Sully hit the button to finish the call. She glanced over her shoulder and backed carefully out of the assigned spot, then drove toward the exit. She glimpsed some of her students headed toward the buses and waved cheerfully at them.

When she reached the strip mall, she parked in front of the salon and went inside. She found Quinn chatting with the receptionist. "I need to call your mom and tell her I won't be there for supper."

"Already done. We're hanging out and waiting for her to go with us. She says you need a grandma's opinion."

"Okay, but we're not telling my mom until after we've made a decision." Sully crossed to the waiting area and sat down, picking up a magazine. "Then, I'll send her pictures."

"Works for me."

The next morning when she walked into the classroom, Sully found Cressida Chapman in the usual short skirt and sweater, make-up perfect obviously watching and waiting. For once, the teen didn't have an entourage of other cheerleaders. Putting down her bags on the desk, Sully crossed to the whiteboard and picked up a black dry-erase pen. "What's going on, Cressy? Where's Mrs. Evans?"

"She went to get coffee when I told her it was an emergency and I had to talk to you." Cressida wrapped a strand of blonde hair around a finger. "What's happening with Quinn? When she got home last night, she said she was going to her Aunt Heidi's next week and she told Dad he had to step up more 'cause she had to do stuff for Uncle Tate. They are so tight. It's just kinky."

Smiling, Sully began posting the daily agenda on the board. "Nothing kinky about it, darling girl. The two of them shared a womb for nine months."

"Ooh, gross!"

"Come on, Cressy." Sully laughed. "You're smart. You know about babies, don't you? Historically, people used to think twins shared the same soul. I don't know if I'd go that far, but Tate and Quinn will always be closer than most brothers and sisters."

"Yeah, but next week is spring break and I have plans. Dad says I have to be in charge of the house and look after my sibs 'cause Quinn won't be around and I don't wanna. The squad is doing a cheer camp at the middle school and Letty's going to horse camp." Cressida stopped, her face paling and she hastily covered her mouth with a hand. "It's a secret. Quinn said not to tell Letty takes lessons. I wasn't supposed to—"

"It's okay." Sully put the pen in the tray and hurried to the teenager, patting her shoulder. "I know your grandmother has issues. I've already stepped on her toes when I said she should let Chantrea learn to ride. Most girls go through a horsey stage and so do some guys. What are Finn's plans?"

"He's signed up for a church adventure camp. It sounds really preachy, but it isn't. They barely talk about God. Mostly the guys ride around on ATVs, swing from ropes, swim, and do a bunch of outdoor stuff. He's super excited, but Quinn told Dad we don't need her. And we do. She always takes us places and listens to everything we do and packs our lunches and fixes us breakfast and yells at us when we screw up and makes sure we do our chores and—"

"You love her, and you'll miss her. Have you told her that?"

"Not all the time, but she has to know."

"How does she if you don't say it?" Sully hugged the girl, a quick sideways *teacher* embrace. "How long have she and your dad been together?"

"Six years, ever since I was seven if you count them dating and her living with us before they got married. And I do. When we visit her, my mom doesn't do half the things Quinn does all the time. She's the one who always volunteers when my cheer coach needs help and it's not just me. Quinn does as much for everybody else, even the techs at the salons. Do you really think she doesn't know how much we love her?"

Sully nodded. "She adores you, Letty, Finn, and your dad. Otherwise, she wouldn't stay with a guy who doesn't want more kids when she always dreamed of having a big family."

"Is that why we don't have more sibs? My mom said Quinn and Dad would be popping out babies all over the place, but they haven't. Is it because my dad is a big, selfish jerk?"

"I wouldn't say that."

"Well, I am." Cressida planted her fists on her hips in a dramatic cheerleader move. "Okay, if Quinn wants a baby, I'm going to see to it that she gets one."

"Be careful what you wish for, Cressy. Twins run in families and apparently there are quite a few in Baker City. You may have two more little sisters or brothers."

"That's all right. We have lots of room in our house and besides

Letty and Finn will have to do more babysitting than I will. I'm going to college in five years and Quinn isn't getting any younger. She needs to get started. So does Dad."

CHAPTER TWENTY-FIVE

The first two periods zoomed by and before she knew it, Octavia Butler, the teen TA arrived and was taking attendance while the students completed their entry task, a written response on what qualities made someone a hero. Sully circulated through the room, ready to stamp pages in their composition books. The classroom door opened, and Principal Ames entered, accompanied by Maureen Evans.

He strolled toward Sully, pausing beside her. "I'm here to observe the class."

"Very well. We're about to do a student-led Socratic Seminar on heroes and if Odysseus should be considered one during his dealings with the Cyclops, Polyphemus."

"You didn't ask me if this was a suitable activity for these students," Maureen commented. "I'd have told you it's too advanced for them and they've never done that type of seminar before. They've barely managed to behave appropriately during class discussions."

Trying not to reveal her instant annoyance, Sully pasted on what she hoped was a professional smile. Keeping her voice low, she addressed the two adults, not the teens, although she knew some would overhear and share her comment later with their peers. "When I sent you this week's lesson plans on Sunday night, I addressed potential issues. We've had two days to prepare, so I think you'll be amazed at how well they do."

"Do you have another copy of the lesson plan and what you're attempting to teach?" Principal Ames asked.

"Certainly." Sully returned to her desk and removed a copy of the day's plan for the English classes from her notebook and handed it to him. Then, she went to the front of the room and raised her hand, waiting for attention. Once she had it, she asked the students to move their desks into a large circle.

When they had, she told them to open their books to the assigned chapter while she reviewed her expectations. "This is a student-led, group discussion about the ideas in the text. Don't use this opportunity to promote your opinions or prove an argument. Practice listening to each other, make solid meanings, and find common ground while you participate in our conversation."

"In other words, we get points for talking," a dark-haired boy in camo pants and a black t-shirt announced. "This is great. I always have a lot to say."

"Only if you're on topic, Tim Garvey." Smiling, Sully gestured to the student TA for third period. "Now, it's your turn, Octavia. Are you ready to record our speakers?"

"I've got your scoresheet right here, Mrs. Murphy." Octavia gave the seventh-graders a stern look. "Remember the rules. If you have an original statement and cite evidence, it's five points. If you elaborate or piggy-back on somebody else's comment, it's three points. If you just agree or disagree without citing a line from the book, it's one point. If you interrupt or are rude to someone, I take off points."

"Any clarifying questions?" When she didn't see any hands raised, Sully went to the first question on her stack of index cards. "What do you think this text means?"

It took a moment or two while the students eyed each other, then Tim said, "Don't piss off a Cyclops or you'll be lunch. Oh, and my evidence is when Polyphemus tells Odysseus that he'll eat him last."

"It totally breaks the rules of *guest-friendship*." Cressida went on to list some of the traits they'd found in previous episodes in the text. "The host is supposed to provide food and drink to the guest, not eat him or his men and Polyphemus forgot all about being hospitable."

"Yeah, but you could say that Odysseus and his crew broke the rules first. They went into the Cyclops' home and ripped him off when they stole his meat, cheese, oil and wine," Danielle pointed out. "I don't think it was necessary for him to be blinded. No wonder he begged his father, Poseidon to punish Odysseus who was totally bragging about what they'd done."

The discussion continued for the rest of the hour with Sully asking guided questions whenever student interest faded or seemed sidetracked. Five minutes before the end of the period, she had them replace their chairs in the assigned positions and handed out large, printed notecards.

"Now, I want you to answer two questions. First, what did you think of your first seminar? Second, how did it go? Finally, rate your specific performance on a scale from one to five. Be sure to sign your name so you get credit for today."

Standing by the door, she collected the cards as the students left the room, still arguing about what kind of person serves up a guest for dinner. She laughed when she heard Tim Garvey suggest *Hannibal Lecter.* Turning, she accepted the scoresheet Octavia offered on her way out of the room.

"Well, that was interesting." Principal Ames nodded to Sully, sauntering toward the hall. "I'll email my feedback to you. I'll look forward to observing when you actually teach a class."

Sully counted silently to ten, then twenty so she managed to sound calm and in control, grateful her lesson plan template from the university had a spot for justifying the reasoning for the class she'd designed. "Data has shown American industries are seeking employees capable of critical thinking skills. Correctly used, the Socratic Method is one way to encourage student engagement in the process of analyzing literature, pushing them past comprehension to reflection and introspection. I believe this class did a very credible job for their first seminar. Through practice, their skills will improve until they can fully utilize the methodology."

"Intriguing viewpoint." Principal Ames left the room, accompanied by Maureen Evans.

Sully took a deep breath, struggling to swallow the lump in her throat. *Damn them,* she thought, battling the urge to cry. Now, she had to eat lunch and prepare to do another seminar in front of Leslie Dunaway and hope it progressed as successfully as those in the previous three periods since her university supervisor would be filming the class discussion. *Bathroom first, then food.*

Almost three hours later, she sat down with the university professor and mentor teacher to hear their remarks about the seminar in the 4th period English class and the reports on outside sources from the Washington State History students. In addition, they needed to complete her mid-term evaluation.

"Let's talk about time management. We have approximately an hour to discuss the classes that Sullivan taught and do her mid-term." Leslie Dunaway gestured to the outsize clock on the wall. "How long do you think it will take to complete the evaluation? Sullivan sent me her section yesterday when she forwarded it to you, Maureen."

"I skimmed it last night. She certainly has a high opinion of herself and her abilities."

"From what I saw today, her teaching skills have improved in the past week. I wasn't sure about your decision to throw her in at the deep end of the pond and see if she'd swim or drown, but it certainly has forced her to do more than dog-paddle." Unsmiling, Leslie tapped a pen on the desk. "Of course, it isn't what the university likes to see their student teachers do, but Sullivan has certainly done her best to meet the challenge of teaching full-time with minimal mentoring or preparation."

Sully straightened in her chair and watched the two older women verbally spar. She hadn't expected that much support from her college supervisor, but obviously she should have. When Maureen complained about the use of the Socratic Seminar, Leslie said it was a technique the university encouraged their education cohorts to utilize instead of the traditional class discussion format and she felt it'd been appropriate for the material, time, and middle-school students.

Maureen continued to vent about the use of outside materials in the history class, saying that for years the school depended on the assigned textbooks. Leslie pointed out that if there was an issue, the time to bring it up was when Sullivan sent in lesson plans on Sunday night, not three days later. Neither woman could pitch a fit about student behavior because the teens had been on task and totally engaged in the learning process during the two periods.

Sully counted herself lucky on that point. They were kids and things changed with them hour by hour, minute by minute, and often second by second. However, the sniping between the other two women didn't cease as they worked through the university mid-term rubric, scoring her performance in a variety of ways. She'd rated herself highly on preparing materials and presenting them to the students. She'd been more critical about the lesson plans and forwarding them to Maureen and Leslie because that was a new addition.

When she gave herself credit for grading their assignments and posting those scores in the online grade book in a timely manner, Maureen pitched another fit. "Student grades are slipping since Sullivan took over the classes. She'll need to contact parents by Friday and let them know their children will be failing English and History since we only have a week until the end of the quarter when they return from spring break."

"Why do you think that's happened, Sullivan?"

Sully eyed the university professor. "I can only grade what the students turn in and several have missing assignments or projects from earlier in the quarter. It didn't matter until I started entering grades throughout the past four weeks. Now, that I've posted all the scores, the chickens are coming home to roost. Those who haven't submitted any work are seeing zeros where their peers have points and the average class scores show that."

"Makes sense," Leslie nodded. "What is the failure rate for these five classes?"

"Anywhere from ten to fifty percent," Maureen announced gleefully, "which is why she shouldn't get credit for student achievements this quarter."

"Really? And what was the failure rate before Sullivan arrived at the beginning of this month?"

That question silenced the mentor teacher and Sully pulled up the reports on her laptop. "Anywhere from twenty-five to seventy-five percent across the board."

"I'd say we have a marked improvement during this past month. Sullivan, while Maureen and I finish her portion of the mid-term, would you please create a blanket email to forward to the parents of the students in academic jeopardy? After we approve it, then you can send it before you leave today. If they have any questions, the parents will be able to contact Maureen by phone or email so include her contact information. We need to remember that this is her room, her students and she will be responsible for their achievements this year."

"Yes, ma'am."

"After all, she's going to take over again when you finish in May."

"Yes, ma'am." Sully suppressed the urge to jump up and down and cheer. It was wonderful having the university supervisor as an ally. "By the way, will I be able to apply for an extension on my emergency teaching certification, so it includes the Lake Maynard school district once we complete the mid-term? Then I'll get paid when Mrs. Evans is out of the room and I'm the acting teacher?"

"That's the standard for student teachers," Leslie agreed. "We'll see how it goes."

While Maureen Evans squawked in protest, Sully focused on the laptop screen. Oh yeah, she could so do a *happy dance* right here and now. '*Suck eggs, you witch!*'

After they completed the forms and the blanket email was sent to parents, Sully left the school with Leslie Dunaway. They headed to a nearby coffee shop where they discussed the remainder of the practicum and arranged dates for continued observations as well as the final evaluation. Although Leslie didn't offer an apology for the internship, she'd arranged with such a control freak of a so-called, mentor teacher, she did provide more strategies for dealing with the situation.

On her way home, Sully decided she should get a special award for listening to the advice and not throwing a temper tantrum. She turned off the highway into the driveway at Cedar Creek Guest Ranch and headed for Margo Endicott's cabin. The officer must have arrived home a short while before since she was sitting on the porch, still wearing fatigues and combat boots.

Sully parked next to an older Ford Taurus and approached the steps. "How's it going?"

"It's going." Margo rocked in her chair and called over her

shoulder into the house. "Ann, we have company. Bring Sully one of those ginger ales in the fridge."

"We have more glasses and I'll share the wine." Ann Barrett, a curvaceous brunette in camos and boots strode out of the cabin. "It was almost a *need a man* moment, but then I opened the bottle myself."

Sully laughed and sat down in the Adirondack chair, taking the soda Ann offered. "Glad you made it home. Let me know if you need help with Army finance."

"I've got it covered," Ann said, amusement glittering in her leaf-green eyes, pulling up another chair. "No worries. I graduated at the top of my class. Margo says you're doing your last student teaching stint with the *wannabe*, Wicked Witch of Lake Maynard. Wow, I hate that woman. Tell me about it."

"Only if you tell me about your Army school." Sully twisted the cap off the bottle and sipped the ice-cold soda. "I did my mid-term today and she lowballed my scores, but I passed anyway. She tried to blame me because many of the kids are failing English and Washington State History. I only started a few weeks ago."

"What did your supervisor suggest?" Margo sipped her wine while continuing to rock in her chair. "I'm sure she had ideas."

"Well, she didn't believe her, so she had me send out a blanket email to the parents of the seventh-graders in academic jeopardy explaining what assignments their kiddoes need to do to pass this quarter. I'm covered and I'm out of there for a week and a half until spring break ends."

Margo and Ann exchanged glances and then the officer spoke. "I think she needs your *C.Y.A.* letter."

"Sounds like it to me. What's your email address? I'll send a sample to you and then you can revise it for your students."

"What's a *C.Y.A.* letter?"

"Pretty simple." Ann poured more wine into her glass. "It's a letter each student writes, then takes home to Mom or Dad. After the parents read it, they sign off and the kid brings it back. I always gave it 10 points credit in the online grade book, so I'd be sure to have all the letters returned before grades went out."

"How does it work?"

"On the Monday after spring break, you use the document camera and post the sample on the screen. The kids write the letter on a blank sheet of paper. They begin by addressing it to their parents or guardians and tell them what their expected grade is for your class. If there's a lot of behavior issues, I generally make them add a line about being a credit to family expectations."

"In my case, should I have them say they are a credit to Mrs. Evan's teaching this quarter and Lake Maynard Middle High? I've barely had them for a month."

"I would," Margo said. "That's why we call it a *C.Y.A.* letter. You're covering your butt. Keep going, Ann."

"That's the first paragraph. In the second one, they list three reasons why they earned the grade they did. They say things like not completing assignments or turning them in late or not being a team player or disrupting the class or not working up to their capabilities. Your students are probably like mine were. They know the buzzwords."

"Better than most adults, teachers, and administrators, I'll bet," Sully said.

"Undoubtedly. In the last paragraph, they tell the parents what they expect to earn for a semester grade and three ways they'll achieve their goal. They finish by signing the letter and leaving space for their parents to comment." Ann laughed. "Back in the day, I had a drama diva who felt the letter was a waste of time and energy because she was an *A* student so she wrote that she expected to fail my class at the end of the school year."

"O.M.G., are you serious?"

"Yeah, so I told her she should rewrite it and she refused. She took it home. Her mother read it and wrote in the feedback section that if she expected to have a life, she'd better make wiser choices. Otherwise, her dad would have a major fit and she'd be in summer school."

"So, did she get points for the letter?" Sully asked.

"Oh, sure. She did her part, her mom did hers, and it all worked out great. She actually had an *A*+ that June."

"The letter sounds do-able." Sully leaned back in the chair. "I really appreciate all the advice from the two of you. This must be the worst practicum I've ever endured. So, when do you start as the unit clerk or Active Guard-Reserve for our company, Ann?"

Another long look between the other women and then Ann said, "I don't. Army Reserve HQ back East chose a man for the job. He's arranged for me to work at the base until I get a different full-time position and I'm trying to make his life a living hell."

Sully shook her head ruefully. "Is that really fair when he undoubtedly didn't know you wanted the position?"

"Too bad, too sad. He's going down in flames, but he doesn't fight fair!"

"What does that mean?"

Margo laughed. "She barely admits it, but she thinks he's hot."

"Do not!"

"Do too!"

PART III

APRIL 2019

CHAPTER TWENTY-SIX

The university seminars for her teaching cohort didn't start until late Thursday afternoon, so Sully waited until after the morning rush-hour traffic subsided to drive south. She arrived shortly after lunch, early enough to visit the apartment first and unpack the Mustang, putting the food Bronwyn sent in the fridge. Then, Sully took the rest of the fresh veggies from the greenhouse to Heidi.

"It's good to see you." Heidi greeted her with a hug while the collies swirled around them, tails wagging. "How is the student teaching going? Come have a cup of tea and tell me all about it. I'm excited Quinn is coming to visit for a few days. She's always so busy that I barely get to see her. She says we're going shopping this weekend for your new house."

Deciding it was time to break the news of her pregnancy, Sully drew up a chair, pleased when Diddly plopped down beside her. "I'm just past the first trimester so we're actually looking for nursery furniture. Tate picked out the set he wants and sent me the link, but the little branch store at the outlet mall was closed when we visited, so it's a girly raid on the bigger main one here. Bronwyn told me she's bringing the girls and joining us for the day."

Heidi put a plate with a selection of homemade chocolate chip cookies on the table and hugged Sully again. "I couldn't be happier for you and Tate. After we eat, you can help me change the sheets on the beds in the other two guest rooms since I've already tidied the one for Quinn. I'll vac and dust and promise to keep the dogs out of them."

"I don't think Bronwyn plans to stay overnight."

"Tough. My baby sis can get over herself. I'll call and invite her and tell Joe that he must cook for himself and Lock on the weekend. Worst case scenario, they can go to Pop's Café for dinner. That way he won't have to worry about Bronwyn driving home late."

"Way to go." Sully high-fived Heidi. "This will be the most fun ever. I love Tate's family."

"Shouldn't we invite your mom to join us?"

"I don't want her to be rude to any of you." Sully eyed Heidi warily. "Sometimes and I mean all the time, she's my harshest critic. I haven't told her yet that she's going to be a grandma. I guess I'm afraid of the fall-out."

"You have your phone. Call her tonight. She can choose whether she comes or not. If you ask her, she won't think the Murphy clan is trying to steal her daughter. You don't need to worry about me and Bronwyn. We're grown-ups and we can outfly any other witches on our new broomsticks."

Sully hesitated, then forced a smile. "Okay, I'll call her when I get back from my class."

That evening, she cuddled with Bo and Diddly on the couch in the living room. She had a bowl of buttered popcorn, a bottle of icy-cold ginger ale and she was ready to binge-watch the *Criminal Minds* marathon as soon as she'd called her mother. She pulled up the contact list on her cell phone and chose that number.

Helene answered quickly. "It's been more than a month since I've heard from you, Sullivan. What have you been doing? Why haven't you stayed in touch?"

"Because I've been up to my eyeballs student teaching." Sully opted for her most reasonable tone. "The school is on spring break and I'm staying with Tate's aunt and uncle for the next week while I take classes at the university."

"Maybe, we can get together for lunch next week."

"That's why I'm calling. I wanted to invite you to join me and Tate's mom, aunt, and sisters. We're spending Saturday shopping down here. I have a guest room in our apartment, and you could stay over with me."

Absolute silence for an exceptionally long moment and then Helene said cautiously. "I'd like that. Will you give me directions?"

"Sure." After a bit more chat, Sully ended the call. When she put her phone on the coffee table, Diddly lifted her golden head and yawned, showing off a wide grin. Her brother continued to snooze; his head pillowed on Sully's lap.

"I know. I didn't tell her about the baby. I'll do it when she gets here before we go to the furniture store."

Friday morning meant two doctor appointments at the Army base. To Sully's pleasure, she was told she no longer needed to wear the brace but could start wearing two shoes again. She still had to keep the cane and use it as an assistive device. She glanced at her favorite nurse, Jeannie Sanders. "This is wonderful. I'm so excited about having two *real* feet again."

"Low-heeled, supportive shoes only," Jeannie said. "Don't be stylin' in high heels. If that leg gives out, you'll fall and that might hurt the baby."

"I'll be careful." Sully smiled at her friend. "Do you have plans for the weekend, or would you like to go shopping with us?"

"Who is us? You and the baby daddy?"

"Me and the baby daddy's family. He's training in Kentucky and he'll be home in two weeks. He sent me links for nursery furniture. I have to go see if we're on the same page."

"Sounds fun. I'm in if we can look next week. I have duty this weekend, so I'll be stuck on base."

"Works for me. Let's do lunch and shop on Monday before I go to the university."

It'd been forever since she'd gone to the movies so once she left the military base, she headed for the nearby mall and theater. On her way into the lobby, she shut off her cell phone. Then, it was time to buy a ticket, binge on popcorn, soda, and bypass the chocolate she adored, so she wouldn't have heartburn. *Oh, what I do for you, kid. You'll owe me big time in five and a half months.*

After the show, she stopped to pick up pre-made combo pizzas at

Tate's favorite deli on the way home. Heidi had barely put the pizzas in the oven when Quinn arrived.

Offering to help her unpack, Sully followed her to the guest room. "Your aunt is excited about having you here all week."

"She's not the only one." Quinn slung her suitcase onto the double bed. "The kids informed me that they'll miss me a bunch and they're sorting out their parents while I'm gone."

"What does that mean?"

"Well, Cressy told me that after seven years they should be calling me something other than my first name, like Mama-Quinn because I take so much care of them. The three of them decided we should add to our family. Letty wants a little sister to boss and Finn said it wasn't fair since the girls already outnumber him. When Lyle tried to explain that we didn't want more kids, the three of them asked me if it was true."

"Did you rat him out?"

"He's their father so I just refused to play along or address the subject. Their dad was the one who made this life decision, not me, but I didn't say that either. I told all of them I was coming here to be with you for a week and help you choose furniture for your new house."

"That should do it." Sully plopped down on the bed and watched Quinn open the suitcase. "Cressy told me that if you wanted a baby of your own, she'd see to it that you got at least one. I'm not surprised she's involved her sibs. They want you to be happy."

"I am happy."

"Really?"

"Okay, so I want a bigger family and at least one baby of my own, but I'm not willing to lose Lyle over it. He has to want it too, not feel forced into anything by me or the kids, so I'm not engaging."

"That's very mature." Sully doubted her sister-in-law's veracity, but she certainly wasn't going to call Quinn a liar. Instead, they talked about the nursery set, closing on the new house, and what time Bronwyn would arrive the next morning. "Heidi suggested I invite my mother to join us too. So, I did. It's probably the right thing to do since she'll be the other grandma."

The comment earned a long, steady blue-eyed look from Quinn who finally said, "Sounds like I'm not the only adult in the room."

"Yeah, but why is it so hard to be a grownup?"

"It's a question for the ages. Let me know when you find the answer."

They returned to the kitchen in time to meet Helene Barlow. She'd dressed down for the visit in jeans and a sweater in her favorite soft green. Sully waited until her mother finished petting the various collies and then hugged her.

Helene tucked an arm around Sully's waist. "Heidi tells me she has puppies in the laundry room. Will you show them to me?"

"Yes, but if you take all of them home, you know Gil will lose it. He thinks three dogs are plenty."

"There are never enough puppies," Helene informed her. "Especially rough-coated collie mixes."

"That's what I tell Arnie all the time," Heidi agreed. "Help me put dinner on the table, Quinn and we'll let Sully entertain her mom."

Later that evening, Sully helped her mother settle into the guest room in the apartment, Bo and Diddly providing doggie company. Afterward, they migrated to the living room to watch television. Sully brought out potato chips, ranch dip, and sodas. "I'm glad you came."

"I'm just as glad you invited me. What kind of furniture are we buying tomorrow?"

"Tate and I are closing on a house in Baker City in two weeks. It basically needs everything, and he wants us to raid his mom's attic. Bronwyn, his younger sisters, and I already did. I found dressers, an antique dining table and matching chairs, bookcases, and bunkbeds, but I still want couches and a pair of recliners."

"You should come home and see what we have to spare."

Sully shook her head, a vehement refusal and hastily bit back the *'No way in hell'*, that almost escaped. She didn't want the *bad ju-ju* of having Barlow belongings in her new home. Instead, she opted for Raven's strategy of throwing her husband under the proverbial bus whenever a family member asked her to do something she adamantly opposed. "I'll have to ask Tate first."

"Good heavenly days. What is wrong with you girls? I loved Raven dearly. I never understood why she catered so much to Kord's whims. I can't believe you're doing the same thing with your new husband. I thought Raven's mom and I raised the two of you to be stronger than that and use your own judgment."

"I'll talk to Tate about it when he gets home from training. We have a few weeks before he goes to Afghanistan. If we have time before he ships out, we'll stop by. I want to have a housewarming, but he needs to be home for that so it may not happen before next spring."

"I'm glad you're thinking ahead." Helene picked up her glass of cola and gazed at the dogs when they pelted toward the front door, barking excitedly. "What's that about?"

"I have no idea. Maybe Quinn came to join us." Sully rose and followed the two young collies. She stopped abruptly in the hallway when she saw Tate leaning down to pet the pups. She nearly rubbed her eyes, uncertain of whether he was really here or not. He looked so amazing in camos and jump boots. "O.M.G., what are you doing here? Am I dreaming? You're not due back for another two weeks."

He laughed, turning to close and lock the door behind him. "My deployment was cancelled which meant the training was curtailed and they sent us home early. One of the officers pulled a few strings so I caught a military flight here."

"That's wonderful." Sully hurried forward, bypassing the dogs to fling her arms around his neck and kiss him. "I'm glad you're home safe."

"Is this the same woman who told me to *soldier on* and focus on the training?"

"Certainly, I did." She trembled when he framed her face with calloused hands. "I wasn't wimping out on you."

"Good to know." He kissed her again, then drew back to study her. "You have on two slippers."

"I saw the doctors today and I'm cleared to walk with them, even though I can't run miles yet." Sully heaved a sigh and pressed close against him. "Everybody's coming to shop tomorrow. Your mom and your sisters are here. My mom is too. Now, you can join us and show off that bedroom set you want."

"I have to report in at the base and I don't know how long it will take to sort out the details of my next assignment. You go and I'll catch up with you if possible. If not, I'll see you when you get back. Did you say your mother was here?"

"Yes." Sully glanced cautiously over her shoulder, then lowered her voice to a whisper. "I haven't told her yet."

His dark blue eyes narrowed, and he nodded. "We'll do it together."

He'd tried calling her from the plane as well as at the military airport when he landed, but she hadn't answered. He'd wait to bring up the subject until they were alone. He hung the garment bag holding his dress uniform in the entry closet, then picked up his Army duffel and rested his free arm on her shoulders. "Let's go be sociable."

She heaved a sigh and he felt the tension seep from her body. "I really missed you."

"It's mutual, sweetheart."

In the living room, they found her mother conspicuously watching a murder mystery on TV. She turned down the volume and smiled politely. "Well, this is a surprise."

"A good one, I hope." Accompanied by Sully, he carried his duffel to the bedroom. "What was for dinner?"

"Pizza. Your aunt sent the leftovers home with me in case I wanted a snack later. I'll go heat up a few slices. Do you want a soda or a beer?"

"A soda."

"I'm on it."

When he joined her in the kitchen a few minutes later, he asked, "Is something going on with your phone? You didn't answer when I called earlier."

For a moment, she continued dropping ice cubes into a glass, then added cola. She stopped and crossed to the table where her purse sat on a chair, and pulled out the cell phone to look at it. "I charge it every night. O.M.G., I forgot to turn it back on when I left the theater today. My bad. Why did you call?"

"For a ride," he said gently. "My truck is still parked here, but one of the crew dropped me off, so no worries."

"I'm sorry." She grimaced, concern sliding across her face for a moment. "I'll check it more often. I'm sorry."

"No worries," he repeated and went to the microwave when it buzzed. "Things happen, Sully. I've done that myself. Who hasn't?" She still looked upset and he sought for a way to distract her. "Tell me about your classes at the university while you're out on spring break."

"I think Dr. Dunaway was on a mission to save me from Lake Maynard Middle High." Sully tore off two paper towels from the roll, passing them to him. "When I got to the campus yesterday, I learned that we have classes to prep for our certification test two nights a week and format our research papers the other two nights. She told us to choose our topics over the weekend and then be prepared to present them on Monday. We're not supposed to begin compiling sources until the cohort and of course, our professor approves the subjects so it's a kick-back weekend for me since we already filmed one of my English classes."

"Have you picked a research topic?"

"Effectively utilizing Reading Circles to teach literature. I watched another teacher use them in an earlier practicum, so I've got hands-on experience."

He pulled a chair out for her and waited while she sat down at the kitchen table before he joined her. "Having your subject already means I should arrange for leave next week when I check in at HQ tomorrow."

She flashed a cheeky grin. "Only if you want, Master Sergeant Hot Stuff."

"Oh, I definitely want, Mrs. Murphy."

CHAPTER TWENTY-SEVEN

Saturday morning, he switched off the alarm before it rang, leaving her to sleep. He showered, shaved, dressed in a clean set of fatigues, and went to the kitchen to make breakfast before he left for the base. He turned on the coffee to brew and filled the teakettle putting it on the stove to heat.

Diddly and Bo trooped into the room, then escorted him to the front door where he let them out, watching them trot down the stairs, heading to the back of his aunt's house. He knew she'd feed them with the rest of the canine contingent after they did their business in the yard. The collie pups would undoubtedly return for a snack later.

When he returned to the kitchen, soft footsteps on the tile alerted him. Tate glanced over his shoulder to see his mother-in-law. Like him, she was already dressed but in jeans and a tunic print top.

"Good morning." He opened the refrigerator. "What do you want for breakfast? I'm figuring scrambled eggs, bacon, and toast."

"Sounds wonderful. How can I help?"

"Set the table and make the toast." When her eyebrows shot up, he remembered she was a civilian and added, "Please."

"Sullivan seems to be sleeping late."

"Looks that way." The teakettle whistled and he added hot water to the cup where a peppermint teabag waited, allowing it to steep. "She'll be along."

More footsteps, these hurrying to the bathroom and he heard the door slam. "Excuse us."

Helene froze, then followed him. "What's wrong?"

"She'll tell you in her own time." He opened the door and closed it behind him.

Still standing at the vanity, Sully barely glanced sideways at him. Instead, she finished brushing her teeth and rinsed her mouth one final time. "I thought I was over this. Granted, I've been skipping breakfast because I have to be at the school so early and by lunchtime at ten-thirty, I'm not calling for Ralph or cursing you because I'm puking."

"Doesn't sound healthy to me when you're eating for two as my dad says. What did the doctor think yesterday?"

"I've gained four pounds so he's not bitching yet. Neither should you." Taking a deep breath, she brushed by him and headed toward the kitchen, a bright purple fleece robe swirling around her. "He scheduled an early ultrasound next Thursday. Don't give me a ration of crap first thing in the morning, Murphy."

"If I don't, who will?" He chuckled, amused by the snarky attitude. He caught up, cupped her elbow, and guided her to a seat at the table, dropping a kiss on top of the brilliant red hair. He picked up the cup of tea, a jar of honey, and put them in front of her, following up with a spoon and saucer. "Dry toast? Or do you want butter?"

She considered the question while stirring honey into the tea. She still hadn't answered when Helene placed the bread, butter, and homemade strawberry jam on the table.

"What's going on with you, Sullivan?"

A long silence followed by a hefty sigh and then Sully said, "Congratulations, Mother. You're going to be a grandma."

Later that morning, she showed off pics of the Craftsman-style house and the furniture gifted by Tate's family. For once, Helene hadn't griped non-stop about the heavy wooden antiques Sully preferred. Granted she'd made a few snide comments about dust catchers, but those ended when Bronwyn offered to send Tate's sisters to clean once or twice a week.

Naveah happily agreed if it meant she could play with the baby and Chantrea wanted to know how much they'd be paid for housework. Taking care of their new niece or nephew didn't require wages. Sully hugged both teens and told them she loved having two more sisters. When they arrived at the next specialty shop, a custom furniture gallery, a salesman led them through the various displays. The elaborate nursery set Tate wanted drew oohs and aahs from his family.

Helene Barlow rolled her eyes at the hand-crafted dark maple crib, changing table, bassinet, toy chest, bookcases, mother's rocking chair, and two matching dressers. "I could ask if he bought you a house to wrap around this stage set, but apparently he already has."

"We bought our new home in Baker City together, Mother."

"Other people have babies without being so extravagant, Sullivan."

"They can use the same set for the next baby, Helene." Bronwyn slipped an arm around Sully's waist. "It's not as if they'll stop with one child. Joe is refinishing Tate's highchair for them, so they don't have to buy one unless they expect twins."

"Are you serious?" Helene's eyes widened. "Sullivan, how many kids are you planning to have?"

"I don't know." Sully opted for what she hoped was her sweetest smile. "He's supremely hot so I intend to jump Tate until he dies of exhaustion."

That silenced her mother and Bronwyn burst into laughter. "Oh, honey. I went through that with his father and we started with six kids—"

"And then you had a bunch more after we grew up," Quinn pointed out, gesturing to the teens. "One of these days we'll have to tell you where children come from."

"You know what Arnie claims," Heidi added, "one of these days is actually none of these days."

Increased laughter from her audience and Sully relaxed, grateful that her mother hadn't been allowed to ruin the afternoon. Yet, the woman wasn't entirely wrong. The entire nursery set did cost a small fortune. Sully removed her cell phone and shot a quick text off to Tate, verifying that he knew the prices.

His answer came back moments later. He did and if she liked it, he said to place the order since they'd have to wait three to four months for the pieces to be made and delivered. Sully shook her head at the response, then asked the salesman if Tate was correct about the timeframe. It amazed her to learn he was, and they'd need to provide a hefty deposit with the balance due on receipt.

"Are you ready to complete the paperwork?" Quinn stroked the finish on the crib. "It's beautiful."

"It is, but it's really expensive," Sully said, turning back to the salesman. "What about the mattress?"

"It's included and the price includes a military discount."

"I still want to think about it," Sully told him.

"Try out the rocking chair," Bronwyn suggested. "You'll spend a lot of time in it and if it's not comfortable, you need to know."

"Good point." Sully sank into the comfortable flowered cushions. *Oh yeah, I could so get used to this.*

It hadn't taken as much time for in-processing at HQ as he'd expected. Major Harper had left a note for Tate to be reassigned to his former job instead of being sent off to limbo somewhere on post. He should want to work with the Rangers at Fort Clark, but truth be told he missed his old patrol and there wasn't any chance of reconnecting with them. After the last tour when Zeke Garvey died, too many of the others had been reassigned or retired. Helping the Major supervise training of potential officers would be more enjoyable than trying to find the proverbial military home.

Tate spotted the bright pink Mustang strategically parked in the lot near the furniture store and pulled in beside the classic vehicle. He found Sully, her mother, and his relatives congregating around the nursery set he'd chosen. "What do you think?"

"I didn't know you'd won the lottery," Helene said. "It's beautiful but too expensive."

"My baby is worth it." Tate leaned down to kiss Sully. "What about you?"

"I love it." Sully smiled up at him. "Are you sure you want to go this route? We have time to shop around and look for pieces at garage and estate sales."

"Then, you could personalize them for the baby," Bronwyn agreed. "Have you decided on a name yet?"

"Raven," Sully said.

Tate rested a hand on her shoulder. "And Garvey for a middle name."

She tipped her head slightly. "It's perfect."

"Yes, and now let's select a design and complete the order for the nursery furniture." He held out his hand and helped her stand. "Mom, why don't you and Quinn take everyone to see the recliners and couches?"

When it was just the two of them, he eyed Sully. "What bothers you most about the nursery set?"

"The price."

"I'm the one buying it so get over yourself, Mrs. Murphy."

"In case you didn't know, I'm entitled to my opinion. You're not the boss of me except on base. And you won't be after I get my next promotion to Master Sergeant."

"I've got news for you, sweetheart. I'll still have more time in grade than you will, so I'll still be in charge."

"And you'll be sleeping alone for the next fifty years. Let's shop around a while longer."

"Let's not and say we did." He guided her to the desk where the salesman had placed a book filled with designs. "I'm buying new for our baby, not recycling someone else's leftovers. At least, we can look at the catalog and see if we agree on a crib."

"I'll agree to that much."

―――――――――――

That evening she escaped to the gazebo with Bo and Diddly leaving Quinn to entertain the womenfolk with her quilting projects. His uncle dragged Tate off to do preventative maintenance on their rigs, both men knowing better than to touch the Mustang. The young dogs seemed to understand how overwhelmed she felt. They plopped down on the floor to snooze and didn't plague her to participate in games of tug-a-puppy where they fought with each other over tennis balls, flying discs, and rope toys.

The stars played peek-a-boo among the clouds and she barely glimpsed the shape of the new moon. She heaved a sigh. *I must be the world's biggest bitch. I didn't want anything bad to happen to Tate when he deployed. I worried non-stop while he was training because sh— happens in the field. Why am I freaking out because he's home for the duration? His trying to run the world is annoying, but I can't be that insecure.*

She rested a hand on the faint rise of her abdomen. It wasn't a baby bump, at least not yet. She wasn't angry because he was stepping up to be the best daddy in the state, was she? She needed that for their daughter or son, didn't she? She considered the questions for a few minutes. *Oh sure, I want it for you, kid, but I'm still not ready to live with the man ordering me around twenty-four, seven even if he puts down the toilet seat.*

"Is this a private party or can I join you?" Heidi entered the small pavilion, carrying two glasses. She passed one to Sully. "Sometimes, I just come here to read a book and hide from Arnie. What's going on?"

"I'm glad Tate's home…"

"But?"

"He's so bossy. He thinks he's the man in charge and I want to—"

"Smack him upside the head?" Heidi sipped her drink. "Do you need my permission, or shall we ask Bronwyn for hers?"

Sully laughed and tasted her own drink. Ginger ale. "I love both of you. Thanks for the sympathy."

"It's fine. What did my nephew do to piss you off?"

"It's the nursery set he wants to buy at that upscale furniture gallery. We agreed on the crib and he paid the deposit, but I'm not sure about the rest of the furniture. He doesn't listen."

"Well, don't count on things getting better. When he showed up right after Joe's heart attack last November, Tate immediately began issuing orders. He told Lock how to run the farm, advising him about the crops and livestock like his younger brother had just left the city. Bronwyn said they almost came to blows. Then, Tate started giving her menus and telling the girls how to clean the house. He also got into it with the other boys and told Egan not to take any long-hauls for a while."

"Wow, you can take the Master Sergeant off the base, but he still does his *soldier in charge* routine." Sully relaxed deeper into the wooden chair. "He's super exasperating and being extremely hot doesn't excuse it."

"That's mild compared to what his family was telling me last year. Things would have ended badly if Quinn hadn't demanded he drive her to the airport before Christmas. Bronwyn said she didn't have time for an intervention when she was spending hours at the hospital and later at the rehab center."

"It seems like everyone is getting along now."

"Yes, because he's fussing over you, not them. Tate doesn't do well when he's scared or stressed, so he makes these command decisions. Woe betide the person who disagrees with him. He feels safest when he controls every situation. He did even before the Army got a hold of him."

"Well, I'm disagreeing." Sully swirled her drink, ice tinkling. "I don't know what I want for baby Raven, but I have time to figure it out before September. He's going to have to chill out."

"Good luck with that." Heidi raised her glass in a mock toast, then leaned over to touch it against Sully's. "I've got your back if you need me."

"Thanks. I'll keep you in mind."

When she and Heidi parted company a short time later, Sully headed upstairs to the apartment accompanied by the dogs. She found her mother watching TV. "Is Tate here?"

"Not yet." Helene patted the cushion on the couch beside her, using the remote to mute the TV. "Are you happy, honey?"

Sitting down beside her mom, Sully silently contemplated the question and finally nodded. "I think I am. Things are weird. I never expected to meet someone like Tate Murphy or have him sweep me off my feet, but I'm dealing."

"It must be an adjustment having him home early."

"Oh, yeah. But it's a major relief too. I didn't know how worried I was until he came back last night. Now, I can focus on the new house and the baby and finishing my degree."

"How's that going?"

Sully grimaced. "I have the mentor teacher from hell at Lake Maynard Middle High, but at least I'm getting great advice from Margo Endicott and Ann Barrett. We were all in Afghanistan together and they've been teachers forever."

"That must be the mentor Raven told me about," Helene said thoughtfully. "I was really concerned she'd break under the pressure especially when she said she was going to insist on a different placement. She didn't want to make waves while the two of you were out of the country, but she had plans."

"That sounds like Raven."

"Yes, and she was like a daughter to me even before she married your brother. I miss her so much."

"I know you do." Sully stood, suddenly tired of all the emotion and fighting the urge to cry. She was done. "I'll see you in the morning."

"I'm leaving early for home."

"I'll be up before you go."

As soon as he entered the apartment, he heard a television drama. He locked the front door behind him and headed into the living room where he found his mother-in-law. No Sully. Her car was in the garage and she hadn't been in the gazebo when he crossed the lawn. "Where is Sully?"

"She's already called it a night and went to bed."

"Really?" Tate glanced at his watch. "It's barely twenty-hundred hours, hardly eight at night for civilians. I'll go check on her."

Diddly growled at him when he opened the bedroom door, but her doggie brother continued to lie on the bed next to Sully who still wore her jeans and a t-shirt. Bo lifted his head, showing white teeth. Tate closed the door behind him. "Looks like all three of you had a meeting of the minds and made a strategic withdrawal."

"She's making me crazy."

"Okay." Tate crossed the room and sat down on the edge of the bed to remove his boots. "Anything in particular or just in general?"

"Raven and I used to laugh about the way my mother preferred her to me, but it's not funny, not anymore."

"I'm sorry." He shifted and drew her close, the tri-color collie lying between them. "You made the overture when you invited her to join you and my family. She's leaving tomorrow and what happens next is up to her."

"Is that your fancy Ranger way of saying to *embrace the suck?*"

He laughed, kissed her forehead. "Yeah, it's time to *Charlie Mike*, sweetheart."

"Continue Mission?" She heaved a sigh. "I'll do better if you bring me one of your fabulous banana splits. I want ice-cream, but not badly enough to leave this room."

"I will as long as you promise not to upchuck it afterward."

A weak laugh. "Okay, I promise."

CHAPTER TWENTY-EIGHT

She found herself alone when she woke the next morning. The dogs had already left the bedroom. Tate had probably let them outside. She slowly eased out of bed, taking time to be certain her stomach wouldn't rebel. Shrugging into her robe, she headed for the bathroom, then went into the kitchen to make a cup of tea.

Tate and her mother weren't around and while she missed him, Sully figured she'd count her blessings and try to come to terms with the pain and guilt she felt over losing her best friend. Contrary to what Helene Barlow claimed, she wasn't the only one who'd loved Raven, Sully thought. No, it wasn't easy, none of this was easy.

She wished again that Raven was around to share the moment and the news about the baby. They'd always intended to raise their children together. *Well, that's hopeless so it's time to suck it up, buttercup and drive on, Sully Rafferty Murphy.*

She sat down at the kitchen table with her peppermint tea and glanced into the living room as Tate entered the apartment, carrying a covered dish. "What's going on?"

"Aunt Heidi was making French Toast, so I brought you some. Do you want syrup or jam?"

"Neither. I'll take butter and sugar." She smiled at him. As always, he looked super sexy in his flannel shirt, jeans, and boots. "What did you do with my mother? Please tell me you shipped her off to Timbuktu or Liberty Valley."

"Not yet." He chuckled. "She's having coffee with my aunt and uncle before she leaves. I told her I'd carry down her suitcase and you'd come to say goodbye." He joined Sully at the kitchen table. "Word of warning. She asked about adopting Bo or Diddly and Aunt Heidi told her they belonged to you."

"My mother makes me crazy at the best of times." Sully sighed and shook her head before she focused on buttering the toast and sprinkling on granulated sugar. Two slices of home-cured bacon lay beside the perfectly browned bread. "She'd better be careful. I'm going to flip on my 'witch' switch if she doesn't stop trying to get at me. I've been good since she got here, but I'm running out of patience."

He laughed. "Want me to rev up your broomstick?"

"Promises, promises."

An hour later, Sully went downstairs to 'do the pretty' and say all the right things prior to her mother's departure. She spotted Helene standing by a late model white Subaru SUV, an upgrade from the Jeep Grand Cherokee she'd been driving before Sully left on her last tour.

Tate stood nearby, a small, blue-wheeled suitcase next to him. As she drew closer, Sully realized he was standing at the position of attention, his jaw set, and blue gaze narrowed on her mother. He was obviously listening to Helene, but not participating in the conversation. *A typical military response*, Sully thought, *compartmentalize your emotions and control yourself and the situation as much as possible.*

"I'm just trying to warn you," Helene kept talking. "Turning off her phone is typically Sully. She's horribly unreliable most of the time and you can't trust her to tell the truth. Unless the doctor's done a paternity test, there's no way to know if this baby is even yours."

"Are you serious?" Sully advanced on the older woman. "Do you actually have the nerve to call me a slut here and now? In front of my husband?"

"It's hardly a secret," Helene protested. "You dated everybody in town as soon as you turned sixteen."

"Only the boys," Sully shot back, "and I never missed any of my curfews unlike Kord and his brothers. Gil didn't have to ground me, so I'd respect the rules."

"Well, I never found birth control pills in their bedroom drawers."

"What about condoms? You pitched plenty of fits about those until Gil told you that he supplied them to his sons." Sully lifted her chin. "You know full well I needed the pills to regulate my periods when I was a teen. It didn't mean I was sexually active."

"That's your story," Helene sniffed.

"Only because it's the truth. If you have questions or doubts, talk to Raven's mother. She always stepped up for me when you didn't and when Gil was too embarrassed to deal with my *girly* problems."

Tate stepped back. "Sounds like you have this situation under control, Mrs. Murphy so I'll let you two finish this in private."

"Good idea." Sully flashed. "Make a strategic withdrawal while you're able."

Once he strode away, she yanked open the back door of the S.U.V. and almost hurled the overnight case inside. "I'm so done with you today, Mother Dearest. Leave while you're able!"

"Sullivan Rafferty—"

"Murphy. Don't leave that part out. I'm a Murphy and that may piss you off, but I don't care. I have a *real* family now and I won't let you destroy it."

"Gil married me before you were born, and he raised you. We're your family."

"No, you're not." Sully met her mother's assessing gaze. "You chose everyone else in Liberty Valley over me and now I'm choosing others over you. Get off my back. Then, I'll pretend you care and keep you posted."

Tears welled in Helene's eyes. "If Raven and your brother had a baby, it'd have been so beautiful with her cheekbones and his thick, curly brown hair." She drew a ragged breath. "I was really looking forward to my first grandbaby."

"It will be here in September." Sully lifted her chin, determined to maintain her composure. "I miss Raven too."

"Why didn't you do a better job looking after her?"

"We were ambushed, Mother. Would it make you happier if she'd come home and I'd been the one in the coffin? Would you be giving her the same kind of hell you give me? I doubt it. You'd probably be visiting Fort Bronson and doing a *happy dance* on my grave."

"Don't be ridiculous. I never said that." Helene opened the driver's door. "Honestly, Sullivan. You're just like your father. He always preferred the Army to me. I thought I'd raised you better than to make my mistakes. You're repeating my life."

"Is that a slam because I was pregnant before we got married?" Sully planted her fists on her hips. "Or are you blaming me because Tate Murphy stepped up and my bio-dad hightailed it out of town rather than make a commitment to you? I can't blame him for that. Guess what, Mother? I'm living my own life with a *real* man, so get the hell off my back."

"Watch your mouth." Helene yanked open the driver's door. "One more word of advice for you to ignore. You're already piling on the pounds. Don't gain too much baby weight if you want to keep your husband. Men don't like fat women."

"Drive safe, Mother. Even though you're a freaking bitch, I love you too." Sully turned and stalked across the yard toward the gazebo. She wouldn't cry in front of the woman who gave birth to her. *I miss you so much, Raven. I wish you were here to tell me what to do.*

He'd seen the SUV leave the driveway, but Sully hadn't returned to the apartment. He wondered if she'd gone to find the puppies at his aunt and uncle's house. When Tate went there, he didn't see her. "Do you know where Sully went?"

"Try the gazebo," Heidi advised as she puttered around the kitchen making some sort of list. "Take Bo and Diddly with you along with a couple of toys. Be prepared to listen, not talk."

"What if Sully has nothing to say?"

"I told you already, Tate Murphy. Listen. All Helene talked about this morning was her daughter-in-law. She didn't say word one about her daughter and she'll never understand that's why I don't have a puppy for her, not now, not ever. Love isn't a water faucet that you turn on and off for your convenience."

Tate nodded, called the two border collie mixes from the pantry where they supervised his aunt, and headed out the back door. Before he left the wrap-around porch, his sister caught up with him. "After Mom and the girls leave, Aunt Heidi and I are going grocery shopping. Ask Sully if she wants to come along. That will give you time to clean the guest room in the apartment."

"Good idea. Then she won't have to tidy up behind her mom."

"Exactly and next time I snivel about ours, kick me in the butt. We're damned lucky. We always have been, Tate, even if we don't always realize it. After hearing Helene's crap this weekend, I'm gonna be a better momma to my kids and never make them feel unloved or unwanted."

"No worries. I've always had your six and I know you have mine."

"You got it."

On his way to the small cedar structure in the middle of the yard, he threw the soggy tennis ball for Bo. The doggie battle continued for the next five minutes and he chuckled when the two young dogs tussled over the lime green ball. Inside the gazebo, he found Sully huddled on one of the benches.

He sat down next to her, put an arm around her shoulders. She glared at him, then shifted away. "Do you want to talk about it?"

She shook her head. "I've got nothing civil to say to you. Go away, Murphy, and let me calm down."

"That's not happening." He leaned back on the bench, trying to guess what was wrong. "Are you mad at Aunt Heidi for suggesting you invite your mom for the weekend?"

"No. I hadn't seen my mother for a month, not since the wedding and I haven't talked to her." Sully slid further away to the other end of the wooden bench. "It was time for a visit. I should have expected her to do her worst, but I never do. At least I had the opportunity to tell her what I thought of her for once."

"Okay, so what gives? Did you really expect me to chew out your mother?"

"Oh, that would have been new and different." Sully jumped to her feet and stalked toward him. "Why the hell didn't you tell her to watch her filthy mouth? What's wrong with you, Murphy? You stood there like a freaking statue and let her call me a whore."

He held up one hand, forcing himself to remain calm. "No, she didn't do that. She inferred it, but she didn't actually say it."

"Well, goody. You can pin an award on the bitch since she's your best new buddy."

"I'm not saying that either." He stood, strode to meet her. "I get it. You're pissed off and you want to fight with somebody, but you'd better choose wisely. I've been super patient with you, Sullivan Murphy. I don't take crap either."

She glared up at him, green eyes dark with rage. "And when the situation goes from sugar to shit, you hightail it. Some Army Ranger. You're supposed to be the bravest of the brave."

He caught her chin, lifted it so their gazes met and clashed. "I won't fight with your mother because that's a '*Catch-22*'. I'd be damned if I did, damned if I didn't. I've got your six the rest of the time and you'd better damn well have mine. Or where are we going with this?"

"I don't know, but I won't be with a man who chooses anyone else over me. I've lived with it my whole life and I'm not *embracing that suck*. You can call your favorite mother-in-law in September when the baby comes. I won't contact her."

"No worries. Whatever you want works for me." He deliberately bent his head and kissed her a little too fiercely. "I'm here for the duration, Mrs. Murphy. I'll be here when you're ready to apologize for expecting me to fight a war with your mother."

"In your freaking dreams." She shoved away from him. "I don't know why I married you. I must have been nuts."

"As crazy about me as I am about you even if that woman did her best to damage you, so you don't trust yourself or me." He saw tears glimmer in Sully's eyes and headed for the exit between the sections of wooden lattice. She'd undoubtedly give him hell later, but she didn't want him around to see her cry. "After Mom and the girls leave, go shopping with Quinn and Aunt Heidi. The fridge is bare, and the freezer isn't much better."

"Are you telling me to make a grocery run, Murphy? You're pushing your luck. Try asking and you'll get further."

"I never ask, sweetness."

"You'd better start. I already said you don't outrank me here."

"When we're out of butter pecan ice cream, I do."

She stormed through the grocery store three hours later, filling the cart with essentials and contemplating leaving behind his favorite butter pecan ice cream. What the hell had she done? He was a stranger. Oh, yeah, he was the father of their baby, but he was still a stranger. He was supposed to be going off to war and she would have his Army benefits for their child.

That was their deal and he'd broken it. Well, the military had broken it for him. Now, she was stuck with him. No, she wasn't. She could file for divorce. She'd have a teaching degree this summer and even if the economy was in the toilet, she could still get a job, with or without tenure. She didn't need him to support her.

But she loved his family. His parents were wonderful. So were all of his sisters, even the ones she hadn't met yet. Bronwyn said she held an open house on the Fourth of July and invited all her foster kids to return along with the rest of the Murphys. Granted, she only knew one of his brothers pretty well. She'd get to know the rest. His aunt and uncle treated her as if she were special from the start. She didn't have to stay with Tate to be part of the Murphy clan, did she? The baby would provide all the entrée she needed.

In the past five months, I survived an I.E.D. attack, lost my B.F.F., came home injured, had a one-night hookup with a hot guy which resulted in a surprise pregnancy. No wonder I'm totally out of whack! What the hell was I thinking?

She'd barely come to terms with any of it and then she'd spent most of the weekend with her mother, the Wicked Witch of Liberty Valley who always judged and found Sully wanting. She'd done what anyone would call 'her duty'. Now, she could do what she'd told Tate and avoid the woman all spring and summer.

When they returned home, Tate came downstairs to carry the bags upstairs. Sully followed him, amazed when she walked inside the apartment. He'd obviously spent the afternoon scrubbing the place from top to bottom. Dishes done, the counters and tile floors gleamed. He'd vacuumed the carpets. He'd even washed the windows.

"Wow, I have to go grocery shopping more often." She wasn't ready to make up with him a hundred percent, but he'd tried to make amends. So, could she, even if she still didn't know where they'd go from here? She kissed him, a teasing brush of her lips over his. "Now, I feel guilty for only buying a quart of ice cream because we'll be going back to Baker City next weekend."

"If we run out, I'll stop by the store." He tipped up her chin and his mouth claimed hers for a long intense moment. "Put away this food and I'll bring up the rest of the bags."

She slid her hands over his chest to his broad shoulders. "I have to talk to your mom and tell her to teach you to say please and thank you."

"Good luck with that."

Two kisses later and he'd headed back downstairs while she unpacked the cloth grocery bags. Okay, so they'd had their first major argument, but anyone who mopped, scoured, and totally G.I.d their living quarters should be cut some slack. The next morning after he headed off to the Army base, she did the breakfast dishes and then went to Heidi's house. Arnie showed Sully to the sewing room while he weeded the garden and trained the dogs. Once there, she discovered Quinn and Heidi sewing squares for the baby quilt.

"Can I help?" Sully asked.

"Sure." Quinn waved her over to the large table. "I'll teach you how to cut pieces of fabric and then we sew different colors together. I'm the recreation director and this is today's activity."

"Sign me up. I'll help for a while before I meet Jeannie for lunch. Do you want to join us?"

"Sounds fun," Quinn said. "Are you coming too, Aunt Heidi?"

"No, I'll stay home with Arnie. The dog trainer is coming today, and we have to work with some of the rescues so we can find them homes."

Remembering her mother's request, Sully tensed slightly and kept her gaze on the older woman. "But not Bo or Diddly? They're not going anywhere else, are they?"

"Nope, they're yours. When she comes on Friday, you can work with her and those two puppies. They never focus when they're on leashes."

259

"Sounds great."

They met Jeannie at an Italian restaurant where they enjoyed salads, breadsticks, and pasta. They skipped dessert figuring they stop at a local bakery for cheesecake after showing Jeannie the nursery set at the furniture gallery. She liked most of it but agreed with Quinn that her brother and father could make a better rocking chair.

"I figure if Tate helps Dad with it, then he won't be harassing Sully on a regular basis."

"Makes sense to me," Jeannie agreed. "What do you think, Sully?"

"I'll talk to him about it tonight." Sully managed to smile at the two of them. She wouldn't tell them that she and Tate had issues and she didn't know if they'd be together when the baby came. *What did I do? O.M.G., what did I do?*

Quinn eyed her with obvious concern. "Are you okay, Sully?"

"I'm fine." Sully slipped her arm through Quinn's. "I agree Master Sergeant Hot Stuff needs a hobby although I have to say coming home to an immaculate apartment was a terrific surprise. Would you believe he even did all the laundry including changing the sheets in both bedrooms and washing the couch covers while we were grocery shopping?"

"Sounds like a hero to me," Jeannie said. "When you get tired of him, send him to G.I. my place. Then I'd definitely pass inspection on Friday."

"In your dreams." Sully heaved a sigh. "Okay, enough with the baby furniture. Let's go clothes shopping while I think about this set. The price is still a major setback for me."

"Didn't Tate say he'd buy it?" Quinn asked.

"Yes, but I'm not into spending all his money."

"You've got a lot to learn about being a wife," Jeannie told her.

"What she said!" Quinn agreed.

"You two are both disgusting. Let's go shopping and then I need cheesecake. I'm eating for two now."

CHAPTER TWENTY-NINE

When she arrived home after class that night, she found Tate sitting in the kitchen working on his laptop. "What's happening? What are you doing?"

"Answering emails." He stood and came to take the bags of clothes she carried. "I was touching base with Dominique about renting our new home before we close in two weeks."

"You still don't want to sleep with me in your mom's house?" Sully laughed, shaking her head. "It may come as a complete surprise, but Bronwyn and Joe know about sex or you and Quinn wouldn't be here. Neither would your brothers."

"I know, but it doesn't mean I want to think about it."

"Okay, but do we want to keep the same colors in the house or repaint some of the rooms? They're kind of blah, but I'm not into beige or white walls. I'm thinking of sunshine yellow as an accent color in the baby's room."

"You're not painting." Tate carried the bags into the bedroom. "You can choose the colors, but that's it."

"Really? Are we back to the telling rather than asking me?"

"You got it, Mrs. Murphy." He came back from the bedroom. "I've been researching, and even latex paint fumes can be bad for the baby."

"So, what are you going to do? Hire painters? Did you win the lottery and never share that news with me?"

"I have brothers and sisters. I'll call out the Murphy army and they can help, but you *will* avoid the house until we're done. We'll spend nights at the guest ranch. I already reserved *our* cabin. "

"Really? More telling, not asking?" She watched him cross to the refrigerator and remove a casserole dish, followed by a green salad. "I had a sandwich in class."

"Not enough of a meal for my kid. Wash up while I fix you a real dinner."

She considered arguing the point, then gave up the battle. First, she was hungry. Second, he might be super bossy, but he cared enough to cook for her even when they were on the *outs* with each other. "You do realize that you're setting a standard for the next fifty years, don't you?"

"What standard?"

"Taking care of me. Nobody else ever has." She paused for a moment. "Well, Raven always had my *six*, but she was the only one."

"She's a tough act to follow. I'm doing my best, so she doesn't come back and haunt my sorry butt."

"I'll keep that in mind."

Suddenly, Sully realized they were talking like they'd done so many times before, lightly, glibly, all on the surface. She hadn't said anything about not knowing where they'd go from here and neither had he. She wanted a man who stood up for her, not one who made all the right noises about being on her side, but then didn't practice what he preached.

After she ate, they cleaned up the kitchen. Then she went to the living room to watch TV and he returned to his emails. She fell asleep halfway through a *Criminal Minds* episode and woke to find herself on the couch, puppies lying next to her and an afghan tossed over the three of them. So, Tate was still maintaining his distance and neither of them knew what came next. She could go to the bedroom, but she didn't. She turned off the TV, cuddled a snoring Bo close, and allowed the tears to slide down her cheeks into tri-colored fur.

Tate had already left for the base when she woke the next morning. She found the tea kettle sitting on the stove and a peppermint teabag waiting in a mug on the counter. Tears stung and she drew a ragged breath. She didn't want to hold a pity party for one, but it was different having him look out for her even if he was annoyed with her.

Helene hadn't been a helicopter mother always claiming to be busy around the house and Gil had the farm to run. Kord and his brothers hadn't been particularly unkind to their little stepsister, although they hadn't paid much attention to her either. Little wonder she spent as much time as she could next door with Raven and the Driscoll family.

A tap on the door interrupted Sully's musings and she went to answer it. She found Quinn on the landing accompanied by Bo and Diddly. They promptly trotted inside and made themselves at home in the living room, plopping down on the rug in front of the couch. Amused, Sully smiled at her sister-in-law. "Good morning. What's new and different in the wide world of sports?"

"Not much. Tate texted and asked me to pop over and make you breakfast."

"Hello, I'm a grown woman you two. I can take care of myself."

"Well, get over that. I'm the auntie and I need to be able to tell Cressy, Letty, and Finn that I'm taking care of you this week."

"Are they calling you all the time? How are they enjoying their spring break?"

"We talked last night, and I heard all about their camps. I promised to be home on Friday so I can attend their various performances. Luckily, those happen at three different times."

"Hmm, sounds like I need to auntie-up and rearrange the dog training with Heidi so I can be there too."

"They'd love it." Quinn crossed to the refrigerator. "What works for breakfast? Tate said I should make you a bowl of oatmeal."

"Only if he's going to eat it." Sully added more hot water to her mug and dunked the teabag in it again. "This *Rescue Ranger* routine gets old, but I'm trying to be patient."

"Let me know when you plan to thump him. Aunt Heidi's started a pool and I picked next Sunday. I want to win everybody's money."

Determined to maintain her composure and not allow her emotions full rein, especially after Heidi refused to let her participate in the *thump Tate pool*, Sully focused on prepping for the university class that day. When she returned home after the three-hour session, she encouraged Tate to share stories about the field assessments of the trainees. In passing, he mentioned Anise Tyler was having a tough time with the reports and Sully offered to help the next day.

It would allow her to avoid the weekend drill with her reserve unit and she wasn't ready to face everyone and hear their comments about Raven. A quick call to the Command Sergeant-Major and Sully gained permission to work at the Army base on Wednesday and Thursday. If she and Tate took a long lunch, she wouldn't need to rearrange the appointment for the ultrasound.

He intended to ask for leave on Friday so they could attend the cheerleader demonstration, the horse show, and the cross-country road rally with Quinn. If the previous owners agreed to let them rent it before the closing, they'd spend the next week or so prepping the new house so they could move in A.S.A.P. Once again, she retreated to the living room and her beloved *Criminal Minds* on television, and once again, she woke to find herself and the dogs covered with a blanket while they slept on the couch.

Anise greeted her warmly Wednesday morning and Sully struggled not to feel guilty. This was for her convenience, not the other woman's or Tate's or the Major's, but everyone seemed so happy that she was in the office. Anise even brought her multiple cups of tea and had lunch delivered to Sully's desk. Tate almost rolled his eyes when he saw the slab of cheesecake, topped with fresh fruit.

"It's dessert," Sully told him. "I had a sandwich and salad, so I earned it."

"Yes, she did." Anise continued filing reports. "I'm so glad she's made time to help me. This is the busiest time of year for us. I wish Sully could be here full-time. Everyone that Mr. Edwards has sent up is like the aide the Major had while you were gone, Sergeant Murphy. It's too much work for them and they bail after a day or two."

Sully shared a look with Tate. "I wouldn't mind transferring here, but I'd only be available two days each month and two weeks during the summer."

"It's one way to stay in *The World*," Tate said. "You wouldn't ship out again, not after already going to war three times and I want you home with me."

"I'll think about it," Sully said, appreciating his tact in not mentioning the baby here, "but I'd want a guarantee that I won't be bounced around the base from office to office."

"I'll talk to the Major about it," Anise said. "If we're all on the same page, I'm sure he'd be agreeable to using his clout."

By closing formation on Wednesday afternoon, Sully had visited Mr. Edwards in his office and completed the transfer request. He hadn't asked why she was looking for a 'new home' as the Army Reserve saying went. He just seemed happy to have someone reliable who wanted to step up and work part-time in the Headquarters building.

Sully told him she was pregnant, so she'd pull a few extra duty days in May once her stint at Lake Maynard Middle High ended. The decision thrilled him. He said having her in Major Harper's office would help when there were more young officer trainees. Afterward, she left for her class at the university branch campus while Tate headed to the apartment. She didn't bother to change out of her fatigues. The rest of the teachers in her cohort already knew she was a soldier, and it wouldn't bother them if they saw again that she actually wore combat boots.

Halfway through the class, Professor Dunaway announced they wouldn't meet the following night since they'd worked through all their breaks and stayed a half-hour late the first three nights. She offered the same option for students who'd be meeting with her in May to finish their final projects and Sully quickly joined the group who signed up for that opportunity. When she arrived home a short time later, she discovered Tate lounging in the kitchen paperwork. He was obviously comfortable in a t-shirt and camo pants since he hadn't bothered to change to civvies. "Now what, Master Sergeant Hot Stuff?"

"Dominique sent me a rental agreement. The previous owners already signed it. Once we do, we can move in this weekend. She said she'd stop by tomorrow afternoon, pick it up and bring by the keys. Major Harper said if I come in early, we can head home after your doctor's appointment."

"I don't do early mornings unless I cut out breakfast. It only works at the school because lunch is at ten-thirty."

"And you know I don't like that, so I told him you'd be in for a half-day and then make it up later."

She put her school bag on the couch and walked over to sit on his lap. She kissed him, then nipped his ear. "You're a bossy guy who thinks he's totally in charge."

"True. I am and I know I run your world, as well as mine even when I try not to overstep the bounds." He feathered his thumb along the line of her lips. "Uncle Arnie warned me to watch my step or you'd throw me out with the trash. Are you going to pitch a fit because I'm not deploying?"

"Not yet." She tilted her head, nibbled the strong column of his neck. "I think you should take me to bed and show me a rough, tough Ranger in action."

He chuckled, shifted on the chair, and stood, holding her. "I can do that. Promise you'll eat dinner after I have my wicked way with you."

"Depends on what you cooked."

"I didn't. I swung by the deli and picked up fried chicken, potato salad, and your favorite coconut cream pie."

"Oh, that's even better. I promise."

The sex was great as always. Afterward, he held her and stroked her hair, and she nestled close enjoying the warmth of his body next to hers. She didn't say she loved him. She couldn't, not when she didn't know if they had a future. He didn't say the words either, so it wasn't really make-up sex. Sully didn't know what to call it. She settled on being happy to be back in his arms and not on the couch.

When they walked out of the clinic the next afternoon, the news they were having twins still overwhelmed and shocked her. They headed toward her car and his pickup parked side by side. She poked him in the ribs. "Stop gloating and tell me what you think."

"About what?"

"Hello, were you even in the same exam room? We're having twins."

His grin widened. "I know. Isn't it great?"

"I was barely comfortable having one baby and now we're having two and from their positions when she did the scans, it was impossible for the tech to tell us the gender of the second one. All we know is that the first one is a girl. And I don't know what other colors to paint the nursery."

"You already said you wanted yellow as an accent and that works for both boys and girls. You pick the shade and I'll do the work."

"No worries. As soon as we get to your aunt's, I'm taking Quinn and we're going to the hardware store. I'm starting a list of things you need to accomplish at our new home in the next four and a half months."

He held the Mustang's door for her. "I'll come too."

"No, you won't. I can't bitch about you when you're there. I want to spend time with your sister and find out what she can tell me about raising twins." Sully slid into the driver's seat, behind the wheel. "You'll just keep smirking about what a stud you are, and I'll have to dig out my cane and thump you."

He laughed but didn't disagree. She closed the door and slid the key into the ignition. She started the engine, still reeling at the news. At the next intersection, she waited for the light to change and gently rubbed her belly. "I can't believe there are two of you. I knew I was naming one of you, Raven. Now, I don't know what to name the other one. Well, I guess I'll let your daddy do the honors. He'll decide he's even more all that and the proverbial bag of chips."

She was the first to arrive at the apartment and spotted Quinn standing in the driveway chatting with Dominique. While both women wore jeans and casual tops, only the realtor had paired her outfit with stilettos. Quinn wore ancient running shoes. Sully parked behind the late model Cadillac and went to join the conversation.

"So, what's the good word?" Quinn asked. "Did you find out if it was a girl or a boy?"

"When your brother gets here, he'll be bragging all over the place. Since he's not, I can tell you we're having twins and so far, I know one is a girl. We'll have to wait until my next ultrasound to find out the second baby's gender."

"Wow, that's a surprise." Quinn's eyes widened. "And you're barely showing. Girl, you need to eat more."

"They weighed me today and I'm on track. I gained another pound this week, but I wouldn't say no to cheesecake so let's go shopping."

"Am I invited?" Dominique asked. "I can come back later to drop off the keys."

"Or you can give them to me, and I'll get you the paperwork. It's upstairs in the apartment. Besides, we need your help. You have pictures of the house and I want to choose paint and new flooring for some of the rooms."

"Sounds like a plan." Dominique promptly handed over the set of house keys. "Are you changing out of your Army duds?"

"No need," Quinn said. "The combat boots support her weak leg better than anything else and she won't have to use her cane so let's go with it. Besides, with her in uniform, we definitely get the military discount. What are we buying?"

"Painting supplies and flooring at the big hardware store by the freeway," Sully said, "and then cheesecake at the bakery and finally I guess we're going back to the furniture gallery to look at that nursery set. With two babies, I need to step up and make a decision."

"Hey, you still have time. They won't be here until September, but I want more material to make another quilt, so let's hit a fabric store too. When are you telling Mom and the girls? They'll be knitting up a storm."

"Tate and I will call them tonight."

The fabric store was close to the furniture gallery, so they were the first two stops. Sully led the way to the corner where they'd seen the nursery set before and came to a complete stop.

Instead of the hand-crafted dark maple crib, changing table, bassinet, toy chest, bookcases, mother's rocking chair, and two matching dressers, she saw a totally different, much smaller version.

This arrangement only had four basic elements, a crib, changing table, bookcase, and one dresser. Because they were obviously machine-made of manufactured wood with a contemporary painted white finish, the price was much lower. Sully looked around for the salesman.

"Don't tell me Tate Murphy liked this," Dominique said. "You'll break my heart. I thought he had much better taste."

"He does and this isn't the one he wanted." Quinn rolled blue eyes. "This is a cheap, crappy version."

"You got that right." When the salesman finally joined them, Sully demanded, "What happened to the nursery set you showed us last weekend?"

"That was last year's model. This is the new style."

"Did you sell the previous ones?" Sully asked. "Where is it?"

"In the back. It'll be sent off to another of our stores in one of the local outlet malls."

"My friend brought me here to see it." Dominique intervened with a super sweet smile. "Can you still show it to us?"

"Of course, but I think they've started wrapping it for shipment."

"Then, they can unwrap it," Quinn said.

Despite his belief, it seemed the workers in the storage area hadn't received word to wrap up the baby furniture. The set was artfully arranged in a distant storage area. Sully caressed the sturdy, dark maple crib. "We ordered one like this already."

"And now you need this one too," Dominique pointed out. "Do you want all the pieces, Sully?"

"Yes, but I don't know what happened to the rocking chair. It was a nice upholstered one."

"It was sold separately, but we can order one made for you."

"No." Quinn slipped an arm around Sully's waist. "Let Dad and Tate make it so they can have some father-son bonding time."

"That works for me and it will undoubtedly save your brother's life."

Dominique eyed the price list still attached to the end of the crib. "Okay, since this is last year's leftovers and you're wholesaling it at the outlet mall, what's the new cost?"

Sully gaped at the realtor but didn't speak.

Negotiations ensued and the exorbitant price began dropping.

When Sully started to agree to the new amount, she felt Quinn squeeze her ribs and remained silent. Dominique continued to bargain with the salesman and at one point, he went to check with the manager.

"I'm thrilled with what you're doing for us," Sully said in a low voice. "This price works for me."

"Not for me. Let's see if we can do better." Dominique narrowed her gaze on the crib. "I love shopping."

The salesman returned accompanied by another man about his age and the dickering continued. Finally, Dominique nodded agreement. "All right. Let's write it up."

"We'll need to add on the cost of delivery."

"No, you won't." Quinn removed her cell phone. "I'll call my brother, Egan. He's a long line trucker. He'll pick it up for us and take it to Sully's new house."

"Let me try Kord too." Sully reached in her pocket. "If he's not on a long haul, he'll come and that'd save us money."

"Of course, your people will wrap up each piece." Dominique sounded like the voice of sugary-sweet reason. "We don't want the baby's new bed marred before she's born."

"What about the crib you and your husband already ordered?" The salesman turned to Sully. "Did you still want that one or should I cancel the order and apply the deposit toward the purchase of the rest of the set?"

"We're having twins. We need both cribs, but they must match."

"Congratulations, ma'am. I'll see to it."

Sully contemplated telling him that calling a non-commissioned Army officer, ma'am or sir was considered an insult but opted to keep the fact to herself. After all, Dominique had about skinned them alive. They wouldn't have much of a profit this time around. Instead, she pasted on what she hoped was a sweet smile. "Thank you. You'll be sure the mattress is well wrapped too, won't you?"

"Of course, we will."

CHAPTER THIRTY

The bright pink car was long gone when he arrived home from the base. He obediently tossed the tennis ball for the two pups on his way to the back door of his aunt's and uncle's home. He tapped on it and walked into the kitchen, greeting his aunt with a kiss on the cheek.

"You want something, or the charm wouldn't be starting this soon." Heidi continued peeling potatoes. "What is it?"

"We're renting the house for the next two weeks before we close on it and I need help painting some of the rooms, laying new tile and carpet, and moving furniture. I'll call my brothers and sisters, but will you arrange for your kids to help me out?"

"Of course, I will." Heidi rinsed the spuds, then began slicing them into a buttered casserole dish. "Are you and Sully joining us for dinner?"

"Yes." Tate poured a cup of coffee. "When I went back to the office after our appointment at the clinic, I talked to my boss and then we went downstairs and discussed it with the head civilian liaison. I'm taking a week's leave to fix up the house."

"Sounds like you have a good plan. Did you talk it over with Sully?"

"Not yet, but I will when she gets back from her shopping trip."

"As I tell your cousins, you have two ears and one mouth. It means you should listen twice as much as you talk. Now, set the table for me, but first, mark off Easter on your calendar."

"Why?"

"If you want me to do something for you, then it must be reciprocal. You and Sully need to come here for the egg hunt and family dinner that weekend."

"Sounds fair. We'll be here that Friday to help prep for it."

His aunt flashed a beaming smile. "That's my boy. Now, be sure to ask your wife if that works for her in case, she planned to visit her relatives. Helene told me they go all out for holidays and you'll want to split time between families."

"We are." Tate kept his tone even and matter-of-fact. "We're with you or with the Baker City bunch. I'll tell Sully the plan. We're not going to Liberty Valley before Christmas and that's non-negotiable."

"Honey, if you want this marriage to work, you need to start asking instead of ordering Sully around. She's your wife, your equal. She's not a subordinate at home even if she wears the same Army uniform. You're only one pay-grade above her."

Raven spotted the bright pink Mustang as soon as Kord pulled into the parking lot at the strip mall. He hadn't driven his big eighteen-wheeler today, borrowing a smaller box truck from Driscoll Hauling to pick up the new set of furniture Sully had purchased. After he parked, he headed inside the store, but Raven drifted toward the classic sports car and slid behind the steering wheel.

Wow, she missed speeding on the local highways even if she'd been pulled over more than once and had to talk her way out of a ticket. She heaved a sigh wishing she could grip the steering wheel, start the car with the key Kord had buried with her, and race out of here. "We had some good times, didn't we?"

She glanced at the store. Time to go see what her bestie bought. She just hoped Sully liked the antique, heavy, solid oak rocking chair that Grandma Driscoll insisted on sending along. Kord had carefully wrapped it in shipping blankets and secured it in the front corner of the truck. Inside the store, Raven found her husband with Sully and a group of people including two salesmen and a couple of warehouse workers clustered around a set of nursery furniture. How had Grandma known that the rocking chair would fit in with the crib and the rest of the elaborate furnishings? The woman was brilliant.

Sully stood next to her husband, his arm around her slightly thicker waist. "You'll be careful with all of this, won't you, Kord?"

"Of course, I will." He took a step forward, close enough to drop a kiss on her forehead. "Don't worry. Where am I taking it?"

"To our new house in Baker City." Sully rested a hand on one end of the dark, wood crib. "I want the nursery painted before it's set up in there so I think the best place for it will be my study."

"I'll meet you there," Tate said. "The two of us can unload everything and then I'll catch up with Sully and Quinn at Lake Maynard Middle High for the cheerleading demo."

"Speaking of which, we'd better hit the road." Quinn glanced at her watch. "My stepdaughter will be having fits if we're late and miss any of the routines she's been teaching the middle-schoolers this week."

"I'm with you." Sully kissed her husband. "Remember, I've checked every piece. A single scratch and you're toast, Master Sergeant Murphy."

He grinned down at her. "I've got my orders and I know how to take them as well as give them. Drive safe. Don't be hot-rodding on the highway."

"Sully never gets tickets in that flamingo car." Kord laughed. "Raven was the one who always drove it like she was in the Indy 500."

"Yeah, well I'm going with her even if she does drive like an old lady." Raven followed her friend toward the parking lot. "I miss my car."

Blue skies, puffy white clouds, and lots of sunshine, a perfect day for a drive north. They timed it correctly to miss most of rush-hour traffic on the way to Lake Maynard. Sully stayed just under the speed limit since she'd seen more than Washington State Patrol vehicle and the last thing, she wanted was a speeding citation. She couldn't bat her eyelashes and get cops to change their minds. "I miss you so much, Raven."

"Likewise. I'd be happier if you could hear me, but I can't wait to see your new house. I'm glad you're living close to the Murphys. You need a real family. Remind Kord to give you the box of snickerdoodles from Grandma."

Sully swiftly glanced sideways at the passenger seat before changing lanes. Did she imagine it, or did she see the faint shadow of her friend sitting there? Raven would be tapping her fingers on her knee and muttering rude things about slugs passing them in a moment or two. Smiling, Sully moved right for the upcoming exit onto the secondary highway that led to Baker City and of course, Lake Maynard.

At the high school, she parked beside Quinn's car in the visitor's lot. Her sister-in-law paused next to the Mustang. "Get your cane, will you? Tate texted me and reminded me to tell you to take it because the ground is probably uneven, and he doesn't want you to slip or fall."

"At some point, I'm going to use this cane and thump your brother with it."

"You know my answer to that. Wait until Sunday so I win the pool."

"What pool?" Raven asked.

"I still don't think it's fair that Aunt Heidi won't let me participate and win the money."

"It wouldn't be right since we're betting on you losing it, having a meltdown, and ripping Tate a new one for being a macho jerk."

Sully caught her breath. They were still living together even if she didn't know what came next and apparently, he hadn't shared their dust-up over her mother, not even with his twin. For a moment, she admired his loyalty and then decided it must be a matter of pride. She was one person he didn't control, and neither was this situation.

"I'm glad you know him so well and won't be turning against me when we have our first big fight."

"How could we when we're fully aware of what a stinker he is sometimes?"

"What if I lose it and leave him?" The question slipped out before she could stop it.

"What if you do? Come sleep in my guest room. I'll use yours when I'm ready to shoot Lyle. We're sisters now and men are the frosting on the cake and sometimes, they're just icky."

"I'll keep that in mind."

Comforted by the knowledge that Quinn was on her side, Sully accompanied her to the football field where they saw seats in the bleachers and prepared to watch the different groups of students perform cheerleading routines.

Before they sat down, Cressida spotted them and raced to greet them, hugging Quinn. "I'm so glad you're home."

"Me too." Quinn glanced around. "Where's your dad?"

"Not here yet." Cressida clung to her stepmother for a moment longer, then turned a dazzling smile on Sully. "How are you? How was your class? Did you do a lot of shopping?"

"I'm fine." Sully smiled at the cheerful blonde. "Class went well. My professor approved my final project and suggested I organize a field trip for the Washington State History class."

"That'd be major fun. We haven't gone anywhere this year. Where's Uncle Tate? Mama-Quinn said his deployment was cancelled and he came home early."

"He'll probably get here at the same time your dad does or he may just meet us at the horse camp." Sully grimaced as she saw the principal nearing them. "Your stepmom and I bought a bunch of furniture. He and my brother are delivering it to our new house."

"Awesome." Cressida glanced over her shoulder as her friends approached. "I'm helping Naveah with the new tile backsplash and the vinyl wallpaper borders in the kitchen, pantry, and laundry room. You don't get to see them until we finish because Uncle Tate says the glue is too smelly for you and the babies."

"Hey, we're the ones who chose the retro-appliance and old-time clothesline paper," Quinn said. "We don't mind missing all the work, but you girls better do a good job, or it'll be a do-over."

"Just like when Sully gives us an essay assignment." With one more wave, Cressida spun and jogged back to the squad.

Quinn smiled after the teen, then hugged Sully. "I owe you. It's the first time in ages that she's shown how much she cares."

"If it weren't for you, I'd need bail money. You make me see Tate as if he's human."

"Well, that's negotiable."

Sully giggled but sobered when Principal Ames joined them. She nodded politely to the stocky man who'd opted for casual wear, slacks, a Lake Maynard Middle High sweatshirt, and a flat tweed cap with the initials of the school on the brim. "Good morning, sir."

"Hello, Mrs. Murphy. I'm sure some of your students will show up today and be glad to see you. How was your spring break? We missed you at the faculty picnic yesterday."

Sully smiled sweetly and murmured something about a doctor's appointment but didn't mention it was for an ultrasound. As the saying went, the man didn't have a 'need to know' her business. His attention soon shifted to Quinn and he began talking to her about what a wonderful student Cressida was. Before the conversation reverted to Sully again, a helpful breeze swept over the three of them, taking his hat with it.

"I don't know why that happened, but I'm glad it did." Quinn gestured to the nearby benches. "Come on. Let's sit down before your leg collapses."

They found seats in the second row and proceeded to watch the broad range of routines executed by elementary, middle school, and senior cheer squads. The girls and boys had obviously worked hard for the last few days to polish the precise movements, jumps, leaps, and diverse gymnastics. Lyle arrived moments before Cressida's group performed. Sully decided it'd save his reputation as a good daddy and hoped Tate would join them soon.

He didn't make it to the school. However, when she arrived at Mindy MacGillicudy's stable a short distance east of Cedar Creek Guest Ranch, she glimpsed his pickup. A tall, black-haired hunk in faded jeans, a flannel shirt, and hiking boots, he made her pulses jumpstart to life. She kissed him, then demanded. "How's the furniture?"

"Just fine. Not a mark on it." Chuckling, he put an arm around her. "And Kord suggested we leave it wrapped up in the shipping blankets for now. The Driscolls sent Raven's great-grandpa's antique rocking chair. I guess you've always loved it and they wanted you to have it."

Tears slid down her cheeks. "I thought they hated me for not taking care of Raven."

"Like Kord says, that wasn't your duty. He was stopping by Pop's and picking up sandwiches. He'll be along in a while to watch Letty do her horsey magick."

"What about your mom? Won't she lose it when she discovers Letty is riding horses?"

"No, because we're not telling her. It's not our business how Quinn and Lyle raise their kids any more than it's their business about how we raise ours."

"I can live with that."

Through the next two hours, they sat next to each other in the guest corral eating sandwiches, drinking bottled water, and watching the riding demonstration. It began with the kids doing exercises on a variety of different sized horses and ponies followed by basic movements and finishing with timed Western games. Afterward, they toured through the barn while Letty took care of her horse and introduced them to her instructor, an elderly white-haired woman who still looked amazing in jeans, a cowgirl shirt, and lace-up riding boots.

Letty hugged her fiercely on the way out of the barn. "I'm going to miss you so much this summer, Mrs. Mindy."

"No, you won't. I'll be here to ride my own horse and check out the new owner. I have to make sure she does things the way I did."

Quinn lingered to embrace the riding instructor as well. "I'm not Letty, but I'll miss you too, Mindy. I'm glad you finally got your price and found someone willing to take over the place."

"And keep my kids' horses alive, well, and working." Mindy grinned. "A bonus is that Herman didn't get the property for one of his awful gravel pits."

"There you go," Tate said. "Everything has a blessing."

On the way to the parking lot, Sully tucked her hand in his. "Is Herman related to Dominique MacGillicudy?"

"Yes, he's her father and the guy has been buying up everything he can in Baker City. The town sits on a gravel bar and he wants to bulldoze most of it and make millions selling the rock."

"Wow, Dominique has more courage than most people if she's flipping houses instead of letting him tear them down."

"Good point." Tate opened the driver's door of the Mustang and held it for her. "I'll follow you to the church camp."

"I'll drive slow so you can keep up."

He bent his head, kissed her quickly. "Good thing I love your sense of humor."

"I'll remind you of that."

"I'm sure you will."

For the rest of the weekend, she struggled to remember that sense of humor while he refused to allow her in the house when he and assorted Murphy relatives painted different rooms. She and Bronwyn drove into Liberty Valley, shopping for curtains, linens, blankets, and towels. When they delivered them to the house, Quinn or one of the teens met the car and carried the purchases inside.

Sunday afternoon, Quinn returned to the Mustang with a handwritten list. "Don't shoot the messenger."

"Why would I?" Sully scanned the note. "What is this? A lunch order? Am I the caterer now?"

"No, you're picking up sandwiches, salads, fried chicken, and everything at Pop's Café. It's just to make sure nothing is forgotten, and the girls want cheesecake. You'll have to swing by the new bakery for it."

"I'm kicking your brother's butt from here to the Army base."

"You can't," Bronwyn said at the same moment that Quinn cheered. "I chose next Friday for the fireworks."

Sully glared at the two women as she turned the key and the Mustang roared to life. "He's so lucky that neither of you is getting a penny."

"Yeah, but I didn't get to pick a date," Raven grumbled from the back seat. "And I've seen plenty of your temper tantrums over the years. The man had better realize that 'duck' is a word of wisdom, not a noun when you get going."

After they dropped off lunch, Bronwyn decided to stay at the new house and sent Sully off to Cedar Creek Guest Ranch to take a nap. Reluctantly, she agreed. On her way through town, she decided she needed her own slice of cheesecake and stopped at the bakery. This time she saw Tim Garvey behind the counter helping customers.

She debated between a slice of the old-fashioned thick cheesecake topped with fresh strawberries or the caramel fudge with a brownie crust. She hadn't quite decided when Tim came toward her. "Hi, how are you?"

"I'm good, Mrs. Murphy. Some of the other guys were freaking out because they had to spend spring break finishing up projects for class, but I didn't. My mom was happy when she heard the other parents got emailed and she didn't."

"How'd you know I had anything to do with that?"

"This is my second semester in that class and we've never had warnings about failing before, and the only thing different is that you're our teacher. So, you did it. There's going to be a lot of work turned in this week."

Sully wrinkled her nose. "That means I'll be the one doing a lot of work, trying to get everything graded before the end of the quarter next Friday. I really need cheesecake."

Tim laughed. "What kind?"

"Two slices. The strawberry and the caramel fudge."

"No worries. You've got it."

She was sitting on the porch in one of the Adirondack wooden chairs when Cat McTavish strolled toward the compact Alpine cabin at the dude ranch. The other woman leaned against the rail instead of opting for the second chair. Sully forked up another mouthful of cheesecake. "Have you been sent to check on me?"

"Nope. Why would I?"

"Because my mother-in-law sent me here to take a nap and I don't wanna."

Cat laughed. "You sound like the twins when Rob decides they're tired and they disagree."

"Does that happen often?"

"All the time. It's part of being a parent." Cat winked. "I think they get it from me. I sulk when he tries to send me off to bed after I fall asleep in the recliner or on the couch."

Sully heaved a sigh. "It's undoubtedly the babies. I need more sleep than I ever did before."

"If you think it's bad now, wait until later." Cat gestured toward the empty chair. "Did you know that you have company?"

"Yes, you're here."

"Besides me. Raven has come for a visit. Is there anything you want me to tell her?"

CHAPTER THIRTY-ONE

Raven watched the color fade from Sully's face before she carefully placed the cardboard container and plastic fork on the small table next to her chair. "That was a shock and I don't think she's ready for it."

"Well, since we can't keep you a secret, she better grow accustomed to having you around." Cat gestured to the chair. "I've been polite long enough and I'm only packing one baby, so move it, First Sergeant Driscoll-Barlow, and let me sit down."

"You pregnant ladies are sure grumpy." Raven stood and crossed to stand by her best friend. "Tell her I'm okay and she'd better not be blaming me for convincing her that joining the Army Reserve was a good idea."

Cat nodded. "Okay, I'll play intermediary for you two." She glanced at Sully. "Your friend wants to be sure you're not mad at her."

A tear streaked down Sully's cheek. "Why would I be mad at her? It's my fault she's gone. I should have insisted we listen to the intel and hold back until we knew for sure the road was safe."

"I'm the one to blame. I wanted the adventure of being in the Army. Sully would have been happy going to college and then becoming a teacher. You've got to tell her I don't want to be the thing that keeps her from being happy," Raven said. "I'm always going to be her family, but she needs more than I can give."

"Wow, that's insightful." Cat heaved a long-suffering sigh. "Anything else?"

"And she also needs to know that moving on doesn't mean forgetting. I've got a lot to tell her."

"Why do I think this is going to take hours to sort out? I hope there's more to eat than cheesecake."

<hr>

Thanks to his large crew, the painting was finished downstairs. Quinn would return in the morning with their brothers' girlfriends and two of their cousins to work on the second floor. It'd take at least two days for the fumes to dissipate which meant the earliest he could allow Sully to move into their home was Wednesday.

He hoped she'd understand and be patient. He'd talk to her about it over dinner and stopped to pick up a frozen pizza at the mercantile on his way out of Baker City.

When he walked into the cabin, he found Sully tearing lettuce for a salad. "What's going on?"

"Isn't that my question?" She flashed a quick smile. "What's the story with the house?"

He filled her in on what they'd accomplished over the weekend. While he talked, she handed him an ice-cold beer, put the pizza in the oven, and then started slicing a tomato.

"You have time for a shower before we eat." She gestured toward the small bathroom. "Hustle up, soldier."

"I thought I was the ranking NCO and issued the orders."

She laughed. "Not here, handsome. You're busted to Corporal as soon as you step over the threshold."

"In your dreams." He kissed her quickly and followed directions.

After they ate, he helped clean up the small kitchen and then they snuggled together on the bed to watch a legal thriller. She didn't last long, falling asleep halfway through the movie and waking up in time to see the credits.

He kissed her forehead. "Do you want me to put on something else? We have several DVDs. You can choose a different show."

"No. I have to leave for school by six a.m., so I think it's time to call it a night." She hesitated, then added. "Your favorite medium came by for a visit and told me Raven was here too."

"Did you believe Cat McTavish?"

"Actually, I did. She knew too many things about us to be faking it. I feel better now that I know Raven doesn't blame me for the ambush."

"And vice versa?"

"Why would I ever blame her? She might have come up with ideas for us to try, but I never argued. I went along because it always sounded like fun and I didn't have much confidence. I was afraid I'd disappoint my mother and I'd hear about it from the rest of the Barlows in Liberty Valley. When I got in trouble for sneaking out, Raven always claimed responsibility for putting me up to it."

He drew Sully closer. "Sounds like typical kid stuff to me."

"Yeah, it was, although my mother always said I was the worst kind of sinner."

"Being thoughtless and taking stupid risks is what teenagers do."

"We'll have to watch the twins, so they don't."

"We will." He smoothed her hair. "It's going to be okay, Sullivan Murphy. We'll be okay."

"I hope you're right, but I'm still afraid."

"You won't be after a few years with me. Trust and love are a two-way street. I can wait for you to realize that."

"Have you always been so smart?"

"I had a good raising by decent people."

"Lucky you." She heaved a contented sigh, her cheek against his chest. "Tell me what you're going to do tomorrow."

"Lock's helping me change out the carpet in the master bedroom to the charcoal wool one you chose for us. It matches the gray patterned ones you liked in the other two downstairs bedrooms. Egan, Garvin, and Dougal are helping Dad install ceramic flooring in the bathrooms, pantry, and kitchen. Quinn's rounded up most of the women to help finish painting upstairs and we'll put down the new blue-gray carpet in those rooms on Tuesday."

"Wow, sounds like I'll have it easier teaching seventh grade English and Washington State History."

"Probably." He smoothed the bright red hair. "What did you and Cat do with Raven? Is she still here?"

"No, she was visiting Cat's family for a while and then going into Baker City to hang out with her ghostly friends. She said she wasn't much for watching me neck with a guy when she was alive, and she didn't plan to do it now that she was dead."

He laughed. "I really like her, especially since she left us alone so I can jump my wife's bones."

"Promises, promises!"

She parked in her assigned spot at the high school and headed inside, grateful she could wear two shoes and only use the cane for emergencies. In the classroom, she found an overflowing in-box piled high with completed assignments. Well, she knew what her life would be like for the rest of the week. Teaching, assessing projects, and posting grades through Friday when the third quarter ended.

The door opened and she nodded at Maureen Evans. "Hello. How was your spring break?"

"Good. I visited my daughters and grandchildren in Idaho, read a book, and went shopping. What about yours?"

"There wasn't much reading for Doctor Dunaway's seminars, but a lot of research for our final projects at the university." Sully went to the front of the room and started writing the daily agenda for the ninth-graders. "I saw my doctor, was cleared to wear two shoes, put in for a transfer to a new Army unit, and did some work at the base."

Maureen nodded. "It must be difficult to transition to civilian life."

"Not too bad when it's the third time I've done it." Sully glanced at the door as Tim Garvey entered, followed by three other boys. "After my first hitch in the *sandbox,* it was hard to adjust at home because I freaked about the fireworks during the Fourth of July. Raven and I headed for the mountains, camping with my brother."

"My dad used to do that with us too," Tim commented while his buddies dropped more papers on Sully's desk. "He always told my mom to get the car packed up so we could head for the hills as soon as he arrived. He'd decompress for a couple of weeks and then be ready to deal with everything when we returned home."

Sully stopped writing as she eyed the young teenager, putting two and two together. "Your dad was Zeke Garvey, wasn't he?"

"Yes. Did you know him?"

"Not me, but I heard about him. My husband was on his Ranger team. He'd have been with your dad when they were hit, except Tate came home early on emergency leave because his father had a heart attack."

Utter silence while all the boys stared at her. She took a deep breath, gestured toward the hallway door. "You guys had better hustle, or you'll be late to first period."

"I told them you'd have all their stuff graded by Friday, Mrs. Murphy," Tim said. "I'm right, aren't I?"

"Yes," Sully said. "I'll undoubtedly be up until oh-two or oh-three-hundred hours every night this week, but I'll get it done."

"Let me know if you need more cheesecake and I'll tell my mom." Grinning, Tim sauntered toward the door, accompanied by his friends.

They'd barely reached the hall when she heard one of them say, "I heard she was in a car wreck and that's how she hurt her leg."

"Yeah, there's a lot of crap floating around this school." Irritation filled Tim's voice. "Cressy Chapman's been passing the word that Mrs. Murphy is a noncom in the Army Reserve and she was injured by an I.E.D. in Afghanistan. It's pretty bad when a cheerleader has to stop the gossip train."

Kids were realists, Sully thought, not for the first time. She might not care for her mentor teacher, but at least the woman had been friendly this morning. Maureen didn't say anything about the lesson plans for the next three weeks or the possibility of a field trip to Underground Seattle. Since she had plenty of work to do, Sully focused on that instead, directing the students through writing their *C.Y.A.* letters justifying their grades at the end of the quarter.

Tate arrived at the cabin after she did, so she took a break from grading to prepare dinner. After they ate, he cleaned up the kitchen, then jumped in to help her. It meant she could follow Margo's advice and enter grades online at the last moment before going to bed.

Tuesday followed the same pattern, but Wednesday, she headed to the new house in Baker City rather than the cabin.

When she drove inside, she found Lock in the three-car garage. She parked, turned off the engine, and watched him for a few moments. He continued putting away new containers of the supplies she used for the Mustang, high-quality handwashing soap, sealants, wax, polish, proper rags, sponges, orbital polisher, wheel care products, chrome polish, and interior conditioner. "What are you doing?"

"Prepping so I can detail your *Barbie* car for the duration."

"Where did you get an insane idea like that?"

"From Tate. He's been researching on the Internet again and says too many of these products might have toxic ingredients that are bad for the babies, so you can't use them."

"That's it. I'm going to kill him." She reached in the back seat, removed her cane. "He's a dead man."

"You can't do it until tomorrow or I won't win the pool."

"Too bad, too sad." Leaving her bags in the car, she started toward the door that opened into the kitchen. It opened before she reached it and she glared up at Tate as he approached. "I liked you better when I thought you were leaving. Now, I'm stuck with you for the duration and you're pissing me off, *Rescue Ranger*. I'm either filing for divorce or seeing Reverend Tommy about an annulment."

Tate winced. "Somebody had a bad day at school."

"No, my day was fine until I got here and discovered the *Internet Doctor* has struck again and thinks he's the boss of me and my car."

"Hey, I didn't say I wanted to drive it." He eyed his younger brother. "You told her, didn't you?"

"I didn't know it was a secret." Lock placed two buckets on the bottom shelf. "I did say she couldn't smack you around until tomorrow."

"Why?"

"Because your aunt started a pool on when I'd lose it and start throwing things at you. She won't let me participate. I need the money to bury you."

He laughed, scooped her up in his arms, and started for the doorway. "Clobber me later, Mrs. Murphy. Right now, I'm carrying my bride across the threshold so she can ooh and aah over her new house and tell me I've done everything she wanted."

"I better be happy or I'm hanging you out to dry." She rested her head against his shoulder, breathing in the lime aftershave. "You're lucky you're sexy."

Behind them, Lock groaned. "Dammit, this means I didn't win the pool."

"And you're also not washing or waxing my car."

"It's still my car too." Raven floated across the garage to study the various automotive supplies. "I may not be able to drive it either, but that doesn't mean any guy in the family gets to put their macho hands on it."

Once she approved of the goods he'd selected for the Mustang, she wandered into the house. She found Sully admiring the oak rolltop desk in the study. The hutch top had a solid roll down tambour and key lock. The desk was obviously a replica since it'd been designed to hold a computer and even had USB ports. There were multiple drawers, two of which would hold files and several traditional cubbies for other supplies.

Spring sunlight streamed through the blinds on the windows. Raven sauntered around the room, eyeing the wooden file cabinets, the bookcases filled with paperbacks and hardcovers, the dresser that held various office materials, and the new laser printer on top of the same dresser. "This guy knows how to appeal to a teacher, doesn't he?"

No answer from her best friend and Raven drifted to the corner and the antique rocking chair by a pole lamp. She sat down, leaning back to watch her friend check out the room. "If Kord had done this for me, I'd call in sick at the school and take him to bed for the next three days. You picked a good one even if he does try to run the joint."

Tate lingered near the study, waiting for Sully to finish exploring the desk. Quinn had come through for him when she found it at the outlet mall. He owed his twin big-time for the rescue. Without her, Sully undoubtedly would still be giving him hell over leaving her out of redoing the house and not letting her help paint or put down carpet or move in the furniture. She stroked the wood one more time, then glanced at the rocking chair that moved on its own in the corner. "Apparently, we have company."

"Undoubtedly." He leaned against the doorframe. "Do you want me to contact Cat McTavish and ask her to run interference?"

"Don't be silly. It's Raven and she's always welcome here."

"Good to know." He followed Sully out of the study and across the hall to the first of the two bedrooms. She frowned thoughtfully as she inspected the layout of some of the nursery set. The crib, changing table, bassinet, and one of the dressers was in the sitting area of the master suite, but the rest was here. There was still room for the second crib in their room when it arrived. "Do you like it, or do you want me to move things around?"

"I'll think about it. I haven't decided."

"Okay, that works for me."

A long, slow look before she went to check out the second bedroom. Light blue-accented one wall, but the other three were still soft ivory. Panel curtains hung at the windows over the mini-blinds. He hadn't changed out the gray patterned carpet. "I thought we could bring over beds, a desk, and a large dresser from the attic at Mom and Dad's so we'd have a guest room in case the girls want to come for a night or two this summer."

"I like that idea." She strolled to him, brushed her lips across his. "It's a good thing you're smart and sexy, Master Sergeant Hot Stuff."

He chuckled, rested his hands on her hips, and brought her closer. "And we've just gotten started. You haven't seen the rest of the house yet."

"I'm enjoying the tour." She laced her arms around his neck. "I think you should really kiss me instead of playing around."

"I can do that." Twisting a hand in the bright fire of her hair, his mouth claimed hers.

For the rest of the week, she enjoyed the nesting process as they settled into their new home. Just for fun, she gave herself points when she jumped him in each of the rooms. Lock brought over furniture from his parents' house and helped Tate arrange it. When he returned to the base on Monday, he promised to be back as much as possible, thanks to Major Harper. Chantrea and Naveah hung curtains, unpacked dishes, helped make the bed in one of the upstairs rooms. With Joe's and Bronwyn's able assistance, Sully turned the other one into a suitable man cave for Tate.

When they talked on the phone, she told him how much she loved his relatives and they certainly seemed to return the favor. They called or visited almost every day. When they didn't come to her house, she went to Bronwyn and Joe's. She could tap on the back door, walk in and be greeted as if she were another of their actual children, not a daughter by marriage.

Sully didn't mention how often she walked into the various rooms at their new home and found the flat-screen TV playing a Hallmark movie, or heard the comfortable sound of the ABBA CD on the stereo, or turned to see the rocking chair in the study apparently moving by itself while she prepared for class. It was wonderful having Raven for company even if her best friend couldn't be seen, at least not by Sully.

She thought about Raven's advice often, that "moving on didn't mean forgetting." It was okay to have a new family, one that loved her for who she was. She might not know where she and Tate were going or if they even had a relationship beyond this odd marriage of convenience, but she was falling in love with him. She hadn't told him that of course. If she did, he'd probably run for the hills. She'd learned a long time ago that she wasn't loveable.

Stop it, Sully remembered what Raven had told Cat more than once. *It's time to be happy. I haven't lost my B.F.F. Even if I never hear from people in Liberty Valley again. I have a new life here. I have a good man and a good family. Soon, I'll find a good job too. And I'm going to be a great mom. I'll do the opposite of everything Helene Barlow did and my babies will be sooo happy.*

The three weeks of student teaching in April zoomed by. Most of the seventh-graders had turned in their work in time to have it affect their quarter grades. Maureen Evans hadn't said a word about what Ann Barrett called the *C.Y.A.* letters and hadn't pitched a fit when Sully gave the kids credit for bringing back the copies signed by the parents.

So far, so good, Sully told herself. The Washington State History class was excited about the upcoming field trip at the end of the week. However, she still hadn't received authorization from the administration for a bus to take them to Seattle. She glanced at the calendar. Four more days. She could do that standing on her head. Granted, they needed to film a lesson in the History class, but Dr. Dunaway would do it when she came to assess Sully for a final observation.

Her cell phone buzzed, and she eyed the screen. Odd. Why would Command Sergeant-Major Jenkins be calling? She hadn't heard back from him about the transfer, but he also hadn't turned her down. "Hello, Sergeant-Major. How are you?"

"I'm good, Sergeant Barlow-Murphy. Just checking in to see if you heard from Master Sergeant Waller."

"Why would I?"

"He and Sergeant Colter, the new Active Guard-Reserve company technician are putting together a training exercise for this Saturday. They need an OPFOR. He thought you might want to lead it."

"Why would I?" Sully repeated the question. "I've requested a transfer."

"I know. I saw the paperwork. Leave in a blaze of glory, Sergeant Barlow-Murphy, and have the satisfaction of ambushing the cadre who set you up. Not that I'd say such a thing of course."

Sully gaped at her phone, stunned by the opportunity to wreak vengeance on the officers who'd cost Raven her life. "I've got to think about it."

"That's why I called. It's Tuesday. Let me know by Friday. Waller suggested you round up your brother, Falcon Driscoll, and Bianca Powell."

"I need to include Tate. He'll have a fit if I do it without him and it's not worth a fight on the home front."

"Something I need to know about him, Barlow-Murphy? Is there some reason he won't let you out of his sight?"

Sully glanced cautiously at the closed hallway door, then lowered her voice to just above a whisper. "We're expecting twins in September and he's in full-blown daddy mode."

"Oh, I remember those days. Tell him, it doesn't get easier. I have four daughters. Like my wife says, 'the more the merrier.' And call Waller."

CHAPTER THIRTY-TWO

She thought about the Army Reserve training exercise for the rest of the afternoon while she graded papers and entered scores in the online program. When she packed up at the end of the day and headed downstairs, she still hadn't decided if she wanted to participate although she'd texted the others the Sergeant-Major suggested.

She forced herself to stop thinking about the military and focused on the job at hand. Most of the students in the Washington State History class had turned in their permission slips for the field trip. She knew the rest would undoubtedly come in before Friday's trip. In the office, she waited for Della Lowry to finish a phone call and the secretary approached the front counter, with a friendly smile.

Sully nodded a greeting. "Hi, Della. I'm still waiting to hear about the bus for the field trip. Have you heard anything?"

Shock and concern filled the older woman's face. "Didn't they tell you? Principal Ames turned down the request. He says we don't have the funding."

"It's a new quarter." Sully took a deep breath. "Is he still here? Can I see him?"

"Let me check with him. I know he has an appointment with a parent, but it doesn't start for a few minutes."

As usual, when it came to seeing her, the principal wasn't alone.

Maureen Evans sat in one of the chairs facing his large oak desk. Sully nodded to both of them and then asked about the field trip and a bus.

"Mrs. Evans says she told you that we're low on funding for special events and this counts as one. Activities like a trip to Seattle need to be arranged at the start of the school year." Principal Ames folded his arms, resting his elbows on the desk. "Maybe, we can do it another time."

"Except that my last day is next Monday," Sully reminded him. "I won't have another opportunity to take them."

"Well, I suppose you and Dr. Dunaway should have thought of that before."

"I see." Sully eyed the pair once more before she focused on Maureen Evans. "Will you tell the students or is that my responsibility?"

"It was your plan. You get the honors."

"I see," Sully repeated. Tears burned but she refused to let them fall. She'd been sabotaged before and Raven had died. "I'll handle it tomorrow."

Still stunned and bewildered, she left the office and headed for the parking lot. Safely in the car, she sent a text off to Tate who'd returned to the Army base early Monday morning. She missed him. When he arrived on Fridays, she often found him puttering around the house and making it perfect for them. He always had an afternoon snack prepared for her when she walked in the door and the two of them sat at the table in the kitchen to talk about their week, Bo and Diddly snoozing underneath.

He didn't answer right away. He must be in the field, his phone out of range and he'd get back to her. Meantime she sent a note off to Dr. Dunaway letting her know they'd need to reschedule the final student teaching exam because the woman didn't need to accompany them on the now cancelled field trip. Why did some people enjoy hurting others? Sully could handle the disappointment, but what about the kids? Why knock them down when they were so engaged in the idea of a living history trip?

She really needed to talk to other teachers, so the last message went to Margo Endicott and Ann Barrett. Sully offered to meet them at Pop's Café for dinner, saying she wanted to pick their brains for a make-up lesson now that she couldn't take her class to tour the remains of the pioneer city. They'd been entranced when she explained how Seattle was rebuilt over the top of the burned buildings and they'd be able to see some of the historic structures.

She tucked her phone away and headed home after a quick stop to top off the gas tank in Lake Maynard. Once she arrived, she parked the car near the garden hose, then took her school supplies inside and let the puppies out to play. After she changed clothes, she went back out to wash the Mustang, her go-to activity when she was upset. Bo brought his favorite tennis ball and between bouts of scrubbing, she threw the ball toward the outbuildings. He and Diddly had learned to stay with her and away from the road.

Her cell vibrated and she pulled it out of her jeans to answer the message from Ann. She and Margo would meet her in an hour and a half at the café, depending on traffic. The next note came from Dr. Dunaway saying that full-time teachers often had their plans thwarted by those in power, so it was time to improvise. She'd rearrange her own schedule and look forward to seeing what Sully devised on Thursday when they did the final assessment.

Sully sent an acknowledgment and then replaced the phone in her pocket. She returned to her chore of washing the Passionate Pink hood of the classic Mustang. The half-grown pups romped on the grass near her, then bolted past the car to bark at the pickup pulling in the drive.

She wished it was Tate, but it only took a moment to recognize his younger brother. She dropped the soggy sponge in the bucket of soapy water and advanced on Lock. "Hi, how's it going?"

"I got a message from Tate. He told me to come over and help you detail the car."

"Don't you have pigs and cows to feed?"

"Not for a couple of hours and Dad will get the girls to help him if I'm not back." Lock looked down at the soggy tennis ball Bo had dropped at his feet. "What do you want?"

The two young dogs crouched, tails at full wag, and barked in pure excitement until he surrendered. He bent, picked up the ball, then winged it toward the barn. They tore off in hot pursuit. "I've got to get a dog."

"I heard you didn't like them."

"What? Who told you that?" Lock removed his baseball cap, ran a hand through dark, curly hair, and then replaced the hat, putting it on backward. "I don't want untrained, nasty little yapping dust mops who upset my sows when they're about to farrow or my cows when they're due to calve. I told Aunt Heidi if she came across an Aussie Cattle Dog to let me know."

"Aren't they nippy?"

"Yup and they round up kids if there isn't any work to do. They're real dogs, not phony-baloney ones."

Sully hid a smile as he threw the ball again and the dogs chased after it. "These two are half-heeler and half-collie."

"I know, but they're yours so I can't take them to the farm." One last throw and then he picked up a sponge from the supplies in the tote box. "Let's get busy and you can tell me about your day. Tate's out camping with what he calls his princesses and cell phone service is erratic, so I've been drafted to do the listening thing."

"Okay, but first I have to say how much I love your family."

"We love you too." He winked at her. "You fit in perfectly."

In a shining bright pink, freshly washed, and waxed Mustang, Sully drove through town to the café a short time later. She was the first to arrive, but Margo and Ann showed up within ten minutes. Soon, they were all in a booth, Ann enjoying a glass of her favorite white wine while Margo and Sully opted for ginger ale. Once they'd ordered dinner, she brought them up to speed on the latest contretemps with the mentor teacher and principal from Hell and the canceled field trip.

"So, now I have to come up with something else for the kids to do on Thursday when Dr. Dunaway comes to film the class. Ideas?"

"Is there a virtual tour of Underground Seattle?" Ann sipped her wine. "And if not, can you create one?"

"Good idea."

"She's full of them," Margo said. "What are you going to tell your students tomorrow? It may not be super professional, but I'd find a way to throw Maureen Evans and Principal Ames under the bus they won't let you have."

"She's right," Ann said. "Nothing is worse than a bunch of pissed-off middle-schoolers. They'll get you and you don't want to see their teen version of pay-back. Talk about *fubar*—you'll be *embracing the suck* for days."

"Thanks for the warning." Sully smiled at the waitress when she arrived with their food. "Let's eat and then come up with more strategies."

She wasn't nearly as exhausted as she'd expected when she drove home three hours later. She still had enough energy to begin work on the new lesson after she fed the dogs. They kept her company while she designed a worksheet containing the various links to different websites about Underground Seattle. She didn't hear from Tate, but then again, she hadn't anticipated she would after his brother said he was camping out with the students at the Army base. He'd probably call tomorrow or Thursday when he was back at HQ and she could talk to him about the upcoming training exercise with her old Army Reserve Company.

Sully wasn't surprised to find Maureen Evans in the classroom when she arrived. She put her bags on the desk and proceeded to write out the daily agenda on the whiteboard. "Did you hear from Dr. Dunaway? She moved up my final assessment to this Thursday instead of Friday."

"You haven't received appropriate recommendations from anyone in the administration or from me. We really don't feel you're ready to be certificated yet."

"I'm sorry to hear that." Sully kept listing the schedule. "My last day is Monday and even if I'm forced to appeal your decision, I can always apply for positions as a Science teacher since I've already met those prerequisites."

"That isn't a wise choice."

"It's the one I've already made." Finished with the list, Sully turned on the overhead projector and put up the entry task for first period. They'd finished reading *The Odyssey* and she was reviewing the key points in the epic so Maureen could test the students on their knowledge after Sully's departure. The older woman stalked out of the room before the bell and the day started.

In Washington State History, Sully announced that plans had changed. They would have a virtual tour of Underground Seattle since the school administration said Lake Maynard Middle High couldn't afford a field trip. Moans and groans erupted along with more angry responses, but the students settled down after a few minutes of furious venting, especially when Sully promised to bring popcorn to go with the movies and computer exercises.

During sixth period, Sully continued her usual routine of grading assignments and posting the scores online. She missed Tate. Without his help, this last segment of student teaching would have proven impossible. She didn't know any other man who'd have helped with the work dumped on her. Raven had never said whether Kord backed her up or not and he hadn't either. Sully decided to ask when she called him. As if the thought conjured him up, her cell buzzed, and she answered.

"Hey, I was just thinking about you."

"Good things, I hope," Kord said. "Raven's mom wants to know if you'd like the antique china hutch for your dining room. It wasn't our thing and she says if she gives it to one of her sons, it'll be busted up for firewood."

"We'd love it. Once we have the house totally revved up, we'll be having a housewarming and I want to invite the Driscolls. Do you think that will make waves with the Barlows when I don't invite them?"

"Who cares if it does? They've always treated you like a second-class citizen. Just be sure to include me, Dad, and our brothers. Helene is still miffed because you barely call her. Did you really chew her out?"

"She was obnoxious when she visited during spring break and I'm not putting up with her driving away Tate."

"All right. Way to go!"

Sully glanced at the door when she heard the tapping of heels on tile and saw Sandra Young coming into the room. "I've got to return to grading, Kord, but I heard from Sergeant-Major Jenkins yesterday and he wants me to lead an OPFOR team this Saturday afternoon."

"Why? What's up with that?"

"It's a training exercise for my battalion at Fort Bronson. Want to help?"

"Why would I?"

"As Dad would say, we're *spinning the helmet* on the Colonel and his cadre. If things go as usual, we won't be using live ammo, just paint guns. Are you in?"

"Oh yeah, I'm in. Got somewhere for me to bunk Saturday night?"

"You bet. Ask Falcon if he wants to play."

"I don't even have to ask. He'll be in too. We'll kick some butt that day."

"Good to know." She ended the call and turned her attention to the Humanities Department Chair. "I have Army Reserve duty this weekend and I've been put in charge of the OPFOR team. Thanks for waiting."

"What's an OPFOR team?" Sandra drew up a seat on the other side of the desk. "Are you sure someone in your condition should be doing that?"

"OPFOR is an abbreviation for Opposing Force and basically we sneak around the woods and attack different small groups of the reserve unit." Sully wrote down the score at the top of the page. "And what condition are you talking about? My physical therapist encourages me to exercise my leg, so I build up strength and muscle."

"You're pregnant." Sandra picked up the graded paper and scanned it. "Maureen may not be announcing it, but I have three boys and two girls. I knew right away. Is running around the woods playing soldier a great idea?"

Sully laughed. "It'll be fun, and I can't leave my husband home when I'm doing it, much less my brother. With those two, I'll be lucky if they let me do anything but sniper duty."

"As long as somebody watches over you, it will be fine." Sandra replaced the paper. "I heard from the kids that you're finishing up your student teaching soon."

"Next Monday."

"That's not much time. I'll be in to observe your class tomorrow so I can write a recommendation. I'll send along some of the other teachers too although Maureen claims you're staying through June because of your abysmal performance."

"No, I'm going on Monday. That's when my university supervisor says I'll be done. I don't want you getting in trouble because of me."

"Don't worry about that. I wouldn't have my job if I wasn't

comfortable making trouble. Some people like surprises, but I have a hunch you don't. We'll be celebrating your accomplishments at lunch this Friday and afterward, you can go home early."

"Wow, I'm thrilled. I didn't expect that."

"You should have. Remind the kids you'll be leaving on Monday. Some will want to bring you cards and going away presents. After all, many of them wouldn't have passed last quarter without your hard work."

PART IV

MAY 2019

CHAPTER THIRTY-THREE

Before school Friday morning, she found Maureen Evans in the classroom. Placing her school bag and computer tote by her desk, Sully nodded a greeting. When she spotted two stacks of papers, she paused. "What is this?"

"Pop quizzes for the students."

"What?" Sully froze in her tracks. "The university and Dr. Dunaway believe those are an ineffective assessment tool. She told my cohort there isn't any point in catching the kids off guard and it doesn't make them better prepared."

"That's one person's opinion and this is my class. I'll be taking over next Tuesday since she insisted on giving you a passing grade on yesterday's evaluation. I don't think you're ready to leave here, especially since you haven't finished the unit for English Seven or Washington State History, and I want to be sure they know the material."

Sully counted silently to ten. "Are they allowed to use their chapter notes?"

"What would be the point? Then, they'd be cheating and definitely don't remember anything they've been studying."

"Wow, no wonder Raven was determined not to come here." It was a low blow and Sully watched the older woman stiffen in obvious shock. "I thought it was beyond the proverbial Pale when you didn't come to her funeral or memorial, but you really didn't like her either."

Maureen sputtered for a moment. "I didn't know she'd died. Nobody did."

"Her obit was in all the local papers and on the news." Sully folded her arms, looking the other teacher up and down. "I understood why Dr. Dunaway didn't make it. She always goes to Ireland for Christmas, but you—"

"I didn't know."

"You just keep telling that story and I'm sure you'll find someone who believes it."

Sully watched the older woman leave the room. Okay, so it'd been a totally bitchy thing to do, but did she have any regrets for abandoning the high road? No, she thought, and she was sure Raven would have been cheering her on because her best friend didn't like pettiness of any sort.

Taking a deep breath, Sully picked up the quiz on *The Odyssey* and skimmed the twenty multiple-choice questions. They'd covered the entire epic from start to finish and she silently congratulated herself for reviewing it with the students. If they'd been paying attention in class, most of them would be able to zip through the test. They knew the setting, the characters, the timeline, themes, common descriptions, and metaphors.

The warning bell rang, and she collected a handful of quizzes. She walked to the door to meet the incoming students, handing out tests as they entered. "This is a half-day and you know the drill. We have short periods. You don't have a lot of time, so get started right away."

"You've never given us one of these before," one of the boys complained.

"It was Mrs. Evan's idea." Sully passed out more papers. "She'll be taking over your class on Tuesday because I'm almost done student teaching."

"That's not fair." This time it was a girl.

"Life isn't and you'd better get started. The clock's ticking, folks."

While they worked through the test, Sully quickly created an answer key for the TA to use during the next period. If everything was graded during the day, she'd be able to enter the scores online tonight.

Next Monday, they'd review the quizzes and she'd make that last for the entire class period. There wasn't any point in assigning something she wouldn't be here to assess.

What should have been a pleasant morning wasn't. The students felt betrayed and cheated as they sullenly took the quizzes. Instead of being her usual sunshiny, cheerleader self, even Cressy sulked on her way out the door. Sully sighed, feeling like *Public Enemy Number One*, and prepared for more teen drama.

Luckily, the older teens seemed a bit more understanding as they graded the quizzes. "Don't stress, Mrs. Murphy," Octavia said, heading to lunch. "They'll figure out eventually that it was Mrs. Evans who tried to trick them and sabotage you. Everybody in second period passed the quiz and these guys are sharper. I know they did better."

"I hope you're right." Sully closed the classroom door and went to eat her own snack. Two more classes and she'd be done. Then, all she had to endure was the lunch with the other teachers and hope their farewell party remained somewhat civil. Despite Sandra Young's promise, only two of them had shown up on Thursday to observe the classes and Sully figured she'd better not count on letters of recommendation from either instructor. They had to stay here and get along with the administration. She didn't.

Shortly before noon, she headed for the parking lot carrying a bouquet of mixed flowers. She'd tucked the box of chocolates in her school bag, figuring she'd give them to Margo Endicott. She stopped suddenly when she saw Bianca Powell standing by the Mustang, Dak Marshall next to her, his hand clamped on a dark-haired boy's shoulder.

Sully started forward, increasing her pace as she saw sunshine break through the clouds to reveal broken eggs splattered across the bright pink hood. Bright yellow yolks ran down the windshield and over the roof of the fastback. She gasped, shaking her head in denial. "It can't be. What the hell? My car. My Mustang. Raven—"

"Somebody was obviously angry with you." Dak urged the teen in a torn black t-shirt and sloppy camo pants forward. "This is the one we caught."

Struggling to breathe, Sully looked past the pair to the broken rear-window and the slashed, left-front tire. "O.M.G., why? When did it happen? This doesn't make sense."

"I'm sorry, Mrs. Murphy, but a bunch of the guys got mad about the surprise tests today." Tim Garvey tried to pull away from the security guard but Dak's hold tightened. "I keep telling them it wasn't me that trashed the car. I tried to stop it, but they—"

Sully glanced at him, seeing the bruise forming on his cheek, blood dripping from his nose, and the dirt-stained shirt and pants. "Let him go. He's right. I had him in class earlier today and he didn't look anything like this. Who was it, Tim?"

"I'm not ratting them out. I wouldn't mess with your car, but I'm not a snitch."

"Whoever did it broke this security camera first, but we have others," Bianca said. "I'll check with the chief and we'll get names and try to file charges."

A sudden coldness washed through her and Sully shuddered, fighting to control her emotions. She didn't know if she wanted to cry or scream or throw things. She squeezed her eyes shut for a moment. *Breathe*, she told herself sternly. *Just breathe and drive on. You've been through worse. You can deal.*

Somehow, she managed to pull out her keys without dropping the stupid flowers. "I've got to change that tire and get my car home so I can wash it. Those eggs will destroy the paint job."

"Do you have a jack?" Bianca approached and took the keys. "Where is it?"

"In the trunk. So is the spare."

"We'll change it." Dak pushed Tim toward the rear of the vehicle. "You do a report with Bianca."

Sully managed to nod again. Her voice shook. "It was my last teaching day here."

"A helluva parting gift." Bianca opened the notebook she carried and removed a form. "Let me get some facts."

"Okay." Sully lifted a hand to keep the other woman from getting too close. "Did you get my message about helping with the training exercise at Fort Bronson tomorrow?"

"Yes. Dak and I will be there." Bianca uncapped a pen. "Tell me about your classes today, Sully."

A cool wind blew through the broken back window and ruffled her hair as Sully drove toward Baker City. Tears rained down her cheeks. Why did they hate her so much? She'd busted her butt to teach them, to be kind but fair, to make sure most of them passed English and History. It wasn't right. What they'd done wasn't right. Oh sure, Tim Garvey claimed to have spoken up, but he'd chosen his friends over her. He'd allowed them to trash her car, her beautiful car, the one thing she had left from her time with Raven.

She pulled into the driveway and parked by the garden hose. She had to wash the car, had to get the eggs off it before they ruined the paint. She supposed she should be grateful that Sandra had allowed her to leave early. If it'd been a regular Friday, she wouldn't have been out of the school for at least another three and a half hours and her Mustang would be totally ruined.

She turned on the water and adjusted the sprayer at the end. Then, she began rinsing off the hood. She didn't dare pick off the pieces of the shell stuck to the metal. Gravel crunched and she saw Tate pull in the driveway. He parked his truck behind the Mustang, got out, and came toward her, a lethal, dark-haired figure in camos and combat boots.

"What the hell? Who did this?"

"Middle High School 101." Sully handed him the hose. "Keep rinsing them off while I get some vinegar. Don't remove the broken eggshells or you'll pull off the paint."

"I'll take care of this for you."

"No, you won't. My car, my responsibility. You can help, but you're not doing it for me." Before he argued the point, she spun around and hurried into the house. She opened the kitchen door for the dogs to run in the fenced back yard. She didn't have time to walk or pet or play with them right now.

She found a plastic bottle and filled it with distilled white vinegar. That done, she collected soft white towels from the linen closet and hustled back to the car. Tate had continued rinsing off the Mustang. She began spraying the remaining eggs with vinegar, then dampened the first towel with more vinegar before gently wiping away the stain and pieces of shell. Thankfully, none of the paint came with it. She whooshed out a sigh of relief and continued hunting down the eggs.

"I knew you were almost done teaching." Tate allowed the water to flow over the roof, careful to keep it away from the broken window. "I thought I'd get here in time to take you out for a steak dinner."

"That would have been nice." She kept dabbing at a stubborn yolk. "Maureen made me give pop quizzes today and some of the kids took offense."

"That's no excuse for property damage. Did you call the cops?"

"I didn't have time. I had to get the car home."

"Did you take pictures of the damage?"

"Hello! Are you listening to me at all? I told you I didn't have time. I have to get the eggs off before they wreck the paint."

"You can repaint the car, but you need pictures in order to file charges. Get your phone and take them now or I will."

"Damn you, Tate Murphy. Save that command voice for when you're on post. I don't want to hear it. Besides, Bianca Powell the security officer at the school took photos when she wrote up an incident report."

"Good. Email her and tell her to send what she has to Dick O'Connell, the police chief here."

"Are you freaking listening to me? I'll do it after I finish cleaning my car."

"You'll do it now, Sullivan Rafferty Murphy." He turned off the nozzle on the hose. "There are consequences and these kids need to learn that before they get any older. You're a teacher. This is what you call a teachable moment. Step up and teach."

"But my car." Tears rose along with her temper. She wadded up the towel and threw it at him. It smacked against his broad shoulder, vinegar splotching onto the camouflage shirt. "It comes first."

"No, sweetheart. You come first." He pulled out his cell phone and pressed buttons. "I'm calling the police chief. He can come here and write a report, then follow up with the school."

"I hate you."

"I know." He paused and waited for someone to answer, then identified himself and told them the situation. "We need Chief O'Connell to come now before my wife destroys the evidence."

His next call was to the school where he left a message for Bianca Powell to email him the original photos of the vandalism and to also send them to the cop shop in Baker City. "Were there any witnesses?"

"Tim Garvey." Sully snatched up the hose, turned on the water, and began rinsing off the eggs she'd saturated with vinegar. "But he won't rat out his friends. He claims he stopped them before they slashed more tires and didn't let them break more windows."

"Zeke's boy?" Tate asked.

When she nodded, he pushed more buttons on his phone. "Twila, this is Tate Murphy. We have a problem and I know you'll want to deal with it before Chief O'Connell gets there."

Sully glared at him as she rounded the car and started working on the passenger side. He obviously didn't understand the situation. He didn't grasp how important it was to take care of the Mustang first and then deal with recalcitrant teens that didn't hesitate to do property damage. She rinsed off the car, letting the gentle spray soak the door panel.

Her fury escalated as he strode toward her, putting the phone back in his shirt pocket. "Twila will talk to Tim and get names."

"Well, aren't you the big man?" She swung toward him, the hose in her hand. Before she had time to consider her actions, she turned the nozzle on full blast and let him have it from beret to combat boots.

He backed up and she followed, soaking his shirt and pants again. He reached the outdoor faucet before she did and pushed down the handle on the stand-pipe. "You're out of ammo now, sweetheart."

"I'm not done."

"Oh yes, you are." He snagged her wrist and pulled her hard against him.

When he lowered his head, she punched him in the ribs. He gasped for an instant, then laughed and kissed her, a fierce possession. She tried to twist her head away, but his mouth remained on hers. The pressure forced her lips apart as he staked his claim. She ought to keep fighting, but she couldn't.

She gasped for air when he lifted his head and smirked down at her. She kicked him in the ankle. "Gawd, how I hate you."

"Too bad, too sad, Mrs. Murphy." He traced a line down her nose with one finger. "I love you so much. You're never getting away from me."

"You married me because I'm pregnant."

"No, I married you, so you'd stay with me." He drew her tight against him. "I could have just paid child support and demanded visitation if I was only stepping up to do the right thing. I lost you once when you disappeared like smoke in December. I'm never losing you again."

"I love you too, but I can compartmentalize with the best of them." She lifted her chin, measuring the sincerity on his rugged features. "I'm still mad at you."

"I know." He trailed a series of kisses along her neck. "You're cute when you're mad. I have to piss you off more often."

She shivered, suddenly aware that her blouse was wet and clinging. So were her slacks. His clothes were soaked from the hose. Hers were from the way he'd shared the moisture when he dragged her tight against him. "My car still needs to be washed."

"I know. Damn those kids." He nipped her ear. "I want to take you to bed and I can't because I have to get those eggs off before they wreck the paint."

"I thought you were waiting for the town cop."

"I am and he's here."

She glanced over her shoulder, heat flooding her face when she saw the police cruiser in the drive. "I've got to change clothes."

"Yes, you do." He stepped between her and the officer. "Come join us afterward so you can talk to him."

"My car."

"You don't have to spend the afternoon washing, sealing, and waxing your Mustang. I already told you I'd take care of it."

"O.M.G., not more of your soldier in charge of the universe crap." She stomped toward the house. "I'm telling you again that you're not the boss of me."

"Want to bet? When Dick leaves, you can take a nap while I clean up the Mustang."

CHAPTER THIRTY-FOUR

It'd taken several hours to detail the Mustang. Quinn came by with takeout Chinese food for dinner and stayed to help wax the classic vehicle. Once it was safely locked in the garage, they called it a night. Tate carried her off to bed where he proceeded to rock her world until she admitted she was no longer angry with him.

On Saturday, Naveah and Chantrea came over to babysit the puppies while Sully and her OPFOR team headed for Fort Bronson to help with the training exercise for the battalion scheduled for thirteen-thirty, military time; one-thirty in the afternoon, civilian. When they arrived shortly before lunch, Derek Waller, the lead civilian technician explained the parameters of the camouflage, escape, and evasion class.

"Sergeant Barrett will supervise the small groups preparing to cross the obstacle course. They're going through the woods back to the office buildings the battalion uses for regular duty hours," Derek said. "We'll ambush them on the way. Master Sergeant Colter will lead one OPFOR patrol and I'll lead the other."

Tate eyed him. "Great, just as long as you realize that Kord and I are on Sully's team or this is a no-go."

Sully waited for the older non-com, a solid, muscular man whose worn features looked as if he'd won more fights than he'd lost in his thirty-plus years of military service to assert his authority, but he didn't.

He nodded agreement instead. "Works for me. The Command Sergeant-Major already gave me a sit-rep." He glanced around the breakroom where they waited, Bianca and Dak obviously just hanging out until the action started. "It'll be fun. I watched this old *Patrick Swayze, Gene Hackman* war movie last weekend, so I'm adapting their tactics. I made a few signs for the really stupid folks to wear."

That brought a few chuckles, but Sully didn't smile. She folded her arms, sweeping the three macho men with an icy gaze. "If you get in my way when the officers come through the woods, you'll wear more paint than they do. That's non-negotiable."

Kord chuckled and bumped Tate's arm with his. "Just remember you wanted to marry her."

"She's spunky, but she's all mine." He dropped an arm over her shoulders. "And so are our twins. I don't care what she says. If you see her doing something that could hurt her or the babies, you stop it, or I will."

Sully elbowed him in the ribs. "Thanks a lot, Murphy. What are you going to do next? Take out an ad in the paper? Yes, I'm pregnant, but I'm not helpless. The Army taught me to kick butt and that's my plan today."

Falcon Driscoll, a lean, dark-haired fighter, grinned appreciatively. "She and Raven were always meaner than the rest of us, so I'd listen to her if I were you, Murphy."

"I always do."

Sunday, she slept late. When she woke, she wrapped up in her robe and headed for the kitchen padding along in her slippers. Bo and Diddly kept her company. She found a teabag waiting in a mug by the stove. With a cup of peppermint tea and two pieces of cinnamon toast, she started for the back deck. She stopped when she saw a set of keys and a note waiting on the center island.

Sweetheart, didn't want to wake you and the twins. I took the

Mustang to Lake Maynard for a new tire and a rear window. Drive my truck until I'm back. Love you.

Rage followed initial shock. Damn him! It was her car, not his.

She spotted her purse and yanked out the cell phone. She was the only one who drove the Mustang, nobody else. He had no business taking it anywhere. She had to look up the number. When she found it, she called the police and filed a stolen vehicle report. She was done with one arrogant Ranger.

Two hours later, she still didn't have her car. She loaded the pups in the truck and drove to his parents. She'd been working with the dogs on wearing their harnesses and walking on their double hook-up leash. They seemed to have the knack of heeling beside her.

She stormed up on the porch, barely knocking before she entered, slamming the door behind her. "Enough is enough! I'm finished with him!"

Bronwyn stared for a moment, then rose gracefully from her chair at the foot of the table where the rest of the family had gathered for a mid-afternoon snack. "Sit down, honey. Tell us all about it. I'll get you a plate and a bowl of homemade chicken noodle soup."

"He stole my car!"

"He's a dead man." Lock stood, came around the table to take the leash. He leaned down to pet the wag-a-tail collie pups. "I'll put these two in the mudroom while we eat and then they can go with me to tour the farm."

"Are you listening? He took my car!"

"We hear every word." It was Joe's turn. He advanced on her, put his arms around her offering a warm hug. "You can't kill him on an empty stomach, Sully. Eat something and I'll help you hide the body."

"Seriously?"

"It's the least I can do after winning Heidi's pool. Everybody said I was nuts for picking the first Sunday in May, but I won. I'm using all the money to buy things for my newest grandbabies."

"Dad, if you start doing your grandpa dance again, Naveah and I are filming it and putting it on the Internet. I bet it goes viral." Chantrea pushed the platter of toasted cheese sandwiches toward Sully. "We checked out the garage yesterday and saw your car. We're so sorry. Middle schoolers suck."

"Yeah, she's right." Naveah leaned over to pat Sully's shoulder. "You should create a slide show all about Raven and the car and make those slimeballs watch it over and over."

"How could I when tomorrow is my last day and I have to finish grading their stinking quizzes and enter their scores online?"

"Naveah and I will help you after we eat."

"Good idea." Bronwyn slid a bowl of golden soup with chunks of chicken, vegetables, and thick noodles in front of Sully. "Do you want tea or milk?"

"Tea." Sully bit into the sandwich, chewed and swallowed. "I'm still killing him."

"You go, girl!" Bronwyn stroked her hair. "Just remember I want more daughters-in-law like you before the day is done."

"Thanks, Mom." Lock winked at her. "What did we ever do to deserve that?"

"You're all as arrogant, charming, and sexy as your dad, so I need sassy gals to kick your tails," Bronwyn informed him as Chantrea and Naveah burst into laughter.

He'd left at oh-dark-thirty this morning arriving at the tire store in Lake Maynard as it opened. The weekend supervisor had put the Mustang up on the overhead rack and inspected all the tires before he pointed out that two others had been damaged even though the sidewalls weren't completely punctured like the one in the trunk.

Four tires later, Tate drove to the glass repair shop only to learn they didn't have the kind of glass required for the back window and it meant a trip to the Ford dealership in town. The manager almost cried when he saw the busted rear window. He had his people clean up the rest of the broken glass in the back of the car while he made some calls and arranged for a friend to open his vintage car restoration place in Liberty Valley.

By late afternoon, the Mustang was its pristine self again. Tate drove toward Baker City, listening to the oldie rock and roll station. He preferred country music but somehow the radio never remained where he set it but constantly reverted to '60s rock. He wondered if he was alone in the rig or if he had company, but he wasn't Cat O'Leary McTavish so he couldn't talk to the person he thought was riding shotgun.

It wasn't his car, and he carefully stayed under the speed limit. The sound of a siren startled him. He glanced in the rearview mirror before moving over to the shoulder and stopping. He unrolled the window and watched Dick O'Connell adjust his belt with all the paraphernalia that a police officer needed as he walked toward the Mustang. Broad shoulders filled out the blue uniform shirt tucked neatly into dark blue slacks. Short black hair liberally sprinkled with white was barely visible under his western hat, modeled after the Canadian Mounties' version.

Tate nodded at the tall, older man when he approached the driver's side of the car. "Hey, Dick. What's going on?"

"I've got a stolen vehicle report on this rig." Amusement filled Dick's blue eyes. "Son, did you forget to ask your wife before you absconded with her Mustang?"

"She was asleep when I left this morning." Tate tapped his fingers on the steering wheel. "She's pregnant and she was worn to a frazzle after Army drill yesterday. You saw how heartbroken she was by what some of her students did to her car and she needs to go to the school tomorrow. It took longer to get the repairs finished than I expected."

Dick chuckled. "When those pregnancy hormones are going, anticipate fireworks, but don't tell my wife I said that. The dog doesn't want me sharing his house. Where are you headed?"

"Home."

"She's not there. She's at your folks' place. Your momma called to tell me where to find her when I located the car. I'll follow you."

"They'll be on Sully's side since she's the mother of their latest grandkids. I bet I'm grounded for the next month."

"Not for the first time, I'm sure." Chuckling, the police chief turned and strode back to his cruiser.

"Women should come with warning labels," Tate muttered.

"What's the point when guys don't read them?" Raven asked from the passenger seat. "You're busted, Ranger. Sully is going to make you suck more eggs than those thrown at our car."

When they arrived at the three-story Murphy house with the tower, balconies, and wrap-around porch, Raven followed him up the steps. She paused to look back and spotted the police chief turning his vehicle and driving away. In the kitchen clustered around the end of the table, she saw her bestie, Tate's parents, and foster sisters focusing on a laptop screen. She recognized the photo as one she'd taken the first day, they got their car.

"You've got to realize finding any kind of Mustang in a wrecking yard is rare," Sully said. "Raven claimed the shell of our car as soon as Grandpa Driscoll received it."

"It wasn't in great shape," Raven admitted, "but it was useable."

"We had to rebuild it from the ground up," Sully continued.

Chantrea typed away, before asking. "I paraphrased what you said, adding it to the slide. Does it work?"

Sully skimmed the sentences and then nodded in agreement. "It does."

"What's the plan?" Tate asked, stopping behind her.

"We're making a documentary about the Mustang for Sully to show her classes on Monday," Naveah said. "You look pretty good for a dead guy."

"I haven't killed him yet." Sully held out her hand. "Keys."

He passed them to her. "It took longer than I thought it would to find a vintage car lot and have the rear window replaced."

Tears welled in her eyes and one streaked down her cheek, followed by a second. "You could have just had it repaired at any auto glass outlet."

"No, I couldn't." He drew her against him, smoothing her hair while she buried her face in his t-shirt. "Then, it wouldn't be perfect, the way it was when you and Raven restored it."

"I want to be mad at you."

"I know." He rested his chin on top of her head. "We have a lifetime to share. I promise I'll make you angry again soon. You're super-hot when you rampage around the house."

She sniffed hard. "I filed a police report so Dick would arrest you for stealing my car."

"He told me." Tate's arms tightened. "He said it was just the pregnancy hormones talking and tore up the complaint when we arrived here, once he knew you had your car. I'm not getting locked up in the Gray Bar Hotel and you won't have to spring for my bail."

"What if he comes after me for filing a false report?"

"He won't. You're a Murphy and he saw how devastated you were on Friday. He certainly understands how you feel about your car. Besides, he's never come after Mom or Quinn when they throw rigging fits."

"What's a rigging fit?" Sully asked.

"It's what Murphys call temper tantrums," Joe explained. "It's not macho for boys to have tantrums so I always called them that. Sometimes when you're rigging up a fence or a truck or cables, stuff happens."

"And we've all had our share of them," Tate said, dropping a kiss on her hair.

"Stop that. If you two are going to start kissing, we'll never finish this presentation," Naveah informed them. "As long and hard as you two worked to repair that car after what her students did Friday, those kids need a major slap down for dissing Sully's sister and the Mustang."

"She's right," Chantrea agreed. "Tate, you have to arrange for guards in the parking lot at Lake Maynard Mid High tomorrow and then nobody will mess with the car while Sully's kicking butt."

"How do I do that?"

"Ask Kord." Sully shifted slightly and looked up at him, green eyes still damp. "He knows a ton of guys and gals at Nighthawke Security."

"Good idea," Raven agreed. "I was glad to be with him last night. I'd have left with him this morning, but I want to see Sully's last day, so I'll go home tomorrow after school."

"I ran into Corporal Ferguson at HQ last week and he was going on leave. He gave me his cell number and said if you needed a babysitter for the Mustang to call him. Of course, I didn't know about it being vandalized then but I'll touch base with him and see if he's still available."

She headed off to school before Tate left for the Army base. "He's a good guy. I can't believe he used up yesterday fixing the car."

"You would if you'd been there," Raven said, riding shotgun. "I know you loved me, and I loved you. We've always been sisters of the heart. It's okay if you love him, Sully. He's a stick-and-stay kind of man."

Sully heaved a sigh as she drove out of Baker City. "I know what you'd say, Raven, if you were here. You'd tell me not to be such a chicken-goober and to step up. You'd have laughed your backside off if you saw Colonel Stewart when we got done with him on Saturday. He was covered in red, yellow, and orange paint and Derek stuck a cardboard sign on him that read, "*NOT EVEN CLOSE!*"

"I was there even if you couldn't see me. Tate had your six. He respects the fact that you'd have stood by him if he went to war and he stands by you. Remember what I said before. I'm not being the thing that keeps you from happiness. Let me go. Stop blaming yourself. Step up, Sullivan Rafferty Barlow-Murphy."

At the school, Sully turned into the parking lot and headed toward her assigned spot. She gasped when she saw people waiting for her, some attired in the distinctive Nighthawke Security blue and black uniforms. She recognized Bianca Powell, Dak Marshall, and their boss, Durango Hawke. They shifted enough that she could pull into the waiting slot.

Sully turned off the engine and slid out of the Mustang, looking around. Her stepbrother, Kord in jeans, a flannel shirt, and boots stood next to Corporal Ferguson. "What's going on?"

"We're here to make sure your car is safe and remains that way for the next few hours," Kord said. "If I go home and let those kids near it, Raven will tear our house apart."

"Good idea. Too bad I didn't think of it," Raven said. "Next time you act stupid, I'll do more than haunt your butt."

Sully hugged him. "Thanks, Kord. I feel better about leaving it now."

"Hey, Murphy isn't the only one who has your back. The rest of us do too." Durango drawled. "And Kord tells me there will be more of us soon. His brothers, Falcon Driscoll, and the rest of the Driscoll guys will be here before school starts."

CHAPTER THIRTY-FIVE

Della Lowry eyed her cautiously when Sully signed in at the office. "Chief Wright would like to speak to you before school. He's a bit concerned about the people in the parking lot."

"Really? I'm a bit concerned about who vandalized my car last Friday." With that snarky comment, Sully walked past the counter, down the corridor to the Security Office. She nodded to the man behind the desk, studying the rows of computer screens. "Did you have any luck discovering who trashed my Mustang?"

"Not when they took out the cameras in that part of the lot." He rubbed his buzz cut. "Principal Ames wants me to intervene and get rid of the guards near your car today. He says they'll intimidate the students."

"Good, maybe they'll leave my car alone." Sully kept her tone even. "I'll be leaving after fifth period today. I'll drop off my ID badge then and the security team, with my Mustang, will go at that time too. I suggest you tell the principal if he wants to keep Nighthawke around to protect school property, he'd better not tug on Durango Hawke's cape."

"That gives me a way to go. Thanks."

Sully spun around and headed for the elevator. She was the first one in the classroom. *No surprise*, she thought. After instigating so much trouble, Maureen Evans undoubtedly wanted to be least in sight today. Turning on the lights, Sully crossed to her desk. She hadn't brought her school bag today, just her laptop. She unpacked it, then checked emails. No response from Dr. Dunaway yet. Another shock since Sully had sent the pictures of the Mustang to the university supervisor last night, along with a note that she'd be leaving today right after Washington State History.

However, there was one from Margo Endicott asking Sully to reconsider her transfer and remain with her original Army Reserve unit. They needed her and so did Margo since she was taking over command of the company and she wanted Sully to come on board as the new First Sergeant. It'd been Raven's job to look after the enlisted troops, but now it was Sully's. *Yes*, she thought, *After Saturday, I know I'm ready to be back with my own folks, but I can still help out down at Major Harper's office.*

She turned on the overhead projector and connected the cables to her laptop, loading up the special presentation. The warning bell rang, and she watched the students quietly enter the room, wondering which of them vandalized her vehicle.

Taking their assigned seats, they eyed her warily and one brave soul raised her hand. "Don't we have an entry task or an agenda to copy in our logbooks today, Mrs. Murphy?"

"No. It's my last day and I have something else to show you."

More silence as the middle-schoolers stared. The last bell rang and while Principal Ames droned through the morning announcements and flag salute, Sully took attendance. When he finished, she clicked onto the first slide, a simple title, "*Serving with First Sergeant Raven Driscoll-Barlow.*"

"Who is that?"

"She would have been your teacher," Sully said. "She should have been instead of me."

Next came a picture of the Mustang in all its Passionate Pink grandeur. "It was her idea to snag the car when it came in the wrecking yard." Sully clicked through the photos of the car project from start to finish, from Raven pointing to the shell to the two of them installing the motor, the transmission, and step by step, restoring the classic vehicle.

Once they'd painted it, the pictures changed from rebuilding their new treasure to incorporating it into their high school life. They'd gone together to their Prom, Raven driving and Sully riding shotgun, their dates in the back seat. Parties, watershed moments like graduation, and the Mustang was always there. It was at the recruiter's office when they enlisted and Kord picked them up at the airport after basic training. More photos of their life as best friends followed including those of Raven standing by the car on her wedding day.

"She took it on their honeymoon," Sully said, struggling to keep the emotion out of her voice. "She wouldn't let my brother behind the wheel. It was our girly car from the very first day."

"Where is she?" someone asked—a boy this time.

Sully didn't answer. She clicked the mouse, showing more slides. These were of their Army Reserve drill days, the Mustang waiting in the lot, always a shining pink, always glamourous. The same couldn't always be said of her and Raven who usually wore camouflage fatigues and combat boots while they performed their military duties, from standing in formation to marching to office work.

"When we went to Afghanistan the first time, Kord and Raven were engaged. He took care of our car for us. He started it every day, but he only drove it back and forth to the gas station. He took care of it the second time we went too. Then, came the third time."

Someone, Sully didn't know who had taken a picture of her holding a folded American flag, standing in the rain at the airport last December while she waited for Raven's coffin to be unloaded.

"Oh no!" a girl wailed. "Oh no, Mrs. Murphy."

"Yes." Sully clicked the mouse and the next slide showed the flag-draped coffin at the military cemetery, the Mustang parked close by. "She was supposed to be your teacher."

The following slides showed the damaged car sitting in the school parking lot on Friday. Raw eggs splattered across the hood, both sides of the car, the roof. The Mustang slanted downward on a flat tire and broken glass from the rear window shimmered in the afternoon sunshine.

"This is her car." Sully paused. "And mine. She would have been your teacher, but she was always my best friend, my sister even before she married my brother."

She pushed the button on the mouse and there was a picture of the white marble headstone with Raven's full name, her rank, U.S. Army, Afghanistan, her birthdate, and the day she died at the Fort Bronson military cemetery. "She was twenty-nine years old and I miss her every day."

Deliberately, Sully brought back the picture of the damaged car leaving it on the screen as the bell rang. "You're excused."

The seventh-graders fled from the room, one nearly running into Maureen Evans who brushed by them. Sully hit the exit button on the slide show, preparing to start it over again for the next period.

"I didn't get a lesson plan from you over the weekend," Maureen said.

"I had Army duty." Sully waited as the next group of students came into the room and found their assigned seats. She clicked on the first slide, *"Serving with First Sergeant Raven Driscoll-Barlow."*

"What are you doing?" Maureen asked. "She's not here."

"She should have been their teacher, not me." Sully calmly took attendance. "And this is what I call a teachable moment after last Friday."

"What about that day?" Maureen glanced around the room at the students. "What aren't you sharing?"

"Oh, I'm sure your kiddoes have a lot to tell you. They are, as Sergeant Ann Barrett would tell you, a credit to your teaching." Sully gestured to the front corner where the TA stood. "Turn off the lights, please. You're welcome to stay or go, Mrs. Evans, but we are about to have a show."

At the end of the hour, she finished up the presentation, once again showing Raven's headstone before she clicked back to the photos of the damaged car. The bell rang and she glanced around the room at the students. "You're excused."

Like the kids in the first period, this group hightailed it for the door. Maureen Evans gaped at the departing seventh graders, then turned her attention to Sully. "You can't think I'd condone that sort of behavior."

"I don't know what you'd consider particularly heinous or what you'd tolerate." Sully switched to the first slide as she waited for third period to begin. "You haven't been here during the past eight weeks to teach me anything."

From the way the students cautiously came through the door and eased into their seats, they definitely knew something was up. Apparently, the gossip train was full steam ahead and running strong. Cressy didn't hold back. She stalked up to the front of the room, giving the older teacher the stink-eye. "I hope you're happy now."

"What are you talking about, Cressida?"

"My mom says she's pulling all of us out of Lake Maynard school district. After she saw what was done to that car, Mom told my dad this is our last week. My brother has already been enrolled in the new Baker City School and as soon as they have teachers for me and my sister, we're going too. Mom says she's not raising hoodlums or miscreants, whatever those are and we gotta go someplace civilized. When I said I want to keep being a cheerleader, she said for me to get over it. There's more important things than cheer."

Maureen blinked, then glared at Sully. "You told Mrs. Chapman about the accident?"

"Wrecking the Mustang wasn't an accident," Cressy snapped. "Bad kids did it because they were pissed about the tests you made us take. And now my mom is calling the parents of my friends and saying this is no place for us."

"What goes around, comes around." Sully glanced around the room at the other seventh-graders while Octavia took attendance. "By now, I'm sure all of you know what happened to my car last Friday. However, I don't think you know the story behind that car and I'm going to show it to you."

Cressy planted her fists on narrow, teen hips and eyed her. "I know already. My mom told us when she drove me and my friends to school today. You and your best friend bought the Mustang together when you were kids and fixed it up. You did everything together in your car. Then, you went into the Army and went to war. Together. You got hurt bad and she died—"

"Her name was Raven Driscoll-Barlow." Danielle gestured to the screen. "And she wasn't just your best friend. She married your brother, so she was like your sister. This is majorly sad, Mrs. Murphy, and we didn't have anything to do with trashing your car. We talked about it with the other cheerleaders and if anybody on the junior or varsity squad hears anything, we're telling Chief Wright."

"I see." Sully ignored the distressed teacher beside her and focused on the students. "Is there anyone else who wants to follow the cheerleaders' example and demonstrate the qualities of heroes?"

Almost a third of the seventh graders raised their hands and Sully nodded approval. "In that case, you're excused. You don't have to stay and watch this presentation. Octavia, would you please escort them to the library? They can check out books and do silent reading or homework."

"You got it, Mrs. Murphy." Octavia collected the clipboard they used when they went to the resource room to track student activities, gesturing to the volunteers. "And most of the juniors in my classes are on the same page as the cheerleaders. So are the rest of the upper-classmen. We hear anything and we're sharing it. The people who did this deserve to go down in flames."

Tim Garvey didn't speak, just stared at the notebook on his desk.

Sully crossed to him and said softly, "You don't have to stay. I know this is going to be painful after what happened to your dad. Go to the library with the others."

He shook his head and whispered, "No, Mrs. Murphy. I'm staying. Maybe, the people who did it will have their consciences raised, but even if they don't, I can't snitch on them."

"Okay, but if you decide to take justice into your hands, walk softly and watch your back."

"I will."

She returned to the front of the room and began the slideshow. Halfway through, Dak Marshall slipped into the room, followed by Chief Wright. They didn't interfere, just stood, and viewed the presentation. When it was over, they left, taking three boys with them. Tim Garvey wasn't one of them.

He paused by Sully and Maureen. "That's not all of them."

"I'm sure," Sully said. "Be careful, Tim."

"I will. I promise. I'm sorry about your sister."

"And I'm sorry about your dad."

When they were alone in the room, Maureen asked, "Are you joining the teachers for lunch?"

"I haven't in more than two months. Would your friends welcome me today?"

Maureen winced. "I deserve that. I haven't been fair to you."

"No, but that was your choice, not mine."

Maureen left the room, but Sully opted for her usual pattern of hitting the restroom and then eating in the classroom. After lunch, there were more visitors during the fourth period, two teachers and Principal Ames. Dr. Dunaway arrived in time to see the presentation. She cried, not making a show of it, but silent tears. At the end of the period, she told the students that Raven and Sully always drove the Mustang to their university classes, often arriving before she did.

When the students left the room, Principal Ames approached Sully and Dr. Dunaway. "Everyone regrets what happened last week, but hasn't this drama gone on long enough?"

"Not yet," Sully said. "I have one more class."

"I'm staying for it," Leslie Dunaway told him. "After that, I'll meet you in your office so we can discuss any future student teaching placements."

"We've already invoiced the university for payment for next fall."

"Yes, and we'll talk about that in an hour."

At the end of Washington State History, Sully shut down her laptop, gathered her belongings, and headed out the door. "I'm done here."

"You've certainly earned your certification." Dr. Dunaway walked beside her to the school office. "Now, I'm going to crush Ames' pretensions and tell him he isn't getting any more student teachers. I don't have anyone else with your capabilities. You did very well, Sullivan. I'll see you at the university in two weeks to finish up your certification."

"I'll be there." Sully lingered long enough to drop off her ID Badge and sign out at the front counter, then strolled out the door into the May sunshine. She glanced across the parking lot and saw the entourage guarding the Mustang. They'd been joined by one more soldier, Tate Murphy, standing tall in his fatigues.

Her pulses thudded in excitement when he turned, saw her, and came toward her. "How'd it go?"

"Well. It went really well." She stepped close, reached up to rest her hands on his broad shoulders. "I love you."

"I know." He leaned down to kiss her, a quick warm touch.

"How do you know when I barely say it?"

"You married me. You wouldn't have if you didn't really love me."

"Why wouldn't I when you've always had my six even if you didn't fight with my mother during her visit? I've thought about it and you were right about that."

"An apology?" He held her close. "I know we'll fight sometimes, but it doesn't mean I'm not here. I don't have to be back at the base until tomorrow. Let's go home, Mrs. Murphy."

"I'm ready."

<hr />

A week and a half later, on a sunny Thursday afternoon, she planted flowers in front of the house with doggie assistance. Bo happily buried his beloved tennis ball in between the begonias and geraniums with Diddly retrieving it so they could have collie battles over the muddy toy. The tug-a-puppy war ended when they found someone new to throw the ball. Sully shifted to watch Smitty O'Sullivan approach. "Hello there."

"Hi." He accepted the dirt-encrusted ball and tossed it across the lawn which sent the young dogs racing after it. "Margo Endicott and Ann Barrett have started teaching at Baker City School and they sent me to hire you. I missed you at Lake Maynard Mid-High last week."

"My mentor teacher and the administration aren't happy with me." Sully patted damp earth around the clump of red flowers. "I kicked butt and took names."

"I'm not surprised. That's what soldiers and teachers do." He held out his hand to help her rise. "Got time to talk?"

She nodded, accepted his help, and stood. "I made lemonade and snickerdoodles. Let's go chat in the kitchen."

That evening, she tore lettuce for a salad. Potatoes baked while steaks marinated, ready for grilling on the outdoor barbeque. Cheesecake from the town bakery waited in the refrigerator for dessert. The dogs barked and she gazed at Tate as he came toward her, Bo proudly toting a new stuffed lamb while his sister had a matching one. "Somebody went shopping."

"Good practice for when the twins get here." He kissed her. "Got your text about the teaching job. Are you good with being in Baker City for the duration?"

"It's home." She put the tomato on the counter. "Wherever you are is home and I'm finally home. With you. All of you."

He chuckled, put a big hand on the baby bump. "I know."

THE END

Keep reading for a sneak preview of Josie Malone's upcoming *Ghost of the Past*, book four in her *Baker City Hearts & Haunts* series!

Don't miss out on your next favorite book!

Join the Satin Romance mailing list
www.satinromance.com/mail.html

THANK YOU FOR READING

Did you enjoy this book?

We invite you to leave a review at your favorite book site, such as Goodreads, Amazon, Barnes & Noble, etc.

DID YOU KNOW THAT LEAVING A REVIEW...

- Helps other readers find books they may enjoy.
- Gives you a chance to let your voice be heard.
- Gives authors recognition for their hard work.
- Doesn't have to be long. A sentence or two about why you liked the book will do.

GHOST OF THE PAST

BAKER CITY HEARTS & HAUNTS ~ BOOK FOUR

Baker City, Washington ~ August 2014

"I'm done coming second in your life, Durango Hawke."

"Say again, babe. I didn't get that."

"You heard me." Heather McElroy shifted on the corral rail where she'd perched so he could snap her photo. She eyed the tawny-haired man twenty feet away. Six foot, six in his socks, broad-shouldered, narrow-hipped, he still carried himself like the Marine he'd been for six years.

She'd followed him far too long. It was her turn, damn it. She tossed her head, long copper hair flying in the warm breeze. "I'm through nursing you after your stupid adventures."

"Thanks for the support." Sarcasm laced his bass rumble.

She took a deep breath and watched the storm build in his navy eyes. Irritation made his rugged, handsome features harder to resist. Blue jeans, boots and a faded, sleeveless chambray shirt increased his resemblance to a Madison Avenue cowboy. But there was nothing plastic about her man!

Deliberately, she concentrated on the bandaged left shoulder. Any lower and the bullet would have hit his heart. As cantankerous as he was though, he'd have survived long enough to take out the attacker.

She wouldn't let him see how he affected her when he lowered the *Nikon* and strode toward her.

"I mean it." She raised her chin. "No more system support, Hawke. If you return to Columbia, I'm outta here. Someone else will have to patch you up. Just remember doctors must report gunshot wounds and all cops aren't stupid. One might not believe you were hit in a drive-by shooting at a construction site."

"Don't threaten me." He stalked closer, menace in each step. "I've never taken your crap. It's why we've stayed together this long."

"We won't be together if you leave me again." Her ultimatum didn't appear to faze him. His face was expressionless, a mask that hid any and all emotion. "I mean it."

"Watch it. You don't want to piss me off."

She shrugged. "I'm not scared of you. Save the macho act for the bunch of mercenaries you run with or one of your cousins."

She didn't want to know how many soldiers of fortune died in the South American jungles. It was bad enough knowing he might. He was pretty annoyed with her. She could tell by the edge in his deep voice and the tight line of his strong jaw.

Too bad, too sad! After those tours as a combat nurse in Afghanistan, does he honestly think his tantrums frighten me?

He stopped in front of her. The shirt left unbuttoned and open because of the injured shoulder revealed his neck and tanned chest. Her gaze narrowed on the bright red scar that ran from his right shoulder in a diagonal six-inch line toward his left nipple. The injury two years ago had been her introduction to his illegal, dangerous hunt for his younger brother.

She pointed to the healed knife wound. "Remember when I stitched that with an upholstery needle and dental floss. I cleaned it with alcohol first. You yelled like a stuck pig. Without anesthesia, I know everything I did must have hurt like hell."

"Yeah," he grunted agreement. "Your point?"

"You didn't learn, jarhead. You still think you change clothes in a phone booth. I'm not *Lois Lane* to your *Superman*." She trembled when he gripped the fence, resting large hands on either side of her. "I'm right, damn it."

"You always tell me so." He leaned nearer. "It's why we fight so much."

She tried to turn her head, but he caught her chin in calloused fingers. "Don't. I'm not in the mood."

Of course, it's all too easy for him to get me in the mood.

"I won't force you." He chuckled. "I don't have to and we both know it. This is your pride talking. It's why you've slept on the couch for the past three weeks."

"Like you cared." She trembled when he feathered his thumb over her lips. "You've ignored everything I said. You won't admit how wrong you are."

She glanced past him to the overgrown rose garden in front of the old Victorian house where her grandparents had lived. The scent of flowers wafted her way on soft wind. The four-hundred plus acre farm waited for her uncle to return.

Fenian McElroy had disappeared on a covert Army mission back in 2010 with Durango's brother, Waco. There was little hope her uncle would come home to claim his inheritance. After all the U.S. didn't even admit they had troops in South America fighting the drug lords. Too much attention was taken up with the war in the Middle East.

When Durango trailed one finger down her neck to the gold chain she always wore along with the special four-leaf clover he'd given her as a gift on her sixteenth birthday, she glared at him. "I've told you a hundred times. I'm not interested."

"You want me, babe." He nipped her ear, kissed the spot below it. "You're too damned proud to admit it. You figure if you don't let me make love to you, I'll kowtow to your demands."

"I'm not *that* manipulative or spiteful. Even if I were, you'd deserve it. You walked into the house leaking blood like a saturated surgical sponge and terrified me."

"You didn't show it. You fixed me up." He pressed another kiss to her neck. "You're one in a million and way too good for me, *Empress*."

The nickname offended her. She wasn't as capricious or arbitrary as he made her sound. She pushed him away. "At least, we agree on something, jarhead."

She jumped off the fence, heading toward the blanket she'd spread on the grass. "Let's go. Your idea of a picnic on the old McElroy homestead was only another try to get me in the sack."

"We haven't eaten yet. I want to take some pictures of you with my new camera."

"I'm not in the mood," she repeated. "I'd have more luck talking to a rock. No wonder your mother claims, "bigger is dumber". For once, she's right."

"Funny. You never say that in bed. You always beg for more."

A blush scorched her cheeks. "Damn you!"

She whirled to confront him. He was right behind her. Surprised, she fell back a step, the blanket beneath her shoe. "I won't sleep with you until you're home for good."

He grinned down at her. "Want to bet, *Empress*?" He hooked a hand around her neck. "I haven't given you a birthday present yet."

"My birthday isn't until next week. You'd better be here for it." When he didn't answer, she stiffened. "I said, no."

"I heard you." He brushed her lips with his. "I fully intend to get started on your present today."

"Oh, really? What do you plan to give me?"

"What do you think?" He lowered his head. "The same thing I've given you for the past eight years, multiple orgasms. I'm going for a new record, twenty-nine of them, one for each year."

She shuddered, trying to ignore the heat in her face. "You can't. It's physically impossible. I'll die of exhaustion ."

"You haven't yet." He laughed. "Let's check it out."

She hesitated. She wanted him as badly as he wanted her. She'd ached for his touch, longed to go to him and forced herself to maintain a safe distance. Would surrender work any better? Could she entice him to stay home with her?

It was worth a try. At five foot, eight, it wasn't much of a stretch to tiptoe up and tease his mouth with hers. "Want me?"

"You know it." He pulled her tight against him. "I've missed having you hog all the covers."

"Not enough to come out to the living-room and charm me."

"It wouldn't have worked until you were over the snot-slinging, foot-stomping hissy fit."

"I don't have tantrums anymore."

"When I got home, you tipped a table full of food on me. Laredo hit the door a-running."

"That was the plan," she said in her sweetest voice. "I couldn't let your baby bro see you were a bloody mess. If I had, we wouldn't be arguing. You'd be in a hospital, then jail. You got off easy."

"Says the woman into pay-back. Vengeance is always yours, baby."

"I'm not petty."

"You'll go to hell for lying." Durango kissed her brows. "You threw your engagement ring at me for a week straight. I kept putting it back on your finger."

She tipped back her head and met his gaze. "I didn't ask for it. I offered to bring you a jar of *Vasoline* so you could shove it where the sun doesn't shine."

Another laugh before he dropped a kiss on her nose. "You make me glad to be alive except when all you give me to eat is potato soup."

"It was good for you."

"I hate the stuff. Then, you made peanut butter cookies for dessert." He stroked her hair. "How many times have I told you that peanut butter makes me gag? And you refused to make me chocolate chip ones no matter how many times I asked."

"Making you suffer was the general idea."

"You went for two and a half weeks without speaking to me. Must have been a new record." He rested his chin on top of her head. "You're an ornery woman, Heather Marie McElroy."

"As if you'd want any other kind." She closed her eyes and leaned against him, relishing the hard, solid feel of his body. Did he realize how close he'd come to dying? Tears burned her eyes. She blinked them away, determined not to reveal the weakness. "You're mine."

"I always have been." His mouth claimed hers. "Ever since we were kids."

When the kiss ended, he lifted his lips a few inches from hers. Before he spoke, she slowly slid his shirt down the muscled arms, letting it fall onto the grass. "I've given you all of me. I want all of you."

"You have me. We'll get married as soon as I bring Waco home."

"He's gone by now. We have to let him go and Fenn too."

"I don't believe that. I've got to keep looking for the two of them."

"All right, lover. You think what you need to think." She stopped him with a kiss. "I wish there were an O'Leary in Baker City to find Waco for you, but there isn't, and he means more to you than—." She paused. "No, I won't say that. I won't spoil this moment, but I'll agree we'll both do what we have to do."

As soon as he parked the rental car in the driveway, he knew she was gone. September leaves covered the unmown lawn and weeds shared space with the bright marigolds in the flowerbeds. Rolled up newspapers littered the front porch. Envelopes overflowed from the small mailbox beside the screen door. Proof of her departure from his life as if he hadn't gotten a clue when she wasn't at the airport to meet him.

"I don't need this crap, Heather Marie."

He left the bouquet of golden roses, the box of her favorite chocolate-covered macadamia nuts and the small sack from the jewelry store on the passenger seat. He'd expected her to be angry. She always got mad when he left on a trip to South America, but this tantrum was ridiculous for a twenty-nine-year-old woman.

He reached in his back pocket, pulled out his wallet and flipped to the last picture he'd taken of her. Vibrant red hair cascaded to her narrow waist. High cheekbones, a pointed chin, and huge green eyes reminded him of a cat, but there was nothing tame about his Heather. She was wild, feral, and downright vicious at times. *My kind of woman, long on guts – short on self-preservation. She'd charge hell with a bucket of water.*

It was the low, rich taunting voice he always missed most. She might tear strips off him with her words, but that voice was saturated with sex. He wanted to fall into the photo, grab her and hold her forever. He'd just hold those tall curves against him. She was the perfect size for him, heart-high. In the picture, she leaned against the corral rail, wind ruffling her hair.

He'd told her to say, *'cheese'.* She hadn't, of course. She'd never followed his directions in her entire life. She'd looked him straight in the face, smiled dangerously and purred, "But, babe. I don't want cheese. I want you."

His hands shook when he snapped the photo. It was pure luck, not skill it'd come out this good. He'd assumed their wild lovemaking meant everything was great between them. She'd stopped complaining and calling his hunt for his brother the definition of insanity. She'd even driven him to the airport, kissed him goodbye like they were going to jump back into the sack, not like they'd just left it.

How was he supposed to know she intended to leave?

He flung open the car door, paced to the trunk and removed his duffel bag, a leftover from his stint in the Marines. He slung the carrying strap over his shoulder, slammed the trunk and went around the house to the back door. The kitchen was dark. Daylight filtered through the door behind him. Some came through the window about the farmhouse sink.

What happened to the curtains? He flipped the light switch by the door. Nothing. Had the bulb in the overhead fixture burned out? He turned, saw the note taped neatly to the outside of the breaker box.

Durango, call to have the utilities turned on when you want them. That includes the landline. You never phone me, so I won't worry.

"Damn it!" He tore down the note, wadded it into a ball and looked for the wastebasket.

Gone. He walked further into the room. The table and chairs were missing too. So were all the appliances, the electric range, fridge, washer, dryer, and dishwasher. No microwave. He grimaced, grateful they'd totally furnished the rental. At least, he wouldn't have to listen to the landlord pitching a major fit.

The cupboards were bare. Another note lay where the dishes used to be. *I gave away the groceries. You had more important things to do than be here for me or the meals I cooked for you.*

"You little wildcat." He shook his head. He was cracking up. Imagine arguing with a piece of paper.

He stormed through the house, searching the rest of the rooms. She'd stripped the place. The furniture was gone, everything they'd bought together. A manila envelope was taped to the bedroom door, obviously where she'd left her engagement ring. Another note fluttered beside it.

I got rid of the bed. I didn't want you to share it with someone else. Your clothes are at the cleaners down the street. You can pay them to wash and iron for you. I'm outta here. So long, lover!

Liberty Valley, Washington ~ May 5th, 2015

He'd spent the day on the construction site, too busy working on a new strip mall to check messages. Finally, back in his office, he crossed to the desk, picked up the landline and called the automatic answering service.

Her mocking voice filled his ears. "Durango, sorry I missed you. Happy birthday, lover."

He froze, pressed the button to repeat the message. *It's not my birthday. She knows better than anyone that's in March. What the hell is going on? What game is she playing now?*

ABOUT THE AUTHOR

Josie Malone lives and works at her family's riding stable in Washington State. She's taught children to ride and know about horses so long that she often discovers she's taught three generations of their families. Her life experiences span adventures from dealing cards in a casino, attending graduate school to get her Master's in Teaching degree, being a substitute teacher, and serving in the Army Reserve all leading to her second career as a published author.

Contact Josie at:
josiemaloneauthor@outlook.com

Find her on Online at:
www.josiemalone.com
www.facebook.com/JosieMaloneAuthor

ALSO BY JOSIE MALONE

Baker City Hearts & Haunts

My Sweet Haunt

More Than a Spirit

Family Skeletons

Liberty Valley Love

A Man's World

Cowboy Spell

Made in the USA
Columbia, SC
01 May 2021

36634426R00207